BETRAYAL

OF

FAITH

MARK M. BELLO

A Zachary Blake Legal Thriller

Published by 8Grand Publications
West Bloomfield, MI 48322

Printed in the United States of America

ISBN: 978-1732447196

This book is dedicated to Betty, Dianne, and their sons, whose experiences and bravery inspired it; you are in my thoughts, still, after all these years.

Chapter One

It was a beautiful spring day in Michigan. Flowers were beginning to bloom, and buds were blossoming on once-barren tree branches. The snow disappeared for another season, and the temperature climbed above sixty degrees for the first time. Jennifer Tracey drove her 2013 Chevy Tahoe south on Farmington Road toward the church. She thought, *what a great weekend for a camping trip. The boys needed this. I hope they like Father Gerry.*

She pulled into the parking lot of Our Lady of the Lakes Church and School, parked, exited the old truck, and headed for the rectory. She spotted the group almost immediately. Actually, she spotted a bunch of backpacks, camping equipment, pop bottles, shoes, socks, and other debris strewn across the lawn of the rather impressive two-story brick home. She was the first parent to arrive, not surprising considering she was a half-hour early.

Jennifer was excited to see the boys. This was their first overnight since Father Bill's transfer. Father Bill was the only man the boys warmed up to since their dad, Jim, passed away. *My God! Has it been three years already?* She remembered the day of the accident like it was yesterday—a phone call from the plant with shocking news and the rush to Botsford Hospital. The family gathered for an all-night, prayer-dominated vigil until, finally, the doctor came out of surgery shaking his head—"I'm terribly sorry. We did all we could."

She remembered trying to explain to the boys, nine and eleven, that their father was called to heaven and that God worked in mysterious ways. Jake, her sensitive nine-year-old, wanted to know if he could visit. Kenny, her eleven-year-old, sat stunned, staring at the sky with piercing green eyes, wondering why the Lord chose to take his father when he needed him most. Life seemed so unfair.

Jim's loss was incredibly hard on the boys. They were bitter

and sullen until they met Father Bill. Bill transferred from a
parish in Pennsylvania when Jim's accident occurred. After
Jim's death, Bill made the boys his special project and, in a short
time, became something akin to a 'substitute' father. He took the
boys to Detroit Tiger ball games, played ball with them, took
them camping, and even let them sleep overnight at the rectory.
They became altar boys and were beginning to adjust to life
without their father reasonably well. Then, one day last month,
Father Bill came by the house and announced he'd been
transferred to a parish in Virginia. He spent three years in
Michigan, and it was time to move on. The boys may as well
have heard Father Bill had died, like their dad. Father Bill's
farewell *celebration* was more like a wake. He took the boys
aside and tried to explain that he was required to do God's work
wherever the church sent him. He said he'd try to visit as often as
possible, but the boys were unconvinced. The looks on their
faces when Father Bill drove off were almost as sad as the day
they heard the news of their father's death.

That was why this outing with Father Gerry was so
important. Gerry was Bill's replacement and had been at
Lakes—the parish nickname—less than a month. This camping
trip was Gerry's first chance to spend extended time with the
boys away from parish responsibilities. Jennifer knew it would
take some time, but she hoped the boys would at least like him.

She climbed the porch steps and knocked on the door of the
large bricked colonial. It was a typical suburban Michigan
home—two stories with red, white, and black reclaimed brick
and white aluminum siding. The grounds were massive since the
house stood on church property. The lot was heavily treed, and
the grass had been freshly trimmed. Jennifer could smell the
fresh-cut grass, one of the beautiful smells of spring in Michigan.

Father Gerry came to the door and invited her in. Boys were
running all over the house, chasing each other. The noise was
deafening. Jennifer scanned the crowd but could not locate Jake
or Kenny.

"Nice to see you again, Jenny," Gerry chirped.

"Nice to see you too, Father. How was the outing?"

"The boys had a great time. They're still having a great time, as you can see. Jake and Kenny are in the backyard. I'll go fetch them for you."

"Oh, don't trouble yourself, Father. You have your hands full here. I'll get them."

"No trouble at all, Jenny. Wait here. I'll be right back with the boys."

Jennifer would have preferred to get the boys, given the noise level in the house. Instead, she walked out onto the front porch to wait in the sunshine. In 'no time,' as Jake would say, Father Gerry appeared with her two sons. The contrast between Jake and Kenny and other boys was absolutely startling. Her boys were sullen, gloomy.

"Here they are, safe and sound," Father Gerry reported. "Boys, say 'hi' to your mom."

"Hi, Mom," Kenny managed, his voice barely audible.

"Yeah, hi, Mom," Jake grunted.

"What's the matter with you guys?" Gerry inquired. "Did I tire you out that much?" To Jennifer, he advised, "I ran these kids ragged—hiking, calisthenics, canoeing, all night stories, you name it. They're tired. Take them home and put them to bed. They'll be fine in the morning."

Jennifer was shocked. The other boys were none the worse for wear. What was wrong with hers?

"Thank you, Father," she managed. "I'll do just that."

The Tracey family climbed into the wagon, and Jennifer headed for home. The boys sat in the backseat together. Usually, they fought over who would sit in front. Jennifer's concern level increased.

"Did you guys have a good time?"

No answer.

"How was Father Gerry? He seems quite nice. Is he as good a camp director as Father Bill?"

No answer. Jennifer was almost in a panic.

She adjusted her rearview mirror to look at her two silent sons. Kenny was glaring at Jake fiercely with one finger to his lips, silently ordering him quiet. A single tear ran down Kenny's cheek. The family drove home in silence. Something was terribly wrong.

Chapter Two

Father Gerry Bartholomew was enjoying a conversation with new Lakes members Spencer and Sherry Reed and their teenage boys, David and Justin. The Reeds lost a child to cancer and were trying to organize a charity event for St. Jude Children's Research Hospital, where their Jeffrey lost his final battle with the dreaded disease. The family was touring the vast campus of Lakes, enjoying the beautiful spring weather. The boys were tossing a football. The ball eluded one of the boys and rolled up to Gerry. He picked it up and launched a perfect spiral to David. David glanced at Justin with an expression of surprise at Gerry's quarterbacking proficiency.

"Nice throw," Justin marveled. "Where did you learn to throw a football like that?"

"Oh," Gerry explained, "I played football at the seminary, and I coach our parish team in the local junior football league. You guys should try out. We have many other activities, including camping—my personal favorite—swimming, baseball, and choir. Can you guys sing? We also do a lot of charity work, especially with kids your age. Charity is one way God gives us to demonstrate our love and compassion for others. It is but one of the many miracles of pleasure God wants us to experience. After all, love of man is love of God. Don't you agree?

"Doing what we love makes us happy, and I adore bonding with happy teenagers. We have a close-knit group. Much of my time here at Lakes is spent with our young people, and I love it. We'd love to have you join us." Gerry was thoughtful and spiritual. When he spoke, one could almost hear the voice of God.

The boys promised to consider Gerry's offer, and their parents were excited by the prospect of their boys participating. Gerry walked them to their car and waved as it disappeared down the road leading from the parish to the main highway.

Gerry Bartholomew was recently the assistant pastor of St. Patrick's Parish in Ohio. He was thirty-six, approximately six feet tall and well built. He had dark brown, almost black eyes. One could hardly make out his pupils. He had long brown hair and a pale, almost milk-like complexion. He had two major passions: camping and teenagers. His sermons were powerful and memorable. He was charming—everywhere he'd been, parishioners loved him. The father of a fourteen-year-old boy once loaned him his camper to take his son and some other boys on an overnight camping trip. Activities and interactions with teenagers were the highlights of his priesthood.

Gerry didn't want to leave Ohio or St. Patrick's, but the church hierarchy decided it was time for him to move on. He fought reassignment. His work with parish teenagers was unappreciated and misunderstood. Gerry Bartholomew was sure he was going to be assigned out of parish work, perhaps to do charity work overseas, or to counsel the frail or sick.

In fact, his personnel records contained copious notes with strong recommendations that he receive these types of assignments. To his surprise, the notes were ignored. Gerry was placed at Our Lady of the Lakes. He was in Michigan. There were lush campsites all over the state, excellent sites within twenty-five miles of the parish. There, he met the Reed brothers as well as Jacob and Kenneth Tracey. Gerry Bartholomew was beside himself with joy.

Chapter Three

"Order! Order!" the Voice commanded. "Come to order."

The group of five men was silent almost immediately. The room was dimly lit, which kept its opulence from intruding on their meeting.

"We have assembled again because we have another crisis at the parish level."

"What now?"

"Father Gerry has been active again."

"Shit! When? Where?" The member was angry and perplexed.

"Gerry was recently transferred, wasn't he?"

"Yes."

"Wasn't the placement supposed to be away from children?"

"Yes, it was."

"Well, then what the hell happened?" Another member demanded.

"I don't know—we're still checking who made the placement and why."

"This is disastrous. I presume the victim was male?"

"*Victims*, plural—two boys, fourteen and twelve, it happened on a camping retreat."

"They sent Gerry on a camping retreat? Didn't they read our report?" *Unbelievable!*

"Obviously not," the Voice sighed.

"What do you propose?"

"I think we should stay calm and ascertain the facts before deciding on a course of action."

"Makes sense." Calm began to rule. The Voice was pleased common sense would prevail.

"Where did this happen?"

"In Farmington Hills, Michigan, the Detroit Division."

"Does the pastor know?"

"He's the one who contacted me. He overheard some kids."

"Whom do we have in Detroit?"

"We have a top-notch investigating firm, Parks and Associates, and a silk-stocking law firm, Brodman, Longworth and Darling."

"Get them on this. We need serious damage control this time."

"We should have defrocked him after the first time."

"The situation hasn't changed. There's still a shortage. We have too many parishes and too few priests. Besides, Gerry's psychiatrist gave us the green light."

"Yeah, as long as the placement didn't involve kids," a member snarled.

"It's hard to place someone in parish work that avoids kids."

"How about an all-girls school?"

"Funny."

"No, seriously, why parish work? Why not a teaching position at a seminary or something?"

"I agree with you. Someone botched the placement. We're looking into it. The mandate was clear, yet ignored, and the opposite occurred. The process is flawed. We need a detailed review."

"Issues for another day. For now, get the law firm and the investigator together with the pastor. We escaped inexpensively on Gerry's last one. If anyone discovers this placement followed that one, the sky's the limit."

"Whatever happens, the defense fund can handle it."

"Has the Holy One been informed?"

"Didn't see the need. Let's have the specialists handle the situation and see where we are afterward."

"Another 'accident' perhaps?" Heads turned to the speaker then back to the Voice. *Would he agree?*

"Premature at this point," the Voice declared. "We'll keep all options open. Agreed? All in favor?"

"Aye."

"All opposed?"

Silence.

Chapter Four

Jennifer Tracey and her two sons lived in a small tri-level in Farmington Hills. Money was always tight, but following Jim's death and the subsequent lawsuit and settlement, the money dwindled, and it became increasingly difficult to make ends meet. Jennifer worked as an editor for a neighborhood newspaper and grossed about forty-five thousand per year. Her house payment, utilities, groceries, taxes, and religious school chewed up her spendable income.

Widowed at thirty-seven, she had platinum-blond hair, high cheekbones, and peaches-and-cream skin. She could pass for twenty-seven with signs of age beginning to show around her sparkling blue eyes. She had a broad, sensual mouth with full lips. At five foot three, her legs were slender and athletic from daily aerobics. Jim was the only man she'd ever been interested in. The couple met in high school and dated through college at Oakland University in Rochester, where she received her bachelor's degree in English, and he received his in engineering.

Jennifer wanted to marry Jim from the moment they met, but he was the voice of reason. He wanted his degree and a good job first. Jim would support her without parental assistance; thank you very much. He was a very proud and good man. She missed him terribly. She was beautiful, and there were many potential suitors. However, the thought of dating made her cringe. A couple of dates ended with her apologizing to the men. They claimed to understand. She didn't care either way.

The only thing she cared about was the welfare of her boys, Jim's boys. Two weeks after the camping trip, they were still distraught.

She knocked on their bedroom door and walked in without an invitation.

"I didn't hear anybody say, 'Come in,' did you, Jake?" snapped Kenny.

"Well . . . uh . . . I'm so sorry," stammered Jennifer, surprised at her son's tone.

"Yeah," Jake grumbled, looking at his brother for direction.

Jennifer collected herself and scanned the room. It was a boys' room, to be sure, but it's disaster level at that moment irritated her almost as much as the boys' attitude.

"Lose the attitude, gentlemen," she ordered. "Are you going to spend the rest of your lives in this room? Why don't you get out and enjoy the fresh spring air and sunshine? It's a beautiful day! Why don't you see if there is a pickup game at Lakes or something? You used to love the outdoors. Now I can't get you to leave your room. And this room! It looks like a cyclone hit it! I want these games, cards, and balls picked up this instant!"

"How's this?" Kenny scowled. He picked up a baseball and threw it at the wall, putting a large hole in the drywall. "See, I played baseball! Happy?"

Jake mimicked Kenny's behavior and swiped at an active Monopoly board, scattering cards, player pieces, and Monopoly money all over the already disaster-zone bedroom.

"That's enough!" cried Jennifer. "You boys are grounded until further notice. I want this room cleaned up immediately or no supper! And, Kenneth Tracey, you better think of ways to earn some money to pay for the repair of that wall!"

"Whatever," Kenny snarled. "I didn't want to go outside in the first place, and I sure as hell don't want to go to Lakes."

"Yeah," Jake offered, attempting without success to equal his brother's animus.

Jennifer left the room and slammed the door in utter frustration. What was going on with these two? They hadn't been themselves since the camping trip. In fact, they hadn't even unpacked their backpacks. She saw them, amid the rubble, in the corner of the room, opened but still fully packed. They loved the outdoors and church activities. Now she couldn't get them to leave their bedroom—and the anger, the sadness . . .

Jake's cheeks were often red and wet. Jennifer tried to comfort him. "Jake, honey, I love you. Please tell Mommy what's wrong."

Jake shook his head no. Jennifer reached out, hugged him, and looked into his eyes. There was a haunting sadness in his beautiful blue eyes, his mother's eyes. These days, they exhibited only pain.

Kenny was quiet, aloof, and angry. Jennifer tried to talk to him, but he was combative. She observed him staring into space, scowling. She looked into his eyes, Jim's eyes, and saw unbridled hatred. He spent hours in his room, speaking to no one, doing nothing. His anger was escalating. He threw a ball through his bedroom wall! His younger brother was trying to imitate him. Something was seriously wrong. But what could it be?

The boys' antisocial antics were abrupt and inexplicable, but their origin was somehow related to their recent camping trip. The trip was the key. She was convinced. Maybe some camper embarrassed one of her sons in front of others. But why would such an incident make Jake so sad or Kenny so angry? She decided to visit Father Gerry to see if he could shed some light on the situation. She made the short drive to the church and found him tending the garden.

"Jenny!" Gerry chirped. "How nice to see you. I haven't seen you or the boys in church lately."

"Father," Jennifer responded, getting right to the point, "I am very concerned about my boys. They've been acting very strangely since the camping trip. Jake is sad and tearful. Kenny explodes, tells me to leave him alone, and storms off to his room. They don't do anything except go to school, come home and mope. Did you notice if anything bad happened on that trip?"

"Nothing I noticed," Gerry considered. "Would you like me to talk to the boys?"

"Oh, yes, Father, that would normally be fine, but I can't get either to come to church. I've been trying for two weeks."

"That does sound serious," Gerry pondered. "How about I come over to your house and talk to the boys?"

"Would you, Father? It wouldn't be too much trouble? I'd be eternally grateful. Maybe they'll open up for you. The past two weeks have been living hell, and I'm getting nowhere."

"It's no trouble at all. What time would you like me to come by?" He would talk to the boys and do what was necessary.

"Why don't you come for dinner? I'm making their favorite, spaghetti and meatballs."

"Why that's my favorite too," Gerry lied. "What time do you

want me?"

"How's six o'clock?"

"Sounds fine. I'll be there. Do you need me to bring anything?"

"Just you . . . and . . . perhaps a prayer or two," she smiled.

"Prayer helps whatever ails you. I'll see you at six."

"Bless you, Father, and thank you," Jennifer sighed. She turned and walked to the car, feeling upbeat and hopeful for the first time in two weeks.

Gerry Bartholomew watched Jennifer's van disappear down the road and cursed under his breath. *These boys need to understand God loves them, wants them to enjoy the outdoors, and wants them to understand love of God is often demonstrated through love of man.*

***

Gerry arrived for dinner promptly at six. Jennifer didn't advise the boys of his impending visit. She hoped to surprise them. She took Gerry to the living room and invited him to sit. She called the boys to dinner. As had been their practice for the past two weeks, they were holed up in their bedroom playing board games or creating scrapbooks for their baseball card collections. They liked the security of their room these days. It was the only place they seemed remotely comfortable.

As the two boys bounded down the stairs, Kenny spotted Gerry and stopped dead in his tracks. He stuck out his arm sternly, like a traffic cop, stopping Jake on the stairs. Jake was terrified at the sight of Gerry and immediately hid behind his older brother.

"What's *he* doing here?" Kenny demanded.

"I invited him to have dinner with us. You haven't been to church in two weeks, and Father Gerry misses you. I made your favorite, spaghetti and meatballs. Come and eat."

"We're not hungry," Kenny spoke for both of them. He and Jake then turned their backs and started back up the stairs.

"Kenny and Jake Tracey!" Jennifer cried. "You get back here this instant and eat your dinner! And apologize to Father Gerry! You're being rude, and I don't like it! You've been moping around for two weeks now, and it's breaking my heart, but I won't let you take it out on Father Gerry!"

"You want us to say we're sorry to *him*?" Kenny cried. Tears rolled down his cheeks.

"Right this instant!" Jennifer refused to soften her stance.

"He's the one who should be sorry," Kenny shouted, continuing to shield his brother. He and Jake turned away and started back up the stairs. Jennifer began to protest again, but Gerry stopped her.

"Let them go, Jenny," he suggested. "I'll go up and talk to them. Maybe I can get them to come down."

"Oh, thank you, Father. Perhaps, you can find out what's troubling them."

"I'll sure give it a try."

She watched him go up the stairs, and something in the back of her mind was worried about the impending interaction. A few stray thoughts began to coalesce into an idea. What if the boys' current behavior had its genesis on the camping trip with the man she sent upstairs? The boys were indeed not themselves. *What does this have to do with Father Gerry?* She shook those thoughts away and went back to preparing the dinner.

Gerry somehow persuaded the boys to come to the table. Dinner was uneventful. Jennifer and Gerry engaged in light conversation about nothing in particular. Kenny and Jake ate almost nothing in complete silence.

Shortly after dinner, Gerry arose to say goodbye. As he left leaving, with Jennifer's attention momentarily elsewhere, he flashed the boys a sinister glare. Jennifer sent the boys upstairs to wash up for bedtime. After doing the dinner dishes, she started up the stairs toward the boys' room. She heard the two boys talking.

"You've got to be brave, and you've got to be quiet," she heard Kenny say.

"But I'm scared, Kenny," Jake murmured. "Really scared."

"I know, but I won't ever let him hurt you again," Kenny assured.

"You promise?" Jake managed.

"Cross my heart and hope to die," Kenny promised.

"You can't die, Kenny," Jake panicked. "Daddy died, and Father Bill left us. Don't leave me all alone."

"I won't die, Jake. I love you. I will never leave you alone." He spoke in a calm voice well beyond his years.

"I love you too, Kenny," sobbed Jake.

"Good, now get under the covers. Mom will be in to say goodnight."

"Okay," Jake calmed, regaining self-control.

Outside the door, Jennifer listened in horror. What was it? Someone hurt them. Who? Her thoughts were gathering, inching toward a conclusion, but she resisted. Did something happen at school? Was someone being bullied? The camping trip was fun, wasn't it?

She decided that the boys needed professional help but not that night. That night, she would hug them, kiss them, and put them to bed. That night, she would simply love them with all her heart.

Chapter Five

The telephone rang in Father Jonathan Costigan's private office. He answered, "Our Lady of the Lakes, Father Jon Costigan speaking."

"Hello, Jon," a deep male voice greeted him. "What's the current status?"

Oh God, not him! This character was a member of the church hierarchy, partly responsible for Bartholomew's transfer to his parish. They shoved this bastard down Jon's throat. His identity was a mystery—clergymen who had contact with him referred to him simply as "the Voice."

Jon wanted to appoint his own assistant pastor. When he protested this forced transfer, he was offered a transfer of his own, to a northern Canadian parish. His Lakes parishioners were the only 'family' Jon had. He had no choice but to accept Bartholomew.

Jon was disgusted the church would endanger his parish to accommodate a predator. He privately wished a church pastor had more authority. Alas, such was life in an organization as large and complex as the church. A parish priest, even the head pastor of a parish the size of Lakes, had little control. *Am I not competent enough to interview and hire my own assistant?*

"Well . . . Gerry visited the family last night. He convinced Jennifer to let him up to the boys' room to talk to them in private. Little did Jennifer suspect that the problem *is* the priest," Costigan snarled.

"Cut the theatrics, Jon. How did the meeting go?" The Voice wasn't in the mood for a lecture from a *subordinate*.

"Gerry thinks it went well. Apparently, they had a nice chat about spirituality and acceptance of God's love," he grumbled.

"Get a grip, Jon."

"I want this son of a bitch out of my parish, *ASAP*."

"We can't do that, Jon. Too soon, it will arouse suspicion."

"Who are you people? Who cares about arousing suspicion? I care about safety and welfare, especially of the children. Who is concerned for *their* well-being?" Jon demanded. He didn't care about chain of command.

The Voice softened. "You do, Jon. All of us do. A mistake was made in this case. But, we must look at the bigger picture. A scandal would be very detrimental to the church *and* your parish. It would affect the future of *all* our children, not just these two. Do all we can to help the Tracey boys? Absolutely, but we must proceed in a very discreet manner. We must limit Gerry's contact with children to only public events. This can't happen again. I'm counting on you to keep him under control."

"That is easier said than done, sir. He didn't tell me he was leaving last night. I didn't even know he was gone until I noticed the VW missing."

"We knew he left and where he went. We're watching him, Jon."

"You guys seem to have all the answers. You have the situation under control. Why do you need me?"

"We need him observed at the parish. Carefully schedule his time and activities. Keep him away from kids. Can you do that, Jon?"

"I'll do my best, but not for the likes of you. I'll do it for the safety of the kids."

"Very well then," the Voice was placated. "We'll keep in touch. And, Jon?"

"Yes?"

"Communication is a two-way street. Keep us informed."

No answer.

"Jon?"

"Yes?"

"Can we count on you?"

"Yes." Jon shuddered at the realization that these men, whoever they were, were probably powerful enough to expel him. *Who would watch over the children then?*

"Oh, and, Jon? Pay a visit to the Tracey family. Offer your assistance. Tell Jennifer Tracey that the church knows where the boys can get excellent psychological or psychiatric counseling. Convince her that we know good people and that we'll pick up the bill."

"Why would we do that? Won't that arouse suspicion?" Jon was surprised by this sudden gesture of kindness.

"I think not. Besides, it's the right thing to do. If we can get the boys to *our* mental health professionals rather than one of her choosing—a loose cannon, so to speak—we can monitor the boys' progress much better."

"You mean brainwash them," Jon charged.

"You watch too much television, Jon. Brainwashing? Absurd. Concentrate on your duties."

"Thanks for the advice. Are we finished?"

"For now, Jon. You'll be hearing from us again. Good-bye. God bless."

Father Jonathan Costigan hung up the phone and glanced at his watch. He had time before his seminar to drive over to Jennifer's. He'd known her a long time, baptized both boys, and watched them grow. He knew Jim even longer and mourned with the family when God called him to heaven. Jon had always been there for the Tracey family, providing spiritual and friendly guidance when needed. Now, his superiors wanted him to spy on them and make sure they sought treatment from practitioners loyal to the church. He was to help brainwash them and assist in a cover-up.

He rationalized his assignment. *The boys will get the help they need. A scandal would be harmful to all parishioners— adults and children. Perhaps if we can get them discreet counseling, it would be to everyone's advantage."* Father Jonathan Costigan was a man trying to convince himself of the truth of a false assertion.

Chapter Six

"This is a special Sunday. We are pleased to officially welcome Father Gerry Bartholomew to the pulpit to deliver his first Sunday message to the congregation . . ."

Father Jon almost choked on his words. He'd been instructed to offer words of welcome to set the stage for Gerry's first sermon. He was repulsed but did his job. Gerry sauntered to the pulpit, too cocky for Jon's taste. Gerry raised his arms for quiet, and the congregation grew silent.

"Thank you, Father Jon, and thanks to all of you. I cherish my first opportunity to address you. I'd like to explain why I became a priest . . ." Gerry began.

"When I was young, I thought I'd finish school, grow up, go to college, get married, start a career, start and build a family. God chose another path for me, and I have never turned back or been sorry. I have a much larger family and many children whom I can help shape. Children are the Lord's most precious creatures, and I humbly accept my role in shaping their hearts and minds. This vital work with children is the principal reason that I became a priest. Children represent our future, the future of any race or religion.

"Psalm 127:3 says, 'Certainly sons are a gift from the LORD, the fruit of the womb, a reward.' In other words, God blesses people with children and children are a blessing. The following verse 4 says, 'Like arrows in the hand of a warrior are the sons born in one's youth." As arrows are in the hand of a mighty man; so are children of the youth.' Again, the theme is that children are an asset and a blessing . . .

"In the Bible, God uses the simple but essential word *children* a remarkable 1,650 times. The term *child* is used another 190 times. Three of the Ten Commandments are devoted to sanctifying and safeguarding the family. It is safe to say that God loves children.

"How many parents enjoy the simple pleasure of watching their newborn child sleep? This is a profoundly boring activity, yet parents derive great delight from it. When you have your own baby, when the grumpiest among us observe the interaction of a small child with his or her parent—even the cranky heart becomes full of warmth.

"Children are amazing. All of us have a responsibility to treat them and handle them as blessings. As I gaze out at the congregation, I am pleased to see so many blessed children. You are, indeed, a blessing from God . . .

"It is easy to devote my ministry to children. Church doctrine precludes me from marrying. Priests are required to remain celibate. We will have no children of our own. Why? Because *you* are my family, your children are my children. The church endues the title of 'Father' on priests, and I am honored to be a 'father' to your children. I have wonderful, pleasurable activities and events planned for them. I enjoy sports, travel, camping, and preaching the gospel. Hopefully, I can provide spiritual guidance and enlightenment to your children as they grow from child to teenager to adult. I especially enjoy being a role model to teenagers, counseling them, advising them, shaping and molding young minds, attitudes, and sharing the wonders and experiences of life.

"As children grow into teenagers, I plan to be, if you will permit me, an important part of their lives. Leave them to my care. Trust them to my embrace. As your children are a blessing to you, they are a blessing to me.

"Today, I invite you to focus on important ways to treat our precious children. First, we must give them understanding. They are gifts from God, miniature replicas of each of you. You want to see yourself? Look for yourself in your children. Children are warm, and they bring warmth to us. They have the ability to make parents and grandparents melt in their hands. We feel that warmth when a baby reaches out with his or her little hand and touches our faces or looks into our eyes. We melt when they first say, 'Mommy' or 'Daddy.' When they're young, they're not ashamed to hug or kiss their parents. I am a firm believer in and practitioner of hugs, in physical love, physical displays of affection." Gerry flushed with desire. The congregation could not detect this subtle hint of his sinister nature.

"Parents teach their children. These are blessings because children are tomorrow's teachers. And so it goes, generation to generation. Most of us live simple lives. There are no statues erected in our honor. But many of us will have children, and they will carry on our name and our legacy. This is the special blessing of ancestry.

"Grow closer, express more love to one another. Children and parents must develop trust in each other, a consequence of which is to grow in love. We want our kids to seek *our* advice rather than getting it on the streets from those of dubious character. Many teenagers view the home or the church as a prison cell, with parents and priests serving as their guards. However, many of their problems would be solved if they became closer to God and the church.

"If understanding is not found in the family, the safest place that a child knows, where can it be located? In Corinthians 13:11, the apostle Paul says, 'When I was a child, I spoke as a child, I understood as a child, I thought as a child; but when I became a man, I put away childish things.' If we want to reach our children, we must try to think as they do. We must put ourselves in their shoes.

"Second, we must communicate with our children. With both parents working in most twenty-first-century families, would you be surprised if I told you that moms spend less than an hour a day with their children and fathers less than a half-hour?

"Deuteronomy 4:7 says, 'You shall teach them diligently unto your children, and shall talk of them when you sit in your house and when you walk by the way, and when you lie down and when you rise up.' Spend time with your children, talk about a quality life through spirituality. Parents and grandparents alike have a responsibility to teach children the principles of a quality life. Communication is an essential tool in exercising that responsibility.

"Here is a suggestion. Offer your children an hour a day of your time. Tell them that it is their time with you to do or say anything they want, go anywhere they want to go, play anything they want to play. And I will make you this promise—despite my busy schedule, any parent of any child who asks this of me; I will pledge an hour to you or your child. Parents and priests are busy. We are here, there, and everywhere, taking care of this crisis or that one. However, I urge you to make the one-hour pledge to your children and to honor the commitment. It is crucial they know you care, that you love them and will be there for them in times of need.

"Third, we must provide for our children. It is our responsibility as parents to provide a loving and happy home. It is most important to demonstrate relationships by example in a committed and happy marriage. In many ways, this example of commitment is even more important than the relationship between parent and child. We must provide food, clothing, and shelter, of course, but the atmosphere in which our children grow up is of the utmost importance. However, some marriages fall apart, even when husband and wife have the best of intentions going into them. If that fate falls upon you and your children, please call on me to counsel your sons, to guide them along the paths of righteousness and love, especially if this happens during their teenage years. Trust them to my loving care . . ." *Would they? The parents must trust me.*

"Fourth, we must set a good example for our children. In other words, we must not only talk the talk; we must walk the walk. If we expect our kids not to smoke, not to drink, and not to do drugs, we must refrain from those activities ourselves. Children will often do what they see others doing. What I would like to see is child after child deciding to seek the counsel of the Lord, through private and privileged counsel with me.

"Finally, number five is to love your children. Show them genuine affection. Children need to be loved, cared for, felt, and touched. I am pleased to help in this endeavor, as I am a very hands-on person. I pledge, with all my soul, in all that I do, to love your children. And studies show that physical love is important, even in the first days after birth. Research indicates that female infants less than a year old receive five times more physical affection than boys of the same age. Is that why younger boys have far more emotional and psychiatric problems than younger girls? A child growing up with physical contact will be more comfortable with themselves and others. I promise, with all

my heart, to shower your children with affection, to guide them
to a greater good, through love, touch, feel, the church, and the
grace of God."

Jennifer Tracey attended church services that morning. She
dropped the boys off at her sister's house and arrived early. She
wasn't aware that Father Gerry would be delivering his first
sermon. These last statements compelled her to leave. She didn't
understand why but knew she must. She rose and walked up the
aisle toward the exit. Gerry paused and watched her go. Heads
turned. The sermon seemed to come to an abrupt halt. Jennifer
walked out the door, and it clicked closed behind her. Gerry
struggled to understand her departure and promptly lost his
composure. He continued, more tentatively, as Jennifer exited
the church building.

"Okay . . . now . . . uh . . . I would like to address the children
. . ." *Why is she leaving? Was it something I said? Did the boys
say something to her? Shit!*

"For you to remain blessed . . . for you to . . . uh . . . continue
to be a gift from God, I have three suggestions: Try to learn
about God from your parents, the church, Father Jon, and me,
and, most important, read your Bible. Remember that, according
to scripture, Jesus learned of God at the age of twelve. You can
learn of God as well. Be grateful to God and your parents for all
the nice things that happen in your life. Tell those who do nice
things for you, including your parents, how much you appreciate
their kindness. Learn to say a simple thank you when people do
nice things. Food does not miraculously appear on your table at
mealtime. How did your bed get made and your clothes folded
and put away? Have you ever thought of saying thank you to
your mom for simple acts of kindness? Give thanks for the
kindnesses extended to you and the things you receive. Count
your blessings." Gerry was finding a stronger voice, more
control, following Jennifer's abrupt exit. *I can finish this.*

"Be willing to experiment. Dare to try something different.
Try to do things outside your comfort zone. I specialize in
helping teenagers experience God's love in unique ways, and I
pledge to assist you in any way I can to achieve grace through
love. I am here for you. I am a very valuable resource. Use me as

often as you choose.

"Remember, dear family and friends; children are a blessing and the future leaders of our church, our community, our country, and our world. And they are the future leaders in the kingdom of God and heaven. Thank you, and God bless you and your precious children."

Chapter Seven

Father Jon gave Jennifer two names and numbers. After talking with both clinics, she chose the Beacon-East Counseling Center in Birmingham, Michigan. She liked that Beacon-East had both psychologists and psychiatrists on staff. A Saturday appointment was scheduled for the weekend following her phone call. She was now driving east on Maple toward Birmingham.

Birmingham was an upscale suburb of Detroit. Upscale retailers chose Birmingham for a downtown location, especially following the retail abandonment of downtown Detroit after the 1967 riot. Birmingham has many fine retail shops, restaurants, coffeehouses, art galleries, and theaters.

The city also had many beautiful residential communities and office complexes contained within and surrounding its downtown. Beacon-East was located on Brown Street; two quick right turns from the corner of Maple and South Woodward, Downtown Birmingham's main cross streets. Jennifer spotted the building and the clinic sign as soon as she turned onto Brown. She pulled the Tahoe into the parking lot of the clinic. The kids had not uttered a single word for the entire trip. This morning, she sat the boys down and told them they were going to see a doctor to find out why they were so upset. Neither was thrilled with the idea of seeing what Kenny called a "shrink," but Mom insisted.

Beacon-East was an ultra-modern white-and-glass single-story office building. There were multiple psychiatrists and psychologists listed on the occupant roster. Their appointment was with Harold Rothenberg, M.D., Ph.D. Jennifer walked up to his office counter. A sliding glass window, adjacent a locked door, separated the waiting room from the clinic. The receptionist greeted her pleasantly and handed her a questionnaire to complete. The only highlighted portion of the questionnaire was payer and insurance information. She finished the form, returned it to the receptionist, and took a seat. Kenny and Jake busied themselves with a couple of *Highlights* magazines. She was grateful they were alone in the waiting room.

After a short wait, the locked door opened and a tall, balding man with a flowing white, Santa Claus–type beard asked them to follow him back. Jennifer rose, collected the kids, and followed the man to a smallish room that contained a tiny desk and chair, a recliner, and a couch. There were diplomas, association membership plaques, awards, and certification notices all over the walls. Jennifer took the recliner. The boys jumped on the couch. Santa Claus, to Jennifer's surprise, introduced himself as Dr. Rothenberg and inquired, "What seems to be the problem? How can I help you?"

Jennifer told him about the camping trip, the boys' school situation, and their recent strange behavior. In a series of questions and answers, Dr. Rothenberg also learned about Jim's death and Father Bill's sudden departure. After exchanging a few more questions for answers, Dr. Rothenberg asked Jennifer if he might talk to the boys alone. Kenny shrugged, 'I don't care,' and Jake was okay with whatever his brother wanted. Jennifer and Dr. Rothenberg rose. The doctor escorted Jennifer back to the waiting room and told her that he expected the session to last approximately forty-five minutes.

Forty-five minutes seemed like forever, and when the kids finally came out, Dr. Rothenberg summoned Jennifer in. The boys resumed their *Highlights* reading.

"Sit down, please, Mrs. Tracey."

"Oh, call me Jenny, please," she smiled, taking the recliner.

"Okay, Jenny. This is not a school-bullying situation. Your boys are extremely upset about something that happened on that camping trip. I could not get them to talk about the trip, but the mere mention of it sends Jake into hysterics. It may take several sessions to obtain their trust. I recommend twice per week sessions for now. Hopefully, we can build a trust relationship and learn as much as we can as soon as we can."

"Sounds okay to me, Doctor." *He has a gentle nature.* "May I ask you something?"

"Sure, anything."

"Based on this session and seeing how *upset* they are, to use

your term, do you have any preliminary thoughts on what may
have caused their recent behavior? Do you know if they . . . what
happened?"

"Fair question and one that I'd ask if these were my children.
Any answer would be no more than a guess at this point.
Hopefully, after a few sessions, we'll have some answers."

"Is there anything I can do at home?"

"Hugs, kisses, and lots of love," Dr. Rothenberg smiled.

I like this man.

"Here's my card. It has my office number, cell phone, and
my home number. If anything happens and you need to talk, call
me anytime, day or night."

"Thanks again, Doctor. We'll see you next week." Jennifer
was relieved.

"Good-bye, Jennifer."

Almost immediately after Jennifer left the office, the
telephone in Dr. Rothenberg's office rang.

***

"Good morning, Dr. Rothenberg, here."

"Good morning, Dr. Rothenberg," the Voice chirped.

"What can I do for you?" Rothenberg grumbled.

"How did your session with the Tracey boys go?"

"How did you know the session was over?" *Are these people
monitoring my office?*

"Nothing covert, Doctor. The appointment was for eleven.
It's now noon. You told me sessions last an hour," The Voice
reasoned. "So, again, how did the session go?"

"It went as expected. The boys don't trust me and won't for a
while. Hopefully, in time, I'll be able to gain their trust and be of
some assistance to them and the church." Rothenberg calmed. *I
am a professional. I need to behave like one.*

"How much time?"

"It's impossible to say. This varies from patient to patient. In
this case, though, I have an advantage."

"What's that?"

"I already know what's bothering them."

"True, so what's the prognosis?"

"These are tough cases. It may take months, even years, to resolve feelings of pain and betrayal. A priest is a father figure. The betrayal of trust is enormous, and it takes a long time to rebuild that trust. There are also sexual components. These will manifest themselves as the boys become more sexually aware. Time will tell whether this impacts their sexuality or how they respond to sexual situations. Degree is a factor. In this case, your team has advised that we are dealing with lower-level trauma. While that's a positive, this is not an exact science, and kids react to different things in different ways. Whatever the case, I will do my best to help them."

"We know you will. That's why we chose you. Keep me posted." *I will have measured control of this situation. He is loyal to the church.*

"That, I cannot do."

"What?" *Have I lost control?* The Voice was stunned.

"I cannot keep you posted."

"No? Why not?"

"Doctor-patient privilege and confidentiality. It's very similar to the priest-penitent privilege."

"But the church retained your services, not the Tracey family. Doesn't that change the privilege dynamic? After all, it's our money."

"The privilege belongs to the patient, regardless of who is paying the bill."

The Voice silently seethed.

"Look," Dr. Rothenberg continued, "I promised you when you retained me that I would do my very best to help these boys as discreetly as possible. I intend to keep that promise, but I will not violate doctor-patient confidentiality."

"Understood, Doctor." The Coalition would monitor all sessions anyway.

Somehow he makes 'understood' sound like 'fuck you.'

"Anything else?" Rothenberg wondered.

"Not at this time, Doctor. Thank you and good-bye."

"Good-bye."

Chapter Eight

Jennifer sat in the pew and tried, without success, to let the weight of her children's worries slide off her shoulders. She'd left the boys with her sister Lynne for the morning, hoping that a break from their home environment would help them. Jennifer looked for help from the church.

Father Gerry stood at the pulpit, in full regalia, looking down upon the congregation. His eyes didn't meet Jennifer's, but she hoped he'd noticed her. He began his sermon.

"Today, I would like to talk to you about relationships and anger. Often, we are the angriest at the people we know and love. Take, for example, the relationships between adults and teenagers. What makes a good parent in the eyes of a teen?

"Part of the answer is found in the example you set in your interactions with your spouse. Remember, your kids are watching. They watch, learn, and form their own concepts and opinions of marriage from your example."

Jennifer hadn't been thinking about her late husband or how much help he would have been during her boys' current woes, but now she couldn't avoid it. For a moment, she lost track of Gerry's sermon. Suddenly, his voice intruded into her thoughts.

"If a son watches his father abuse his mother, will the son view this behavior as normal? Will *he* become an abuser? If a daughter observes the same behavior, will she assume that abusive relationships are acceptable?"

Jennifer was uncomfortable. She didn't expect every sermon to contain a hopeful or uplifting message. At *this* moment, however, she wanted the priest to talk about something other than pain.

"There are no perfect adults. We sin constantly and then forgive each other for our sins. There are no perfect fathers, no perfect mothers, no perfect priests."

Why did he have to say that? For the next few minutes, 'no perfect priests' was all she could hear. Gerry continued, but Jennifer lost all sense of his main point.

"Embrace the nuances of others, the imperfections of others. Nobody's perfect, not even you, certainly not me. Psalm 127:3 says, 'Behold, children are a gift of the Lord; the fruit of the womb is a reward.'"

She stared at the stained glass on the eastern windows. A shepherd, a flock of sheep, and an image of heaven shone with the light of the sun, which passed behind clouds and then emerged again as she watched. Did that mean something? Even when the sun was obscured, the colors shone brightly. Father Gerry was concluding his sermon.

"John 4:20 says, 'If anyone says, 'I love God,' yet hates his brother, he is a liar. For anyone who does not love his brother, whom he has seen, cannot love God, whom he has not seen.' So settle things with those who have angered you before coming here to pray.

"Read in verses 25 to 26, Jesus also preached that we should settle disagreements without going to court. I couldn't agree more. 'Settle matters quickly with your adversary who is taking you to court; do it while you are still with him on the way . . .'

"To Jesus, this type of resolution of differences is important. 'Don't wait,' he says. 'Do it now.' Cast away your hostility and inherent desire to win at all costs. Ask God's forgiveness and your adversary's forgiveness for the harsh words spoken against him or her in anger. Love your children and others as you would love yourselves and your God. Resolve those differences that tear you up inside. Cast away your wrath. Respect each other. Love each other. Take care of each other and go with God. Amen."

The sermon did not provide Jennifer what she was seeking, but it *did* provide her with the seed of an idea.

Chapter Nine

Dr. Rothenberg paused, reviewed his notes, and contemplated his approach. He was beginning his thirteenth session with the Tracey boys. The sessions took place over six weeks at two sessions per week. Phone calls from the Voice, after each session, were very troubling, frustrating him as much as the boys' almost complete silence during therapy. He learned the boys hated church. They also disliked school, as it was part of the church. They were angry with their mother for making them go to school and for trying to make them go to church. They were angry with their father for dying and with Father Bill for leaving. They were mad with Father Jon for letting Bill leave and hiring Gerry to replace him. Most of all, they hated Father Gerry, without explanation. He decided today he would take a more direct approach.

Dr. Rothenberg prompted, "Your problems with Father Gerry seem to have developed on that camping trip. Did Gerry do anything on that trip to upset you?"

No answer. Jake glanced at Kenny, eyes pleading for direction.

"Did he speak to you in a mean or sarcastic way?"

"No," Kenny grunted.

"Did he hit you?"

"No," muttered Kenny. He was becoming uncomfortable.

"Did other boys do anything to cause anger?" Dr. Rothenberg probed.

"No," repeated Kenny.

"Did Father Gerry put his hands on you in any way that made you uncomfortable?"

Does he know? I can't tell him, can I? Can I trust this guy? Kenny folded his arms and engaged in internal debate. Jake's eyes met Rothenberg's for a brief moment.

"Do you boys know the difference between good touch and bad touch?" Rothenberg probed.

"Yes," Kenny grumbled, and then he began to cry.

Jake began to cry as well, looking to his brother, silently urging him to unload their burden.

"What's the difference?" Dr. Rothenberg pressed.

"I don't want to discuss this," Kenny groaned. *Do I?* The voice in his head grew louder.

"Why not?"

"Because it's disgusting!"

"What's disgusting?"

"Someone touching you in a bad way,"

"What way would he have to touch you for it to be bad?" Rothenberg was desperate.

"You know," Kenny moaned.

"No, I don't. Explain it to me," Rothenberg prodded.

"I can't," Kenny grunted in anguish, tears rolling down his cheek.

"I can help you," Rothenberg pleaded. "Please, you must trust me."

"I don't trust anyone from the church," Kenny shouted.

"Do you think I want to hurt you?" Dr. Rothenberg inquired.

"I don't know. I don't know you that well. Do you want to hurt me?"

"No, Kenny, I don't. Trust me, please! I want to help you," pleaded Rothenberg.

"Bad touch is when he touches you in places he shouldn't, your private parts!" Jake blurted. He screamed and broke into tears. "But he did more. He hurt me, and he hurt Kenny too."

"Jake, no!" Kenny screamed.

Jake continued, tears flowing in droves. "I *begged* for him to stop. He wouldn't stop. It was awful. I was bleeding and crying. He wouldn't stop. He wouldn't stop!" Jake broke down in uncontrollable sobbing. He buried himself in Kenny's arms.

Rothenberg was dumbfounded, shocked speechless. He was retained to provide treatment in a *fourth-degree* fondling case. This was far worse. *This is a first-degree case. These boys were raped!* The floodgates opened—details were pouring out now. Father Gerry showered with them, forced them to wear nothing but nightshirts as they got into bed, and joined each one in turn.

"I knew we couldn't trust you or anyone! Look what you've

done to my brother!" Kenny charged.

Dr. Rothenberg corrected him. "No, Kenny. Gerry hurt your brother. It's good to get this off his chest and talk about it. It can help you guys begin to heal." He desperately tried to return them to a calmer state.

"We don't need your help," Kenny calmly grumbled.

"I think you do," Dr. Rothenberg countered. "Did Gerry do this to you too, Kenny? You and Jake have done nothing wrong! This is all on Father Gerry." *I have to get them to trust me!* "Kenny, what Jake just said, did Gerry do this to you too?" he prodded, sickened by the thought. *Of course, he did; why wouldn't he?*

Trembling and ready to burst if he didn't talk, Kenny screamed, "Yes!" Tears poured down his cheeks. "Just like Jake said! He wouldn't stop. It hurt worse than anything! He got this stuff all over me, and I was bleeding. He told us, 'The Lord loves clean bodies,' and I'm bleeding all over the place! Then he took us into the shower, cleaned us off, and hurt us again! I hate him! We trusted him. He was our *priest*!" Kenny cried.

"Of course you trusted him," Rothenberg agreed. "Why wouldn't you?"

Both boys sobbed. Rothenberg got up from his chair, sat down between the boys on the couch, and held both of them in his arms. He was devastated and shocked at the scope of the priest's conduct, enraged church officials deceived him, and a parish priest raped two young boys. He could not maintain the discretion the Voice requested and still serve justice.

This monster needs to be locked up. Where did this predator come from? Has he done this before? How many young boys has he traumatized? How could the church expose unsuspecting children to such a man? Gerry has to be stopped. Forget discretion! I'll tell the Voice to fuck off. Rothenberg's head was spinning.

He needed to calm the boys down and speak to their mother. *Oh, my God! Jennifer! Her entire life, especially since her husband died, has been these boys and this church. To have both shattered in such a bizarre fashion . . .* He found himself despising his work. Jennifer required the truth, but he dreaded the moment. She'd been through so much.

And what of these boys? Am I qualified to help them? I've never had a case like this one, this severe. His stomach was in turmoil, his mind filled with self-doubt. Could he find a way? He needed to facilitate the removal of Gerry from Lakes and into a treatment center. The Voice would not approve. *Screw the fucking Voice!*

Rothenberg was skating on thin ice. The Voice seemed to know his every move. *Is my office being monitored? That must be it! God, am I paranoid? Get a grip, man!* He needed an ally, someone he could discuss this with outside of the office. But whom could he trust in this situation?

Father Jon! Jon's a good and decent man. He can't be involved in this. How do I reach him without the Voice discovering the contact? If he's monitoring my office, he's tracking the church as well. Jennifer! I can reach him through Jennifer! Rothenberg realized at that moment that the boys had stopped crying and were staring at him.

"Well," Rothenberg composed himself. "Are you guys okay?"

"Yes, Doc," Jake had regained self-control.

"I g-guess so," Kenny stuttered.

"Do you feel any better unloading all those secrets you've been keeping inside?" Rothenberg probed.

"I'm not sure . . . ." Kenny hesitated.

"Father Gerry is *evil*. He did terrible things. Telling someone, getting this off your chest, is a wonderful first step. Hopefully, I can help get you past this. We need to tell your mother, okay? She is very worried," Rothenberg prodded.

"She'll be angry," Kenny argued. "She'll be mad at me for not protecting Jake. That's my job."

Tough job for someone so young, Rothenberg reasoned. "No, she won't, Kenny. Gerry took advantage. He's the adult. What could you have done? Please, don't blame yourself. That's how guys like Gerry control little guys like you. He makes you believe *you* were bad, that *you* did something wrong. He told you not to tell, right? He said your Mom would be mad, and even *God* would be mad, right?"

"Yeah, he did," Kenny admitted, surprised at Rothenberg's insight.

"If you don't want me to tell your mother, I won't. You're the boss."

"I'm the boss?" Kenny straightened. "Then, I don't want you to tell her."

"Why not?" Rothenberg was taken aback. He thought he had Kenny on track.

"Because she'll be mad."

"No, she won't, Kenny. Trust me, please." He knew it would be difficult for this abused, violated boy to trust a man after what he experienced. He believed the answer would be 'no.' Kenny surprised him.

"Okay," Kenny agreed, "as long as you promise."

"I promise," Dr. Rothenberg assured him. "May I bring her in now?"

Kenny nodded, and Jake mimicked him as usual.

"Yes," Kenny assented.

Kenny was beginning to trust him, something to build on. Rothenberg was buoyed.

***

The doctor left the room and returned with Jennifer. The Voice sat back to listen.

"We've had a breakthrough today, Jennifer," Rothenberg began.

"That's wonderful news, right?" Jennifer exclaimed. "What's happened?"

"Sit down, please," he motioned her to a spot on the couch between her two boys.

"Kenny and Jake have been sexually molested by Father Gerry," he blurted. He could not sugar coat this.

Jennifer sat in silent shock. Her worst fears were being realized.

"Oh, my God," she screamed. "Oh, dear God, no! How did this happen? How could a priest do something like this? Oh, my God, my babies! What did he do to you?" Jennifer was trembling.

She grabbed a boy in each arm and held on for dear life. She and the boys began to cry again. Jennifer's perfectly applied makeup was running down her cheeks. When she realized that she was upsetting the boys, she tried to regain composure and tone down the hostility.

"From the boys' description, there's not much he didn't do, I'm afraid."

"How often did this happen?"

"Many times, but only during that weekend camping trip," Rothenberg explained. The boys nodded assent.

"What are we going to do?" Jennifer demanded. *My boys will get through this, won't they?*

"We are going to continue twice-per-week therapy sessions. The boys feel responsible, typical in child abuse cases. The abuser makes the victim feel guilty, which helps conceal his activities. It's as if the victim is responsible for being chosen by his predator. That's one of the many things we have to work on."

"Gerry is a monster!" cried Jennifer. "Jake, Kenny, you have no reason to feel guilty or ashamed. He's a priest, for God's sakes! He betrayed your trust. He's a terrible man and an even worse priest. He will be punished—I promise you that!"

"Jennifer, betrayal of trust is another issue we need to work on. Priests are often father figures, especially in a fatherless home. These acts are quasi-incestuous and create serious trust issues. The good news is the boys were not violated over a long period. Some molesters are able to obtain victims' silence and assent to repeated assaults over months, even years. The victim is simply too afraid and ashamed to speak. Your boys trusted me, a relative stranger to them, with this secret. They've shown good reason and judgment. Progress over guilt and distrust in these cases is vital because they are major components of the victims' syndrome. We need to continue to work on these two areas as well as channeling anger and pain. This is a breakthrough session."

After an additional period of questions and answers, Rothenberg led the family out to the lobby. He uttered, "Good-bye," and put his finger to his lips, gesturing for silence. To

Jennifer's surprise, he followed her and the children out of the front door. Once outside, Jennifer sent the boys to the car.

"Jennifer, I want you to call Father Jon and arrange a meeting somewhere other than your home or the church," Rothenberg requested, scanning the area, his voice shrouded in mystery.

He was scaring her. *Why did we come outside? What is he hiding? What is he afraid of?* "Please call me Jenny. Everyone else does. Why the meeting?"

Rothenberg continued, ignoring her question. "When the meeting is set, drop off a note—don't call—and let me know when and where. I'll be there. Make sure Jon doesn't put this in his appointment book. Tell him to make sure he isn't followed, and don't do or say anything about Gerry to anyone, including Jon, until we've had this meeting."

"Okay, Doctor, but what's this all about? What's going on? Why are we talking about this out here in the parking lot?"

"I believe my office is being monitored," he confided.

"What?" Jennifer was stunned at the revelation.

"Yes, and probably your house, Lakes, and the rectory."

"But why? Who would do such a thing?" Jennifer puzzled, astonished.

"I'm not sure yet who they are or exactly what their function is. My sense is they minimize the impact of these kinds of events and limit damage to the church," Rothenberg surmised.

"You have got to be kidding!" Her shock morphed into outrage.

"I wish I was. Will you schedule the meeting as discreetly as possible?"

"I'll do whatever you say, Doctor, anything, if it will help Jake and Kenny . . . but . . . shouldn't we call the police?" Jennifer wanted these bastards to pay for what they did.

"At this point, I think we can wait. Let's see how this plays out. Hopefully, we can prevent other boys from becoming victims. And remember, your initial conversation with Father Jon will probably be monitored. I'm not sure we can trust him," Rothenberg warned.

"Who? Father Jon? Of course, we can trust him," Jennifer assured.

"He knew about the boys, Jenny. He's the one who retained me. We need to find out everything he knows," Rothenberg whispered. He knew this would jar Jennifer's psyche.

"Father Jon knew all along and said nothing?" Her face drained of color. She swooned, caught herself, and regained her balance by placing her hand against the wall.

"Apparently so, but we've both known Jon a long time. He's a good man, and my instincts tell me there were reasons for his silence. I want to know what they were and whether he'll help us before anyone else gets hurt, okay?"

"I don't believe this. He sat in my kitchen, ate my food, and recommended treatment for this 'unknown' condition when he knew, all along, that the boys were sexually abused?" Jennifer was nonplussed, betrayed by a good friend.

"Don't judge him yet. He may have a perfectly good explanation."

"He had better." *What explanation could there be?*

"Then you'll arrange the meet?"

"Of course. If we can prevent one more child from going through what my kids are going through, it will be worth it," she decided.

"You are a remarkable woman, Jennifer. Go ahead now. The boys are waiting."

"Thank you for all you've done, Doctor."

"You're welcome."

Rothenberg breathed a sigh of relief as he watched them exit the parking lot. *She still has her faith.* The church brought him this case, but those behind this cover-up were not his patients. *They are my patients' enemies, and I will fight them with every fiber of my being.* This meant exposing Father Gerry and getting him into a treatment program or a jail cell, anywhere away from teenage boys. Jon would assist. Rothenberg was sure of it.

Chapter Ten

The telephone rang. Rothenberg answered. He knew who was on the other end of the line.

"How did the session go, Dr. Rothenberg?"

"It went very well. Today was a breakthrough day in their treatment," Rothenberg seethed.

"How so?"

"I am not at liberty to say."

Defiance? "Do you have any sense of how long treatment will continue?" The Voice inquired.

"This will be a long-term project. Most child abuse victims have feelings of repressed anger, guilt, and a sense of betrayal, especially when the abuser is known to them, or as in this case, is a trusted figure. Getting in touch with those feelings and positively channeling them is one key. Reestablishing trust relationships is another. How long the process takes is anyone's guess."

"Does the mother know about the abuse?" The Voice tested. *Will he lie?*

"Yes, she does. She was informed today. She handled it well. I was able to persuade her that discretion would be helpful to treatment. Nobody wants the boys to become a public spectacle."

"Did she buy it?" The Voice wondered.

"Yes, she *bought it*," Rothenberg grumbled. The more he spoke to this 'Voice,' the more he despised the man. "It's true. Publicity may have a negative effect on treatment."

Antagonism in his voice? "That makes sense. Did she agree to keep things quiet?" The Voice inquired.

"Yes, she did. Anything else? I have a patient to see," Rothenberg snapped, dismissing the man.

"No, thank you again, Doctor. I'll talk to you soon." *And fuck you, too.*

"Good-bye."

The Voice turned to face the other men in the room. They'd heard the conversation.

"So, what do you think?"

"I think Dr. Rothenberg is helping those boys, which is, after all, what he was retained to do. I also think he's done an adequate job keeping this quiet so far. Still, I'm uneasy about him. I don't trust him. We need to maintain surveillance and keep Parks probing for skeletons."

"Anything found in his closet?"

"No. Doctor Rothenberg is either a sincere man or a saint. We haven't found a thing."

"Keep looking."

"Oh, we will."

"What about the mother? She knows now. She could be dangerous."

"Her home and Rothenberg's office are bugged. Parks will maintain twenty-four-hour surveillance on her and the doc."

"Very well, then. We're adjourned."

Chapter Eleven

Pastor Jonathan Costigan was finishing up his sermon for Sunday when his private telephone rang.

"Our Lady of the Lakes, Father Jon speaking."

"Hi, Father Jon. This is Jenny Tracey. How are you?" She fought hard to sound pleasant.

"Jenny! How nice to hear from you. I'm fine, thank you; how are you and the boys?"

"Better, I think. Thank you for asking."

"I presume you didn't call just to say 'hello.' What's up?"

"I need to see you, Father. It's important."

"What about?" Jon was curious.

"I'd rather not go into it over the phone if you don't mind."

"Say no more, Jenny. When would you like to do it?"

"Would now be too inconvenient?"

This must be important. Jon completed writing his Sunday sermon and had a couple of hours.

"Now would be fine. Your place or mine?"

"Would you mind coming here?"

"Not a problem, Jenny. I'll be right over."

"Thanks very much, Father. God bless you." She bit her tongue.

Father Jon drove the old van the short distance to the Tracey home. As he approached the front door, he heard classical music playing at a deafening volume. Before he could knock, Jennifer appeared at the door and stepped onto the porch.

"Let's take a walk, Father," uttered Jennifer, nudging him down the stairs.

She passed him by, ambled down the steps, and up the sidewalk. He turned to follow her. *Curious behavior.*

Jennifer looked up and down her street for suspicious people or cars. When they reached the end of her walkway, she turned up the city sidewalk and continued walking away from her home. Father Jon was bewildered by her behavior but said nothing.

"I believe my house has been bugged, Father, the church and

rectory at Lakes, as well. Dr. Rothenberg says his office is also monitored. That's the reason for the loud music and this walk. With these precautions, I doubt they can hear us."

"What in heaven's name are you talking about, Jenny?"

"You know perfectly well what I'm talking about. The question, before we go any further, is whose side are you on? Can I trust you?"

"Of course you can trust me, Jenny." Jon was confused and upset. "What's this all about? And who's doing all this monitoring you're talking about?" *What the hell is going on?*

"I was hoping you could tell me, Father. Dr. Rothenberg tells me that whoever it is told you to retain him to counsel the boys."

Now he understood. *Rothenberg told Jenny about the Voice and the Coalition, but why? What happened to cause him to cross the Voice? This was a dangerous move—there might be consequences.*

"Rothenberg told you this?"

"Yes, Father. Someone is trying to cover up Father Gerry's abuse of my two sons. Since you retained the doctor at this person's request, it stands to reason you're also involved in this cover-up."

Jon felt incredibly guilty. It was not that way. He had to make her understand he only wanted to help her without jeopardizing his church.

"Jenny, listen to me. I am not involved in any 'cover-up.' Yes, when I found out about your boys and Father Gerry, I called the division office. And, yes, this 'someone' you refer to returned my call and requested I keep this matter quiet. This man works in some capacity with the church hierarchy. He felt it would be in everyone's best interest to prevent this from becoming a scandal, and I agreed. What if they removed me and left Gerry in place? I needed to go along to protect not only your kids but also any other child from Gerry's misbehavior. I insisted the boys receive treatment as a condition of my silence, which is why they were referred to Dr. Rothenberg." *She has this all wrong!*

"How long have you known?"

"Shortly after the boys came home from the camping trip. I

overheard some of the kids talking about someone spending the whole weekend alone with Gerry. When I saw the boys on their return, I put two and two together and reported it to division almost immediately."

"But you chose not to tell their own mother?" Jennifer shook with rage.

"I was told not to, Jen. I was afraid if I didn't go along, I'd be replaced and unable to protect the children. I'm terribly ashamed. You have an absolute right to be angry, but I thought it was in their best interest." He was frantic.

"And the church," Jennifer charged.

"Yes, and the church. A scandal could destroy all that I have worked for. Am I wrong for even considering it? Gerry was at Lakes for a short while. No one from division gave me any reason to distrust him. I couldn't let him bring down my parish. I couldn't let this Voice decide the best interests of one of my kids. I needed to be silent to ensure he trusted me. Now, all I can say is I'm sorry." Jon felt terrible.

Jennifer would not let him off the hook. "But, Father, when you came to my house and offered to pay for counseling, you knew the boys were molested and kept it to yourself?"

"Yes, Jen, that's true. It sounds awful now, but I honestly thought it was in everyone's best interest to keep this quiet."

"Even from me?" Jennifer cried. "How could you? I have been in agony for over a month, trying to figure out what was wrong, and you *knew*? I've known you for most of my life. How can I ever forgive you? Did you think I would run to the press?"

"You're right, Jenny. I'm so sorry. I thought what I was doing was best for all concerned. M-may I ask you a question?"

"Go ahead," she sniffled.

"Why do you think we are being monitored?"

"Dr. Rothenberg says that this man—this Voice—calls him. He knows way more than he should unless he monitors the boys' sessions. I don't know if my house or Lakes is bugged, but the doctor thinks they must be. He wants to meet us at a private location. He thinks you can be trusted. I'm not so sure."

"Jenny, what can I do to convince you? I would never deliberately do anything to harm Kenny and Jake."

"Do you know what that animal did to my sons, Father?"

Jon was very embarrassed, almost red-faced, but he answered her question. "According to Mr. Voice, there was, perhaps, some inappropriate touching. Is that what you mean?"

"He *raped* them, Father," Jennifer revealed.

"Oh, my God!" Jon was stunned. "Jenny, I s-swear, I-I didn't know!"

Jennifer fell into Jon's arms and sobbed. After what seemed like several minutes, she broke the embrace, took out a tissue, and dried her eyes.

"Dr. Rothenberg says I can trust you, Father. I don't know if I agree, but I trust him. If you cross my kids or me again—"

"Jen, I swear, you can trust me. What's the plan?"

"Meet with Dr. Rothenberg and me. We must be discreet because we may be followed. Dr. Rothenberg doesn't want this shady 'Voice' fellow to know we've met."

"You can count on me from this moment forward. Where and when?"

"Tomorrow is Saturday. How about lunch somewhere?"

"Tomorrow and lunch are both fine."

"How about the Little Daddy's on Northwestern Highway, say 1 p.m.?"

"That's fine."

"You must be discreet. Someone will try and follow you."

"I understand. I'll do my best."

"You need to do better than your best. You need to lose them."

"I will, Jenny."

"And make sure you are careful when using the phone. I'm sure it's tapped."

"Unbelievable! I understand."

"Can I count on you?"

"Absolutely."

They walked toward the van in silence. When Jon got to the driver's side door, he stopped and studied Jennifer. "I'm truly, truly sorry, Jenny."

"I know you are, Father," she placated him.

"I will never let you or the boys down again. I want these

bastards to rot in hell."

"Father Jon," she scolded with a wry smile, looking up to the sky. "Such language!"

Chapter Twelve

Little Daddy's is a nice little Coney Island restaurant on Northwestern Highway where Farmington Hills borders Southfield. Jennifer and Father Jon drove separately to different stores, parked, entered the respective store, and quickly exited through the back door.

Uber drivers, summoned by phone, awaited them and drove them to the restaurant. This 'sleight of hand' was Father Jon's idea. Jennifer felt like an actress in a *James Bond* movie, but she appreciated the subterfuge. For his part, Dr. Rothenberg drove around town, made various stops, studied his surroundings, made sudden U-turns, doubled back, and slipped into alleys. It was exhilarating. Surely he gave the slip to anyone who might be following.

Jennifer and Father Jon were seated by the time Rothenberg arrived. Each had a drink of some sort. Rothenberg greeted them and sat down. A waiter approached, and Rothenberg ordered a Diet Coke. After an exchange of pleasantries, the waiter returned with his drink and took their food orders.

"They have good Coney's here," Rothenberg advised. "If you like salad, the Tommy's is the best."

A real connoisseur, thought Jennifer. At the waiter's suggestion, they ordered a gyro appetizer, several Coney dogs, and a Tommy's for two, since the orders were huge. After taking their order, the waiter left them alone.

"Thank you for coming, Father," started Rothenberg. "I'm very concerned about the direction in which the church is taking this incident. My contact remains unknown and is more concerned with keeping this quiet than he is with getting Father Gerry into treatment or making sure his conduct is not repeated."

"I have the same sense," Father Jon admitted. "When he instructed me to retain a therapist, he was more concerned about your loyalty to the church than about your credentials and competence. I was concerned about both, so I made sure that the man chosen was highly competent."

"Thanks for the compliment. I am now convinced this is not the best course for the church, nor is it the best course for the boys. If we remain quiet about this, I am positive Gerry will be transferred, and the parents and children in his new parish will not be advised," Rothenberg warned.

"I think you're spot on, Doctor," Jon agreed. "According to national research on this issue, these cases are disturbingly prevalent. The church's strategy in dealing with these cases is consistent and unfortunate. The priest is privately counseled, released from treatment, and then quietly transferred to a new parish in a new town without warning. We can't derail this policy nationally, but we can try to prevent it in this case."

"How?" Jennifer wondered.

"I say we turn this over to the Farmington Police and prosecute Bartholomew. I'm confident Gerry's done this before; the church must have covered it up. If we prosecute him publicly and notify the press, the church will be unable to transfer him without any new parish knowing his history," Jon posited.

"What makes you think he's done this before? He's not been prosecuted. I'd bet the church could even bury prosecutions if it wants to," Rothenberg suggested.

"You may be right. I have been involved in some sensitive cases where the prosecutor made a plea arrangement that included sealing the file."

"What do you mean 'sealing the file'?" Jennifer wondered.

"The otherwise public record is made private by a judge. If you go to the records to check under the particular criminal's name, nothing appears. He has no record, so far as the public is concerned."

"So, if a molester arranges to have his file sealed in exchange for a guilty plea, he could be transferred by the church, and if the pastor of the new church wanted to check his record, he wouldn't have one?" Jennifer exclaimed.

"Yes, which may be what happened here."

"What can we do about preventing Gerry from doing this again?" Jennifer challenged.

"I like Jon's idea. Publicity should prevent that. Here's what I suggest. Pursue criminal charges and notify the press. Jennifer raises holy hell if any proposed plea bargain includes a sealed conviction. Jennifer and the boys file a civil case against Father Gerry and the church. They make *this* lawsuit *very* public too. Jon testifies Gerry was transferred to Lakes without any prior warning even though the church was aware. What judge would permit a sealed result under those circumstances?"

"I'm willing to testify he was transferred without my being knowledge of prior conduct, but I don't know for sure if there was prior conduct or the church knew of his propensities," Jon cautioned.

"A great lawyer will take care of that. If presented with evidence the church knew, covered it up and transferred him anyway, would you testify?"

"Absolutely."

Jennifer remained quiet and listened, intrigued by the conversation. She was impressed with Rothenberg's two-prong attack. Criminal and civil charges would publicly expose Father Gerry and the church's policy toward pedophile priests. *But, is this right for my family?* The plan was centered on publicity. *Would the boys have to testify? Newspaper reporters would hound them. What would things be like at school? Kids could be so cruel. Would the boys be subjected to cruel jokes about sexual desires and preferences?* Was her imagination carrying her away, or were these realistic fears?

"Jenny? *Jenny?*" Rothenberg interrupted her thoughts.

"Yes?"

"You were a million miles away. Penny for your thoughts?" Rothenberg requested.

"I was wondering about the boys. You originally told me publicity might be harmful. I see reporters, schoolyard jokes, and bullies. I can see how your suggestions will help prevent Gerry from doing this again, but not at the expense of my kids. I'm extremely worried. I don't want any progress they've made in therapy to be ruined by publicity."

"Your concerns are well-founded, Jenny. I certainly did say publicity could be harmful. But I've been treating these boys for almost two months now, and I have concluded they're strong young men. Their anger with Bartholomew is appropriate, yet they continue to blame themselves. I now believe successful criminal and civil outcomes in these cases, prison for Gerry, and a large damages award for the boys, would clarify these issues and assuage their guilt feelings. A guilty verdict in the criminal case and a large civil verdict or settlement would be *double* vindication for the boys. I am almost certain they will be okay with pursuing the civil case. However, to be on the safe side, I suggest you include them in your decision-making. Considering their current trust level, they should have a voice."

"How do you mean?"

"Tell them what we propose. We want to proceed in a very public way, and neighbors and classmates will know what happened. We also tell them Gerry has probably done this to others who most likely agreed to confidential settlements and sealed files. Our strategy prevents this from ever happening again. We seek their prior approval to proceed. We involve them every step of the way."

"That's an excellent idea," Father Jon agreed. "If they have full input and approve the plan, they will be better equipped to handle the publicity. If we go ahead without their permission and they experience ridicule, we will be three more grown-ups who went behind their backs and violated their trust."

"Exactly," Rothenberg concurred.

"I'm apprehensive about this," Jennifer countered. "Aren't they too young? Haven't these events made them too fragile for this kind of exposure or publicity? They are teenagers! Can you imagine how embarrassing it is to admit you've had sex with your priest? How can they face their classmates and friends? Will the trial and publicity make it clear this is all on the priest? He is the criminal and the boys his victims. I am sick with worry over this."

"Again, Jenny, I am not going to tell you there's no risk. But the boys are angry. If the priest goes to prison, there is vindication, a very public statement that the priest is a criminal predator and the boys are victims. They didn't have sex with their priest. Their priest raped them! It's a big difference, no? In the civil case, a large verdict will buttress what happens in the criminal case. A verdict will not only punish the church for concealing these crimes, but it will also serve as further evidence the boys were helpless victims."

Jennifer remained skeptical. However, she appreciated Rothenberg had gone to the trouble of developing this strategy. Her heart ached with concern for her sons' wellbeing.

"I'm still not convinced, but I agree we cannot and will not proceed without talking to the boys, getting their input, answering their questions, and putting them at ease. Their willingness or unwillingness to proceed is absolute. If the boys say 'no,' then it's 'no,' and we continue treatment and devise an alternate plan that does not directly affect them. If they say 'yes' after a detailed explanation of the plan and all its negatives, then we proceed with extreme caution."

"Sounds like a plan. I couldn't have said it better myself. I am pleased to participate in the discussion at whatever level you want me to. I agree we should proceed with great care and caution. Also, be prepared to pull the plug if things get too ugly for the boys to handle. Does anyone have any thoughts on a lawyer for the civil case?" Rothenberg added.

Jennifer placed her hand on her chin, deliberating. "The only lawyer I know is the man who handled my husband's accident. He specialized in accident and injury cases and did a terrific job. I felt he cared about my husband and family. It took a while, but we got all the law allowed. He sat down and educated me, so I was comfortable with my decision. I was very impressed." She smiled at the memory.

"He sounds like our man. What's his name?"

"Zachary Blake."

"Where's he located?" Rothenberg inquired.

"At the time, he had offices in the Southfield Town Center. I presume he's still there. If not, I'm sure he's listed."

"Are you comfortable calling him about this, Jenny, or would you like me to contact him for you?" Rothenberg offered.

"No, I'll do it."

"Make sure you tell him you already have a supportive psychiatrist with a Ph.D. in your hip pocket. Lawyers love it when they can present treating doctors rather than the bought-and-paid-for 'whore' doctors they keep on their payroll,"

Rothenberg noted.

"What do you mean?" Jennifer wondered. *Is he serious or trying to be funny?*

"Many personal injury lawyers have doctors they do business with regularly. These doctors treat clients and do what they can to support their cases. Defense lawyers do the same thing, and judges get tired of seeing the same guys on every case. If a case involves these docs, the case has less credibility. In *this* case, we won't need these doctors. You have me." Rothenberg smiled.

"In other words, I should tell Mr. Blake we already have a 'whore' and won't need one of his?" Jennifer laughed.

Father Jon smiled and wagged his index finger at Jennifer. Rothenberg laughed. "It's great to see you laugh, Jenny."

"It's nice to laugh," Jennifer admitted. "I hope the last laugh is ours."

The food arrived. The appetizer was terrific, especially the tzatziki sauce. Coney Island, as most Detroiters knew, was a guilty pleasure, and Tommy's was indeed the best. Jennifer even enjoyed the company. At long last, there was a reason for optimism.

Chapter Thirteen

There comes a time in the life of every attorney when he or she has two fundamental questions: *Why do I need this shit? Is this why I went to law school?* Zachary Blake was half asleep in a district courtroom, a victim of 'hurry up and wait' syndrome. A judge might order thirty or so lawyers and clients to appear in court at 9:00 a.m. and begins to call cases one by one. If you're called first, great, but what if you're thirtieth? You're in court all day, hence 'hurry up and wait' and 'why do I need this shit?' Zack awoke with a snort when he heard his name called.

"Are we interrupting your late-morning nap, Mr. Blake?" District Court Judge Emma Pearl inquired, with a harsh tone and an insistent expression. "Your client and I are waiting."

"Sorry, Your Honor. I was going over the file. I just received the assignment," Blake stammered.

"You're wasting the court's time, Mr. Blake. How does your client plead?" Judge Pearl demanded.

Blake charged through the swinging door, leading from the gallery to the litigants' tables and the judge's bench. He stumbled as he crossed the threshold, dressed in wrinkled, stained tan dress pants and a faux suede jacket. His shirt was coming out of his pants. The top button was undone, and his tie was pulled up into what could only be called a chokehold in a failed attempt to hide the fact that the top button was missing. He stomped up to the podium. "What . . . what's the charge, Your Honor?"

"You don't know, Mr. Blake?" She was incredulous.

"I just got the file, Your Honor. I haven't really had the chance to acquaint myself with the details." Blake frantically flipped through pages in a file.

"When exactly did you receive the file, Mr. Blake? Arraignment call was at nine; it is now close to eleven. You've had the file for two hours." Judge Pearl was about to explode.

Exactly, bitch, hurry up and wait for two fucking hours! Blake opened his mouth to speak, but the judge usurped him and turned to his client, an accused drunk driver who spent the night in the city jail. He awaited arraignment and a bail hearing.

Suddenly polite and cherubic, Judge Pearl addressed the defendant, a voting citizen. "Mr. Jordan, have you had a chance to meet with your attorney?"

"No, Your Honor. Is this the guy?" Jordan sneered at the disheveled Blake.

"Yes, Mr. Jordan—this is your assigned attorney. You've indicated you can't afford an attorney. Is that correct?" Judge Pearl inquired.

"Yes, that is correct, Your Honor . . . but . . ."

"But what, Mr. Jordan?" Judge Pearl growled.

"Can't I choose a lawyer, like from a list or something?"

"No, sir, you can't. How long have you been here in the courthouse this morning, sir?" She bristled.

"Almost two hours, Your Honor," Jordan estimated.

Judge Pearl turned to her court clerk, the person in charge of doling out the morning court assignments. "Mr. Roman, what time was the file provided to Mr. Blake?"

Roman flipped through his assignments ledger and responded, without looking up, "Eight-thirty, Your Honor."

Judge Pearl turned to Blake and fumed, "Mr. Blake, you have had this file for two and a half hours. You've not met with the client, nor have you familiarized yourself with the charges. While the city pays fixed fees for these court assignments, they are important, and there is a long list of attorneys who are happy to remain in the court's good graces and pleased to receive their assignments. Apparently, you are not one of them."

Judge Pearl again turned to her clerk. "Mr. Roman, you are hereby instructed to remove Mr. Blake's name from my roster of assigned counsel," she ordered.

Turning to the voting citizen, Zachary's soon-to-be-former client, she instantly adopted a pleasant demeanor. "Mr. Jordan, please accept the court's profound apologies. We will get you new counsel. Have a seat in the gallery for a few minutes, and Mr. Roman will get you reassigned.

"Mr. Blake, you are relieved of this assignment and dismissed from this proceeding. Your name is hereby removed from my assignment list. We'll hold this case in abeyance to allow newly assigned counsel to get up to snuff and then we will recall it. That's it for now. Mr. Roman, please call the next case."

"But, Your Honor, I waited two hours—" Judge Pearl abruptly interrupted Zachary Blake. "Mr. Blake!" she shouted. "One more word from you and I will find you in contempt." She shook her finger at him like a mother scolding a child.

Blake turned meekly from the bench. The gallery, made up primarily of other attorneys, whispered, muttered, and snickered. They pointed at him and whispered to each other, hand over mouth. Zachary waded through them, enduring their snickers and taunts in utter humiliation.

He exited the courtroom and walked dejectedly to his car. He started it up, drove to the nearest tavern, and proceeded to get very drunk. *How has it come to this?*

Three years earlier, Zachary Blake was managing partner of Blake, Geiringer, and Schwartz, a law firm that specialized exclusively in personal injury litigation. At its peak, the firm handled over three thousand files. There were four associates—non-partner attorneys—two paralegals, six secretaries, an investigator, and a receptionist.

The main office was on the seventeenth floor of the prestigious Town Center office complex in Southfield, Michigan, a quartet of gold and black glass and steel high-rises that existed primarily for tenants to boast they paid the highest rent in the tri-county area. Each partner had a southern view office on the seventeenth floor of the complex's tallest building.

Since the building sat on the John C. Lodge Freeway, the main thoroughfare from Detroit's northwest suburbs to downtown Detroit, tenants clamored to pay a premium for office space facing southeast, high enough to see the downtown Detroit skyline, approximately twenty miles away. Zachary Blake occupied the firm's largest office, which, naturally, faced southeast. He had a key to the executive lounge and health club and an executive parking space in the underground garage. He wore fifteen-hundred-dollar suits and dined in the city's finest restaurants. Life was good.

Unfortunately, while Blake earned his success in the early

days, with multiple trials and high six and seven-figure verdicts, his partners began to ask, first quietly, and then rather loudly, "What have you done for me lately?"

Zack was at the country club more than he was at the office. He pawned more and better cases off on his partners and associates. This would have been acceptable if Zack was still bringing in high-dollar cases, but he wasn't. His referral sources were evaporating—lawyers and former clients were annoyed Zack wasn't personally handling those cases. He missed appointments, ignored business contacts, and became detached and arrogant. In short, he became a *liability*.

On that fateful day three years ago, Blake arrived at the office at 7:30 a.m., as was his habit. He was greeted by an Oakland County sheriff's deputy, who served him with a lawsuit filed by his partners, alleging violations of the Michigan Partnership Act. He was also served with an injunction, ordering him to remove himself from the premises and preventing him from removing any personal property, including his own office files. The deputy escorted him from the building while obscenities and choice expletives were shouted from all corners of the office.

His now ex-partners planned their coup well. They had signed letters from firm clients, transferring their files to the new law firm of Geiringer & Schwartz. The court ordered Blake to cease and desist from working on their cases. Since the three men were once longtime friends, there was no written partnership agreement—leave it to lawyers to have nothing in writing.

When the dust settled, Zachary retained fifty files and *quantum meruit* in those that remained with the firm.

"You'll land on your feet, Zack," David Schwartz assured when Zack arrived to pick up his fifty files.

"Fuck you!" Zack roared. "I made this firm. I taught you guys everything you know. I gave both of you your first jobs out of law school and taught you how to handle PI files, how to treat clients, and how to deal with opposing attorneys. I demonstrated how to handle judges and clerks and how to try cases. This traitorous palace coup is how you thank me? Fuck the both of you!"

"Look in the mirror, asshole. You brought this on yourself!" cried Schwartz, with the umbrage of a mistreated child addressing his abusive parent. "Yes, you taught us everything, and we appreciate it. We've always appreciated you. But you haven't been *that* Zack Blake in almost a decade. How long are we supposed to carry your dead weight? Five years? Ten? We can't do it anymore, financially, or emotionally. You're a shit example for the associates and the support staff. It's time for the inmates to run the asylum. Seriously, Zack, we are grateful for everything, but it is time for you to go. If you didn't see this coming, you must be totally blind, and I'm really sorry," he bewailed.

Blake was having none of it. "Fuck you, fuck Geiringer, fuck the associates, fuck the staff, and fuck the horses all of you rode in on. You'll never make it without me." He spat all over Schwartz.

"Well, then, that will be our mistake and our misfortune. We wish you nothing but the best." Schwartz folded his arms across his chest, signaling the 'meeting' and conversation were over.

Blake exploded. "Bullshit!" He screamed, again expelling saliva into Schwartz's face. "You hope I fall on my face. Admit it, you ungrateful prick. Well, I won't give you the fucking satisfaction! Have a nice death."

Zachary Blake gathered up his small box of files and stormed out of the offices where he once reigned supreme. As Blake walked away, Swartz pulled a handkerchief from his pocket, wiped spittle from his face, shook his head, turned, and returned to his office. It was time to move on. His decision to part company with his former hero and mentor was appropriate. Still, Zack taught him everything he knew in this business. David was ambivalent about how this decision would affect Zack. He fervently hoped Blake would land on his feet.

From time to time, Blake received a small check from the new law firm of Geiringer and Schwartz. He couldn't blame himself. In Zack's mind, his former partners were fucking him, big-time. But he lacked the inertia to pursue what he was owed. "Let them keep the fucking money," he grumbled. "At least I'm rid of them."

That final surrender was his first of many. Shortly after the palace coup, Blake made some bad stock investments and lost what little money he had left. His 'retirement' land deal investment turned sour. He couldn't pay the mortgage payments on his huge Bloomfield Hills home, and it fell into foreclosure. Blake and his wife put the home up for sale and sold it for less than full value. When the moving van showed up, so did a process server with the divorce complaint from Zack's wife. She didn't want much, only the proceeds from the sale of the house, the three kids, all the furniture, and what was left of the bank account. A temporary support order demanded child support of $1,000 per week. She got it all.

Zack slept through most of the ride from the bar to his office. It was a short trip north on the John C. Lodge Freeway from Downtown Detroit to Zack's office on Eight Mile Road, the highway that separated Detroit from its suburbs and made famous by Eminem. Upon becoming Detroit's first black mayor in the 1970s, Coleman Young told all the pimps, pushers, and prostitutes to "hit Eight Mile Road." That warning was one of the few things Young ever did to combat crime.

On the trip up the Lodge, Zack's Uber passed through old, poverty-stricken, predominately black neighborhoods. Many homes were abandoned; some were falling down from decay or abuse, some were boarded up, and many featured iron bars on their windows. The driver passed through pockets of stately homes and well-kept neighborhoods where residents were proud of and attentive to their homes and gardens. The new mayor announced projects to light every streetlight, reduce criminal activity, tear down abandoned houses, rebuild neighborhoods, and solve the problems of a failing public school system. He was certainly trying, and the residents were responding positively.

Southfield, which bordered Eight Mile Road, and other northern suburban communities were now integrated. The line between the city and its suburbs was blurring. Blake and his fifty files—his wife didn't ask for a cut of the fees—had relocated to a small, one-room office in the low-rent district. A client would push open the door, and there would be Blake—no receptionist, no secretary, no copier, just Blake, an old desk, and a couple of worn side chairs for clients to whine in.

Blake had a secondhand computer on his desk with antiquated word-processing software. His caseload dwindled, and he always took the first dime offered to settle those cases he had left, *donating* all dollars generated to his ex-wife for child support. He was now hustling traffic cases and two hundred dollar juvenile assignments from Oakland and Wayne County Juvenile Courts. But, as Judge Emma Pearl noted earlier that morning, Blake was no longer capable of providing quality representation for cases usually reserved for rookies.

When he wasn't at the office, he could be found at the local pool halls, taverns, or strip clubs that lined Eight Mile on the Detroit side. He would pick up an occasional criminal case from those who frequented the various establishments, but rarely represented them with the skill he once had and rarely for a fee of any consequence. After an afternoon or evening of drinking, playing, or carousing, Blake went home to his one-bedroom, scarcely furnished apartment at the Lodge Freeway and Nine Mile Road and watched TV, bottle in hand.

Zachary Blake lost his practice, his wife and kids, his home, and his money. He was at rock bottom in only three short years. He also lost the most valuable possession of any successful trial lawyer. Zachary Blake lost his will to fight. His luck, however, was about to change.

Chapter Fourteen

"Boys . . . we'd like to talk to you about Father Gerry. We want him punished so he can never do to others what he did to you . . ." Rothenberg commenced a meeting between himself and the Tracey family. The meeting was held in the Beacon East Office Building conference room. Rothenberg was still suspicious his office was being monitored.

"Do you know what a lawsuit is, boys?" Jennifer wondered.

"Like the TV commercials when someone gets into a car accident or gets bit by a dog?" Jake volunteered.

"Yes, something like that," Jennifer smiled.

"People sue for 'combination,'" Jake remarked. Apparently, he watched some lawyer advertisements.

The three adults laughed. Jake looked confused and somewhat embarrassed.

"People sue for *compensation*, Jake, honey," Jennifer corrected. "But you have the right idea."

"Compensation means a person who has done something wrong to someone else must pay money to the person he hurt. In very serious cases, a judge or a jury will give the hurt person more money to *punish* a wrongdoer. The amount of money depends on how serious the injuries are. Sometimes one person is hurt; sometimes, many people are hurt. In some cases, one person causes harm. In other cases, many people are responsible. The point is to hold those wrongdoers responsible for the harm they caused. Get it? What do you think?" Rothenberg explained. He turned his head from boy to boy.

"Sounds right to me," Kenny determined.

"The problem is that some lawsuits, like rear-end car crashes, are rather common. Nobody cares a whole lot, and you don't see anything on the news or TV. Others are very shocking, and you *will* see them on the news and TV," Rothenberg continued. He looked at Jennifer for support. She nodded in return.

"We want you to consider a lawsuit against Father Gerry for what he did, and against Lakes and the church for bringing him here and letting him do what he did."

"Sounds right to me," Jake mimicked Kenny.

"But this would be one of those lawsuits that get on the news and TV," Jennifer warned.

"That's right, boys. And the thing is your names and your mother's name and what happened to you would be on the news, and everybody will know what happened to you on the trip," Rothenberg explained.

"So?" Kenny wondered.

"So . . . we're concerned about how you feel about everybody knowing. We're concerned about how things will go at school. Will you be okay? Will you be teased? Bullied? You'll become known as the two boys who got hurt by the priest. It might be embarrassing or make you uncomfortable. How will you handle all this attention?" Rothenberg cautioned. *Do they understand the issues? Am I getting through to them?*

Jennifer noticed the grim look on his face and chimed in. "I don't want to cause you any more pain than you've already endured. I don't want you to be bullied or teased at school. You've been through a lot. Maybe this is more than you can handle. Gerry should be punished for what he did. No other kid should ever have to go through one more minute of what you guys went through. The church must be punished for letting him get away with this. The public must know about Gerry's behavior, so it can't continue, and so the church can't keep covering it up. But, if you don't want to pursue this, it stops here. We won't go forward." Jennifer studied her boys, gauging their reactions.

"Father Gerry has done this before?" Kenny inquired.

"Yes, we're almost certain he has," Rothenberg declared.

"And he can do it again?" Kenny questioned, with a growing comprehension of the importance of their decision.

"If he goes unpunished or the criminal court allows him to hide his conviction, yes, he could do it again," Rothenberg advised. "He has serious mental issues and needs to be kept away from children. If the public remains in the dark about him, he could easily do this again. He has to be stopped," Rothenberg concluded.

"And we can stop him?" Jake wondered.

"That's our hope. We think we can stop him," Rothenberg suggested.

The boys looked at each other, resolutely, saying nothing.

"This will be hard," Jennifer warned. "It will take a long time. You will be asked a lot of questions, and you will have to give answers. You will have to talk about the disgusting things he did and tell your stories to people you don't know. I won't *make* you do it. I won't even consider going forward without both of you agreeing."

"Can we talk about this a little?" Kenny glanced at Jake.

"Sure." Rothenberg folded his arms, ready for the discussion.

"Alone, please?" Kenny requested.

Rothenberg cleared his throat, unfolded his arms, and stumbled to his feet. "Of course you can," he managed, impressed with the young man's maturity in such a stressful circumstance.

"Do you want me to stay?" Jennifer inquired.

"No, Mom, I want to talk to Jake," Kenny demanded.

Jennifer and Rothenberg made their exit.

"We'll be right outside when you're ready," Rothenberg advised, closing the conference room door.

***

After the adults left, the two boys sat still, in silent contemplation, taking in the weight of what they heard.

"Whaddaya think?" Kenny broke the silence.

"I dunno," Jake mumbled.

"Father Gerry is a piece of shit! I don't want him to get away with this," Kenny snapped.

"N-No . . . me neither," Jake agreed. "But, Kenny . . . everybody will know . . . yuck . . . everyone will know . . . he'll go to jail, right?" Tears welled up in his eyes.

Kenny softened. "Maybe, maybe not. Who knows? Look, we don't have to do it. Mom promised. But I don't want to be the one who let him get away with this, and I don't want to ever hear he did this to someone else or someone else's brother, do you?"

"N-no . . . no, I don't." Jake stammered. *He's still a kid,* thought the *mature* Kenny.

"Well, if we are the ones who can stop him, shouldn't we do it?" Kenny concluded.

"Will Mom be doing this with us?" Jake wondered.

He's coming around. "I think so . . . let's ask her," Kenny suggested. "If she says yes, what do you want to do?"

"Concentration, I guess," Jake decided.

"Compensation, squirt." Kenny corrected his brother. He smiled but quickly changed expression in contemplation of the vital decision they were making and the long road ahead. He demonstrated maturity beyond his years.

"Okay, so if Mom is there with us, we'll do the lawsuit thing, right?" Kenny clarified.

"Yes, Kenny," Jake whispered.

"You're sure? I'm not forcing you, and I won't do this without you," Kenny advised.

"I don't want him to ever do this again. This will stop that?" Jake wanted reassurance.

"That's what Mom and the doc say."

"Okay then," Jake agreed.

The boys rose, opened the door to the conference room, and called for their mother. Rothenberg and Jennifer hustled around a corner and into the room.

"We decided to do the lawsuit," Kenny advised. "But only if Mom is there with us the whole time."

"Yeah," Jake concurred.

"We will both be there the whole time," Rothenberg assured.

"The whole time," Jennifer promised. "I'm proud of you guys. Dad would be proud of you guys, too. I'll talk to the lawyer and get this thing started."

The boys broke off in private conversation, satisfied with their decision to move forward. Jennifer stared at them, through them, trepidation inching into her psyche. *Is this the right decision? Are they mature enough to handle this? Do they seriously understand what they're signing up for? Do I?*

She would be with them every step of the way. If there were any signs the litigation was harming her kids, she'd shut it down.

Gerry Bartholomew! This bastard must pay—he must be stopped. We'll blow the lid off this whole affair . . . won't we?

Chapter Fifteen

Zachary Blake had just returned to his drab, one-room office from traffic court. His *big* cases of the day were ninety-nine-dollar traffic ticket defenses. He had three of them on the docket today, a pretty good payday. He advertised for traffic cases in the newspaper and on the Internet.

He guaranteed prospective clients he would reduce a moving violation to a non-moving or "double your money back." Since the courts had no room on busy trial dockets to try traffic cases, judges instructed city attorneys to negotiate any traffic matters that didn't involve a collision. Zack's 'guarantee' came with almost no risk. He could always plead down these cases and only paid off once. On a good day, he might knock off five or six of these cases, a six hundred dollar payday.

He opened the door and sat down in a broken, old chair at a second-hand desk, exhausted from dispensing justice to a bunch of drunks. He turned on his answering machine. There was a message! Jennifer Tracey, a former client, called to discuss a case involving her two sons. *Jennifer Tracey? Do I know her? Probably another crap case—teenage drunks? I'll call her tomorrow.*

He sat back, reclining in the old, oversized executive chair, one of the few items he received in the partnership breakup. As the chair went back, the tension spring broke, and Zack toppled over. *Figures.* He dusted himself off, righted the chair, and sat back down. He closed his eyes and thought about his two hundred ninety-seven dollar day. In his heyday, each day was worth five grand in fees, maybe more. As he nodded off, the phone rang, startling him, almost toppling the chair again.

"Zachary Blake." He grumbled.

"Mr. Blake? This is Jennifer Tracey. You handled my husband's industrial accident. Do you remember me?"

"Sure," Zack lied. "How are you, Mrs. Tracey?"

"Fine. Call me, Jenny. How are you, Mr. Blake?"

"I'm fine, Jenny. Please call me Zack. What can I do for

you?"

"I'd rather not discuss the matter over the phone. Can I come and see you, perhaps this afternoon, if it wouldn't be too much trouble?"

"This afternoon? I'm afraid I'm booked solid," Zack lied again. "Hang on; I'll check with my secretary to see if anyone canceled."

He put his hand over the mouthpiece and paused thirty seconds. He would have put Jennifer on hold, but he had only one line.

"My secretary tells me I have a three o'clock cancellation. Would you like to come then?"

"Oh, yes, thank you!" Jennifer exclaimed.

"You're welcome. What kind of case is this, did you say?" Zack yawned.

"I didn't. I'd rather not discuss it over the phone."

"I need to know if it's civil or criminal."

"I'm pretty sure I understand what 'civil' means, so it's 'civil' and 'criminal.' But I only need you for the civil."

"All righty then. I'll see you at three. Do you know where my office is?"

"Town Center, isn't it?"

"Ah, ahem, not anymore," Zack whispered. "I'm at 16922 W. Eight Mile, Suite 139, on the Southfield side, between Greenfield and Southfield."

"I'll find it." *Eight Mile?* "Thanks very much, Zack, and God bless you."

He hung up. *God bless? That ship has sailed.*

***

At 2:55 p.m., Jennifer Tracey arrived at the Law Offices of Zachary Blake, P.C. *This is a far cry from Town Center.* It was a small, one-story, puke-green building. The paint was chipping, the parking lot was full of potholes, and the windows needed washing. Inside, the lobby was tired, with dirty beige carpet worn to the pad.

Jennifer walked by rows of office doors, some closed, some

open. The open ones revealed one-room, dingy offices. Was Blake's office like these? How was that possible? What happened to him? *Am I in the right place? Am I doing the right thing?*

She found Suite 139 with a cheap black-and-silver plastic identification sign on the wall next to the door:

Suite 139, Zachary Blake, P.C.
Attorney and Counselor

The door was open, and there was Blake, sitting at his old desk. Some dingy side chairs sat on her side of the desk. The office setting she remembered was the Taj Mahal.

Is this the same guy? He was great in Jim's case. Is he up to the challenge of this one?

"Mrs. Tracey?"

"Jenny."

"Jenny, of course. Did you have any trouble finding the office?"

"No, it was easy, actually."

"Good. Have a seat. What can I do for you?"

"I don't know where to begin."

"Try the beginning. It's a perfect place to start, as my daughter and Julie Andrews used to say."

He looks . . . I don't know . . . off, somehow. The years have not been kind . . . "My husband died three years ago in an industrial accident at White-Chelsea, remember?"

"Yes, I do." *Not really.*

She went through it all for him, starting with the death of her husband and through Father Bill's departure. She sensed he wasn't paying complete attention, but she continued anyway.

"I even invited Gerry to dinner. I hoped he could get through to the boys, talk to them. It only made them worse. At the time, I didn't know why. I do now."

"I'll bite. Why?" Zack fidgeted.

"I'm getting there. Please be patient with me. This is difficult," Jennifer struggled.

For me too, Zack brooded.

"Finally," she continued, "Father Jon came over to see me. That's Father Jonathan Costigan, our pastor."

Zack pulled out a yellow legal pad and pretended to take notes.

"Father Jon asked how the kids were getting along. I told him, 'Not very well.' He offered to recommend a psychiatrist or psychologist and offered to pay for a consult or treatment, which I thought was strange. Jon claimed the church felt responsible because the kids' problems originated with the camping trip.

"I was reluctant to accept what I thought of as charity. My husband would never take anything from anybody. He believed you made your own way in this world. We lived by that rule when he was alive, and I was determined to live by it after his death. Father Jon, however, wouldn't take no for an answer. He finally convinced me to take the boys to the church therapist. That was the only thing I did right. After approximately two months of sessions with Dr. Rothenberg, the boys told him Father Gerry sexually molested them on the camping trip."

Zack suddenly lit up with greedy glee. He sat up straight and scribbled something on his notepad. Jennifer noticed the change. She preferred his sudden enthusiasm to his earlier indifference but was still concerned by his surroundings.

"Has Father Gerry done this before?" Zack inquired.

"We're not sure yet. Dr. Rothenberg is convinced Father Gerry has done this before. He feels we need to investigate this, go to his former parish, and talk to the police and parishioners." Jennifer quavered, suddenly unsure whether she wished to continue sharing information with this man.

"He's right," Zack blurted. "That's the difference between a good case and the mother lode! What else should I know?"

Jennifer now preferred his previous apathy to this sudden exuberance. She hesitated, sighed, and studied the lawyer. Then, Jennifer made a snap decision to proceed. She told him everything—about the Voice, the bugs, the surveillance, the pending criminal charges, everything.

"I will try to resolve this as discreetly as possible," Zack promised.

Jennifer's disdain for this remark was palpable. "On the

contrary, we want publicity. I've talked to Dr. Rothenberg and both of my boys, and we've decided a public airing of this case, embarrassing though it may be, will act as a cleansing agent for Jake's and Kenny's guilt and shame. Gerry will be publicly vilified and proven guilty. Hopefully, he'll serve prison time. If this case and the criminal prosecution are both high-profile successes, my boys will see that Gerry is the criminal and they are victims," she chastised.

Zachary stubbornly persisted, against his own interest and despite her obvious displeasure. "I think you would be far better off, at least in the preliminary stages of this case, to keep things hush-hush. We can use this as a wedge to increase settlement funds. Tell them to give us X thousand more, and we will not publicize the result," he coaxed.

"That is not the way we wish to proceed. We want as much publicity as possible," Jennifer scoffed.

Zack wisely decided to retreat. "Okay, if that's the way you want it," he conceded.

She could tell he was appeasing her. Dollar signs were dancing in his eyes. *What happened to my family's champion from a few years ago?*

Zack rifled through a drawer and produced medical authorizations and a contingency fee contract. Jennifer paused. *What's happened to him? His career? Is he up to this?* Deciding she could terminate the relationship if he proved to be unworthy, she signed each form while listening to Zack explain his fees. He would collect a third of the settlement if he won, but would charge nothing if he lost. It was standard in the business, he explained. He promised Jennifer he would work hard for her and not rest until he got justice for her boys. *Is she buying this?*

Zack listened as Jennifer completed her story and the signing ceremony and rose to leave. She was perplexed. This wasn't how she remembered him. This Zachary Blake was detached, disheveled . . . she wasn't sure what it was. *He seems . . . lost. Can he do the job?*

He'd done an excellent job on Jim's case. She reckoned he wouldn't let her and her boys down, though she wondered what events had landed him in such a woeful office setting. She decided to proceed with caution.

Chapter Sixteen

"A Farmington police detective visited Father Jon," the Voice hissed.

"Oh? What happened?" A Coalition member fretted.

"Jennifer Tracey pressed charges against Gerry."

"I told you she was trouble."

"Who do we know at police headquarters? Have Walsh get Parks on that and see if Father Jon's parish included any local cops." The Voice ordered, all about damage control.

"Good idea. I'll handle that."

"We need to start controlling and spinning press coverage. Dear Jennifer has already scheduled a news conference. This will be all over the papers and television. The key to the spin is to indicate this is an isolated incident, and the church is dealing with it internally and appropriately. The priest has been temporarily suspended—he will be *now*—and is seeking professional help. The official church position is it had no knowledge Gerry was a pedophile, and the church acted very responsibly by getting both perpetrator and victim into counseling as soon as the discovery was made," The Voice declared.

"Sounds good to me." *He is an eerie dude.*

"None of this strikes me as 'good,'" The Voice admonished.

"It's only a figure of speech," the member gulped. "But, you're correct. It's probably not applicable here."

"What about Gerry's last placement? Is that situation under control?"

"Yes, the pastor has been briefed, and the victims well paid for their silence. The criminal file has been sealed, and we were able to persuade authorities over there to seal criminal results. Except for the pastor, the victims, and the cops, nobody over there knows about Gerry. Parishioners think he was transferred in the ordinary course."

"Jennifer has hired a civil lawyer. We haven't heard from him yet."

"Is that right? Who is this guy?" a member queried. "We should check him out."

"I am way ahead of you. Parks handed me his report this morning. Zachary Blake . . ." the Voice began to read from a report. "Born April 2, 1972, married in 1995, to Tobey Kosofsky. Graduated in '97 from Western Michigan Cooley Law School with a C plus average. Worked for a couple of high-volume personal injury firms, then opened his own office with a couple of law school buddies, Stuart Geiringer and David Schwartz. Has a couple of kids.

"Here's where it gets interesting. Three years ago, after building an eight-figure personal injury practice, with prestige offices in a Southfield high-rise, his partners staged a palace coup. Blake gets dumped and never recovers. His law practice and personal life go to shit. His wife cleans him out in a divorce and takes the kids. He's been hustling two-bit, criminal and juvenile assignments or handling traffic tickets ever since.

"He's got a one-room office in a shithole building on Eight Mile, lives in a small apartment in Southfield. He grossed about forty grand last year. He spent it all on child support and office expenses. If he lands a good case, word on the street is he settles on the cheap, for the quick buck. Sources say he's lost his stomach for legal work," The Voice snickered.

"He seems perfect for us. One room on Eight Mile? Quite a fall. Probably needs fast money. We can use that to our advantage and accommodate him." A member laughed.

"Shall we approach him or wait for him to approach us?" Another pondered.

"We wait. This man has skills. You don't build a multi-million-dollar practice by being an idiot. The fact he's had some hard times does not mean we should underestimate him," the Voice stressed.

"You're right, of course. We do not wish to appear anxious."

"Exactly."

"Anything else?"

"Yeah. We are all religious men, correct?"

"Yes," they concurred, in unison.

"Prayer, then. We pray this turns out all right."

"Amen," they whispered, suddenly pious.

Chapter Seventeen

Blake was ecstatic. The church would offer him six figures with little effort on his part, merely to sweep the incident under the rug before the press got wind of it. He'd be reasonably flush again in a matter of weeks. Perhaps he could jump-start a new PI practice. He would send his retention notice and offer to keep a low profile, with settlement terms sealed. *I'll get an extra $50,000 or so in settlement proceeds just for being discreet. Jennifer will be so grateful. This could change everything!* His rotten luck was finally changing.

Blake felt like a lawyer again. He was beyond excited about the prospect of a huge payday but would try to exercise some professional control. He'd go through the motions to appease Jennifer. After all, he did promise her justice for her boys.

The case could play out in any number of ways. *Has the priest done this before?* If not, the church could not have known of his propensities and would not be liable. If so, they could be liable on multiple agency theories, especially if Zack could prove the church camping trip was within the scope of the priest's employment. A viable argument could be made. *If this priest was convicted of similar conduct before assaulting the Tracey boys and the church knew of the priest's predisposition to pedophilia, bingo! The sky's the limit!*

The day after Jennifer's visit, he drafted his retention letter to Our Lady of the Lakes Parish on his antiquated computer.

To whom it may concern:

This office has been retained to represent Jennifer Tracey and her sons, Jake and Kenneth Tracey, for collection of damages arising out of an incident that occurred recently, while the boys were on a camping trip with Father Gerry Bartholomew. The Tracey boys have suffered severe physical and emotional trauma as a result of this incident and their mother, severe emotional trauma.

Please refer this letter to the attention of your liability insurance carrier and ask that the appropriate representative contact me to arrange a private meeting as soon as possible. It is my firm belief that discretion in this matter is best for all parties.

Kindly consider this letter a claim of lien for services rendered on behalf of my client, and please give this matter your immediate attention. I look forward to hearing from your representative.

Thank you for your anticipated cooperation.

Very truly yours,
Zachary Blake, PC

The letter was in the hands of the Voice three days later, and he placed a call to Blake to arrange a meeting. *Turf* is an important issue in the practice of law. Lawyers prefer to negotiate on their own turf. They are more confident in their own surroundings with supportive people all around them. Lawyers always try to have meetings, negotiations, depositions, arbitrations, and the like in their private offices. It also cuts down on travel, which could be a drag.

In this case, however, Blake was embarrassed about his one-room dump of an office. He could not have a meeting at this practice level in a place like that. Thus, he waived territorial preference and agreed to a meeting in the prestigious law offices of Brodman, Longworth, and Darling in downtown Detroit's tallest building, Renaissance Center. Apparently, this silk-stocking law firm represented the church.

The RenCen was built in the Coleman Young era. It consisted of three blue-glass high rises, which forever changed the Detroit skyline. Zack could see the towers from the southern view he used to enjoy from his Town Center office window. General Motors purchased the complex in the early 2000s and relocated its headquarters to the largest tower. This was good for the city, because, like almost every other downtown venture in Detroit's recent past, the building had never been successful.

Following Detroit's historic bankruptcy, a comeback of sorts was occurring. Buildings were being purchased and renovated by

local billionaires. In the same area as its relatively new
professional football and baseball stadiums, a new hockey arena
has just opened for business. Upscale restaurants and "yuppie"
loft-style residences were attracting young people to live and
experience "downtown living."

The Fox Theatre, an old 1920s movie palace, was beautifully
restored to its original splendor and served as a concert and
Broadway play venue. Other theaters had followed suit,
including a new opera theater. Additionally, three Vegas-style
casino developments helped revitalize different sections of the
downtown entertainment district. These developments were the
genesis of a food and entertainment rebirth in Downtown
Motown.

Blake arrived at 9:00 a.m. for his 10:00 a.m. meeting. He was
excited and nervous. Perhaps this meeting would mark the
rebirth of his career. He thought about Jennifer Tracey and her
two sons. *What did she think of me? Could she smell alcohol on
my breath? Did she notice how far I have fallen? Was she
sufficiently impressed with my legal knowledge? Must have been,
she signed the retainer agreement, didn't she? Did she notice
how excited I got when I heard what the case was about? That
wouldn't be good. A big, fat settlement check will take care of
everything.*

Blake parked in the underground parking lot on Jefferson and
walked up the street to the RenCen. He entered and quickly
found a coffee shop. Suddenly the downtown business district
was full of coffee shops. He ordered a flavored decaf and sat
down. No caffeine, he was too nervous. *Calm down, Blake, you
can do this. This one's no different than a thousand meetings
you've attended with a thousand different lawyers.*

But, of course, this *was* different. This was Blake's survival
meeting, his resurrection meeting, and his personal career
renaissance meeting. He laughed to himself. *The renaissance of
Zack Blake at Renaissance Center, what a story! Maybe Mitch
Albom will write a column.*

Blake bought a *Free Press* and read the sports section. *Let
them make the first offer. It might be higher than what I'd
propose. Don't be anxious. After all, this is only the most crucial*

moment of your so-called life.

He went into the bathroom and studied himself in the mirror. He was short, about five feet eight inches, but never found height to be a detriment. He was a lawyer, not a pro basketball player. He'd been a pretty good baseball player in his prime and played on his high school baseball team. His hair was prematurely gray—blame his father—and he was rapidly losing his athletic build.

Back in his Town Center days, he went to the club and worked out every day. He ate well and took care of himself. But that was a lifetime ago. Today, far from the Town Center, lunch and dinner consisted of the nearest fast-food restaurant. Exercise was a trip from his car to the office and from the office to the bathroom. He was overweight. His suit was a bit snug. He needed to go to Men's Wearhouse and take them up on that free 'let-out-your-suit' offer. *Is it still available? I'm still a good-looking son of a bitch, though.*

His prematurely gray hair, combed straight back, was distinguished. It was advantageous when he was younger because clients thought he was older and more experienced. He had crystal blue eyes—his whole family did. Another lifetime ago, Tobey fell in love with those eyes. *After I settle the Tracey case, I'll reclaim some things.*

He splashed water on his face, dried it, left the bathroom, and started for the elevators. He immediately got lost. *Most people get lost in the RenCen—what a confusing building*! All Blake could see was glass and concrete. He couldn't locate a directory or find elevators or stairways. He saw no directional signs, and the three towers each had different addresses. *How does a person know which building he wants? How do clients ever find the office they need?*

Blake conceived a clever business idea. He'd use the Tracey money to open a small RenCen office, stand in the lobby, and direct his competitors' lost clients to his office rather than theirs. *There's no loyalty in this business anyway*. Lawyers were a dime a dozen. Look how easily his asshole ex-partners were able to convince his clients to stay with them.

He found a security guard who agreed to escort him to the

elevators—directions were not enough—and he immediately lifted off on his journey to the thirty-fifth floor. The RenCen had outside-view elevators that provided a beautiful panoramic view of the city of Detroit and twenty miles to the north, ancient history—the Southfield Town Center. A person with acrophobia must turn his back to the view.

He stepped off the elevator and into Brodman Longworth's suite of offices. The firm leased the entire thirty-fifth floor. The reception desk was just off the elevator. He identified himself to the receptionist and asked to see Craig Walsh, who was handling the case for the church. Blake waited a few moments before an attractive redhead appeared. She offered coffee and escorted him to a conference room. *I'll follow you anywhere.* The poetic movements of her beautifully shaped tush hypnotized the lawyer.

Unfortunately, she left him alone. Two men appeared. One, the prototypical defense lawyer, six feet two inches tall, blond hair, blue eyes, and the whitest teeth Zack had ever seen, identified himself as Walsh. The young lawyer had a politician's smile. The other man was not introduced and did not speak. He was shorter than Walsh, with grey hair, a trim beard. He wore a cleric's collar. The three men sat down at a beautiful lacquer conference room table.

"I see Rebecca took care of your coffee, Mr. Blake . . ."

"Yes, she did. Thank you." *Can I get her phone number?*

"I'd like to get right down to business. The church is quite upset about this incident. It is despicable. However, it is the isolated conduct of one rogue priest. The church was unaware of Father Bartholomew's propensities toward pedophilia. As such, this incident took us as much by surprise as it did Mrs. Tracey. In short, Mr. Blake—"

"Call me Zack."

"As I was saying, in short, there is no institutional liability here. The defendant is a priest who has sworn an oath of poverty. There is no collectability," Walsh argued.

"*Respondeat superior* creates liability and collectability." Zack retorted. He knew agency law, and he made sure they knew he knew it. *Respondeat superior* was a Latin term, meaning the superior was responsible for the wrongdoing of an agent under certain circumstances.

Walsh scoffed at the suggestion. "*Respondeat superior* only applies if the offending conduct occurs in the scope of employment. Clearly, child molestation is not in the scope of Gerry's employment as a parish priest."

"But the camping trip was," Zack smirked.

"True, but child molestation is not a necessary or expected function of camping. *Respondeat superior* doesn't apply," Walsh groused.

Zack sensed his rival's growing unrest. He decided to belabor the point.

"How can I be certain the church had no actual knowledge of Gerry's propensities? For purposes of this meeting, I must assume it had such knowledge. These were *children*. How are they supposed to know what religious rituals are without or within the scope of the priest's duties and responsibilities? There is, at least, apparent authority, and they have the right to rely on it." Zack doubled down. He'd researched the issue.

Walsh cringed. "There is absolutely no record of any previous conduct. Bartholomew's personnel file is squeaky clean. He has no criminal record or record of civil suits anywhere. We've checked. We also have a vigorous screening process all priests must go through. He's completely clean. As to apparent authority—"

"What if his priors escaped your screening process? Would you be liable then?" Zack interrupted. The old litigator juices were flowing again. He was enjoying himself.

"I'll concede the argument, but there is no evidence anything of the sort occurred in this case," Walsh grumbled.

"Back to apparent authority, if he used his collar to entice children to sleep with him under the guise, such conduct was pleasing to God, wouldn't that be within the scope of employment?" Zack persisted.

"Of course not." Walsh snapped. "Sleeping with children is not within the scope of a priest's employment."

"But an unsuspecting kid doesn't know that. He trusts the priest to tell him what God likes or doesn't like, isn't that true? This is textbook apparent authority," Zack reasoned. He relished the old back and forth.

"Possibly," Walsh conceded. "But that's not the standard. The standard for the church is whether its hierarchy reasonably could or would have sanctioned such conduct on a camping trip. The standard for the priest is his understanding of expected and acceptable behavior. Without any doubt, this priest knew the church did not sanction his behavior."

"True enough, but with the number of young parishioners being molested by priests throughout the country, wouldn't the church be wise not to send young male parishioners on camping trips with potential pedophiles?" Zack pressed. He could see himself *trying* this case.

"That's nonsense." Walsh sputtered. "When a few rogue priests molest some children in other communities, *all* priests and parishioners are supposed to suffer? These outings are great for camaraderie and enjoyed by all. They help the children to get better acquainted with their clergy and bring all closer to the church and God. Pedophilia is an extremely rare exception."

"I don't think Jake and Kenny Tracey wanted to get *that* acquainted with Father Gerry Bartholomew," Zack quipped. "It is my understanding millions, perhaps *billions* of dollars have been paid out to children as the result of priest-parishioner child molestation. That hardly constitutes a 'rare exception,'" Zack scowled. He prepared for this meeting. It was *that* important.

"Which brings me to the reason for our meeting." Walsh was pleased to change the subject. "The church feels terrible about what happened to the Tracey boys. We are paying for their therapy sessions and will continue to do so until their doctor releases them. Additionally, we are prepared to offer them a little something for their trouble," he floated.

"How do you define a little something?" Zack wondered.

"The church will offer six hundred thousand dollars, two hundred fifty-thousand for each child, one hundred thousand for Mrs. Tracey, and, of course, continuing treatment for the entire family until their doctor releases them for treatment. How does that strike you?" Walsh offered.

Zack was breathless. He felt his professional composure going out the window. He expected and was willing to accept an offer of low six figures. Instead, their first offer was *high* six figures. He hit the mother lode. "The offer seems a tad light," Zack managed to counter. *Was I convincing?*

"What would you recommend?" Walsh scoffed. He wasn't buying Blake's bravado.

"One million dollars," Zack demanded. "I can probably sell four hundred thousand for each boy and two hundred thousand for the mom—that and continued treatment," he bluffed, his stomach churning with trepidation.

Walsh studied Zack and then looked over to the mystery man, who raised his eyebrows. *A signal of some sort?* Zack wondered.

"That's an outrageous figure, Zack. We're being very generous here," Walsh blustered.

"Generous?" Zack gibed. "Your friend Gerry repeatedly does the nasty with two pre-teens, under your very noses, on *your* camping trip, and you think you're being generous? You're wasting my time. I think a jury will love this story."

Zack rose and began to leave. *Please, God, stop me before I get to the door!*

"Hold on, Zack," Walsh pleaded, turning to and conferring with the mystery man.

Thank you, God!

"Let's not be hasty," Walsh cautioned. "I'm sure we can reach some sort of accommodation."

"What kind of accommodation?" Zack challenged.

"I'm not sure. I need to confer with my client," Walsh asserted.

Mystery Man here has the purse strings.

"Zack, would you mind stepping out into the hall? We need to confer."

"Not at all," Zack assented. *Maybe Rebecca is out there.* He was feeling very lucky today. Zack stood in the hallway outside the conference room, alone, for about five minutes. He could hear the muted conversation inside but could not make out the words. Finally, Walsh came out and invited him to return.

"We've decided to accept your counterproposal, subject to one nonnegotiable condition," Walsh declared.

"And the condition?" Zack queried.

"Complete confidentiality. No one is to know about this claim. No one is to know about the settlement. The mother will agree to the conditions of any plea bargain that is worked out in the criminal case. We want this to go away as if it never happened," Walsh insisted.

"Seems to me a condition like that requires additional compensation. Perhaps confidentiality is worth another one hundred grand?" Zack countered. If that's okay, I'll talk to my client and recommend the deal."

Walsh looked at 'mystery man' who nodded his head. "Deal," Walsh assented.

"Anything else?" Zack gasped, struggling to contain his composure.

"No, I think that covers it. Thanks for coming down, Zachary. You've done a good job for your clients," Walsh sighed. He walked to the door and motioned for Zack to leave. "I'll request a check and have releases emailed to you in the morning. The check should be ready by the end of the week. Will that suffice?"

"Absolutely. Thank you," Zack effused. "This is a good resolution for all concerned. It was nice meeting you." *I've got to get out of here before I explode!*

"Likewise," the old man grumbled.

He's a cold, sinister character. The voice was familiar, where had Zack heard it before? *He was the one who called to set up the settlement meeting.* The guy sent an eerie chill up Zack's spine. He was glad he dealt with Walsh.

Zack stepped into the elevator. The doors closed. Zack let out the breath he'd been holding since he walked out of the conference room. *Blake is back*! Zack smiled. He would soon receive an almost four hundred-thousand-dollar fee for an interview, a letter, two phone calls, and a meeting. "I love this job," Zack chortled. He hadn't felt this good in three years. He couldn't wait to get back and call Jennifer with the fantastic news.

Chapter Eighteen

Gerry Bartholomew sat alone in Lakes' smallest chapel. A stone figure of the Son looked down upon him from the altar. Gerry meditated, gazing out at the adjacent courtyard. To him, celibacy meant being single, not having a wife or significant other. It had nothing to do with his sociopathic fondness for children.

What he did with the children was beautiful. It was God's will. *We were created in His image to enjoy marvelous physical pleasure. My calling is to teach the children as many of those pleasures as possible. God demands this of me. I've done nothing wrong.*

Gerry was incapable of guilt or remorse. He was interested only in the physical pleasure of children. At every parish on his journey, he loved his kids, and they loved him back. The church hierarchy, pastors, bishops, administrators, and parents were the problem. They despised Gerry, and he despised them right back.

How could people who never experienced such pure physical love attack his conduct? How could parents chastise his methods of education? God encouraged physical love as a beautiful experience, and made human bodies in His own image, for each of us to share. Would adults prefer to have their children grow up with no emotion, no experience, no understanding of what life and love had to offer? What did these people know?

Of those who were once married, most were divorced. Why? Because most were emotionally crippled, taught at a young age that physical love was dirty, punished for loving each other. Why should anyone be surprised about a rising divorce and suicide rate among the faithful? The teachings of the church were based entirely on making parishioners feel guilty for what they enjoy.

He hated them all. They didn't understand his higher calling. Gerry was answerable only to God. God loved him and approved of his efforts with children. In fact, his first experiences with the children were encouraged by a visit from the Lord. In his vision, the Lord told him to "teach them diligently unto thy children."

He told him young boys needed encouragement near puberty to experience the physical pleasures their young bodies were capable of feeling. Shortly after that, Gerry 'educated' his first child, on a camping trip in Minneapolis. That was almost ten years and twenty-five teenagers ago. His thoughts were interrupted by a knock on his door. It was Father Jon.

"Gerry, there are some Farmington Police Officers downstairs. They wish to talk to you," Jon frowned.

"Tell them I'm indisposed at the moment," Gerry blustered.

"I can't do that, Gerry. They have a warrant for your arrest. I called Walsh. He advises you to exercise your right to remain silent. He'll meet you at the Oakland County Jail and try to arrange for a quick arraignment and bail to minimize your incarceration."

Gerry rose and followed Jon down the stairs. Two uniformed officers put his hands behind his back, handcuffed him, and began to read him his rights. Gerry bowed his head and began to move his lips in silent prayer. The officers led him out of the church and into a waiting police car. A second team of officers handed Father Jon a search warrant and entered the rectory.

***

Father Jon watched the police car disappear down Farmington Road. He could not identify his feelings. He was glad to have this cancer excised from his church. At the same time, he felt profound sorrow.

What a troubled young man. Does he truly believe pedophilia is a priestly calling? He needs psychiatric help. What happened in his life to turn him into a depraved and callous individual? Did he become a priest because it afforded him fertile ground for young conquests? These questions might be answered during the upcoming criminal and civil trials.

He wondered how Jennifer's meeting with the lawyer went. Were she and the boys strong enough to endure the public spectacle that was to come? What did the future hold for them, his church, and for Gerry? He prayed all would come out of this experience intact. Would his prayers be answered?

"Please God, guide this troubled family into better days . . ." His prayer was interrupted by a second set of officers who left Gerry's room. They descended the stairs, carrying a small statue of a man and boy embracing. They carried boxes of pornographic magazines, a computer, and nude photographs of teenage boys. *I didn't even know he had a computer.*

The officers advised the search was not over. They'd be on the premises for most of the day. They demanded a list of families and individuals who were members of Lakes and asked Jon to highlight those who had teenage boys. Jon promised to compile and turn over a list in a couple of days. He couldn't believe this went on in his parish, under his nose, without his knowledge. Neither could the police. They grilled him with questions about his own activities, his knowledge of Gerry's actions, and his efforts to cover for Gerry. Jon almost called Walsh but decided against it. He wouldn't be part of a cover-up. He'd answer their questions. He'd done nothing criminally wrong. His failure was stupidity. *What is the penalty for assuming my parish and I were immune from this stuff? In my stubborn arrogance, these two beautiful boys were physically, emotionally, and religiously scarred for life. Their mother is an emotional wreck.*

What was the penalty for stupidity or blind loyalty? The police finished their questioning and left with their collected evidence. Father Jonathan Costigan was completely alone. He hung his head and entered the rectory. He sat on the couch, buried his head in his hands, and began to weep.

Chapter Nineteen

Blake called Jennifer Tracy and asked her to come by the office. He had 'good news,' he told her. They set the appointment for 3:00 p.m. At 2:55 p.m., Zack sat in his stuffy office, awaiting her arrival. He was surprised she wasn't early.

In civil case legal wars, plaintiff attorneys and defense attorneys have the exact opposite agendas. On the plaintiff side, attorneys work on a contingency-fee-basis, routinely one-third of the damages recovered. Upon settlement or verdict proceeds, the attorney is paid his out-of-pocket costs and one-third of the net proceeds. If there is no recovery, the client owes the attorney no fee. Technically, the client still owes the attorney for out-of-pocket costs, even when the case fails. Most attorneys never see a dime because the typical plaintiff can't afford to pay the bill. It is rare to settle a large case at such an early stage, but Zack didn't mind. *They made a solid offer. Why risk a no-cause or work my ass off for the money?*

On the defense side, the attorney bills insurance companies and other deep-pocket defendants by the hour. Thus, it's in their best interest to drag the case on through endless pretrial motions, depositions, hearings, scene investigations, witness preparations, jury consulting, and so on. These large defense firms bill $350 to $750 per hour. For this reason, civil dockets are quite crowded in Southeastern Lower Michigan courtrooms. Plaintiff lawyers are vilified for filing 'frivolous' suits. But, the truth is, defense attorneys decide based upon the reasonableness of their settlement offers, which cases are filed or tried. In addition, defense attorneys will not settle cases until they have sufficient billable hours in the case. What is sufficient depends upon a firm's pedigree, overhead, and client's deep pockets. How easily can the firm persuade a deep-pocket defendant to believe in its quest for justice, regardless of the hours necessary to achieve that justice?

This was why Zack was ecstatic with the result. *Tracy v. Bartholomew* was a tough, *David v. Goliath* type case. *David*, in this litigation scenario, was Zack and his clients— Brodman Longworth and the church were *Goliath*. The firm featured hundreds of attorneys, high overhead, and the ability to drag this case on for years. Before the settlement, Zack envisioned endless proceedings, motions, and appeals. The church was a deep-pocket defendant, with the resources to delay resolution for years. All the characteristics of a battle royal were there, yet they offered $1.1 million—amazing! He still couldn't believe the outcome. *Jennifer will be so pleased.*

A knock on the door abruptly interrupted his pleasant thoughts. "Come in, please."

The door opened. In the hallway stood Jennifer. She wore a sheer, almost see-through, floral-patterned dress, which hugged the curves of her slender body. Her face was glowing. *She's a stunner!* Zack shook himself to consciousness.

"How are you, Jenny? Have a seat. Thank you for coming on such short notice. I have great news," Zack gushed.

"I'm getting along, Zack. Thanks for asking. I'm pleased you're working on the case so quickly. What's the great news?" His excitement was palpable, contagious. *He seems much better today. He's rather nice looking.*

"I've settled the case!" Zack beamed.

"You've what?" Jennifer grunted. Zack was too emotionally charged to notice her dismay.

"That's right. It's settled," he boasted.

"I thought the case couldn't be settled without my permission," she challenged.

"That is a mere technicality, my dear." Zack rambled, oblivious to her rancor.

"Technicality?" Jennifer questioned.

"I mean, when you hear the terms of the settlement, you'll be ecstatic!" Zack promised.

Jennifer tried to relax. She tried to share his enthusiasm. He was euphoric, and it was contagious.

"I've settled the case for one point one million dollars—four hundred thousand for each of the boys and two hundred thousand for you. And, get this, there's another hundred thousand for keeping this quiet. Can you believe it? Am I good, or am I good?

On top of all of this money, the boys can stay in treatment for as long as they need to at the church's expense. And there are only two insignificant conditions."

"And what are those?" Jennifer seethed. For the first time, Zack noted her displeasure. She was unenthusiastic, raining on his parade.

"I already mentioned confidentiality. We must also agree not to contest any plea bargain negotiated in the criminal case," Zack reported, still elated. He was clueless about the coming storm.

Jennifer paused. She shook from growing rage. "I don't believe this, Zack. Your so-called settlement is completely unacceptable, absolutely out of the question," she snarled.

Zachary was nonplussed. She completely shut down his remarkable achievement. Instead of the jubilation he expected, Jennifer Tracy was *livid*.

"How could you do this?" she demanded. "I gave you specific instructions when I retained you. I wanted a lawsuit filed in a very public manner. I told you I would never settle, and I was clear there would be no confidentiality clause. I also told you, in no uncertain terms: I will never approve any plea bargain that doesn't include prison time. I will not permit this creep's conviction to be concealed from the public.

"Dammit, Zack! I told you my sons, and I never want anything like this to happen to another child, ever! How could you violate every condition we discussed when I retained you?"

"But, Jennifer . . ." he staggered. "I thought you'd be pleased. This is an awful lot of money . . . "

"Damn it, Zack! This isn't about money. It's about justice and prevention, justice for my boys and those who came before them, and prevention for those who may come after. Your crap settlement does not alert the public and allows this animal to continue to violate children," Jennifer raged. "I will not stand idly by for a few bucks and permit this to happen to another innocent child."

"This is a seven-figure result, Jenny. It's hardly a few bucks," Zack grumbled. His get-rich-quick dream was becoming a nightmare.

"Zachary Blake, you are fired, sir," Jennifer ordered.

"Compile a bill for services rendered, and I'll pay it. I have no further use for your service."

"Jenny, be reasonable. Let's not be hasty. Let's not be rash. I'm . . . I'm . . . sorry!" Zack pleaded, ashamed he so completely misread the situation.

She was right to be angry. He *did* violate every condition she placed on the resolution of the case. He never thought she was serious. But she *was*, and his blunder was going to cost him the case of a lifetime. *I can do this her way! If she wants the case to be public, then public it shall be! If she wants to turn down $1.1 million, I'll get her $2 million—whatever she wants! I have to convince her!*

"Jenny, please! I'm truly sorry," he implored. "I admit I misunderstood your feelings on this. I honestly thought, when you heard the numbers, you'd be pleased. I can do this your way. Besides, you're the client. No lawsuit can be settled without your approval. The defense *knows* this!

"I'll prepare a lawsuit. I'll call a press conference when it's ready to be filed. I'll refuse any offer that includes confidentiality, and I'll refuse to cooperate with any plea bargain. I'll hire a top-notch investigator, and we'll get the goods on Gerry and the church. I'm good, Jenny. I'm a great lawyer. You know this—you know my work. Give me a chance, *please!*" Blake argued, fighting for his life. He was near tears.

Jennifer softened, but her tone remained harsh. "And you'll never agree to anything without consulting with me first?"

"I didn't do that this time, Jenny. I told them I needed to consult with you. I swear," Zack pleaded, his demeanor almost juvenile.

Jennifer assuaged and then admonished him. "Against my better judgment, I'll reconsider. But we're going to pursue this *my way,* mister, and if you cross me again, I'll drop you like a hot potato. These are my precious children. I will not permit you to let them down!"

"I won't, Jennifer. I swear to God, I won't," He promised, with genuine remorse.

"I take an oath to God very seriously, Counselor, especially in this case," she taunted.

"So do I, Jenny. So do I."

She paused to study him. *Is he holding his breath? Oh, my God, he is! I should cut him some slack before he explodes.* She capitulated.

"Okay, you're rehired."

Zack was relieved and pumped at the same time. Jenny's unbridled anger and enthusiasm had a profound effect on him. He had trivialized the importance of the case, her kids, and the future of the church. Many lives hung in the balance, awaiting the outcome. This was the type of serious litigation the old Zack Blake used to thrive upon. Jennifer Tracey's passion for justice ignited the spark of Zack's competitive flame. He would be *that* Blake again, the kick-ass trial lawyer Blake. *The church and that piece-of-shit priest are dead meat*!

***

Immediately after Jennifer left the office, Zack went to work. He attempted to structure a rough draft for this rather unique situation by using old complaints he filed in the past. He had minimal success. This complaint had to be prepared from scratch. He wasn't surprised. How were most civil child molestation cases filed against institutional defendants?

He pondered potential theories. Intentional torts were typically excluded from coverage in most commercial insurance policies. Still, he had to include a count for assault and battery. The liability of the church, the principal, was vicarious for the acts of Gerry, the agent. If there was no lawsuit against Gerry, there was no lawsuit against the church.

Next, he tackled agency theories. The church and Lakes employed Gerry. Under Michigan law, they were Gerry's principals, and he was their agent. Agency theories and principal liability for the conduct of agents were the keys to success in this case. The assault and battery case was a slam-dunk. It was worthless, however, because Gerry, unlike OJ, was not collectible. He swore an oath of poverty when he entered the priesthood. For this reason, the agency theories were even more vital, and Zack spent countless hours researching them.

The doctrine of *respondeat superior* provides the act of an employee during his or her employment is legally the act of his or her employer. Michigan case law provides the standard is not merely that the church is the employing entity, but whether Gerry, the employee, was acting in the interests of the employer. While the existence of the agency was a jury question, Zack wasn't worried much about establishing that. Gerry was an employee of the church, therefore, an agent. Zack was more concerned about the 'interests of the employer' question.

He decided to plead the camping trip was in furtherance of a legitimate church function, namely parishioner camaraderie and priest-parishioner relations. As to the victim, the agent was acting in his employer's interest. However, while employers can be held liable for the willful and wanton misconduct of their employees, their criminal acts outside the scope of the master's business, intentionally or recklessly, do not create liability to the master.

Next, Zack tackled the issue of apparent authority. This was the key issue in the case. If he could successfully argue apparent authority, the potential for a substantial verdict against the church rather than the priest was significantly enhanced. The crucial distinction between this theory and the others is it depended on the *victims' reliance.* What was the reasonable belief of the person or persons—Kenny and Jake— when dealing with the agent? With apparent authority, a principal is responsible for the acts of its agent, not actually authorized, but traceable to the principal if they are relied upon by the victims. This was where the boys' ages came into play. If the church sent Gerry on these trips with children and the outings were church-sanctioned or sponsored, it was not unreasonable, especially in the minds of naïve children, to assume the church-sanctioned the actions of the priest. Further, in this case, Gerry injected God into his perversion, advising the boys God considered these acts to be beautiful and acceptable behavior in His eyes. The theory was viable, and Zack decided to base the case on this vital principle of law.

Ideas and theories were now popping into Zachary's head. One he especially liked was called the *agency by estoppel* theory.

Quite similar to apparent authority, the estoppel theory deals explicitly with the conduct of the victim. There are three elements necessary to establish the theory: First, the person dealing with the agent must do so with belief in the agent's authority, and this belief must be reasonable. *This burden is undoubtedly met in this case.* Second, the belief must be generated by some act or neglect of the principal sought to be charged. *A bit more complicated, but his burden could be met with the church's knowledge of prior actions, failure to properly screen or supervise, or, simply, bad policy in sending priests on camping trips alone with the children.* Third, the victim must be justified in relying on the agent's apparent authority. *These were children.* Gerry was their *priest. Who could disagree that these children were not justified in trusting their priest? Nobody!*

The more he thought, the more he liked the approach. While the implied agency could not exist contrary to the express intention of the alleged principal, it could spring from acts permitted by the principal over time through acquiescence.

Zack finished with his agency and intentional acts theories. He developed several more theories, and one week after his meeting with Jennifer, he completed his final draft. The complaint was a seventeen-count masterpiece against Bartholomew, Costigan, Our Lady of the Lakes, the division director of the Detroit Division of the church, and the church. It contained the following allegations:

1. Assault and battery by Father Gerry
2. Intentional infliction of emotional distress by Father Gerry as to Kenny and Jake
3. Intentional infliction of emotional distress by Father Gerry as to Jennifer
4. Negligent assault and battery (The assault and battery was obviously a deliberate act; however, while the act was intended, Gerry did not foresee the resulting damages to the family; thus, he was negligent in creating the result. Plaintiff attorneys used this theory often in an attempt to avoid intentional acts exclusions in liability insurance policies.)

5. Negligent infliction of emotional distress by Gerry as to the boys
6. Negligent infliction of emotional distress by Gerry as to Jennifer
7. *Respondeat superior*—the acts occurred in the scope of Gerry's employment with the church
8. Apparent authority
9. Agency by estoppel
10. Gross negligence/misconduct by Gerry and by the church, which knew or, in the exercise of reasonable care, should have known of Gerry's propensities toward pedophilia and did nothing to stop him
11. Negligent screening of priests by the church
12. Negligent training of priests by the church
13. Negligent transferring of priests by the church when it knew or, with the exercise of reasonable care, should have known of their propensities toward pedophilia
14. Failure by the church to warn its parishioner of the danger posed by Gerry
15. Negligence of the church in covering up Gerry's prior acts
16. Negligent infliction of emotional distress by the church as to the boys
17. Negligent infliction of emotional distress by the church as to Jennifer

The complaint sought damages of $40 million. Zachary invited Jennifer over to the office to review the complaint. She was extremely pleased. The two agreed it would be filed at the end of the week in Wayne County Circuit Court. Even though the offending acts occurred in Oakland County, two of the defendants, the division director, and the Detroit Division resided in Wayne County. Oakland was the much more conservative of the two counties, and Wayne was notorious for substantial verdicts in personal injury cases. Zachary notified the local newspapers and all pertinent radio and television stations. He called a press conference at the home of his client, Jennifer Tracey, to announce the filing of a major multimillion-dollar lawsuit against a major religious institution. The dye had been cast. A long, tough road lay ahead. For Zachary, Jennifer, Kenny, and Jake, there was no turning back.

Chapter Twenty

"Blake's called a press conference."

"What for?"

"To announce the filing of a multimillion-dollar lawsuit against a 'major religious institution.'"

"Wonderful news. I thought you and Walsh had this under control."

"Yes, you told us this was settled."

"It was."

"Maybe you should have offered more money."

"Seriously? Blake thought he was fleecing us. He had no idea how much money was available to keep this confidential. The amount of money we offered had nothing to do with his decision to litigate. Besides, I don't think Blake is behind the rejection of the offer."

"Who then?"

"Jennifer Tracey. I'm certain. Blake was euphoric when he left Walsh's office. He was going to recommend the money *and* confidentiality because confidentiality meant even *more* money. He thought the boys would prefer privacy. My guess is *she* refused the money and the terms."

"But why? It's more money than she's ever seen in her life."

"Because for her, money isn't the issue. This is about revenge, payback, even worse, *justice*." The Voice growled.

"More than a million bucks is an awful lot of justice," a member marveled.

"For some people, maybe, apparently not for Jennifer Tracey. That makes her dangerous," the Voice cautioned.

"How so?"

"This press conference must be Jennifer's idea. She wants to expose Gerry to the whole world."

"Why? What does she care? Publicity is not going to help her boys."

"She doesn't believe that. In the few conversations she has had with Rothenberg and Costigan that we have been able to monitor, she clearly wants to out Gerry as a criminal. Doing so, she believes, will help rid her sons of guilt feelings."

"That's foolish. Why should they feel guilty?"

"Why is not the question; it is, indeed, how they feel. Jennifer and Rothenberg believe the boys' self-esteem will benefit from a public flogging of Gerry," the Voice uttered, with mounting petulance.

"Rothenberg? I thought he was working with us. Did he actually say this in monitored conversations?" The member was aghast.

"No, he didn't. However, Jennifer would never go this route without his blessing. He has to have told her about the effect a public trial would have on her kids."

"Then why haven't we heard any of this on the recordings?" the member persisted.

"Because conversations are being conducted elsewhere."

"But that would mean they know about the listening devices at the Tracey home and the doctor's office."

"I'm afraid so," the Voice presumed.

"It would also mean Rothenberg is working with Jennifer," another member concluded, now acutely aware of the gravity of the situation.

"I'm afraid that is also true," the Voice conceded.

"Well, what are we going to do about it?"

"What would you have me do?"

"Replace Rothenberg with a different therapist?"

"We can't do that," The Voice advised.

"Why? We're paying for the treatment. Aren't we entitled?"

"We might have been able to replace him early on, but not now. The boys are comfortable with Rothenberg. To change now would be too obvious."

"Screw the boys," a member snapped.

"Quite an interesting comment considering our circumstances. Sensitivity training, anyone?" The Voice admonished.

"I didn't mean it like that," the embarrassed member apologized. "I care about all the kids. You know that. I wish we had better solutions to these disturbing events. I wish we could identify, treat, and control these predator priests. I want to root out these demons, so no other children suffer the same harm. On the other hand, I care about our institution and its wonderful humanitarian work around the world. The problems of two children can't be permitted to affect the overall great work the church is doing."

"Here, here," the Voice mocked. "What's your solution?"

"I believe it is time for some aggressive action."

"What do you have in mind?" The Voice was intrigued.

"Go on the attack. Hire the best public relations people money can buy and trumpet all the good things the church does. We have occasional issues with pedophilia in the clergy that we are aggressively working to eradicate. If a priest is accused of pedophilia, we suspend him, get him treatment, and make positive findings as to the truth or falsity of the allegations. That's what we've done in this case.

"We are a caring, giving, charitable, religious institution, and the good we do for society far outweighs the bad. A public spectacle like this deliberate attempt to embarrass the church for the isolated and previously unknown conduct of one rogue priest is unconscionable. It only serves to undermine our ability to do God's work.

"I'd arrange to have some reporters friendly to the church at the press conference. Ask Blake if he has any evidence to substantiate allegations the church is involved in some 'cover-up' here or somehow encourages pedophilia in its clergy. The answer will be 'no.' Demand that Blake publicly apologizes to the church hierarchy if he is unable to sustain the charge. If the boys are truthful and Gerry is a pedophile, we are already providing and paying for the boys' treatment. This course of action has been quite helpful, as Mrs. Tracey will attest. We will also get Gerry the treatment he needs. We are not monsters, and we resent being depicted in such a manner."

"I like that approach as long as we can deliver the message effectively," a member remarked.

"Leave that to me," the Voice assured.

"I still think we could eliminate one of the players without arousing too much suspicion," a member guilefully suggested.

"Who, for instance?" the Voice wondered.

"The mother. She seems to be the driving force behind this. Without her, the whole issue would fizzle out."

"Too risky, in my judgment. Let's try the public relations approach before we consider anything so drastic."

"I agree."

"So do I."

"Me, too."

"All in favor of this approach?"

"Yes," they assented in unison.

"I'll call my friends at the newspaper. There is one problem, however."

"What's that?"

"Aside from our humanitarian work, there's not a word of truth in our proposed public position. If Blake uncovers the truth, the Coalition and, perhaps the church, are finished."

"Part two of this plan, then, is to make sure that never happens."

"How do we accomplish that?"

"By any means necessary."

Chapter Twenty-One

On Friday morning, in the lower level family room of the Tracey's Farmington Hills tri-level, Zack and Jennifer were preparing for the Downtown press conference scheduled for later in the day. Jake and Kenny were sent to sleep over at Aunt Lynne's house. They'd be in safe hands and have ample recreational options. Lynne, Jennifer's sister, had four sons, ranging in age from eight to fifteen years old. Lynne and Jennifer's boys were good buddies. Jennifer's boys always welcomed a sleepover at Aunt Lynne's, until the infamous camping trip. While the suggestion this time did not spark the usual excitement in her boys, Jake and Kenny did appear enthusiastic about the sleepover and the idea of quality time with their cousins.

"Jenny, the boys would love to see Jake and Kenny. How are they doing?" Lynne wondered.

"Reasonably well, all things considered," Jennifer reflected.

"Jen . . . I don't mean to pry . . . but . . . what exactly happened with the priest?"

"Lynne, I really don't want to—"

"Come on, Jenny. I don't want to find out from the papers. What did that son-of-a-bitch do to my nephews?"

Lynne's motives weren't totally pure. She wanted the gossip, but she was right. She should know before the general public, so Jennifer laid it all out for her. It wasn't any easier this time.

Lynne was floored. "Has this guy done this before?"

"We don't know. We think so. We're hiring an investigator."

"I'll bet he has, the scumbag. I suppose you've seen the light and given up this obsession you have with religion?" Lynne groused.

"I am not obsessed, and religion has nothing to do with this. Father Jon has been very supportive, and so have the families at Lakes."

"Jenny, if you weren't religious, this never would have happened. I certainly wouldn't send my kids on a camping trip with some pervert priest," Lynne argued.

"Lynne, 'perverts,' as you call them, come in all shapes, sizes, professions, and religions. This could have just as easily been your boys' baseball coach or teacher," Jennifer retorted.

"But it wasn't, was it? They won't let these priests have normal relationships, and that attracts a unique element to the priesthood," Lynne persisted.

"Thank you, Dr. Lynne," Jennifer chuckled.

"You can be a smartass if you want, but you need to get a life away from the church," Lynne insisted.

"How much do you charge for this advice? I didn't need a therapist; I could have hired my sister," Jennifer mocked.

Lynne softened. "Very funny. As long as I'm giving advice, do you really think going public with this thing is going to be good for the boys? Haven't they been through enough? They're going to take a lot of abuse once the details are disclosed."

"Yeah, I know. I've had second thoughts, but Dr. Rothenberg believes a public airing of Gerry's crimes might actually help the boys. I've asked the boys, and that's how they want to proceed."

"But you could talk them out of it. The boys take the lead from you. I don't think I would embarrass them in public like this."

Jennifer was fed up with the conversation. "You're my older sister, and I love you, but the last thing I need is a bunch of I-told-you-so's or this-couldn't-happen-to-me's. I certainly don't need you telling me what you would or wouldn't do. I'm going to hang up now. Will you watch the kids or not?" she demanded.

"You're right, Jen, of course," she capitulated. "I'm sorry. You're going through hell, and I'm pontificating instead of being compassionate," Lynne admitted.

"Pontificating? Interesting choice of words for a nonbeliever," Jennifer chuckled.

They both laughed, and the tension that had developed between them evaporated as it often did during their childhood arguments. Their mom used to say, "One minute you're mortal enemies, and the next you love each other."

"Maybe I'm closet religious." Lynne laughed. "Of course I'll watch the boys. Being with my boys will do them some good."

"Thanks, Lynne. I'm sorry if I seemed harsh."

"Nonsense, I deserved it."

"You're right. You did."

Both ladies laughed again, uttered their goodbyes, and hung up. Jennifer wondered why the church was where she turned for help before her own sister. Perhaps, that was what Lynne was referring to. Perhaps . . .

"Jenny?" Zack brought her back to the here and now from far away. "Where were you this time?"

"I was replaying a phone conversation I had last night with my sister. Zack, I sought help from the church before my own *sister*. Isn't that weird?"

"I don't think so, Jenny, unless your sister's a therapist or something. I'd expect to get more help from someone who counsels others for a living, like Father Jon."

"I guess you're right, but I sensed Lynne was somewhat hurt."

"Well, that's her problem, and it's a lot less of a problem than those you and your boys are facing."

"You're right again."

Zack, as was his habit lately, was making her feel better. She appreciated Lynne's concern, but she'd handle the situation her own way.

"Jenny? There you go again." He snapped her out of it again. "We have a couple of hours before we head downtown. Do you want to go over it again?"

"No."

"No?"

"No!"

"But, Jenny—"

"Zack, we've been over and over this 'dealing with the press' business. I'm as ready as I'll ever be."

"Just remember, if you don't want to answer a question posed to you, look over to me—"

"I know, Zack." She interrupted him. "You'll answer it for me."

"If they ask you about the boys—"

"They're going through hell, but they're tough kids. They're getting excellent therapy, and we're very hopeful. Still, to have something like this happen at this time in their lives . . ."

This time it was Zack who interrupted. "Coupled with the loss of their father and Father Bill . . ."

"I know, Zachary! I know," Jennifer snapped.

"What's wrong, Jenny?"

"I don't know, Zack. I guess I'm having second thoughts about this publicity thing."

"Why?"

"I'm just not sure it's right for the boys," she moaned.

"Dr. Rothenberg seems to think it may help the boys."

"Psychology is not an exact science, Zack. He doesn't *know* it will help. He sets up scenarios and deals with the results. He doesn't deal with prevention. He deals in solutions after the development of a problem," she reasoned.

"Thank you, Dr. Tracey."

"I said the same thing to my sister only I called her 'Dr. Lynne'."

"Really?"

"Yeah, she called me a smartass," Jennifer teased.

"I get the message. Jenny, it's not too late to cancel the press conference," Zack offered.

"Yes, it is, Zack. I allowed the boys to decide, and they want to go forward. I trust Dr. Rothenberg's judgment. I wish I had a crystal ball and knew things would turn out all right."

"A magic wand would be better." He smiled warmly and took her hand in his.

"Yeah," she agreed, smiling back at him. "I could wave it and make all of this go away like it never happened."

Zack was gently caressing her hand. It had been a long time since a man had caressed her in any way. It was nice. Her eyes met his. *Blue like mine*, she thought. Zack was a handsome man. Under different circumstances . . .

"There you go again."

"What?"

"Wandering off somewhere."

"I wasn't wandering. I was looking . . . at your eyes. You have nice eyes."

She couldn't believe the words came out of her mouth. The timing sucked.

"Back at you," Zack stuttered, surprised and somewhat embarrassed.

He's blushing. So cute . . . stop, Tracey. He's your kids' lawyer. The case is our number one priority. Get your mind back on this afternoon's business.

"So, Jenny . . ." Zack returned to matters at hand. "Yes or no to the press conference?"

"Yes."

"Let me do the talking unless they ask you a direct question. Even then, wait to see if it's a question I want you to answer. Take a deep breath, count to five. I'll chime in before five seconds are up to save the day."

"Ah, my knight in shining armor."

"That's me."

"I'm glad I didn't fire you, Zack."

"So am I, Jen. So am I. Let's get going."

Chapter Twenty-Two

"We have called this press conference to announce this morning's filing of a forty-million-dollar lawsuit against the church, the Detroit Division, Our Lady of the Lakes, Father Jonathan Costigan, Bishop Andrew Glimesh, Father Gerry Bartholomew, and others," Zachary Blake announced to a packed room at the Cobo Center, Detroit's largest convention center.

Father Jon had to be named as a defendant in the lawsuit because Michigan law required all reasonable parties to be joined. Since Jon was Gerry's direct supervisor, he was responsible for his conduct under the aforementioned agency theories. These issues and his status as a named defendant in the suit were explained to him in a private moment between Jon, Jennifer, and Zack. It was no surprise to Father Jon to be a named defendant in the lawsuit. He understood it was necessary and assented to the strategy. Zack scanned the room. All the major players were there. There were reporters and mini-cam operators from Channels 2, 4, 7, 50, and 62. Radio reporters from WWJ, WJR, and various religious stations were present. *Detroit Free Press* and *Detroit News* reporters, local newspaper and religion writers, as well as internet bloggers crammed into the room, recorders in hand.

Zack continued. "I don't know how many of you picked up copies of the complaint filed this morning in Wayne Circuit, but I have several copies."

"Mr. Blake, why was the lawsuit filed in Wayne County?" It was Benjamin, from Channel 7, young, aggressive, and eager to make an impact. "The alleged conduct, the church, and the boys' residence are all in Oakland," he reasoned.

"The church, the division, and Bishop Glimesh all reside in Wayne, which permits us to file there. We're confident we will receive justice from a Wayne County jury even though the events occurred outside Wayne County," Zack explained.

"Aren't you simply forum shopping?" Benjamin charged.

"Wayne County juries are notoriously more generous than Oakland County juries. Everyone knows that."

"I would appreciate all of you holding your questions until I've finished my statement. Thank you."

Benjamin backed off.

Of course, I'm forum shopping! Verdicts are traditionally higher in Wayne than in Oakland. "As I was saying, this complaint alleges seventeen counts of intentional and negligent misfeasance, malfeasance, and nonfeasance by the church and Father Gerry. Gerry sexually molested fourteen-year-old Kenneth Tracey and as his twelve-year-old brother, Jake. The church, pastor, and bishop failed to educate, train, and monitor this dangerous predator. Furthermore, they failed to screen or weed out pedophiliacs in the clergy. Finally, after helping to create this predator and discovering Father Gerry's offensive proclivities, church officials covered up his prior conduct rather than reporting it or exposing it," Blake charged.

This last comment caused a noticeable stir in the bloodthirsty crowd.

"Do you have proof of prior conduct and the church's knowledge of the same?" The question came from an unknown voice in the back of the large assembly room.

"Would you identify yourself, sir?"

"Sure, Al Schneider, *National Religious Reporter.*"

Zack could see him in the back of the room. He was a squirrelly looking guy with thick plastic glasses perched at the end of an ample nose. About thirty-five years old, with kinky hair, he wore a plaid jacket and striped shirt. He wouldn't win a fashion contest. If Steve Urkel was a white man, he'd be Al Schneider.

"Well, Mr. Schneider, thank you for that question. Unfortunately, if I told you, I would have to kill you."

Laughter filled the tense, crowded room. Zack's sudden attempt to add a bit of levity to the proceedings eased tensions.

"Seriously, though," Zack continued. "I cannot reveal certain sources of information at this time. I need to protect confidentiality and confirm the reliability of the sources. You members of the press can appreciate that. Next question?"

"What do the boys say was done to them by this priest?"

"I don't think we need to get into the prurient details. Suffice it to say Father Gerry is guilty of statutory rape." There was another noticeable stir in the crowd. "The acts were deplorable and repetitive. As perverted as this sounds, there is a second violation here. The priest used God as a pretext for his depraved behavior. God sanctioned this; don't you know? Post-incident, two boys' faith in God and their church have been damaged, perhaps destroyed. A male trust figure has betrayed them most egregiously. These essential virtues of childhood will be hard for them to reclaim as adults."

"How do we know the boys are telling the truth?" Harlow, from Channel 4, challenged. She was an anchor. The event attracted all the big guns from Detroit's media community.

"Forensics and common sense will back up their allegations. When you hear their stories from their own lips, you be the judge. When the time comes, read their testimony. I defy you to disbelieve them. Besides, this is now a police matter. Before the civil case ever goes to trial, Gerry Bartholomew will be formally charged with first-degree criminal sexual conduct, will be convicted, or will enter a plea bargain on a lesser charge."

"Mrs. Tracey, in this lawsuit-happy society of ours, why sue the priest and the church? I understand treatment is being provided for the boys by the very entity you are now suing. How is money going to help your kids, or is this just another money grab?" Al Schneider charged. *Did someone put him up to this?* Zack wondered.

Jennifer paused and glanced at Blake for approval. Zack shrugged his shoulders. "Answer it if you can."

"We seek compensation, true, but we also seek to prevent future abhorrent conduct by this or any other priest. We seek to punish a vicious predator of children and the religious institution that stands idly by and watches while a whole generation of God's precious children are physically and psychologically raped of their childhood, their faith, and their trust in role models. This is about a hierarchy whose solution to the problem is to send the offending priest packing, quietly pay off victims, and actively cover up crimes. The cover-up is responsible for a vicious cycle of crime upon crime. This lawsuit says we will not go quietly like those who came before us. The vicious cycle stops here and now."

"How do you mean?"

"This lawsuit will be conducted in *public*. Members of the press will have full access. Gerry Bartholomew can no longer hit and run, as we believe he has in the past. After this case is resolved, the result will follow this predator everywhere he goes. We will not consent to a confidential settlement. Gerry will be branded a child molester, which should have happened long ago. We seek to prevent another child from being molested by this monster."

"Are there any other questions?" Zack inquired, scanning the room.

"Before taking more questions, I want to say one more thing about what this lawsuit accomplishes, " Jennifer interrupted.

Zack shot her a 'sit down, shut up, you talk too much,' look, but he was helpless to stop her. She had a mind of her own, and he admired her more with each passing moment. He gazed at her in the lights of the television cameras. *What tenacity! What spirit! I feel so alive in her presence. I can conquer the world with her by my side.* If she'd let him, he'd violate his rule about becoming involved with a client.

"Go ahead, Mrs. Tracey," he prompted

"If the jury does its job properly, this lawsuit will vindicate my sons and prove they've done nothing wrong . . ."

Zack was astonished. *She just challenged an unpicked jury!*

"My boys have nothing to feel guilty or shameful about. A verdict will prove my sons were victims and Gerry is a criminal predator. He has used his position to prey on the most innocent and helpless in society, our children." Her voice trembled with anger but grew stronger as she progressed. "He and others like him, if not stopped, will create a generation of faithless and trustless adults. We cannot let this happen to our children."

The entire press corps, with the possible exception of Schneider, erupted in thunderous applause. Jennifer blushed, nodded appreciation, and sat down. The rest of the press conference was uneventful. Jennifer Tracey had them eating out of her hand. She was a woman on a mission. It was a nice beginning to a long, hard journey.

When the press conference was over, Zack approached Jennifer. "You were incredible today," he marveled.

"Thank you. You were quite smashing yourself," Jennifer beamed.

"Jenny, have dinner with me tonight," he requested.

"What?" The invitation startled her.

"Come on. The boys are at your sister's. It'll do us both good."

"I don't know, Zack. We should keep our relationship on a professional level."

"Jenny, it's just dinner. If it makes you feel better, we can discuss the case, thus making it a business dinner. We can even split the bill."

"What if someone sees us? We're like celebrities now." She cautioned.

"No, you *are* a celebrity after your performance today. Can't a lawyer take his client out to dinner to discuss the case? Haven't you ever heard of the two-martini lunch?"

"Yes, but this is dinner," she corrected.

"It's the same thing. I looked it up in my *Etiquette and Tax Deductions for Lawyers* handbook." He joked.

"And this book says it's okay?" She rolled her eyes.

"Absolutely, page 357," he whispered.

"Well, all right, Zack. I'd love to." She paused and gazed out at the now empty room.

"There you go again," Zack noticed.

"What, now?"

"Daydreaming."

"I was seeking permission."

"Permission from whom? For what?"

"For dinner, from Jim."

A solitary tear fell from her eye, and she lowered her head. Zack lifted her chin. Their eyes met and Zack saw profound sadness.

"And what did Jim say?" He dared.

She smiled. "He suggested that dinner with Zachary Blake is

a splendid idea."

"Smart man, Jim. There's something I admire greatly about him, although we never met."

"Oh, and what's that?"

"He had terrific taste in women."

Chapter Twenty-Three

They went to Mitchell's, located in the heart of downtown Birmingham. Inside, tables were crammed together in a fashion that required hostesses and dinner guests to zigzag around to get to their chosen table. To the right was a large bar with television sets mounted from the ceiling. The volume was turned off, but captions appeared at the bottom of each screen. The interior was much like the exterior—polished wood, with numerous odd-shaped ceiling fixtures, providing rather dim lighting. The seafood fare was expensive, dinner for two, with drinks, could easily cost over a hundred dollars. The food was excellent and the portions reasonable.

Zack pulled his 2007 Z4—a remnant of his *wealthy* days— over and handed the keys to the valet. He rushed out of the car so he would open Jennifer's door. The roadster was cramped, low to the ground, and difficult to exit. Her low-cut, red satin dress made things worse. She took Zack's helping hand and noticed a couple of men ogling her. She hadn't dated in a while. The attention made her uncomfortable.

Zack wore a pair of black dress pants and a black mock turtleneck with a black-and-white tweed blazer. *He cleans up well.* Jennifer studied the movers and shakers in the bright lights reflecting from the downtown district. This wasn't her style. Evenings out with Jim consisted of buck fifty, second-run movies at Farmington Civic and dinner at the local diner. The couple didn't go out much, preferring to stay home with the kids. *Everyone is staring at me; my imagination?* She took Zack's arm and held on for dear life as they entered the restaurant.

A hostess guided them to their reserved table, and both ordered drinks, a sea breeze for Jennifer and an Absolut on the rocks for Zack.

"It takes some notice to get a reservation here, but I pulled some strings," Zack boasted.

"It's very nice," Jennifer nodded.

"Only the finest, for my favorite client," Zack boasted.

Jennifer smiled, the drinks arrived, and a waiter brought menus. After a detailed discussion of the offerings with the accommodating waiter, Zack ordered sea bass, and Jennifer, whitefish.

"Zack, does this qualify as a date?"

"Maybe. Why?"

"I've only dated twice since Jim died . . ." she drifted. "The dates didn't go too well—they ended in apologies. I haven't been good company since he died. Lack of preparation, I thought Jim would live forever."

"Who prepares for sudden tragedy? If it makes you feel better, I haven't been on a date for over twenty years. My wife and I used to go out to dinner often—Tobey hates to cook—but that doesn't qualify as a date, does it?"

"Well, it might, did you have to ask her to go?"

"I had to beg," Zack kibitzed. "No, it was assumed, sometimes with the girls and sometimes without."

"I don't think that qualifies."

"Then, officially, we're both on our first date in years. Your two don't count because they ended in apologies," he rationalized. Jennifer began to relax.

The waiter brought the meals. They ate in relative silence.

"That was delicious," Jennifer remarked, wiping her mouth with a napkin. "I'm glad I let you talk me into this. I haven't felt this relaxed in years."

"The pleasure is all mine, I assure you. You're the most beautiful woman in this restaurant. All the men are looking at us in disbelief, wondering how a schmuck like me could be dining with a babe like you."

"Babe? Is that term socially acceptable in the new millennium?"

"Absolutely, very politically correct."

"If you say so."

The waiter returned. "Coffee or dessert, anyone?" He recommended Mitchell's dessert special, the Shark Fin Pie, consisting of Oreo Cookie crust and vanilla and chocolate ice cream with a hot fudge topping. The pie was tempting, but they passed on dessert, opting instead to visit one of the trendy coffee shops on South Woodward. They held hands and browsed through windows of closed retail stores. It was a beautiful spring evening. The moon was full, and stars filled the night sky.

"Zack?"

"Yes?"

"How tough will the lawsuit be for Jake and Kenny?"

This was her biggest worry. Rothenberg could tell her a public airing of their grievances would be a net positive until he was blue in the face. She would still agonize over her part in the decision to put her boys through this.

"Most of the way, not very tough at all. Until trial, the most stressful part will be giving a deposition. If the case goes to trial, the boys will have to testify. Until then, it's all grunt work, discovery, deposition testimony of others, records, subpoenas and reviews, and investigations. While their deposition and trial testimony will cause them the most difficulty, most defense attorneys don't lean on kids too hard because it might backfire."

"How do you mean?"

"Walsh won't want a judge or a jury to think he's picking on children. The quickest way to get a kid to clam up during testimony is to bully them. He'll demand answers to his questions, but he'll be gentle in the way he poses them. Understand? Walsh is a pro. The boys should be fine."

"What about how they treat me?"

"About the same. Everyone knows you've had a rough go, losing your husband and now this crap with your kids. If Walsh isn't courteous, he'll lose points with a judge or jury."

"It has been a tough three years."

"Yeah, I know the feeling."

"Of course you do. I wallow in self-pity, but look at you. Your partners cheated you. Your wife deserted you and took your children. We've been leading parallel lives over the last three years," Jennifer realized.

"True, but together, we're going to turn it around. So are the boys."

"Together?"

"Professionally, of course."

"Of course."

"We could explore the other if you're willing."

"I don't know, Zack. There's a lot of emotional baggage. My number-one priority is helping my kids through this ordeal. I don't know if there's room . . ." Her heart was beginning to feel one thing, while her head screamed another.

Zack stopped and pulled Jennifer to a stop as well. He cradled her cheeks with both hands and peered into beautiful blue eyes.

"Jenny, we will see this through, together," he promised. "Both of us have our demons. We've both been cheated and lied to. But fate has brought us together. We need to trust again, to have faith in someone.

"You are an inspiration to me. You made me take a long, hard look in the mirror and I didn't like what I saw. Now, I have a chance to resurrect myself, personally and professionally. One evening with you makes me realize I've not only been a professional cripple but an emotional one as well. It's time to start caring and trusting again. In time, maybe we find love together. To not try would be a tragedy. I'll promise you this: I will pursue this case to the bitter end. I will never, ever let you or your boys down."

"I know you won't, Zack. I'm still glad I didn't fire you," she smiled.

They both laughed. Zack leaned toward her and gently kissed her on the cheek. They locked eyes and lingered in place a few seconds before resuming their walk. Zack draped his arm over Jennifer's shoulders as they continued to the coffee shop in silence.

At the end of the evening, he drove her home and walked her to the door. They bid each other a good night. Jennifer entered the house. Zack returned to the Z4, a happy man. *The beginning of a beautiful friendship?*

Chapter Twenty-Four

"The press conference was a disaster. I thought we were going to have favorable reporters on hand to ask tough questions and expose holes in their case," the Voice grumbled.

"We were, but on such short notice, we could only secure Schneider."

"Even Schneider wasn't very tough or persistent," the Voice seethed. "The tone of the conference was so pro-plaintiff he couldn't get the opportunities he wanted. Jennifer Tracey stole the show. The press was eating out of the palm of her hand. The conference couldn't have gone any better for them if they planted all the reporters. We have to mount a counter-offensive. Is anything in place?"

"We've quietly relieved Gerry of his parish duties and activities. We've banned him from any and all contact with children. His days as a parish priest are unofficially over. We've retained Rashid-Bevak, a top-notch public relations firm. A press conference is scheduled for tomorrow to answer the charges made in the complaint. Walsh is opposed."

"Why?" the Voice wondered.

"He thinks we should formally answer the complaint before making any public statements. He's afraid we may say something that will come back to haunt us."

"Nonsense," the Voice retorted. "He'll answer the complaint in conformance with our public statements. We cannot let this press conference go without response while lawyers take three weeks or more to develop their pleadings."

"I agree. The best defense is a good offense. I say we take Blake to task on some of the allegations of a cover-up and challenge him to reveal his sources or admit he has no evidence of church involvement," a member recommended.

"I concur."

"So do I."

"One word of warning, of course."

"What's that?"

"We're *lying*," a member warned. "Gerry *has* done this before, we *did* know about it, and we *did* cover it up after we botched the transfer. If Blake finds out and can prove it, we'll have only made a terrible situation disastrous."

"That's true, but I don't think we have a choice at this point."

"If I may, I have an alternative," a member suggested.

"Go ahead," the Voice encouraged.

"We admit Gerry is a pedophile who slipped through the screening process. We apologize to the Tracey family and continue to provide treatment. We agree to compensation in a non-discreet fashion. We promise to defrock Gerry, so this never happens again. I understand Jennifer Tracey. This will satisfy her. Give her what she wants," the member reasoned.

The Voice sneered at the member and responded derisively. "That would expose us to tremendous financial risk. We can't take that chance," he argued.

"In my judgment, proceeding in this fashion exposes us to even greater financial risk," the member retorted, not backing down.

"Only if they discover the truth. Berea is wrapped up tighter than a drum."

"I want my vote in opposition noted for the record," the member resolved.

"The record will so reflect," a surprised Voice noted.

"All in favor of the proposed rebuttal press conference?" the Voice polled.

"Aye," several voices concurred.

"All opposed?"

"Nay." With a single vote in opposition, the armor of the Coalition had been dented.

Chapter Twenty-Five

The church held its press conference the following day. Half the reporters who covered Blake's press conference bothered to show up. Somehow, the response wasn't as newsworthy as the lawsuit. The spokesman did a marvelous job responding to the lawsuit, using words like 'conjecture,' 'outlandish,' and 'innuendo.' He demanded Zack Blake immediately produce evidence of prior conduct or cover-up. He demanded a public apology, retraction and promised to seek frivolous action sanctions if Zack failed to comply. In Michigan, the filing of a frivolous lawsuit subjected the filing party and attorney to actual costs of defense and attorney fees. With a case and a defendant as volatile as these, the frivolous filing rule could make sanctions an enormous burden.

The spokesman attacked Jennifer as being unappreciative of the kindness and concern that was shown by the church in providing treatment at its expense for the duration. Under these clouded circumstances, the spokesman wondered, what more could the church have done? The boys were responding to treatment, and Father Jon, the boys' trusted pastor, was providing spiritual counseling.

Reporting in the newspapers and on television lacked the impact and electricity of the lawsuit filing. Still, the church did a masterful job raising doubts in the minds of readers and viewers, potential jurors in both the civil and criminal trials. At issue was whether Zachary had the evidence he claimed. Editorial pages demanded Zachary "come clean" with the information in the interest of justice and expediency. Such allegations tarnished the reputations of men who held high positions with the church hierarchy and did so without substantiation the charges were true. It was an excellent defense argument, and the spokesman used it quite well. The Voice was extremely pleased with his performance.

The following day, Gerry was pre-tried in the criminal case. The main reason for a pre-trial was to find out how much discovery time was necessary before the trial could commence and what evidence the prosecution intended to proffer to prove the charge. The critical evidence for Joseph Saunders, Oakland County's chief assistant prosecutor, was the testimony of the boys. He argued for the boys to be allowed to testify in closed session. The experience would be a bit less terrifying. That motion was denied on First Amendment grounds. If the boys testified in closed session, the press and the public would have no access to their testimony, and only the judge, the parties, and the jury would hear it.

The judge was a tall, lanky, Jimmy Stewart-ish looking old man named Erroll Shipper. He apparently felt the press and public's right to know was more important than the boys' mental health. A trial date was set for September. The judge ruled the criminal case could be televised—score one for the prosecution and for the civil trial. The defense objected, arguing it would be impossible for the defendant to get a fair trial in an impending publicity circus. Judge Shipper pounded his gavel in anger at this suggestion and urged the two sides to get together and work out a plea, thus avoiding the painful and public trial they feared. But, public it would be. With that, he rose and abruptly left the bench.

Gerry, out on bond but prohibited from practicing his profession by the judge, rose from the defense table and stormed out of the courtroom without conferring with his lawyers. Jennifer and Zack were seated in the last row of five polished dark wood benches that extended parallel from one side of the courtroom to the other, leaving an aisle on each side for ingress and egress. As Gerry passed by, he glared at Jennifer. *If looks could kill* . . . Jennifer thought. *How did I miss this side of him?*

Zack eyed Bartholomew and watched the entire scene unfold. After Gerry departed, Jennifer and Zack rose, exited the courtroom, and walked to the Z4.

"I could kill that son of a bitch," Zack groused. "Did you see the look he gave you?"

"I chose to ignore it, though I can't believe it came from a parish priest."

"From a parish priest who *molests children*," Zack reminded her. "The nerve of this guy! He does this to your kids, and *you're* the bad one? I hate that guy!" He growled.

"Zack, don't get yourself so worked up. You'll get even in court," Jennifer assured.

"You're right, of course," Zack calmed. "But I can't stand that creep's arrogance. Blame the mother of the kids you abused? This guy is the poster child for castration in sexual molestation cases."

"So, how's the civil case coming?" Jennifer changed the subject.

"I'm glad you asked me that question. I've got a meeting today with the infamous Micah Love, private eye extraordinaire. He's the friend I've been telling you about. He's the best there is."

"His name is really 'Love?'" Jennifer wondered.

"Yep, and his father and grandfather before him. I don't know what it was like in the old country. His Ashkenazi grandfather, like mine, emigrated from Russia to escape the czar."

"You're Jewish?" She was surprised.

"Yes, is that a problem?"

"Of course not. There have been rumblings about anti-Semitism within the church hierarchy, but it is unsubstantiated. I don't want this to become too personal or religiously difficult for you," she reasoned.

"It's already personal with me, but not for that reason. It's because of you and the boys and what that scumbag did to them. Now, *that's* personal!"

"But, Zack—"

"Jenny, if this case develops anti-Semitic overtones, I can deal with them. I'm a big boy. Sticks and stones can break my bones, and all that shit," he teased.

Jennifer laughed and, just as quickly, was serious again. Zack noticed.

"Jenny, my religion isn't a problem for you and me, is it?"

"I've never dated outside my faith, Zack."

"Well, if it makes you feel any better, neither have I. There's a first time for everything. If someday, a closer relationship develops, religious differences should not stand in our way."

"I guess you're right. It's not like we're getting married or anything."

"We're not? I'm crushed."

"Jesus, Zack, will you stop kidding around? We've had one dinner."

"Jesus? Name's familiar … I can't place it. Wasn't he Jewish?"

"You're impossible."

"Yes, I know. It's what makes me so irresistible to women."

"And that's why you're divorced?"

"Ouch!"

"Sorry. How can I make it up to you?"

"Have dinner with me tonight. I can fill you in on my conversation with Micah."

"And if I say no?" She wouldn't have.

"Then, I'll keep my discussions with Micah to myself."

"Zack, that's bribery."

"Sue me."

Chapter Twenty-Six

Micah Love was a heavy-set fortyish man with hardly any of his gray hair left. He was on the short side, like Zack, and Zack loved to tease him about his *hairstyle*. Micah was bald on the top, so he wore his hair long on one side then combed that side over his bald dome to meet the hair on the other side. Zack never understood why balding men thought this was a good look, but then again, he wasn't bald. He was getting a bit thin at the back of his head but insisted, "I don't have a bald spot," to anyone who called it to his attention. The funny thing about Micah's hairstyle, though, was when the wind blew, the combed-over hair would return to its natural side of Micah's head, completely exposing the dome. It was a funny sight—to Zack, at least. Micah never saw the humor in it.

Despite an obsession with sex and pornography, Micah Love was the best private investigator in the area, and Zack wanted him to handle the Tracey case investigation. The problem was—there was *always* a problem—Zack couldn't afford him, especially now. Unlike Zack, Micah didn't work on a contingency. Micah had the nerve to expect to be paid upfront. He required a retainer. After retainer money was exhausted, Micah expected to be paid his hourly rate on a weekly basis. Miss a week and he abandons the case. Those were the rules.

As Zack approached Micah's office at the Buhl Building, downtown on Griswold, he knew serious groveling would be involved. He hoped he could sell Micah on the seriousness of the offense and the importance of the case. Obviously, he would triple Micah's hourly rate, if he had to, as long as Micah agreed to handle the investigation on a contingency basis.

Zack steered the Z4 into an underground office parking lot next to the building. The sign on the ticket dispenser announced parking was $1.20 per twenty minutes, up to a maximum of $18.00. *I should have gone into the parking lot business, less stress, more money*. He found a spot on the second level near the elevator. *Why walk when you can ride?* He walked the short distance from the elevator to the building entrance and pushed through the revolving doors.

The Buhl was a beautiful old building with an all-ceramic foyer and elevator doors in polished brass. For an added touch of old-world class, building management offered human elevator operators, in uniform, who pressed the floor buttons and escorted visitors to their desired floors.

The elevator door opened to the offices of Love Investigations, which occupied the entire floor of the building. The offices were recently redecorated in today's colors. On Zack's last visit, two years ago, for a simple skip trace on a deadbeat client, the place was burgundy, gray, and black. Today, the decor was mahogany and cream. If the suite number hadn't been the same, Zack would have thought he was in the wrong place.

It was perfect, thought Zack. Even the receptionist was new, a pretty, young, buxom blonde named Eden, according to her nameplate. Micah must have handpicked her from the Garden. She wore a tight cotton dress—if one could call it a dress—that began at the very bottom of her ample breasts and ended just below the crotch. While Zack enjoyed the view, he couldn't believe Micah's poor taste. Clients came in all shapes, sizes, ages, religions, and political backgrounds. *A woman like Eden may appeal to a degenerate like me, but not to a classy client, like Jennifer.*

Alas, this was vintage Micah. He lived to please no one but himself. Zack knew this was what made Micah such a great detective. The personal satisfaction he derived from his success in a particular case—screw whether the client agreed or disagreed. If you satisfy yourself, you satisfy your client. Zack thought about his own practice. He hadn't satisfied himself for a long time. In fact, seated in the new, perfectly redecorated waiting area of Love Investigations, Zack couldn't remember the last time he satisfied himself professionally. *How pathetic is that?* His return to the quality practice of law required Micah Love. Jenny and the boys deserved a commitment to excellence.

The thought of Jennifer caused his mind to wander. He couldn't wait for the evening and their dinner plans. *What will she wear? How will her hair be styled?* Zack hadn't felt like this in a long time. Micah Love interrupted his thoughts with his usual gruffness.

"Whadayawant this time, Blake?"

Love was standing at the door leading from the reception area to the offices. He wore a dark-blue suit, white shirt, and burgundy-and-blue tie. His hair was neatly groomed in non-wind-blown over-the-dome style. Zack couldn't remember the last time he'd seen Micah in a suit.

"Did you dress up for me, Micah?" Zack teased. "And these new digs, they for me also?"

"Don't flatter yourself, asshole," Micah grunted. "The suite and the suit—hey, that's cute—are for my classier clients. You don't qualify."

"And the babe?" Eden blushed.

"Out of your league, pal," Micah winked at Eden.

She smiled. Only Micah knew whether he was being complimentary.

"Come on in, lowlife. How ya' been? You're a big TV star now. I caught your performance the other day. Not bad . . . but the babe! Where did you find her? She's outstanding!"

"She is something," Zack sighed.

Micah motion Zack into the suite. They walked to the conference room and sat down in executive chairs upholstered in the same pattern as those in the reception area. Ten chairs surrounded a beautiful black lacquer conference table. A matching black lacquer bar stood at the back of the room, open, displaying any kind of liquor imaginable. Micah's office suite was trendier than Brodman Longworth's offices. Micah was the best at his profession and enjoyed showing off.

"You've got a thing for her, don't you?" Micah teased.

"I'm not sure. I'll tell you this—she's quite a lady."

"That's a lawyer's answer. You're bonking her, aren't you?"

Zack was annoyed by Micah's bawdiness. "Micah, our relationship is professional. I like her and her kids very much."

"Sure, it is. Why don't you explain these?" Micah pounced. He opened a thin manila envelope and removed pictures of Zack and Jennifer, walking down South Woodward. Zack's arm was over her shoulders, and one of the photos showed him kissing her on the cheek. Zack felt violated.

"Where did you get these?" Zack demanded.

"It doesn't matter. Some investigators have divided loyalties. I got them. That's all that matters. Query? Do you think it's wise, in such a high-profile case, to play kissy-face in public with your beautiful client?" Micah sassed.

"It was just a client dinner," Zack countered.

"It looks like more than that to me, compadre, and, most likely, to the church as well. The press would have a field day with these."

"Would have?"

"I purchased exclusive use, aside from the church, of course."

"The church wouldn't publish these, would they?"

"Who knows, Romeo? I doubt it. Why embarrass the lovely lady? What would that accomplish? I only showed them to you, so you'd be aware you are being followed and to be careful," he warned.

"Thanks, pal. I knew there was a reason I once liked you."

"Don't mention it. Now, what do you want from my life?"

"I want you to work on the case." He implored.

"I charge five hundred dollars per day, plus mileage and expenses. A case this size requires a fifteen-thousand-dollar retainer."

"What happened to the 'friendship' discount?" Zack pleaded.

"What friendship? I never see you unless you need something. You never call. You never write, not even a birthday card. I feel so . . . *used*!" Micah burst into fake sobs.

"But I still love you," Zack played along.

"But do you respect me?" Micah removed a hanky from his pocket, blew his nose, and pretended to dry his eyes.

"I respect you, Micah," Zack rolled his eyes.

"Good," Micah chirped, suddenly brightening. "Then, I know you don't expect me to do this for nothing."

"The thought never entered my mind, just nothing *down*," Zack begged.

"You have got to be fucking nuts. How much money do you

already owe me?"

"Not that much. I haven't used you in two years or more," reasoned Zack.

"That's because I cut you off for nonpayment. Shall I get the ledger?" Micah grumbled. He enjoyed making Zack miserable.

"No, that's not necessary. Look, man, this is different, important, not the usual nickel-and-dime stuff. This is the biggest case of my life. This can jump-start my trashed career.

"These boys were *raped,* Micah. This priest is the smuggest scum-sucking pig I have ever encountered. I *need* this. I'll pay you more than your regular rate out of case proceeds if you do this. Please," Zack pleaded. "I'm begging you."

"Begging? You must really be hot for this broad." Micah softened.

"I like her, Micah," Zack conceded. "Are you satisfied? But not in the way you think and, besides, that's not the reason why I need you to say 'yes.' It's this case, these kids, this priest, and the way the church handles these matters."

"What do you mean?"

"A guy like Gerry is transferred into town, endears himself to the community and befriends some kids, usually kids from a broken home or the victims of some tragedy. He uses the rectory or a local campground. He abuses the kids. He gets caught or doesn't. If he's caught, the church steps in—victims and cops are paid off, pleas are taken, criminal files and records are sealed, and the priest is transferred to the next parish where this asshole sets up shop all over again."

"You have got to be fucking kidding me!" Micah cringed.

"I wish I was. But that's the pattern. I don't have enough evidence yet to prove it, but there's some kind of cover-up operation within the church hierarchy. These people bug offices, homes, and churches. They snap photos like the ones you have. I need you to dig around. Visit this priest's previous placements. Ask questions. See what you can discover. Something happened somewhere, and the church covered the whole thing up. Who's responsible for these cover-up operations, and how do we get to them? I want to expose all of them," Zack hissed.

"The first will be easier than the second. This is un-fucking-believable," Micah huffed.

"Then, you'll do it?"

"Did I say that?" Micah hardened. "Ask me nicely and promise to pay me whether you win or lose. Where am I going, by the way?"

"Will you *please* help me? Berea, Ohio," Zack pleaded.

"Of course, I will. All you had to do was ask."

"Thanks, Micah. Thanks a million," Zack sighed, genuinely relieved to have Micah on board.

"From your mouth to God's ears. Let's get these bastards."

Zack pulled out his already thick case file and spent the next three hours bringing Micah up to snuff. The more Micah heard, the more wrathful he became.

Chapter Twenty-Seven

Micah Love dove full throttle into the Tracey investigation. He reassigned all the files he was personally handling to an associate investigator. Two days after his meeting with Blake, Love was driving his Lincoln MKZ down I-75 toward Toledo, one hour south of Detroit. Berea was a small town situated near the Michigan-Ohio border, off Route 2, the route a traveler took to Ohio from Michigan, before the interstate system. Berea was a typical Midwest industrial town with a quaint downtown area.

Micah was seeking St. Patrick's Church and School, apparently, the only church in the downtown district. He pulled into the church parking lot and wandered inside. He found the pastor's office and knocked on the door. There was no answer. It didn't matter. He didn't expect the pastor's cooperation anyway. He wandered down the hall toward the sanctuary and noticed a janitor mopping the lobby floor. The janitor, an older man with one eye noticeably higher than the other, heard the sound of footsteps. Startled, he glanced in Micah's direction.

"Hi," Micah chimed. "How are you doing?"

"I'm fine, thank you. How are you?" the janitor hesitated.

"Is the pastor in?"

"Not at the moment. I'm the only one here." He advised.

Perfect, janitors know everything that goes on. Or, they at least hear all the appropriate rumors and gossip. There's no one here to keep him in check. This was an investigator's wet dream. "Do you mind if I wait for him?" Micah cajoled.

"Suit yourself. Can I get you some coffee? I just made a fresh pot."

"Coffee would be great. Thanks a lot."

The janitor left the lobby area and returned shortly with a cup of steaming coffee.

"I forgot to ask how you take it."

"Black is fine, thanks. Did the pastor say when he was coming back?"

"I'm not sure. He went to make a condolence call. One of our longtime members and supporters passed away over the weekend. The funeral was yesterday." He explained. His suspicion radar was weakening. He became more relaxed and forthcoming.

"How old a man was he?" Micah feigned interest.

"Ninety-seven years young, God bless him, and rest his soul," he mourned.

"Amen to that," Micah sighed. It seemed an appropriate response. "May I ask you a couple of questions?"

"What about?" the janitor wondered.

"About six months ago, a priest named Gerry Bartholomew was the assistant pastor of this parish, right?"

"Yeah, that's right. What's this about? Has he done something wrong?"

"What makes you think he did something wrong?" Micah demanded.

"I don't know," he lied. "Man I've never seen or heard of comes around asking questions, makes me think something's wrong. What's your name anyway?"

"My name is Micah Love. Here's my card." Micah handed him the card.

"I'm Gus." Gus looked at the card. "Love Investigations. Are you a private eye? Man, I never met a private eye before. Are you investigating Father Gerry? Why? What's he done now?" Gus slipped.

"What do you mean 'now'?"

"Whaddaya mean whado I mean?"

"You said 'now' after asking 'what's he done.' What did the 'now' mean?"

"Nothing. You just took me by surprise, is all." Gus was panicked. Micah could see it in his eyes.

"Has he done something before?" Micah softened.

"I don't know what you mean. What kind of something?" he grunted.

"Something he did here he would not be proud of, members of your church would not be proud of, and both would want kept secret. Something like that," Micah persisted, trying to appease the old man but still needing the answers.

"I don't know nothin' like that, and I shouldn't even be talkin' to you. Please, excuse me. I got work to do. You can wait over there," Gus pointed to an old wooden bench against the wall.

Micah walked over to the bench and sat down. *Gus obviously knows something. I need to talk to the pastor before Gus does.* Micah fell asleep on the bench. Two hours later, Father William Foley, pastor of the parish for the past thirty years, gently shook Micah awake.

Father Foley had oily white hair, streaked with yellow. Micah didn't know whether priests were permitted to smoke, but this guy was a chain smoker. Not only was his hair yellow, but Foley also reeked of cigarette smoke. He had a reddish, pockmarked complexion and the wrinkles of an outdoorsman whom the sun prematurely aged. Micah guessed him to be about sixty-five years old, medium build, not heavy but not thin either. The only thing that seemed old about him was his weather-beaten face. Other than that, Micah was confident Father Foley was in better shape than he was, although that didn't take much.

"Gus says you're looking for information about Father Gerry. Is there something I can help you with? Is he okay?" Micah detected slight defensiveness, but Foley was far better at concealment than Gus.

"Physically, he's fine. Father, I'll come right to the point," Micah rose and willed the cobwebs of sleep away. "Father Gerry was transferred from your parish to one in Michigan."

"I know. I approved his transfer," Foley looked confused.

"What do you mean approved?" Micah inquired.

"The church transfers him, and it's my job, symbolically at least, to let him go. It's more or less a rubber stamp."

"Did you have second thoughts about letting this one go?"

"No. As I mentioned, it's mostly symbolic. Assistant pastors never stay longer than three years unless they are being groomed for a position as pastor," Foley explained.

"Can you describe his three years here? Were they successful? Did he connect with your parishioners?"

"Yes, they were quite successful. The parishioners loved him." Foley crossed his arms and assumed a defensive posture.

He glared at Micah with cold eyes. "I don't understand all of these questions. What's going on? What is your name, and why are you here, asking all these questions?"

"My name is Micah Love. I'm a private investigator," Micah grumbled. *The best defense is a good offense.* "I've been hired by the mother of two teenage boys to investigate allegations of sexual abuse by Father Gerry Bartholomew. I understand this was his previous parish."

Father Foley was either a great actor or legitimately didn't know anything. He looked shocked.

"I can't believe this!" exclaimed Foley, stunned at Micah's disclosure. "Gerry would never do anything like that. Hurt a kid? No way!"

"The boys identified him. He did unspeakable things, Father. If you know anything, please tell me. It's your duty," Micah demanded.

"How dare you profess to tell me my duty," Foley challenged, clearly offended.

Micah struck a nerve. Foley's eyes were blazing.

"I want you to leave now. I've known Gerry for almost four years, and I've never known a finer man. He'd never do anything like this. He is a fine priest and a good friend. Please leave." He gestured toward the door.

"One more request: May I have a copy of your parishioner list?" Micah requested.

"Absolutely not," Foley rambled, now in full combat mode. "I will not have you running from parishioner to parishioner, asking these questions and making these horrid accusations. Please leave, *now.* "

Micah refused to back down. "Okay, Father, I'll go, but I'm not leaving town, not until I get answers that make sense. A sexual predator doesn't spend three years in one place without incident, and then move and immediately commit offenses. Something happened here. I know it, and so do you. I will find out what, when, and to whom. Apparently, I'll have to find out the hard way, but I'll find out. Good day, Father," he scowled. He turned and began to walk away.

"Good day to you too, sir, and I wouldn't waste too much

time in Berea. We have no secrets. These boys in Michigan ought to be investigated first," Foley spouted.

Micah left the church the same way he entered. As he walked down the front steps and across to the parking lot, he sensed someone staring at him. Micah turned to the church and searched its windows. He caught some movement on an upper floor and saw the janitor staring out at him. When Gus realized Micah saw him, he turned away.

He knows something about Bartholomew. Something happened here. I feel it in my bones. Micah determined he would find out exactly what happened and to whom. His determination kept him in Berea for three days. He went to the public library and reviewed local newspapers on the internet for the three years Gerry was at St. Pat's. There were articles about church functions, weddings, and so on. Gerry was present or officiated at some of these. He was mentioned several times over his three-year stay. All the articles were positive, not a single word in any article was remotely negative. The final piece announced his transfer to Michigan. At a party in Gerry's honor, Pastor Foley and several prominent parishioners were quoted praising the wonderful job Gerry had done and how much he would be missed. Micah copied the names of every person named in every article.

He left the library and borrowed a local shopkeeper's telephone directory. He began looking for the names he'd copied from the newspaper articles. There were fifteen names. He found each one, still listed, still living in Berea. He visited each of the homes and found someone home in all but two. Everyone was cooperative and friendly, all were parishioners of St. Pat's, and all had glowing things to say about Father Gerry. There wasn't one suspicious comment in the bunch. Micah began to doubt the boys.

The thirteen parishioners he talked to mentioned the names of at least twenty more. Micah duplicated his telephone directory search and was amazed to find all twenty were still listed and living in Berea. *Stable town.*

He visited the homes of each of these residents to put faces and voices to them. They were good, honest, and hardworking folks, and no one had a bad word to say about Father Gerry Bartholomew. *Weird—no one is this popular.* There wasn't a single negative comment, which made Micah even more suspicious. *Some sort of parishioner conspiracy of silence? Could the church organize everyone's silence on a grand scale? Can all church members be this loyal? Were they paid off? What the fuck is going on here?*

The questions were entering his consciousness in rapid-fire succession. Not a single negative? It was too convenient to be true. Somehow, he'd locate a parishioner list and visit them all if necessary. There were previous placements to visit and the seminary where Gerry received his training. Perhaps his fellow seminarians, wherever they were now, knew something. Micah would continue to question people, review local newspapers, and probe until he developed a positive lead. Something was out there somewhere. He'd find it. He was Micah Love, after all, and he was, simply, the best.

Chapter Twenty-Eight

The phone rang at the secret office of the Coalition. The call was transferred to the Voice.

"Hello?"

"Hello, this is Father William Foley, Pastor of St.—"

"I know who you are. What can I do for you, Father?"

"My church received a visit from a private investigator."

"Oh? When?"

"Today."

"What did he want?"

"He asked our custodian and me several questions about Father Gerry and his behavior while he was an assistant pastor here at St. Pat's. He seemed to know all about his conduct. He advised that Gerry is being accused of sexually molesting two boys in Michigan. That same behavior got him into trouble here. In light of his situation in Berea, I was assured any new placement would be away from children. I'd like an explanation. What the hell happened?" Father Foley demanded.

"To be honest, we're not sure. Someone botched the placement or didn't review Gerry's record. We're still reviewing this placement and others to fix the glitch and correct it in the future," the Voice conceded.

"This is a horrible mistake," Foley ranted. "Thanks to those loyal to the church, this creep escaped with a slap on the wrist in Ohio's criminal court system. We arranged a quiet surrender, with no embarrassment to the church, and complete secrecy regarding his conviction. Quite a miracle, if you ask me. One would think the church would have praised the Lord and been very careful with his next placement."

"You are absolutely correct, Father, but, as I indicated, the system failed. We are trying to deal with the consequences, and we need your help." The Voice appeased. He owed Foley no explanation but wanted to keep him in line.

"What can I possibly do?" Father Foley calmed.

"Tell me everything you, the custodian, and the investigator discussed. Don't leave anything out." The Voice implored.

Foley repeated his conversations with Micah and the janitor, almost verbatim. He also read Micah's name and business address from the business card Micah provided.

"From what you've told me, the church has not been compromised. Is there any possibility a parishioner would talk to Love?"

"No. At least, I don't think so. The affected families have all been relocated. The few that know anything have been well compensated for their silence. They wouldn't breach pledges of silence and risk forfeiting that compensation."

"What about the local police?"

"Complete confidentiality, a gag order, so to speak, was a promise of the plea bargain. The department is liable for damages if it breaches the gag order. I suppose a rogue cop is a possibility, but a remote one."

"What about the janitor? What does he know?" The Voice inquired, concerned about loose lips.

"Nothing. He wasn't questioned or involved in Gerry's criminal case, subsequent plea or transfer. He knows nothing of Gerry's proclivities or this situation," Foley ventured, aspiring to reassure his superior while protecting a treasured employee.

"Is he the type to gossip?"

Foley paused and considered his answer. *What is most important here?* "Yes, I'm afraid he might be," he finally acknowledged.

"Then we need to take care of him," the Voice intimated.

"What does 'take care of' mean?" Foley gulped.

"Nothing to be concerned about, Father. Perhaps a transfer or paid retirement to a warmer climate?" the Voice reassured.

"Well, he's an old man. Maybe he'd welcome a suggestion like that," Foley placated himself.

"I'll take care of it with Ohio personnel," the Voice promised.

"Shall I talk to him?"

"No, we'll handle everything from here. Are there any others we need to be concerned about?"

"I don't think so."

"I don't think so is not reassuring." The Voice cautioned.

Foley was befuddled. The Voice was a frightening man. Foley willed himself to calm. "I *know* there is no danger," he lied. "There's no one else left who knows anything, other than cops. Church operatives did a wonderful job of keeping this quiet. Hardly anyone in town knew anything happened."

I know, the Voice reflected. *I was in charge of damage control. One of my special talents is to not take anything for granted. Berea's collective mouths must be kept shut.*

"They *did* do a great job," the Voice agreed. "There are people within the church who specialize in minimizing unfair slander. Thanks to their efforts, we should be fine. Thanks for the call."

"Will there be anything else?" Foley feared the response.

"No, Father . . . well, yes . . . there is one more thing," the Voice decided.

"What is it?" Foley wondered.

"If the investigator comes back or if a parishioner indicates he has contacted him or her, will you please call us again?"

"Absolutely, I will," Foley sighed, relieved. "We can't have one rogue priest's problems causing a major scandal." *Why don't you send this guy to a monastery or something?*

"My thoughts, exactly. Good-bye, Father," the Voice charmed, as much his personality could allow.

"Good-bye."

As the Voice hung up the phone, he turned to the members.

"Love visited Berea. He's asking questions. He spoke to the St. Pat's custodian. Whether the guy knows anything or not, we've got to get him the hell out of there."

"I'll get Parks on it," a member responded, eager to please.

"He needs to be gone by tonight. Offer a financial package and a new identity. Does he have a family?"

"No idea."

"Check back with the pastor. Tell him he needs a new custodian."

"Will do. Anything else?"

"Yeah, have Parks get surveillance on Love."

"Do you think that's wise? Love is a trained investigator.

He'll spot a tail in a second."

"I don't care if he knows we're following him. I want to know where he is at all times."

"Okay."

"That's it. Get going."

The member was already out the door.

Chapter Twenty-Nine

Following his rather unpleasant conversation with Father Foley, Micah spent several days in Berea, canvassing the neighborhood around St. Pat's. He'd uncovered absolutely nothing. He sat in his car in the parking lot of the local McDonald's, sipping a scalding cup of coffee. He knew why that lady who sued McDonald's had third-degree burns on her crotch. *This stuff is hot! Damn it!*

Gerry was active in this town. Micah knew it. *How could the church buy off a whole town?* Maybe the townspeople really didn't know anything. Could the families of abused kids be the only ones who knew anything? How would he locate these people? He had no leads. Even in a small town like Berea, the chance he would happen to knock on a previous victim's front door was quite remote. *The church shipped them out of here, far, far away.*

"Wait a minute. That's it. They don't live here anymore! Assume the church paid them off and shipped them out. Who moved out of town at the same time the priest did?" Micah postulated, aloud. *City hall!*

He placed his coffee cup in the MKZ's fancy cup holder and drove off. *If the woman who sued McDonald's had an MKZ, she'd never have burned her crotch. Then again, she'd never have sued, and she wouldn't have all that dough. She could afford a Lincoln now.*

A few minutes later, he pulled into the parking lot next to city hall. He walked into the century-old building, checked the directory, and took the stairs to the second floor to the register of deeds office. The clerk was a bored, nice-looking brunette. As Micah approached the counter, the woman straightened, smiled, and looked directly into Micah's eyes.

"May I help you with something, sir?"

Micah was mesmerized. Nice-looking women were a weakness. "Y-yes, I-I was wondering if you could provide me with a list of names of people who sold their homes in Berea from 2010 to 2015? I'd also like to know the prices they received for their homes. I am mostly interested in the neighborhood near St. Patrick's Church," he stammered.

"May I ask what this is for?"

Is she curious or nosy? "It is my understanding these are public records. I don't need to have a reason now, do I?"

"Well . . . no, you don't. I just thought . . ." she blushed.

"Hey, don't worry about it," he chirped. "I was only teasing. I'm actually a real estate agent," he lied, "and I'm thinking of opening an office here. I'd like to know what prices the homes are selling for and how long it takes the owner to sell. That's why I need the names. If they moved out of town, I'd like to contact them, maybe find out if there is anything about Berea that caused them to leave. I'm cautious about where I open an office."

"Sorry if I was nosy, bad habit," she admitted. "I can get you that information. Berea's a great place to live. Property values are increasing all the time. You'd be very successful here. We have only two real estate agencies downtown, and the owner of one of them is almost ninety years old."

"Thanks. I'm sure you're right. I like what I've seen so far, very quaint, very quiet," he lied. Micah hated small towns. He couldn't wait to get the hell out of Berea and back to Detroit. *Why couldn't Bartholomew transfer from Chicago or New York? Now those were towns!*

"Back in a minute," she promised.

He watched her walk to the file room. *Nice ass. I could enjoy spending time with her if she didn't live here.* He heard her punching computer keys, establishing the perimeters of her search, and then the loud whine of a machine. *They need new equipment.*

"Here we are," she reappeared from the file room. She handed Micah the list. He gave it a quick scan. *Perfect!* The list contained fifty names or more. Some had addresses, some didn't. Most were from the area around St. Pat's. It would be relatively easy to find them. He glanced at the clerk. *Even nicer from the front, nice tits, full lips, beautiful eyes, long jet-black hair . . .*

"If you need anything further, my name is Jessica."

"Jessica—thanks for your assistance."

"My pleasure," she chirped. "Oh, one more thing."

"You owe me ten dollars for the records search."

"Ten dollars?" he yelped.

"That's what the register of deeds makes me charge. It's not my fault," she tensed. Jessica didn't realize he was teasing. Apparently, ten dollars for a records search was a big issue with the locals.

"Lighten up, Jessica. I'm just teasing. Ten dollars is fine," he turned on the old Love charm.

Jessica smiled, relieved. She took his ten and prepared a receipt.

"Is there anything else I can do for you?" Jessica purred.

"Can you answer a few questions for me?"

"I can try."

"Are you a member of St. Pat's?"

"Yes."

"How long have you been a member?"

"All my life, almost thirty years."

"Are you married?"

"No, divorced."

Good. "Can you look at this list and tell me if anyone was a member of St. Pat's?"

"Sure. I don't know everyone, but I'm sure I'll recognize some of the names. Let's have a look." Jessica was eager to help. "Let's see," she studied the list. "MacLean, O'Connell, Jacobson, Pelto, this one, that one, and . . ." Jessica fell into a silent study, circling names. When she finished, Jessica handed Micah back the list.

"That's about it," she confirmed.

"Do any of these names stand out in your mind? Did they leave suddenly or suspiciously?"

"I'm not sure what you mean."

"Without much notice, neighbors who had no plans to move put their houses up for sale. The houses get sold quickly, and the neighbors leave town without saying goodbye to anyone."

"Why would anyone do that?" Jessica wondered.

"Not sure, but those are the questions I'm asking. Are you

being nosy again?"

"Oops, I guess I am." She giggled.

Cute laugh, too. Micah would like to get to know her better. He'd have to make a return visit.

"What about it, Jessica? Anything like that happen with anyone on the list?" He coaxed.

She paused, thinking, finally replying with zeal. "As a matter of fact, yes! The MacLean family left town just like that! They hardly talked to anyone. Put their house up for sale one day, sold it quickly, and took off, like in the middle of the night. A small town like this and nobody even saw a moving van? One day, the family was here. The next day, they were gone. It was bizarre."

"There's no address on the list. Do you know where they went?" Micah had his first serious lead.

"No idea."

Micah thanked her and walked out, yet wishing he had more time. He drove to the family's former address and canvassed the houses in the area, looking for anything anybody could tell him. He was stumped at every turn. No one had any idea why the family moved. They left no forwarding address, no phone number for friends to keep in touch, no . . . nothing. His bullshit meter told him no one was stonewalling. These neighbors had zero knowledge of this family's whereabouts.

He *did* learn the MacLean's had three boys, ages sixteen, thirteen, and eleven. That was something, but not much. In the end, he returned to city hall, where Jessica seemed to be waiting for him.

"A couple more questions," he smiled. "Did the MacLean's have any family in the area?"

"No, they moved here from out of town. They have no family here."

"How about good friends, people who might know more about things than you do?"

"What does this have to do with selling real estate?" She challenged.

"You're being nosy again. As I mentioned, I'm just trying to find out if there is anything about this town I should be concerned with," he fibbed.

"Oh, I'm sorry. I guess I'm just naturally curious," Jessica explained.

"Me too," Micah concurred. "You'd make a good detective."

"Do you really think so? That would be exciting," she gushed.

"Not really," he ruminated. *The grass is always greener on the other side. This is beyond exhilarating. I get to spend several worthless days in this for-shit small town, eating breakfast, lunch, and dinner at McDonald's.* Jessica was the only pleasant thing Micah had encountered.

"Let me think for a second . . ." She returned the Maclean family situation, posturing, hand on her chin, index finger grazing her mouth. Suddenly, she shouted. "Good friends, yes! The O'Connell family!"

"Where do I find the O'Connell family?"

"You don't," she sighed. "They're on the list too. In fact, they left almost as abruptly as the MacLean family."

"What do you mean?"

"Shortly after the MacLean family left town, the O'Connell's left town—almost the exact same scenario."

"Almost? What's the difference?"

"The O'Connell's lived here all their lives. They've got family here."

"Where do I find them?"

"I'll get you names and addresses. I believe Pat—that's Mr. O'Connell—has a brother and parents living here. Pamela— that's Mrs. O'Connell—has a sister and brother-in-law living here."

"Let me guess. The O'Connell's had teenage sons too, right?"

"Yes, they have two boys, fifteen and twelve."

Micah was elated. "Jessica, I love you," he gushed. "You've been very, very helpful. How can I repay you?"

"How long are you in town? You can take me to dinner," she flirted. Micah was unsettled.

Chapter Thirty

While Micah was finally making headway in Berea, Zack was busy noticing up depositions of Gerry's current and former supervisors. Zack's strategy in deposing the priests and bishops was threefold: First, establish knowledge or notice of Gerry's predisposition to pedophilia and a lack of action by his supervisors to remove him from contact with teenage parishioners. Second, prove a policy of institutional denial by the church that several members of the clergy were pedophiles, the numbers of pedophile priests and incidents of molestation were increasing, and, as a result of its denial, no policies were developed to deal with the consequences of their actions. Third, prove Gerry engaged in this conduct with other young parishioners before his placement in Farmington and the church's official response to his prior behavior was to transfer the priest and cover up the crimes.

A beautiful conference room in the Brodman Longworth law offices—on the thirty-fifth floor of the RenCen—served as the site of the initial depositions taken in the case. The room faced south with a spectacular view of the Detroit River and Windsor, Canada, across the river. Walsh was present as the principal legal representative of the priest and the church. A couple of church officials were present and were ordered to keep quiet throughout the proceeding. Jennifer was also present. She insisted on attending every hearing, motion, and deposition.

Father Jonathan Costigan was Zack's first deponent. Costigan testified he knew several priests in parishes throughout the world were homosexual, but it was a giant leap to assume homosexuality was a precursor to pedophilia. He testified that nothing in Gerry's transfer file from Berea indicated anything that would have alerted him to the possibility that Gerry was a pedophile.

Zack interrogated Costigan carefully. He was acutely aware Costigan was friendly to Jennifer and helped her uncover the truth. Still, it was imperative Costigan testify in a manner depicting him to be a loyal member of the clergy, ready and willing to protect his brethren. His testimony would establish, as Gerry's immediate supervisor in Farmington, Jon was provided no information about Gerry's history of pedophilia. As soon as he discovered Gerry molested the Tracey boys, he notified church officials. Gerry was suspended, and the Tracey family was offered therapy. Zack continued the questioning.

"How did you discover the Tracey boys were sexually involved with Father Gerry?" Zack demanded.

Costigan squirmed and rocked in one of the many executive swivel chairs that surrounded the conference table. He looked to the sky and considered his answer, started, paused, restarted, paused, and finally responded. "When the kids returned from the camping trip, I overheard a couple of them remark about how strange it was the Tracey boys spent almost the entire weekend alone with Father Gerry. The other kids were jealous that they were excluded. I looked in on Jake and Kenny and observed their behavior. I feared that something serious might have happened, so I notified the diocese."

"Why did you notify the diocese?"

"I was afraid Father Gerry sexually molested the boys."

"What led you to that conclusion?"

Costigan continued to squirm and rock in the executive chair. "These cases are not common. I want to stress that. However, I've seen enough of them to recognize symptoms. In this case, the fact the boys spent the weekend alone with the priest and were acting sad, aloof and angry, I felt notification was warranted."

"But you didn't feel notification to Mrs. Tracey was warranted?" Zack pressed.

"That's not true," Father Costigan challenged.

"Did you notify her of your suspicions?"

"Not right away."

"When did you tell her?"

"Recently. About two months after I notified the church."

"Two months? Why did you wait so long?"

"I was concerned about my church," Father Costigan conceded. "Gerry had been at Lakes for all of a month. I've been building this parish and parishioner relationships for over *thirty years*. A scandal like this could destroy everything I worked so hard to build. I discussed it with the hierarchy. It was decided the best thing for all would be to suspend Gerry, provide treatment for the boys, and avoid scandal by keeping things quiet. After a while, I notified Jennifer." He lied to himself, trying to justify his behavior in his mind.

"Whose idea was it to keep silent?" Zack continued.

"A member of the church hierarchy. I don't know his name."

"You are under oath, Father," Zack warned.

"I swear. I don't know his name. His identity is unknown. All I know is he handles these things for the church."

"Let me get this straight," countered Zack. "You're telling me there is some secret fellow in the church whose job it is to deal with molestation cases when they occur?"

"Objection! Calls for speculation," interjected Walsh.

"I remind you this is discovery, not trial. I'll take the answer," admonished Zack.

Father Costigan stuttered, "Will you repeat the question?"

"Yeah. Is there some secret guy who handles molestation cases for the church on the sly?" Zack charged.

"Same objection," interjected Walsh.

"Yeah, yeah . . . answer the question, Father," Zack insisted.

Father Costigan hesitated. "The answer is a qualified yes."

"What's the qualification?" Zack bore in.

"I don't know if his role is limited to molestation cases. He might investigate other matters for the church, some sort of security man," Costigan speculated.

"Have you ever dealt with him before on any other matter?"

"No."

"And you simply did whatever this mysterious, unknown guy told you?" Zack pressed.

"It wasn't like that," Costigan wailed. "My bishop instructed me to follow his orders for the good of my church. When I found out what Gerry did to the boys, I realized it was a flawed policy. By then, however, it was too late."

"Too late for what?" Zack implored.

"Too late to help the boys. Jennifer told me the scope of

Gerry's conduct, as the boys told their therapist. Until then, I didn't really *know*. Perhaps I could have spoken up earlier, told Jennifer. But, she discovered how serious this was before I did. The boys were already in therapy, and their therapist knew everything. At that point, it was too late for me to correct my mistake. I've apologized to Jenny. I am truly sorry," Father Jon lamented.

"As a parish priest, have you been advised of the existence of, or ordered to attend any seminars on child abuse by members of the clergy?"

"No."

Zack continued to attack. "Have you received any literature from the church on how to deal with these situations if or when they arise?"

"No."

"Has there been any official position taken by the church either orally or in writing on how to deal with the issue of pedophile priests?"

"No."

Mr. Walsh interrupted, demurely, attempting to interrupt cadence. "Objection. This line of questioning is highly speculative. This man can only testify to whether he has seen such a document or been advised of such a policy, not whether the same exists."

"Okay," Zack declared, enjoying his moment of triumph. He rephrased for Walsh's sake. "Father Costigan, have you been advised by church hierarchy of the existence of an oral or written policy on how to deal with pedophile priests? Yes or no?"

"No."

"One more question . . ." *the coup de grace.* "Who advised you to call this mysterious security man who handles clergy pedophile cases for the church?"

"Objection. Mischaracterization of his testimony."

"Excuse me," Zack chided, slighting the objection and rephrasing. "Who advised you to call this mysterious security man who seems to handle private investigations that *include* clergy pedophile cases for the church?"

"My superior, Bishop Glimesh," Costigan admitted.

"Thank you, Father. I have no further questions at this time. I do, however, reserve the right to recall this witness after further discovery is conducted."

"No questions," Walsh sighed.

Bishop Andrew Glimesh was the next deponent. In responding to Zack's questions, the bishop admitted church teachings affirm a moral responsibility for appropriate sexual behavior. Within the clergy, the vow of celibacy prevents a priest from engaging in sex with any partner, including a same-sex partner. He also admitted the church understands sin more in relation to the sinners than to the victims of sin. In other words, counseling efforts were concentrated on one who confessed to having a problem rather than on those who may have been harmed because of the existence of that problem. He admitted there were many gay members of the clergy, but the subject was rarely discussed.

Glimesh testified to the existence, among priests, of a rigid code of discreet, gentlemanly behavior. The most vital standard of that code was to minimize risks of disclosure. Pedophilia violated that code since it was quite risky behavior. It also violated all moral teachings as well as the vows of celibacy and chastity. Additionally, homosexual acts were clearly condemned in the Bible, he concluded. He indicated that, according to statistics, the number of pedophilia cases involved a minuscule amount within the total number of priests. He also noted, however, pedophilia in the priesthood was "a very serious problem."

Zack realized the importance of the testimony he elicited, important evidence on the church's position on homosexuality, sexual activity, and pedophilia among priests. To this point, however, he'd received no information regarding the church's policy on treatment and placement of a priest who was known to be a pedophile. He decided to explore those issues with the bishop.

"What do you know or feel would be the penalty for violation of these promises?" Zack probed.

Bishop Glimesh chuckled. "Eternal hellfire. I—you know, what's the penalty? Put in that I laughed."

"At the question or the answer?" Zack smirked.

Bishop Glimesh sighed, "There is no penalty. The penalty is simply the moral failing or fault with the person."

"Do church laws recognize any penalty for homosexual conduct of any kind aside from those contained in the Bible?" Zack demanded.

"Yes. Homosexuality is grounds for a marriage annulment."

"Is that it?"

"As far as I know," the bishop appeared to search his memory.

"So the church is more concerned with how homosexuality affects a marriage than it is with how it affects its clergy, is that correct?" Zack remarked.

"No, that is not correct," Glimesh snarled.

"Name me one passage of law or rule from any church codification that deals with the issue of homosexuality or pedophilia in the priesthood."

"I can't," Glimesh conceded.

"How about a position paper?" Zack fumed.

"Not that I know of."

"Have you ever been officially advised in writing of any official position the church has taken concerning pedophilia in the clergy?"

"No. The church's position about such vile behavior is obvious," Glimesh suggested.

"Have you ever been advised that an official position exists?"

"No, I haven't."

"And there are no penalties you are aware of, correct?"

"Objection! Asked and answered," Walsh interjected.

"I'll take the answer," Zack demanded.

Bishop Glimesh's arrogant and defiant manner evaporated. "No. I already told you, no," he whispered.

"Then any priest, gay or straight, could violate his oath of celibacy or chastity, pick up, and carry on, and the church would do nothing?" Zack pressed.

Glimesh took a deep breath, again, attempting to unbend. "No, it would be up to his bishop to determine the appropriate discipline," he opined.

"Oh, and where is that written?" Zack huffed.

"It isn't written; it's understood." His frustration was palpable.

"And how would the individual bishop determine punishment?"

"Based upon the harm caused, probably," the exasperated bishop sighed.

"Harm to whom?"

"I don't understand what you mean."

"It would depend on whether it caused a scandal and whether the scandal was significant and public, wouldn't it?" Zack charged.

"Objection. Counsel is badgering the witness, and the question calls for speculation," Mr. Walsh interjected.

"Speculation as to what?" Zack retorted.

"In the absence of a specific policy on how to deal with this issue, how a particular bishop would deal with a situation that he has not yet encountered, would be speculation, at best," Walsh argued.

"You're right, Counsel. That's exactly why such a written policy should exist. If the church had a consistent and no-nonsense policy to deal with situations like this one before they happened, many of them wouldn't happen. Thank you for pointing that out."

"That's not what I meant..." Walsh stammered.

"I'm not interested in what you meant. I'm interested in what this witness meant. Whose harm were you talking about, Bishop?"

"Why . . . uh . . . both . . . yes . . . both, the church and the victim," Glimesh capitulated.

"And the harm you are concerned about regarding the church is the potential of public scandal, isn't that correct?"

Glimesh lowered his head and whispered, exasperated, "Yes, I suppose it is. But that is not outweighed by our concern for our young victims."

Zack continued to hammer away. Walsh continued to object. Zack's final victory came as Glimesh, in response to a blistering attack, testified he wasn't notified of any tendency toward or prior conviction for pedophilia on Gerry's part. Zack knew this was perjury, a trump card he would play when needed. Despite placing many objections on the record, Walsh, wisely, opted not to question the bishop.

***

After the depositions were completed and the witnesses were dismissed, Zack remained in the conference room at Brodman Longworth to review his notes. Discovering prior conduct was the key to this case, the key to unlocking its riches. The church's defense would be that it could not prevent what it did not know. It could not counsel or train avoidance of a malady that wasn't evident in the history of this individual. If Zack could prove there was a history and the church was aware of it, the sky was the limit on a jury award.

What was going on in Berea with Micah? Zack hoped progress was being made toward discovering Gerry's history in Berea. Zack needed to get back to his office, type deposition memos, and get ready for dinner with Jennifer. This would be their third date. They were to meet at Mezza in West Bloomfield at 7:00 p.m. It was 4:00 p.m., so he had to hustle. It would be at least forty-five minutes in rush hour to get back to the office up the Lodge. If he left now, he might beat the heavy traffic . . . His thoughts were interrupted when Walsh returned to the conference room.

"You want to rent space until this case is over, Blake?" Walsh chuckled.

"Funny," Zack snickered. "Not a bad idea. I'm sure I can trust your office staff to respect my privacy when I'm in court."

"Absolutely, you could. After all, we're all officers of the court."

"Yeah, well, just the same, I'll pass. Thanks for the offer, though."

"Don't mention it. By the way, speaking of offers, do you have a demand on this case?"

"I thought the official position of the church was 'as much as necessary for treatment, but not an ounce for tribute,'" Zack chided.

"Positions change. Defense costs and attorney fees will be enormous with this type of litigation. The church may be persuaded to apply an economic reality test to the case, especially if I tell them the depos did not go well."

"Thanks for the compliment," Zack noted.

"It wasn't meant as a compliment, asshole. You didn't do shit today. But my client doesn't know that. If I say, for instance, you scored some points on issues of priest training or screening, they'll believe me, even if it's not true," Walsh quipped.

"But, of course, it's not true. I scored no points in those areas?"

"None that will have any effect on the results of this litigation. You and I both know the smoking gun, and you'll never produce it. No smoking gun, no case against the church and a big hit against an uncollectible priest," Walsh gibed.

"So, what are you suggesting?" Zack wondered.

"I can probably convince them to resolve this case to avoid a lengthy discovery period and public trial. The criminal case would have to also go away quietly," Walsh suggested.

"Jennifer will never agree to anything like that. There has to be some public admission of liability and a public conviction so Gerry can no longer be transferred without new parishes being made aware of his propensities," Zack explained.

"The church will never agree to that."

"That's what I thought. I guess we'll proceed then."

"Take your client the offer. It's your duty," Walsh warned.

"What, specifically, is the offer?"

"Five million. Complete confidentiality. Criminal conviction sealed. Promise by the church, but not in writing, that all subsequent placements will either be away from children or with prior notice of Gerry's condition."

Zack didn't flinch. He was damned excited, but he couldn't let on to Walsh. Besides, he knew Jennifer wouldn't accept any amount that required confidentiality.

"Five million dollars is an awful lot of money for a case I'm not winning. I'll take it to her, but she won't accept it. For Jennifer, this case isn't about money, never was," Zack advised.

"What's it about, then? Revenge?" Walsh vented.

"No, justice, simple justice. We tend to forget we went to law school to pursue justice for our clients. We get so caught up in the *game* of the law, we forget the purpose."

"Excellent oratory," Walsh snickered. "Take her the offer. If she's amenable, I can get the money. If not . . . perhaps certain pictures may come to light. Perhaps neither of you would want that?"

"Whatever money can't buy, a little leverage *can* buy, right?" Zack bristled.

Walsh shrugged and chided. "I've yet to meet what money can't buy."

"You've met it. You just don't know it yet," Zack warned.

"What's that supposed to mean?"

"We know about the pictures. We don't care. Jennifer can't be bought with money or threats. She wants this predator stopped. She wants the church to stop protecting or covering up for him. Settle this reasonably with no gag order or confidentiality clause. Do the right thing for a change. Only then will she consider a settlement." Zack advised.

"See you in court," Walsh sighed.

Chapter Thirty-One

"Boys!" Jennifer called from the bottom of the stairs to the upstairs bedrooms. "Your supper is getting cold. Come down and eat."

She received no answer, so climbed the stairs and knocked gently on their bedroom door. Jake invited her in, voice quiet, almost in a whisper. "Come in."

She opened the door. The boys lay in their separate beds, facing the wall.

"I have dinner for you guys. It's getting cold."

"We're not hungry, Mom," Kenny murmured.

"What have you been doing all day? You've hardly left this room. It's a beautiful day, and there is still an hour or so of daylight left. How about we go to the park after dinner? You guys can toss a football or something." She prodded.

"We're not in the mood," Kenny sulked. "We're tired. We'll just lay here until we fall asleep."

"Yeah," Jake agreed, mimicking his brother's mood.

"But it's Saturday! You guys love the park, and it really is beautiful outside," she encouraged.

"Not today, Mom, we don't feel like it," Jake whispered. "And I don't feel like seeing anybody I know. Another time, okay? I'm tired."

"I think I will go to services tomorrow. Father Jon is speaking about tomorrow's opportunities. Come with me?"

"Get serious, Mom. I don't think so," Kenny scoffed.

"No, thanks, Mom," Jake concurred.

Jennifer gazed at the backs of her boys. "Okay, guys. I won't force you. May I have a hug and kiss?"

"Not tonight, Mom," they sighed in unison.

"Way too tired," mumbled Jake.

"Me too," managed Kenny.

Jennifer backed out of the room, heartbroken, and gently closed the door. Was the lawsuit a mistake? Would they ever recover from this nightmare? *Oh, Jim! What should I do? What would you do? Give me a sign, any sign.* She turned and headed down the stairs to clean up the dinner dishes.

Chapter Thirty-Two

Micah sipped his coffee in the living room of Pearl and Julius O'Connell. He approached them with a story about the church being sued by some former parishioners of St. Patrick's for the possible disappearance of a large sum of money from the St. Patrick's covenant fund. They invited him into their rather plain split-level home. This was a grandparents' home—photos of grandkids adorned the walls.

Something was amiss with these two, and the pictures gave it away. According to Jessica, their grandchildren would be fifteen and twelve, but the photos didn't show any kid over the age of ten. The couple was friendly enough. That wasn't the issue. They seemed to be forthcoming, so that wasn't it either. Their story didn't add up. According to Julius and Pearl, their son and daughter-in-law called one day and announced they were moving to Florida. Pat claimed he was transferred. The company bought their home, and the family was leaving for Florida right away.

A week later, the whole family—Pat, Pam, and the two boys—showed up at the house late, about 10:00 p.m. to say good-bye. They were leaving immediately. They had a long drive ahead of them and wanted to get a few hours down I-75. They would call with an address and phone number. Pat called a few times since, but he wouldn't give either of them an address or phone number. 'It's better this way,' Pat claimed.

Pearl was incredibly hurt. This elderly couple was completely shut off from their son and grandchildren. But, there was something about the story Micah couldn't wrap his arms around. It sounded like a fairy tale, a story a grandmother would tell a grandchild. Micah wondered whether the Florida part of the story was true.

"Did your son and his family belong to St. Pat's?" Micah queried.

"Yes. They were devoted members of the church. The boys were altar boys and sang in the church choir. We went to services every Sunday to watch and listen. Such a moving service . . ." Pearl sighed and tailed off.

She wore the pants in this family and did all the talking. That much was obvious. Micah wished he could get Julius alone for a few minutes. The old man stayed quiet and looked uncomfortable.

"Oh, how often did you attend?"

"Every time the choir sang, at least twice a month."

"Did the boys have contact with Father Gerry Bartholomew while he was at St. Pat's?"

"Oh, yes. What a nice man!" Pearl gushed. "He was wonderful with the children. We were all sad to see him transferred. He took the boys on camping trips to Cedar Point and overnights to Cleveland or Michigan. Everyone loved him. Most of us silently prayed he'd take over for Father Foley when he retired."

Sure, folks, that would have been great. Gerry would have loved it. "Were you and Julius members?"

"All our lives," Pearl reminisced. "Julie and I have lived in Berea all our lives. We were high school sweethearts." She smiled at the memory.

"Is that right? Pat and Pamela live here all their lives too?"

"Yes, they did," she brightened. "And they were high school sweethearts too. Isn't that something?"

"It sure is," Micah prodded. "Considering their roots here, their leaving so abruptly must have been quite a shock to both of you. Julius, have you done anything to try and locate them?"

Julius opened his mouth in surprise at having a question directed at him.

Pearl interrupted. "No, we've decided to respect their privacy, as much as it hurts. When they're ready to see us or share their lives with us again, they'll call."

"But they'd both lived here all their lives. Wasn't leaving difficult?" Micah probed.

"Didn't seem to be. Pat got transferred one week, and the next they were gone," Pearl reflected.

"Did you know the MacLean family? Apparently, they were friends with your son and daughter-in-law."

"Yes, we knew them very well. John MacLean and Pat

worked together. John was transferred along with Pat."

"Same location?"

"I don't know. Pat hasn't mentioned them since he moved." Pearl drifted off to a faraway place—Florida, perhaps? A tear welled in her eye. She blinked it away and smiled. Julius stared into space and remained silent.

"Two lifelong residents of Berea suddenly get transferred out of town at the same time, probably to the same place, with no time to get their affairs in order, in the middle of a school year, and no time to say goodbye properly to their families. Strange, don't you think? Without a whimper of protest from anyone, don't you think that's strange, Julius?" Micah prompted.

"No, we don't," Pearl interrupted again, just as Julius opened his mouth. "Transfers happen in business, or so I'm told. The company bought their house, bought them a new house. Pat claimed everything was all set up for them. They didn't need much time to get acclimated." Julius shot Pearl an unpleasant glance.

"What company does your son work for?"

"Stone Tablet Publications. They publish books, computer programs, apps, that sort of thing."

"What does your son do for them?"

"Pat's a computer whiz. He develops software," she boasted.

"What kind of software?"

"Stone Tablet is a religious publications company. Pat develops religious software for children to use on their home computers. The Old Testament stuff he created is amazing. Bible stories come right to life on your computer or tablet screen. The children learn while they have fun. My son also helped to develop the company website. He's *very* talented. We're proud of him."

"I'm sure you are. Do you know who owns Stone Tablet?"

"No, we don't."

"Company still in town?"

"It's never been in town. It's in Toledo."

"About the time Pat and Pam announced they were going to be transferred, had you noticed anything strange or different about them or the boys, what were their names?"

"The boys' names were Jordan, Matthew, and Justin. I'm not sure what you mean," Pearl snorted.

"Were the boys angry, unusually quiet, upset about the move, anything you may have noticed? A bad attitude, perhaps?" Micah continued to probe.

"Well, if you were a teenager and suddenly told you were leaving the town you grew up in, all your friends and your grandparents and you weren't even given a week to say goodbye, wouldn't you be upset?" Pearl reasoned.

"Were they?"

"Of course they were," she argued.

"No, they weren't, Pearl." Julius had heard enough.

"They certainly were. They were angry and extremely quiet when they came to say goodbye," she recalled.

"True, but that's exactly how they'd been acting for at least six months before they moved," Julius insisted.

"That's not so," Pearl demanded. Tears began to trickle down her cheeks.

"They hadn't uttered a word to us in six months," Julius bristled. "Something was terribly wrong, but we couldn't get the boys or Pat or Pam to talk to us. Suddenly, they were gone, transferred, no forwarding information. What the hell?" Julius trembled.

"Have you tried talking to anyone at the company?" Micah probed. *Keep talking!*

"Yes, and they don't have an office in Florida, dammit! Apparently, my son lied to us. The company claims Pat came in one day, without notice, and quit his job. I don't know where my son is, Mr. Love. I don't know whether he's in Florida or somewhere else. I don't know who you are or why you're interested in my son and his family. But, find him, Mr. Love. And while you're at it, find out why he did this and what's wrong with my grandsons. I'm begging you!" Julius cried.

"I'll do my best," Micah promised. "I'll need all the information you have, photographs, birth certificates, Social Security numbers, license plate numbers, school records on the kids, credit card numbers, anything."

"You shall have it." Julius wore the pants, after all.

"How often does your son call you, Mr. O'Connell?"

"That's the one thing he's reasonably good about. He calls once a week from a blocked number."

"Good. We'll install unblocking equipment right away. If he calls, we'll be able to find out the area code and number he's calling from."

"Really? You can do that?" Pearl marveled. "Modern technology is incredible. I'm so proud of my Pat. He's up on all the latest technology. He helped create . . ." Pearl trailed off, in pain.

Micah rose to leave.

"Find my son, Mr. Love. I'll be forever in your debt," Julius implored.

Julius rose and reached out to shake Micah's hand. The meeting was over. Micah reached out and shook his hand. It was trembling, ice cold. A winter chill shot up Micah's spine. He walked down the porch stairs. It was hot as hell outside. The chill was immediately a memory. He glanced at his Movado, 4:00 p.m. He still had time to see Pat's brother and Pam's sister, if he could catch them in.

He thought about Jessica—a breath of fresh air in this hell-forsaken town. He'd enjoy dinner tonight. First, though, he'd find out all he could about the disappearance of Pat and Pam O'Connell and their family. It was necessary for the case, but also for Julius, this sad old man, made to stand by, in silence, while the church destroyed his relationship with his children and grandchildren. If only this staunch supporter knew the truth. His life was being destroyed by the organization's stubborn refusal to eradicate pedophilia rather than cover it up.

Micah was certain Pat and Pam were transferred and paid off by the church, and sure their children were Gerry's victims. If he could find them and persuade them to testify, he'd blow the lid sky-high off this scandal. He had to find this family. Lives could depend upon him. Julius and Pearl deserved answers.

Chapter Thirty-Three

Jake Tracey was late for class. He rushed down the hall, focused on getting to his destination, scarcely aware of his surroundings. He carried a load of books under his arm. A student Kenny's age, much bigger than Jake, came up behind him and pushed all the books out of his arm. They scattered all over the floor. Jake was already late. Now he was angry. He stared down his attacker, two years Jake's senior, five inches taller, and fifty pounds heavier.

"Pick those up," Jake demanded.

"Make me," mocked the bully.

Jake charged at him, and the kid stepped aside like a matador sidestepping a bull. He stuck his foot out and tripped Jake as he went by.

"Faggot," the bully grumbled. "When's your next camping trip?"

Jake stared at him in disbelief. Did the whole school know? Was he bluffing? Guessing? Or did all the kids know about his and Kenny's encounter with Father Gerry? Jake was beyond furious. He charged the boy again and met a roundhouse right fist to the jaw that knocked him to the ground. He was dazed, confused, and disoriented, and he was in serious pain. A counselor happened by and found Jake lying in the hallway. He took him to the counseling center and called his mother. Jake was beside himself in grief and pain and in near hysterics. He was demanding to see his brother, so the counselor decided to call Kenny out of class. Kenny arrived before Jennifer. He took one look at his brother and began to fume.

"Jake, who did this to you?" Kenny sputtered.

"Drew Moss," Jake sobbed, relieved to see his brother.

"His ass is mine," Kenny threatened, furious.

"Hold your horses, young man," the counselor cautioned. "Your mom is on her way. We'll deal with Drew. He'll be punished, suspended, and he'll never bother Jake again. But more violence is not going to solve anything."

"I promised my brother I would never let anyone hurt him ever again," cried an enraged Kenny.

His anger turned to shame. He addressed his younger brother. "Jake, I am so sorry I let you down again."

"What could you have done, Kenny?" Jake consoled. "You were in class. You weren't there."

"I should have been. We knew this would happen. Nobody can help us. We've got to help ourselves!" Kenny shouted. "Let's get out of here."

He turned to the counselor.

"Are we free to go?"

"As soon as your mom gets here. You boys can go home with her," the counselor soothed, a calm voice in a growing storm.

The counselor briefed Jennifer as soon as she arrived. He told her about the altercation, the punch, and the offensive language and behavior that sent Jake into hysterics. She demonstrated a brave front but was dying inside. *How much pain must my boys endure? Is this how it is going to be from now on? Will we have to transfer to a different school?* She was glad they had an upcoming appointment with Rothenberg. She spoke briefly to the counselor, who assured her swift and severe punishment was coming to young Mr. Moss. Jennifer signed the necessary "child released early" papers and took her boys home.

Chapter Thirty-Four

Kenny and Jake Tracey arrived at Dr. Rothenberg's office for their weekly session. Therapy was going well. The boys were making remarkable progress. Rothenberg videotaped all sessions at Zack's suggestion so a potential jury could see their pain and track their very gradual healing, the slow release of their anger and sense of betrayal.

On this particular day, Rothenberg began by asking the boys to discuss anything they wanted. They always came together and stayed together, ignoring any suggestion that individual or private sessions might be preferable.

"How's it going, guys? Good to see you, again," Rothenberg began.

"Okay, I guess," Kenny murmured for both of them. He did that in session, quite often.

"What do you want to talk about today?" Rothenberg prompted.

"I don't know, nothing, I guess. Why do we have to come here, anyway?" Kenny protested.

"You don't like coming here, Kenny? What about you, Jake?" Rothenberg wondered.

"No," answered Kenny.

"Not sure," Jake grunted.

"I realize we sometimes discuss unpleasant things, but I thought we'd reached an understanding that discussing them helped you guys. You don't believe that anymore?"

"We discuss the same crap over and over. Nothing's changed. I still feel the same way. Father Gerry's a bad man, an animal. I'll never forget or forgive what he did to my brother and me. Why do we have to talk about this all the time?"

"Yeah," Jake mimed, as usual, after a Kenny rant.

"Well, Kenny, I can certainly understand your reluctance to forgive Father Gerry, but have you been able to forgive yourself?" This struck a nerve.

"Forgive myself?" cried Kenny. "He hurt both of us. I let my brother down because I was afraid. I should have stopped this guy! It's my fault! I knew, but I couldn't move. Some shithead called my brother 'faggot' in school and punched him in the face! What did Jake do to deserve that? I should have been there to protect him," He sobbed. "I'm really sorry, Jake. How can I protect him, Doc? How can I prevent people from hurting my little brother?" Kenny demanded.

"It wasn't your fault, Kenny," Jake consoled. "It was Gerry's."

"Listen to him, Kenny," Rothenberg pleaded. "Your little brother makes a lot of sense. He doesn't blame you. Why blame yourself?"

"He doesn't understand!" Kenny screamed. "He's too little."

"Sounds to me he understands a lot more than you give him credit for," Rothenberg whispered. "He understands what happened to you guys is the fault of only one person, Father Gerry."

"Don't call him that," Kenny scorned.

"Call him what?" Rothenberg inquired.

"Father. He doesn't deserve to be called what we called our Dad and Father Bill."

"You're right, Kenny. I'll never call him that again. I'll call him Gerry like you guys do. Is that okay?"

"I could think of better things to call him," Kenny groused.

"Like what?" Rothenberg masked his amusement. He knew what Kenny meant.

"Mom says not to talk like that," Kenny grumbled.

Rothenberg suppressed a smile. "I won't tell Mom anything you say if you don't want me to."

"Call him 'Gerry,' if you want. That will be okay," Kenny calmed.

"Okay with you too, Jake?" Rothenberg wondered.

"Yeah," Jake snapped, emulating his brother's demeanor.

Rothenberg changed the subject. "Have you guys been to church lately?"

"We don't go there anymore. Mom says we don't have to," Jake sneered, trying too hard to be as scornful as his brother.

"Do you want to go?"

"No," snapped the boys. It was the first time this session they answered in unison.

"When you consider how you feel about going to church or about priests, what does that feel like?" Rothenberg probed.

Kenny looked down, up, and around the room. "Sad, sad and pissed," he sighed.

"Yeah," Jake huffed.

"How do you feel about your mom?" the psychiatrist wondered, eyes moving from boy to boy.

"What's she got to do with this?" Kenny growled.

"Nothing, Kenny, nothing at all. It's a simple question. Will you answer it for me?"

"I love my mom," Kenny smirked.

"Yeah," Jake sputtered, again attempting to replicate his brother.

"Do you kiss and hug your mom as much as you used to?"

"Yeah, sure," Kenny indicated.

"Yeah," mimicked Jake.

When the session was over, Rothenberg brought Jennifer outside to their customary spot away from the surveillance equipment.

"The boys are making progress, Jennifer. Their anger is appropriate and aimed at the priest and the church, also appropriate. In time, with continued therapy, they should be able to deal with it. Many victims of child sexual abuse will have nightmares, and some will have relationship difficulties. I'd be remiss if I didn't warn you to watch for signs of suicide ideation or possible drug abuse, but I see no evidence of anything like that. How are the boys at home?"

"Quiet, aloof, not as fun-loving as they once were. There's an air of caution in everything they do. They won't go to church. They've abandoned their friends. I can't get them to kiss me goodnight. They say they are too old," Jennifer scowled.

"I can't tell you exactly what they told me. It would violate patient-doctor confidentiality, but they were not truthful in describing their relationship with you. Were they physical with you before this incident?" Rothenberg wondered.

"Oh yes, tons of kisses and hugs for their dad and me,"

Jennifer advised.

"I have another appointment, Jennifer. We must assume therapy will be long-term. The boys must continue to appreciate who is responsible and channel their anger appropriately. By word, it seems they have. By deed, I'm not sure. I'll continue to follow this and do my best to help them through," Rothenberg encouraged.

"Thank you, Doctor." Jennifer appreciated the honest appraisal.

"My pleasure."

Chapter Thirty-Five

Micah visited Pat's brother and Pam's sister and came away with nothing new. Neither knew where their siblings were. Both thought Father Gerry was a fine priest, and both heard from their brother and sister about once a week. They were very cooperative and encouraged Micah to find them.

They were glad to hear that 'Mom and Dad' 'hired' him. Both agreed to have a caller ID block installed in their homes. Neither could believe he or she hadn't thought of that. Micah was sure he'd have a phone number for the missing families within a week. It wasn't as easy as it would have been if he'd been on his home turf, where he could call in a favor or two and trace a cell phone signal.

Nonetheless, with an area code and phone number, finding them would be a piece of cake. He loved modern technology. If for some reason the caller ID block bit didn't work, there were methods available to defeat it. Besides, a computer search of credit cards, Social Security numbers, and so on would find them. There was always some electronic paper trail in the twenty-first century.

That night, however, he put the case and technological advance aside for a different type of progress. He planned on putting his best moves on beautiful Jessica. If he had to stay in this town, he might as well get laid, and Jessica was his best prospect in years. She was as pretty and sexy as any of those girls in his magazines—more beautiful, even than the one in the movie he watched on pay-per-view the other day. Well, not quite pay-for-view. Micah had one of those devices that allowed him to steal premium cable channels. *The air is free*, he figured. He ignored all those warnings before every show that cable theft was a crime punishable by fine and imprisonment. He had the same attitude about this as he did about porn. What a grown man did in the privacy of his own home was his business and could not be a crime. Former cops could be so arrogant about their own violations of law.

Micah found the address and pulled the MKZ into the driveway of a modest bungalow with a large front porch. On the porch were some old patio furniture and a swinging couch. Micah parked in the driveway and walked up the steps to the porch.

"Hi." Jessica chirped.

Micah jumped. She was sitting in the shadows and scared the shit out of him.

"Did I scare you?" Jessica purred.

"Uh, n-no," Micah lied.

"Yes, I did," she teased. "A trained investigator can't sense someone is sitting in the shadows?"

"I knew you were there," Micah contended.

"Sure you did," she laughed. "That's why you're white as a sheet. You just about crapped your pants! So how goes your real estate research?"

"It's going fine," Micah recovered his wits.

He gazed at her, trying to focus in the dark. She had this silly, self-satisfied, smirk on her face. The cat had swallowed the canary and Micah knew he was the canary. He flushed when he suddenly realized Jessica referred to him as a 'trained investigator.' He couldn't believe she unmasked him. He felt violated and embarrassed like he suddenly discovered his fly was open.

"How did you . . .?"

"Easy-peasy. You look like the big-city type. The nearest big cities to Berea are Cleveland and Toledo. No Micah Love in Cleveland or Toledo. The next nearest big city is . . ."

"Detroit." Micah completed her sentence.

"Bingo," she taunted. "There's only one Micah Love in the Detroit area, and he is the president of a large private investigating firm downtown," she crowed.

"Go on . . ." He was no longer embarrassed. He was *impressed.* He enjoyed her initiative in sniffing out the truth.

"I called the number and asked for Micah Love," she continued. "I got someone named Eden. Not too bright, is she?"

No, but she's got great tits, Micah smiled. "Whatever do you mean?" He teased.

"Well, it would seem to me the activities of a hot-shot investigator should be discreet, no?"

"Yes."

"When I asked to speak to you, do you know what Eden told me?" Jessica persisted.

"No, but I'm sure I'm about to find out," Micah grunted, rolling his eyes.

"She claimed you weren't in, but you'd be calling in for your messages."

"What's wrong with that?"

"I asked when you'd be in."

"What was her reply?" Micah played along. Jessica enjoyed the exercise, and Micah enjoyed her enjoyment.

"Mr. Love is out of town on a case."

"What's wrong with that?"

"Nothing. Then I told her I was Jessica Klein, from Berea. Guess what she told me?" Jessica snickered.

"I can't guess."

"She got all excited. She likes you." Jessica giggled.

"Oh yeah, she loves me," Micah sighed.

"Well, anyway, she kind of gushes and says, 'what a coincidence! Micah's in Berea working on a case.' Isn't that wild?" She exclaimed.

"Yeah, wild," Micah grumbled, getting annoyed.

"I say, 'wow, that is a coincidence. I can talk to him about my case right here!' I pretended to be excited to find out what a deceptive bastard you are." Jessica snapped, suddenly angry.

"Jessica—" Micah started to apologize.

"So I requested your hotel room number and phone number, and guess what she does?"

"What?"

"She gives it to me! Can you believe it?" She chuckled.

"Unbelievable." Micah rolled his eyes.

"After I hung up, I thought to myself, 'Maybe there's another Micah Love in the real estate business who happens to be in Berea at exactly the same time as the investigator Micah Love,'" she pretended to pretend.

"But you decided against that possibility?" Micah guessed.

"Yeah, I pretty much ruled that out. You're a liar, you son of a bitch!" Jessica fumed. "You lie like a rug!" Seductive and sarcastic morphed into fury. Micah stepped back.

"Jessica, come on. I'm in an unfamiliar town, on a case of major importance. The case is extremely sensitive and volatile. Can I trust anyone? I met you today. I've got a client to protect. I'm suspicious of everyone I talk to. It's the nature of my business. Please understand. I couldn't tell you why I needed those names and addresses and I still can't." He pleaded.

He sat down next to her and picked up her left hand, holding it in both of his. He gazed at her with pleading eyes.

"Relationships must be honest. They should start with simple honesty and integrity," she guilt-tripped.

"Relationships? I thought we were having dinner," Micah gasped.

"Well, you never know . . ." She shot him a seductive look.

Micah was getting aroused. "I'm sorry, then. I don't want our *relationship* to get off on the wrong foot. You know the truth now. May I *please* take you to dinner?" He groveled.

"Are you buying?" She purred.

"Absolutely." He assured.

"Okay, let's go. I know a quaint little place by the river . . ."

Just like that, she returned to the seductive, effervescent Jessica he met that afternoon.

***

While Jessica was chastising Micah, Zack arrived at Jennifer Tracey's home to escort her to dinner. It was a beautiful early summer evening. The sun was high in the sky at 7:00 p.m., a benefit of daylight savings time. Jennifer was full of questions about the depositions. They drove down I-275 South toward Canton. Zack had lowered the convertible top on the Z4, and the wind howled around them.

Jennifer chose her favorite Chinese restaurant in Canton on Ford Road. There was a theater nearby. They made plans to catch a late show if they finished dinner in time. Jennifer had to shout her questions over the wind. She finally decided to give up and wait until dinner. Zack pulled into and parked in the restaurant parking lot. He jumped out and hurried around to the other side to open her door, as was his habit. Jennifer smiled. *Chivalry is not dead.*

The restaurant wasn't crowded. A Chinese host smiled, bowed, and muttered something neither could understand. He escorted them to a booth, handed them open menus, and announced the specials. He left them momentarily and returned with water, hot tea, and dinner rolls, those delicious, hot ones that are only served at a Chinese restaurant. He hovered over them, eager to take their order.

Jennifer and Zachary watched him leave, simultaneously turned toward each other, chuckled, and bowed slightly.

"Nice place," Zack looked around. "Great service. Do you come here often?"

"Not often enough, the food is awesome."

"This isn't exactly near your home. How did you discover it?"

"My brother used to work for the company that owns the theater down the street. Jim and I used to take the boys to the movies for free. We . . . sort of . . . stumbled on this place."

Zack glared at her, lost in thought.

Is he listening to me? She decided to change the subject. "So, tell me, what happened today?"

He came out of his trance and brought her up to speed. She was immediately sorry she changed the subject.

"This is outrageous, Zack. Why would a religious institution need a secret police-type guy? Why would they have such a person on their payroll?"

"Oh, I can see many legitimate reasons for his existence— bomb threats against churches, assassination attempts on high church officials, the security of clergy and parishioners in general. I guess this man and his organization were created for these legitimate reasons. They were logical choices when pedophilia began to surface in the priesthood. What, ultimately, seems to motivate everyone on the defense side, though, is preventing a public scandal. That's why every offer we've received includes nondisclosure of settlement figures, a sealed court file, and a hushed-up criminal conviction and plea bargain."

"That's exactly why we can't let that happen in our case. He'll get transferred somewhere else and do this again. This must be *public*, Zack, to protect the kids, not only from Gerry but from who knows how many other sick priests who are doing this to kids," she grumbled.

"I hear you, Jennifer, but I also got a new offer from Walsh." Zack brightened. "I'm duty-bound to convey it to you."

"Oh, what's the offer?" She inquired, genuinely curious.

"It includes all the privacy features I just mentioned," he tested the waters.

"Not acceptable," she snapped.

"They have offered five million dollars, Jen." He dropped the bombshell.

Jennifer was sipping her tea and almost choked on it.

"Five million dollars? You're kidding!" she exclaimed.

"I'm not kidding. However, you'll have to agree to drop the case, sign a nondisclosure agreement, and allow a non-public plea bargain."

"That's an enormous amount of money!"

"Yes, it is . . . " he admitted, surprised she seemed to be considering it.

"My boys and I—and you—would be set for life," she speculated.

"I don't know about 'set for life,' but it's a lot of money. Take me out of the equation. Worry about you and your boys."

"But it's a lot of money for you too, and you've worked so hard and been through such difficult times . . ." she considered.

"This decision is about you and the boys. You need to do what's right for your family. Nothing else matters." He meant it. This 'new' Blake surprised even him.

The waiter returned with their meals, and they ate as they talked.

"This is delicious, the best Chinese I've ever had."

"I told you so. Zack, what do you think I should do?"

"Jenny, I can't tell you what to do, but you keep saying you're doing this for the boys," he suggested.

"I *am* doing it for the boys," she insisted.

"Well, do the boys benefit from this policy of nondisclosure?"

"I-I don't know what you mean," she stammered, confused.

"The church will pay you more for nondisclosure than they will if this case continues to be conducted in public. Further, they will probably start a public attack on you and the boys. Your decision to conduct these proceedings with maximum press coverage might cost you money and actually hurt you and your kids' reputations. If this is about the best interest of *your* children, it may be best to move forward the way the church desires. I can probably get even more money."

She lowered her head and shook it, wistfully, from side to side. "It's hush money, Zack. They wouldn't be paying for the harm they caused. They'd be paying to shut me up."

"That's true, but what the hell do you care? You and the boys will be set financially for life, and the boys will receive treatment for as long as necessary," he emphasized. He had her attention.

"It's very tempting, Zack," she ruminated. "But what happens with Gerry? He just transfers somewhere else and does this to someone else's kids?" She stammered.

"He would be in the hands of the church. You'd have to trust the church to get him help and place him in settings where he couldn't harm children," Zack reasoned. He knew where the conversation was headed.

"But I can't trust the church," she concluded.

"Why can't you trust them? Do you think they want him to molest children?"

"No, of course not," she scowled.

"What then?" He pressed.

"You are convinced he's done this before, right?"

"Yes."

"If the church had control of his placement and could be trusted to get him the help he needed, why was he transferred to Lakes?"

She'd make an excellent lawyer. "A mistake, probably. He slipped through the cracks somehow," he reasoned.

"Do you suspect his previous victims settled in the manner

you describe?"

"Yes," Zack admitted. Jennifer would turn down this indecent amount of money and more, put her own kids through a public trial, to protect other kids from experiencing the trauma they suffered. *Incredible!*

"Can we get some assurance that no mistakes will occur?"

"I don't see why not. I can try." *Why didn't I think of that?*

"Try then. I also think it's too early. I'd like to see more deposition testimony, perhaps this secret police guy. Let's see where they lead. The money will still be there, and we don't have to be extremely public about the depositions. I'll give you my decision after that," she concluded.

"Sounds like a plan," Zack assented, not enjoying the prospect.

The waiter returned, took their plates, and brought back carryout bags and fortune cookies. Jennifer cracked open the cookie and pulled out her fortune. "You will find peace and riches beyond your dreams." Jennifer laughed out loud as she showed the fortune to Zack.

"Peace before riches, I hope," she prayed.

"Amen to that, but riches aren't too bad," Zack laughed.

"That's true. I could deal with riches," she joked.

"Let's see what mine says."

"Okay."

"You open it," he prompted, straining his neck to view the message.

Jennifer cracked the cookie open, read the fortune, and smirked.

"What does it say?" Zack squinted.

"You will find success in your chosen profession," Jennifer chuckled.

Zack smiled. "From the fortune's mouth to God's ears."

He paid the bill and thanked and tipped the waiter. They left the restaurant together. The sun was setting beautifully, *like a red rubber ball.* Zack thought of the old song by The Cyrcle. They decided against the movie. The evening air was still warm, and they drove in silence with the top down to Jennifer's house.

***

As Zachary was driving Jennifer home from Canton to Farmington, Micah was paying the bill at Antonio's, a small typically Italian restaurant with white stucco walls, hanging, empty wine bottles, and jammed-in tables with red-and-white checkerboard tablecloths covering them. The servers had to maze around, looking for an opening, to arrive at the table they needed to serve. Some of the waiters would break out in song when the violinist, whose job was to visit each table and inquire of and play patron requests, played one of their favorites. The ambiance was terrific and the food superb. Micah had underestimated Jessica. She was a woman of great taste, in food, at least.

He hoped she was not as discriminating in seeking male companionship. She was out of his league. *She's gorgeous, perfect. What would she want with a schlump like me? Bald head, fat stomach, bad comb over.* Micah found himself wishing he could be Channing Tatum or Chris Hemsworth, anyone with hair and a body, for just one night.

"Was I right, or was I right?" Jessica gloated.

"Absolutely delicious. The spiedini was the best I've ever tasted, even better than Maria's, in my neck of the woods, and the veal was outstanding. Would you like coffee or dessert or an after-dinner drink?"

"No, thanks. I'm stuffed. So, tell me, what's this big case of yours about?"

"I can't tell you—it's confidential," Micah claimed.

"Confidential, smonfidential," she needled. "You're discussing it with some people around town because you're trying to locate their children. Parents won't tell you a thing unless you tell them why you were asking."

"You'd be surprised what people will tell me. I'm very good at what I do," Micah boasted.

"I'll bet you are. I'll bet you're good at many things. Now give! What's this case about? Maybe I know something. Did you ever think of that? I could be a witness," she insisted. She'd wait and pester all night, if necessary.

"If I told you, I'd have to shoot you," he joked.

"I look forward to that, as long as it's blanks," she purred.

Micah's pants stirred again.

"Now give. What's going down?"

Was she really angry? Micah capitulated. *Besides, maybe she knows something.* She'd done a terrific job tracking Micah down.

"I'm here on a child sexual abuse case," he conceded.

"Child abuse?" She was genuinely shocked. "Where? Who? MacLean? O'Connell?"

"I don't know yet. I think their kids are involved. The two families just picked up and left without even giving their families forwarding addresses and phone numbers. And the kids are the target age and sex."

Jessica looked perplexed. "I don't get this at all. Why would an investigator from Detroit be interested in two domestic abuse cases in Ohio?"

"Oh, no, you've got it all wrong. Not domestic abuse, clergy abuse," Micah advised.

"Clergy? At St. Pat's?" Jessica was stupefied.

"I believe it happened at St. Pat's or St. Pat's functions."

Jessica was miffed. "That's ridiculous. Micah, you can't march into a small town like Berea and make these kinds of accusations. Almost everyone in town belongs to that church," she defended.

"It's not the church itself or anyone currently associated with it; it's a priest who used to work there," Micah expounded.

"Who?" She demanded.

"Gerry Bartholomew."

"Gerry fucking Bartholomew?" She was incredulous.

"Yes, Gerry fucking Bartholomew."

She shook her head, astonished by the revelation. "But, . . . Gerry was a great guy and an even better priest. Most people around here wanted Foley to retire so Gerry could take over."

"Well, I hate to burst your bubble, but Gerry sexually molested at least two teenage boys in Michigan, and we believe he did the same thing to the O'Connell boys and the MacLean boys—same age, same situation."

"How do you know this?" She hugged herself.

"The boys named Gerry as the perp."

"What's a perp?" She wondered.

"The perpetrator of the crime," he explained.

"Oh, the *perp*," echoed Jessica, abashed. "What did the MacLean and O'Connell families tell you?"

"Same thing you did. Gerry's a great guy, a model citizen, the next coming of Jesus H. Christ. They also told me the boys acted strange for weeks, and both sets of parents suddenly got 'transferred' out of town. They left in the middle of the night without providing a forwarding address or telephone number to any family members."

"I'll admit that's strange behavior, but what does this have to do with Gerry?"

"Coincidence. The grandparents don't realize it, but their grandchildren were silent, angry, and aloof for at least six months before the family left. Both sets of boys went on camping trips and overnights with Gerry at or near the time they began to have problems. My client's children, also teenage boys, exhibited these exact symptoms, following an extended camping trip *they* took with Gerry. Gerry is transferred to Michigan while the two families disappear at or near the same time. Interesting coincidence?"

"It could be just that, a coincidence."

Micah could tell, while she suggested a coincidence, she didn't honestly believe it. She was struggling with the truth. She liked Gerry.

"Could be, but I doubt it. The man is not who you think he is," he disclosed. "Whether you choose to believe me or not, Bartholomew is a child molester. He uses his position to lure children into his bed or his shower and commits unspeakable acts under the guise of religious ritual, in the name of God. Church officials don't deny he abused the Tracey kids. There are *criminal* charges in Michigan, Jessica. I believe there were criminal proceedings here, too, but they were covered up."

Jessica remained stunned. "This is . . . unbelievable, so abhorrent! How could a man of God do such terrible things to children?"

"This is not a man of God, Jessica. Maybe he once was, but no more. Now he's an animal, posing as a man of God."

"I just can't . . . this is so . . . my God, Micah, he forced teenage boys to have sex with him?"

"I'm afraid so, Jessica."

"I can't help you, Micah. I had no idea," Jessica admitted. "I'm like everyone else in town who thought he was a great guy and a great priest, transferred only because his time came up before Bishop Foley was ready to retire."

"Jessica, maybe you *can* help. You know everyone in town, right?"

"Pretty much. Why?" Jessica brightened.

"How well do you know the custodian at St. Pat's?"

"Gus? I've known Gus all my life. He's been the custodian at St. Pat's forever. What does he have to do with this?"

"I think Gus knows something. He started to confess something to me, but caught himself and clammed up. I'm sure the church has gotten to him and told him I'm dangerous or something by now, but if you were to talk to him . . ."

Jessica was assertive now. "I'd be happy to, Micah. I know where he lives. I know his route home. I know where he goes to eat. I'll talk to him."

"Wonderful," Micah cheered. "I'm particularly interested if he knows why Gerry was transferred, what happened on those camping trips, and what higher-ups within the church knew about him or were responsible for his transfer."

"Geez, Micah. He's the janitor—he doesn't run the place!" Jessica snickered.

"I know, but you'd be surprised what janitors hear roaming the halls. Besides, what's the harm in asking? And don't forget, initial denials don't mean he doesn't know anything," Micah tutored, sleuthing 101.

"Micah," she purred, rubbing her leg and hand up his thigh under the table, "I have ways of getting even the toughest nuts to crack."

Micah gulped and then jumped, as her grip tightened. *She is an interesting woman, this Jessica Klein. I have to get to know her better.*

"I'll leave it in your capable hands." He looked down. Her grip tightened.

The waiter appeared with the bill. Micah paid it in cash and requested a receipt. Jessica held onto him, firmly, the entire time, while Micah tried to maintain composure. Finally, Micah rose, unable to take any more, forcing Jessica to release her grip. He immediately sat down, red with embarrassment. Nobody noticed his 'condition,' but Jessica chuckled. Micah waited until his 'excitement' subsided. He glared at Jessica, helped her out of her seat, and escorted her out of the restaurant and into the parking lot. He took her into his arms and kissed her. It was thrilling! He'd been celibate for too long! Doing was much more satisfying than watching. Both finally came up for air.

"What was that nonsense in there?" Micah demanded.

"What nonsense was that?" Jessica teased.

"Oh, never mind, the night is young. Where to, now, in your fair city?" It didn't seem so God-forsaken anymore.

"How about my place?"

Micah thought about those four-hour erections from the commercials. *Who needs Viagra when you have Jessica?* His would not subside. *We could bottle her and make a fortune!* He was putty in her hands.

"Whatever you say, my dear. You're in charge. I give up," he conceded.

"My place, then. We'll plot strategy and begin a physical investigation."

"Sounds great to me," he surrendered.

"Let's go, then."

"Let's go, then," he gestured.

They got in the MKZ and roared off into the night. He'd never driven so fast in his life. He prayed the cops would be somewhere else. His prurient prayers were answered in one, spectacular evening.

***

Blake pulled the Z4 onto Jennifer's driveway and looked at her. She was staring at him.

"What is it, Jenny? What's wrong?" Zack fretted.

"Nothing, Zack. I'm proud of you, that's all," she praised.

"Proud? That's not the emotion I was hoping for," he

cringed.

She blushed. "Zack, I'm flattered, I really am. I don't think the timing is good. Maybe after the trial or settlement?" Jennifer leaned toward him and held out her arms. Zack leaned in and banged the side of his ribs on the protruding emergency gearshift. "Shit!" he cursed. Jennifer laughed, the first time in a long time. Although he was in pain, Zack laughed too. He repositioned himself around the shift mechanism, and he took her into his arms for a brief embrace. Jennifer invited him inside for a cup of coffee.

"What about the neighbors? What about the boys? What about the case?"

"I don't care about the neighbors. You think a cup of coffee would hurt the case somehow?"

"And the boys?"

"They're probably sleeping."

"Let's go see, then."

They exited the car and approached the side door. Jennifer fumbled with her keys, finally inserting them into the lock. Jennifer opened the door and pushed her finger to her lips, begging for quiet. Zack stopped and listened.

"Not a creature was stirring . . ."

"Let me check on the boys," she cautioned.

"You go check on the boys. I'll go freshen up."

"You do that. The bathroom is down that hall. The family room is at the end of the hall. There is a bar in the wall unit."

"Would you like me to fix you something, my lady?" He offered, gallantly.

"Yes, I would. Do you know how to make a Sea Breeze?"

"With or without cranberry?"

"With."

"You got it."

Zack went into the bathroom and studied himself in the mirror.

"Not bad, for an old guy," he primped. He took a pocket brush out of his back pocket and ran it through his gray hair. When it was perfect, he spread his arms out at the mirror, like Henry Winkler used to do in *Happy Days*. He walked into the family room, found the bar and made himself an Absolut on the Rocks and Jennifer her Sea Breeze.

As Zack turned toward the couch, he caught her, standing at the threshold of the room. The soft light glowed off her porcelain skin—she looked beautiful. *Control yourself, Blake. She's a client.* She had freshened her makeup and hair. Her beauty and sexuality enthralled Zack. He downed his entire drink, staring at her. Then he walked over to her and handed her the sea breeze.

"I take it the boys are sleeping?"

"Yes, they are," she whispered.

This time, it was Zack who quashed any attempt at intimacy. "Where's the kitchen?" he gasped. "I'll make coffee."

Their eyes met for a moment, and she sensed his discomfort, a conflict between the personal and the professional. She pointed out the kitchen, and he sauntered away. The rest of the evening was spent discussing the boys, the case, the church, the offer, and where the two of them might be headed sometime in the future. Zack was pleased, glad he maintained a level of professionalism. *This is a solid beginning.*

They walked into the family room and turned on the television. *Murphy's Romance* was on HBO. James Garner was telling Sally Field that he would stay for dinner, but only if she'd make him breakfast the next morning . . .

Chapter Thirty-Six

Zack opened his eyes to an absolutely beautiful morning. The sun peeked into the room through Venetian blinds. *Where am I?* He realized he was still at Jennifer Tracey's house. He had fallen asleep on her family room couch. But, where was Jennifer?

Jennifer awoke in her bed, upstairs. She stretched and immediately remembered she left Zack on the family room couch, fast asleep. *How do I explain this to the boys?* She was slightly embarrassed but realized she had no reason to feel that way. Zack had a couple of drinks, started to doze off, and she couldn't possibly send him out to drive. If something happened, she would never forgive herself. There was a light tap on the bedroom door.

"Mom? Mom, are you there?" Jake whispered.

"Yes, honey, I'm here. Wait a second. Let me get my robe."

Jennifer rose from the bed, retrieved and donned a bulky terrycloth robe, which covered her nightgown completely. There was a man downstairs. She thought of the old *I Love Lucy* television show and the Desi Arnez line: '*Lucy, you have some 'splaining to do.*'

Jennifer went to the door and opened it. Jake was standing there, with a strange look on his face. Apparently, he had gone downstairs and found Zachary Blake sleeping on the family room couch. Where was his mother? He was pleased to discover her in her bedroom, alone, with the door locked.

Blake sat up on the couch and tried to clear his head. *How much did I have to drink last night? I need some coffee . . .* He heard voices upstairs, then footsteps coming down the stairway. He jumped off the couch, ran to the bathroom, and locked the door. He went to the sink and splashed water on his face, lingering there, allowing water to cascade down his neck. *Nice evening. I must have fallen asleep. How is Jennifer going to explain this to the boys? Ah . . . Jennifer . . .*

He could hear the sound of her voice in the kitchen, talking, he presumed, to the boys. He wondered what she was telling them and whether he should intrude. Did she want him to wait here? His cell phone was in the inside pocket—he used it to dial Jenny's number.

"Hello?" Jenny answered.

"Hi, it's me," Zack whispered.

"Zachary? Where are you?"

"In the bathroom off the family room. Is it safe?"

Jennifer laughed out loud. "Of course, it's safe. I can't believe you called me on that thing from the bathroom!"

"I didn't want to interrupt your conversation with the boys. What are you telling them? How will you explain me being here this morning?" Zack blubbered.

"Why don't you come out here and find out for yourself, Mister Tough Guy. Are you this intimidated in court?"

"Okay, smartass. Shoot me for being sensitive to the boys' feelings. Call me *pisher*."

"Call you what?"

"*Pisher*. It's a Yiddish thing. It means . . . never mind. I'll be right down." *Cultural differences*.

Jennifer reflected upon Zack's use of the cell phone from the bathroom and decided his sensitivity was adorable. *What a lovely man . . .*

"Hi, guys."

Zack entered the kitchen to find the Tracey family seated at the kitchen table. He could smell bacon cooking and observed a large bowl of scrambled eggs on the kitchen table. There was a pitcher of orange juice and a full pot of coffee on the counter. The table had four place settings, one of which was unused. Jenny and the boys had obviously started without him. The remaining place setting told him he was expected. The phone call was unnecessary. He sat down, slightly embarrassed.

"Hi, Mr. Blake," Jake muttered.

"Yeah, hi," Kenny grumbled.

Zack ignored the hostility and helped himself to generous portions of eggs, juice, and coffee. Jennifer rose, retrieved the bacon, and brought it to the table.

"Call me, Zack, boys," he gestured. "How's everybody this terrific morning?"

"We're all fine," Jenny smiled. "And how are you?"

"I couldn't be better."

"Mom told us you slept over last night. Does that mean you're her boyfriend?" Jake pondered.

"Shut up, Jake," Kenny scolded.

"Kenny, please don't talk to your brother like that," Jenny scolded.

She handles the boys with such grace, Zack marveled.

"Sorry, Mom," Kenny apologized.

"Not to me, to Jake, Kenny."

"Sorry, Jake," with less sincerity.

"Okay, Kenny." If Kenny hurt Jake's feelings, it was not evident in his demeanor.

"Well," Jake turned to Zack, "does it?" Zack couldn't read him. *If we were a couple, would he be pleased or displeased?*

"No, Jake. I'm not her boyfriend. I just fell asleep on the couch. After this case is over, I might like to get to know your mother better. Would that be all right with you?"

"What were you doing on the couch?" Jake snickered.

Zack laughed. "Nothing like that, Sherlock. We were going to have coffee. I turned on a movie and fell asleep."

The boys chuckled and went back to their breakfast. *No big deal, I guess,* Jenny smiled. They chatted, joked, and laughed all through breakfast.

Chapter Thirty-Seven

Micah stirred in Jessica's small, uncomfortable, double bed. His eyes opened, and he checked the alarm clock—8:30 a.m. He sat up. His head throbbed, and he lay back down. He turned to Jessica and discovered she was gone. He called out to her. Maybe she was in the bathroom. He discovered a note on the pillow.

Micah: I had a wonderful time. You're terrific. I had to go to work. I couldn't bear to wake you. You looked so cute, sleeping with your hair coming off the top of your head and down in your face. Call me at the office or stop by.
Love & kisses,
Jessica

Micah instinctively straightened his hair as he read the note. "She thinks I'm terrific," he boasted. He hauled his ass out of bed, marched into the bathroom, and took a cold shower, courtesy of Jessica's defective hot-water tank. Afterward, he dressed and ate a quick breakfast at a local coffee shop.

He had work to do. He needed to purchase equipment to defeat a caller ID block, check computer records, and develop, with Jessica, an approach to take with the janitor. That would give him an excuse to see her. What a night! It might have been the best night of his life. Jessica was amazing. He was still alive! He loved sex, doing it, watching it, reading about it, but never, *ever*, had he experienced anything like Jessica Klein.

After breakfast, Micah returned to the hotel to check for messages. Nothing. He walked over to city hall and the register of deeds office. Jessica was at the front desk, dressed to kill. She wore a tight-fitting, very low-cut teal silk dress. Micah couldn't believe the city permitted her to dress like this. He didn't mind. In fact, he imagined her without the dress. Last night's memories were vivid.

"Hi," she greeted him.

"Hi, yourself," he smiled.

"Did you sleep well? I didn't have the heart to wake you. You looked so cute and peaceful," she grinned.

"Thanks for the consideration and the compliment," Micah noted.

"What brings you here this morning?"

"What kind of question is that?" Micah babbled. "You, of course."

"I know. I just wanted to hear you say it."

"If you'd like, I'll say it again."

"No, that's not necessary. Once is enough."

"Once will never be enough for me, when it comes to you," he swooned.

"How sweet. Micah . . . I need to say this . . . Last night was wonderful, but . . ." She hesitated.

"But what?" he tensed. *This girl is a roller-coaster ride.*

"But there are no strings, no attachments. I know you're going to finish your work and return to Detroit. I don't want you to feel you owe me something. I had a great time last night, and I hope you did too. But if that's where it ends, I'll understand," she assured.

"Jessica, I don't think you understand. I didn't have a great time last night." Micah lowered his head, sad-faced.

"Oh, I just thought . . ." Jessica blushed.

"I had a terrific time, a marvelous time. I was in ecstasy. I never met a woman like you! 'No strings' is totally unacceptable to me. Don't say anything like that again. I still can't believe a knockout babe like you would even *consider* a *schlub* like me."

Jessica was relieved. "A what?" she queried, confused.

"*Schlub*. A *grubba-ying*. You know," Micah explained.

"No, I don't. What language is that?" She wondered, still perplexed.

"Yiddish." Not Jewish? He didn't care if she was PLO. He was in lust.

"What's Yiddish?"

"It's a slang language Jewish people use."

"You're *Jewish*?" Jessica exclaimed.

"Is that a problem?"

"No, just a surprise. There aren't very many Jews in Berea."

"Well, there's a decent amount in the Detroit area."

"Will you teach me stuff about being Jewish?" she desired.

"Stuff?" he wondered.

"Yeah, you know, rituals, holidays, services—stuff."

She should have chosen a chosen one who was more into the traditions. He hadn't been to a synagogue in years. Could a *schiksa* be responsible for his return to *shul*? His religious mother would turn over in her grave.

Jessica patiently awaited his response.

"I would be happy to," he promised. "Although I'm no expert."

"I'm sure you know more about it than I do," she stated the obvious.

"I suspect I do." He changed the subject. "Jessica, I need to talk to you about the janitor."

"Talk," she ordered. She didn't care for the sudden topic change.

"When do you plan on talking to Gus?"

"This evening," she grunted.

"What approach do you plan to take?"

"Invite him to my place, rip his clothes off, and screw the truth out of him," she deadpanned.

Would she actually sleep with this old guy for the sake of the case? "Speaking from experience, I am positive that approach would be successful. But, can you suggest a more sensible plan? Save the other as a last resort?" Micah shuddered.

"Actually, I was going to use the direct approach. Ask him questions and get the answers we need."

Micah was relieved. "Do you think that's wise?"

"Micah, I know Gus. Very few people in this town even know he exists. Of those who do—very few are nice to him. I'm one of the few who takes the time to say hello, find out how he's doing. If he opens up to anyone, he'll open up to me."

"Okay, Jess. The prospect of you sleeping with that weirdo did not excite me anyway," he cringed.

"Oh? But, I specialize in weirdoes. Why just last night . . ." she teased.

"Okay, okay, I get your point," he sighed. *She's a pistol!*

"No, you don't, Micah, like everyone else in this town. Someone's a little different and, all of a sudden, he's a weirdo. Gus never harmed anyone, never uttered a bad word to anyone. He does his job and is pleasant and respectful." She was suddenly judgmental.

"Jessica, I didn't mean—"

"Yes, you did, and I get it coming from you. You're investigating a case. He works at the place you're investigating, and he's a little strange. It's natural for you to feel the way you do. It's the others in this town who piss me off—the ones who snicker at him behind his back. Kids pull practical jokes like dumping trash cans in rooms he's just finished cleaning or writing disgusting references about him on bathroom partitions. They empty soap and towel dispensers and then stand around looking for a reaction from him. The kids are reported to the pastor or the parents, who promise discipline but do nothing, and the kids then repeat the behavior. Why Gus sticks around is beyond me."

Jessica was disgusted. Micah respected her concern for someone a bit different. He'd let her deal with Gus any way she wanted. If Gus had been a victim of the type of nastiness she described, perhaps he'd open up to her, someone who *didn't* treat him poorly. Maybe he'd view the MacLean and O'Connell children as victims too, and be angry enough at the church for not doing anything to help them.

"All right, Jessica. Have it your way. I'll leave you to decide the approach. Some advice?"

"Sure."

"Gus is a victim. So are the MacLean and O'Connell folks. The church let bad things happen, same with Gus and those kids. The church stands by and does nothing for people who are mistreated. Good approach?"

"That has potential. I'll consider it."

"Well, thank you very much. What's your timetable?"

"We go home the same way. I'll try tonight, make sure the timing is right, walk alongside him, and strike up a conversation."

"You don't think he'll be suspicious?"

"He'll talk to me, Micah. Trust me. Whether he's suspicious or not, he'll talk to *me*," she concluded.

"Okay, Jessica, he's in your hands. Can we get together later to discuss your meeting?"

"Yeah, we can get together. You may wine, dine, and seduce me again," she taunted.

"Who seduced whom?" He was a quick study. He learned to play her game.

"Well," she teased. "Maybe this time, I'll let you seduce me."

"It's a date," Micah saluted. "When and where?"

"Be in your room at seven, showered, dressed, and ready to go."

"You got it," Micah promised, aroused.

Chapter Thirty-Eight

Jessica Klein finished work for the day and hurried outside. She wanted to reach the park before Gus walked by. It was 4:45 p.m. Gus usually came by around 5:00 p.m. She hurried out of the old county building and fast-walked to the park—arriving at approximately 4:53 p.m.

It was a beautiful summer evening. Trees and flowers were in full bloom, and a nearby creek crackled water, which slowly ran toward the river. A slight summer breeze ruffled her hair. Had she not been anxious to see Gus, she might have taken an evening nap on the park bench.

It was 5:05 p.m. Gus was late. He was never late! At 5:15 p.m., she decided, *He's not coming. Something's wrong. Where's my phone? I have to call Micah.* She ransacked her purse, trying to locate her phone in the rubble. A powerful-looking stranger walked by. He glanced her way, serious as a heart attack, and walked on. She froze, quickly collected herself, located her cell phone, and called Micah.

"Hello?"

"Micah? Thank God you're there. Gus didn't come," she fretted. "He's never late. He never misses work! Something's terribly wrong. I can feel it. I *know* it!"

"Okay, Jess, okay, calm down," Micah reassured. "Come on now. I'm sure everything is fine. He's late. That's all. No big deal."

Jessica's hysterics scared Micah. She was not prone to panic. She was strong, sure, and forthright. He kind of enjoyed her sudden vulnerability, being the strong one, and comforting her.

"Don't patronize me, Micah Love!" Jessica bristled. "Everything is not 'fine,' damn it! I'm going over to Gus's place right now! Am I going by myself, or are you coming with me?"

So much for vulnerable Jessica . . . "Of course, I'm coming with you," he promised. "Where are you?"

"At the park, First and Elm."

"Stay right there. I'm on my way."

***

Micah met Jessica at the park. They drove together to Gus's apartment house. Micah parked and ordered Jessica to stay in the car. Of course, she refused. They crept to the building and inspected the directory. Jessica located Gus's name and pressed the appropriate buzzer. No answer. Micah tried the entry door. Locked. He reached into his back pocket, pulled out what looked to be a large wallet, unfolded it, and revealed a set of small tools.

"You're going to pick the lock?" Jessica cackled. "Just like on *Castle.*"

"Quiet, Jessica. You'll alert the neighbors," Micah scolded. He began working on the lock. Within seconds, Jessica heard a *click,* and the door opened. They stepped inside a dim hallway and located Gus's apartment. The door was demolished. Micah pulled out his gun. He shoved Jessica behind him—there was no use asking her to stay there—and leaned through the open threshold. He and Jessica crept inside and observed a neat, sparsely furnished one-room apartment. Other than the broken door, nothing appeared out of order. A small television faced them from the back wall with a large couch in between. Gus lay on the couch. *Asleep?*

Micah came around to the head of the sofa and gently shook Gus's shoulder. Nothing. He checked his pulse. Nothing. Micah turned to Jessica, who was already in tears.

"He's dead," Micah confirmed.

"Oh, my God!" cried Jessica. "Who would hurt a sweet, innocent old man like Gus?"

"We're dealing with some very serious people over some very serious money and negative publicity. I wouldn't put this or anything past them," Micah warned.

"A church would murder someone?" Jessica squealed.

"Not the church itself, Jessica, but the church's secret problem solvers? Absolutely, while the church pretends to be deaf, dumb, and blind." Micah groused.

"What are we going to do? We can't just leave poor Gus like

this." Jessica wiped the tears from her eyes, took a tissue from her purse, blew her nose, and glanced at Micah.

"We're calling the police, Jess. Do you know the number?"

"Yeah." She sniffled. "Nine-one-one."

***

Philip Jack waxed prototypical thirty-year police vet. He gruffly introduced himself as a detective lieutenant of the Berea Police Department. Approximately five feet ten inches, he had a bit of a beer belly but was, otherwise, well built. His hair was kinky and graying, and he had a full mustache and goatee to go with an otherwise three-day growth of facial hair. He looked tired.

"You two found the body?" he presumed.

"Yes," Micah advised, sizing up the veteran cop.

"What were you doing here?"

"We were concerned about Gus," Jessica blurted, sobbing.

"And what caused you to be concerned about old Gus?" Jack yawned.

"I'm a private detective from Detroit," Micah disclosed. "I've been here in Berea, working a case. This man was a potential witness. We came here to talk to him and found him here on the couch, exactly as he is now," Micah explained. He glanced over to the couch. Evidence technicians were feverishly working, wandering all over the room, dusting for prints, searching for evidence. The medical examiner and his team hovered over the body.

"How did you get in, Mr. Detective?" Jack snarled.

He's more observant than he appears. "I picked the outside lock when nobody responded to the buzzer. Gus's door was smashed in when we got here," Micah admitted.

"I'll ignore the B and E for a second. What kind of case you workin' on?" Jack pressed.

"I'm not at liberty to say," Love remarked.

"Not at liberty? Sheeit!" Jack growled. "You can tell me now, or we can go downtown, son."

"I'm not your son," Love snipped.

Jack stared him down, and then glanced at his watch. He'd wait all night for an answer.

"The case involves a former priest at St. Pat's," Love finally conceded.

"What former priest?" Jack persisted.

"Gerry Bartholomew."

"What's he supposed to be involved in?"

"Child molestation." Jack reacted—Love had his attention.

"Not here, not now." Jack scanned the room, distrustfully, checking for eavesdroppers. His sudden change in behavior did not escape Love's notice. "Let me wrap things up here, and I'll meet you at Beans in a half an hour," Jack muttered. "Now, get out of here," he commanded. "I'll take a formal statement downtown tomorrow morning."

Micah and Jessica walked out into the night air.

"Beans?" Micah wondered, confused.

"'It's the Beans,' Berea's downtown coffee shop. Everyone calls it 'Beans,'" she explained.

"Jack knows something," Micah postulated.

"That's obvious, but what?" Jessica pondered.

"No idea, but we're going to find out real quick. Let's head over there."

Chapter Thirty-Nine

Micah and Jessica waited half an hour at Beans. Micah ordered an espresso and Jessica a flavored latte. Jack finally dragged himself in, sat down at the next table, and ordered the house blend, black. He cased the place for gossips. Satisfied the conversation would be private, he looked straight at Micah.

"Okay, hotshot, give. What exactly are you investigating?" a command, not a request.

Love didn't appreciate Jack's tone. He paused, sizing up the veteran cop. *Can he be trusted?* Love wasn't intimidated by Jack's threat to question him downtown. He'd spent time in more dreadful lockups than Berea's. His concern was client confidentiality.

As Love studied Jack, he realized the church already knew everything he'd discovered so far. What confidences could he possibly breach? Deleting client names from the story, Micah spilled his guts. He emphasized the sudden departure of the O'Connell and MacLean families—kids abused, parents paid off and shipped out of town. Now it was Love's turn to ask questions.

"Was there a criminal investigation on the MacLean or O'Connell matters?"

"I'm not at liberty to say."

"Not at liberty? Sheeit," Micah chided. "Come on, Detective. Does this shit sit well with you? I'd bet the farm the church plea-bargained for the priest and promised to keep Bartholomew away from kids, right? So, that condition's been breached, which gives you enormous *power*. Unless you do something to blow the lid off this bullshit publicly, these church guys will keep transferring him from place to place, abused helpless kids, and ruining lives. We need to stop them, *now!*"

Jack sighed. "You're right. I know you're right," he conceded. He drew a deep breath. "I should have known this wasn't over. The guy is sick. Perverts like him don't stop when they're caught. They can't! It's not in their DNA." He took another deep breath.

"Here's the straight scoop, Love. I handled the original investigation. Orders came down from the top, very hush-hush, right from the get-go. The only ones who knew anything about the case at all were high-ranking church guys, the kid's parents, my captain, and myself. Later, the prosecutor and the judge were made aware of the circumstances because the plea had to be placed on the record.

After Gerry pleaded guilty, the record was sealed. Anyone with any knowledge was ordered by the court to observe a vow of silence. Never seen anything like that, before or since. The church here is *that* powerful."

"What was the original charge?" Micah demanded.

"First-degree criminal sexual conduct, two boys, two counts."

This meant the boys were *raped.* Penetration had occurred.

"What was the plea reduction?"

"Fourth degree — two counts. No jail, three years probation, record sealed. The plea was taken in chambers, after hours, for privacy," Jack lamented.

Fourth degree was simple genital touching. Gerry received a slap on the wrist.

"Then he's violated probation with these new charges in Michigan," Micah opined.

"Yep, true, *if* he's found guilty," Jack agreed. *I hadn't thought of that.*

"If he's found guilty, how much time would he serve on the previous guilty plea?" Micah continued, a germ of an idea forming.

"Five to ten."

"In addition to whatever the Michigan sentence is," a statement, not a question. "Worse, unless I miss my guess, Gus's autopsy results will result in a murder investigation. Child sexual abuse and *murder*—enough is enough, don't you think, Lieutenant? We've got to find the MacLean and the O'Connell families. Their lives may be in danger. We need your help. Do you have any idea where they've relocated?"

"No, I honestly don't. I wish I did. I'm as concerned as you are," Jack vented. "Once the guilty plea was entered, the family was no longer needed and were free to leave. So they left, in the middle of the night, leaving no forwarding address. Have you tried other family members? Some still live in town."

"We tried. No addresses, telephone calls from the kids, but always from a blocked number. We've installed unblocking equipment to try to get a location."

"Great idea, Love," Jack praised. "You're alright, after all. I'll put their names out over the wire. We'll see what comes up."

"Nothing. That's an easy one to answer. I'm guessing there's a name change."

"You're telling me the only ones who know who and where they are, are the people who may be after them?" Jack groaned.

"We've got to find them, *fast*."

"How can I help?"

"Contact the Farmington Hills Police. Let them know there's a prior incident and arrest in Berea. Contact attorney Zachary Blake. I'll give you his card. You can testify in the civil case."

"I can't do either of those things," Jack grumbled.

"Why not?" Micah looked confused.

"Because it violates the plea agreement. Until this scumbag is convicted on the Michigan charge, he hasn't violated probation."

"What if I get you statements from his Michigan victims?"

"Can't do it. Look, I know this is frustrating, man. How do you think I felt when they rammed this plea agreement up my ass? I've got thirty years on the force with a pension at stake. Until Bartholomew's convicted of a related crime, my hands are tied. Department brass is in bed with the church."

"Having worked this case, I can believe that," Micah groaned.

"Locating the victims is your best bet," Jack theorized. "They are under no similar constraint."

"Unless their silence has been bought. The money is conditioned on silence," Micah speculated.

"You mean the church paid 'em off?" Jack huffed.

"And paid for them to disappear," Jessica chimed in.

"They're in danger and don't even know it," Jack warned. "We've got to find them."

"Unless the call unblock stuff works, I wouldn't even know where to begin," sighed Micah.

"You have to try, Micah," Jessica pleaded.

"Yeah, you never know unless you try, my mama used to say," Jack smiled.

"You had a mother?" Micah gasped.

Jack laughed. "Scary, ain't it? I'll run the wire, and we'll see where it leads. Where can I reach you?"

"I'm over at the inn, or you can just contact Jessica. She knows how to find me."

"Oh, so that's how it is?" Jack glanced at Jessica. "This guy? Seriously? How come you pretty young things never give us locals a chance?" he winked.

"Why, Detective . . ." Jessica purred. "You've never shown an interest. Why you're about the cutest detective lieutenant I've ever known."

"I'm the only detective lieutenant you've ever known."

"Technicality," she murmured, rubbing up against him, 'Jessica-style.'

"Let's break up this budding love affair before it begins," Micah interrupted. "We've got to get to Pearl and Julius."

"Why don't you run along without me," Jessica teased.

Jack was about to have a coronary. Micah dragged Jessica out of the booth. "Come along, Jessica. Pearl and Julius will be much more cooperative if you're there."

"Yes, run along now," Jack huffed. "At my age, I couldn't handle the like of you. Besides, I might have a homicide to investigate."

"Trust me, Lieutenant," Micah assured. "You'd be wise to limit your investigation to the homicide, and it *is* a homicide. I'd bet my license on it." With that, he pulled Jessica to her feet. "Keep in touch. Let us know if you find anything."

"Will do. You do the same, hear?"

"Will do."

Chapter Forty

"Come to order," commanded the Voice.

He waited for the group to quiet, much like a grade-school teacher would wait for an unruly class to settle down. After a while, the members felt his scorn and silence reigned.

"Very well," he began. "We have solved one problem, but a new one has arisen. The custodian issue is resolved, but the MacLean and O'Connell families present a problem."

"How has the janitor been dealt with?" a member demanded.

"Better you don't know. Assume his silence has been guaranteed."

"What's the problem with the two families?" Another member changed the subject. "They received everything they asked for and more. They have a new life in a beautiful new area, a new identity, absolute financial security—what more could they possibly need? How can there be a problem?" he wondered.

"They haven't complained. They don't even know there is a problem."

"How can there be a problem they don't even know about?" The members were stunned. The Voice pounded the table and demanded silence.

"Trust me. There's a problem," he sneered. "I want the authority to deal with these families by any means necessary."

"Sounds ominous."

"Not to worry about my methods, just approve the exercise. The consequences will be mine and mine alone. Your consciences are clear," he assuaged.

"This is getting completely out of control. I voiced my concerns on the last vote, and I dissent again." The sole dissenter from the last vote rose in protest. "Protecting and absolving these revolting pedophiles, 'dealing' with people, making others 'disappear,' I can no longer tolerate these activities!"

"What do you propose?" the Voice queried.

"Same as before—We admit Gerry's past transgressions, continue the Tracey boys' treatment with Dr. Rothenberg, and pay any compensation the family deems satisfactory to resolve this matter. Gerry pleads guilty in the criminal matter, places himself in a long-term care facility, and never engages in pastoral work again. Take this approach, my friends, and no one else will need to be *dealt with* or *disappeared*. Your solutions disgust me. I will not be a party to them."

The Voice dismissed him with a wave of his hand. Too late for that—anyone else want to voice an opinion?"

Silence.

"Let's put it to a vote. All in favor of allowing me to handle the potential problem as I see fit say, 'Aye.'"

"Aye," came the collective response.

"All opposed?"

"Nay," two voices this time.

"The 'ayes' have it," declared the Voice.

"May God forgive you." The original dissenter growled as he hastily exited the room.

"I am concerned about him," warned the Voice.

"He disagrees with your methods. That is his right. He's loyal to the church. He won't betray us."

"Perhaps we shouldn't take the chance."

"What do you have in mind?"

"Nothing, nothing much. Keep an eye on him. Set up surveillance."

"Spy? On one of our own?" The member gasped.

"Just to confirm he's still one of our own," the Voice reasoned.

The member capitulated. "I can't see what harm it can do, err on the side of caution."

"I agree."

"Surveillance it is then. I'll arrange it with Parks, at once."

"Very well, then. Anything else?"

Silence.

"Then I move to adjourn. All in favor?"

"Aye," the members chimed.

"All opposed?"

Silence.

"We're adjourned."

Chapter Forty-One

Zachary Blake was in his office late, burning the midnight oil. The *Tracey v. Bartholomew, et al.* civil trial was two weeks away. He hadn't heard from Love. If Micah didn't find prior victims or witnesses to the prior bad acts of this lowlife disguised as a man of God, Zack would be unable to prove the church was responsible for his conduct. If that happened, the church would have no financial obligation to pay the jury verdict. A huge verdict against Bartholomew was worthless due to his vow of poverty. The phone rang, startling him.

"Zachary Blake."

"Hi, Zack, Micah here."

"Micah!" Zack exclaimed. "Where have you been? What's going on? I've been calling you all weekend. Do you ever check your messages? Talk to me, man. Give me some good news!"

"Well, I've got good news and bad news," Micah explained. "Which do you want first?"

"Give me all of it! I don't care about the order. What's going on? I've got a trial in two weeks!" Zack urged.

"Two weeks, huh? That's a new development."

"Yeah, and here's another one. Bartholomew copped a plea."

"You're shitting me. What'd he cop to?"

"Criminal sexual conduct, fourth degree."

"Only fourth? That sucks!" Micah groaned.

"That's not the worst of it. He gets to enter the plea off the record, at night, in a judge's chambers—no jail time, three years probation. Jennifer is through the roof. She's allowed to speak at the hearing under the Victims' Rights Statute, but it's a formality. According to my sources at the courthouse, it's a done deal." Zack groused.

"The identical thing happened in Berea," Micah grumbled. "He got the same Goddamned deal. The in-charge detective thinks the judge and the prosecutor are in bed with the church."

"It would seem the same scenario exists in Oakland County."

"There's more," Micah continued. "Bartholomew molested

the children of two families here. He was caught. The result was the plea I told you about. But, get this! Nobody in town knows about the incident. The kids' grandparents don't even know. All they know is their children and grandchildren have disappeared."

"Disappeared?" Zack sputtered.

"Yep. Shortly after Bartholomew pleads guilty and gets transferred to Michigan, the two families take off in the middle of the night, 'For Sale' signs in front of both houses. The cops believe they've been bought off and moved by the church. They have new identities. Their parents don't know where they are. They quit good jobs. It's all very convenient for the church. Only two people in town seemed to know about the incident and why the priest and the two families left town."

"Good. Then we have witnesses. Who are they?" Zack wondered.

"I hate to burst your bubble, Zack, but we have a problem."

"What's that?" Zack fretted.

"One's dead—janitor at the church where Gerry did his dirty work before Michigan. Died yesterday. We think he was killed, but autopsy results are inconclusive. They've ruled out homicide, and the official cause of death is 'cardiac arrest.'"

"The church strikes again? People are being murdered?" Zack seethed.

"I don't know. It sure looks that way."

"Who's the other witness?"

"The investigating cop, Phillip Jack."

"So, he can testify, right?" Zack presumed.

"Wrong. He claims his captain, the prosecutor, and the judge have ordered any violation of the plea agreement of silence will result in termination and loss of pension. He's got over thirty years on the force. He's not talking," Micah retorted.

"You mentioned there was good news? Hopefully, you haven't given it to me yet."

Micah was upbeat. "No, I haven't. I have located one of the families, the name is O'Connell, although they've changed it."

Yes! Zack was pleased to finally hear positive news. "That's great news! Have you talked to them? What did they say? Will they testify?"

"Hold on, Counselor; hold on. I indicated that I've *located* them, not that I've *talked* to them."

"You've set up a meeting, right? When is it? Should I be there, too? Of course, I should. I'll get in the car and meet you out there. Where am I going?" Zack rambled—processing what seemed like a million thoughts at once.

"Hold your horses, Counselor," Micah reasoned. "The family lives in Coral Springs, Florida. They've been given a new life, a new identity, new careers, and, probably, a shitload of money. I'm flying down there first thing in the morning. They're unaware anyone, other than the church, knows their whereabouts. They don't know me. They certainly don't know I'm coming. I doubt it will be easy to get them to talk, but that's not my main concern at the moment."

"What do you mean? What else trumps getting them to talk? Without someone to testify to prior incidents and church knowledge, I'm going to be up shit's creek without a paddle," Zack cried.

"How about their *safety*, Zack? The janitor's death was no accident. These two families are the only ones who can link Gerry and the church to Berea. They're in *danger*. I can feel it. If I'm right, I've got to get to Florida, quickly."

"Of course, you're right. No flights tonight, huh?"

"No such luck. Delta has a 6:00 a.m. nonstop out of Metro to Ft. Lauderdale."

"How far is Ft. Lauderdale from Coral Springs?"

"Fifteen, twenty minutes. With no delays, car rental, and everything, I should be at their front door by 10:00 a.m."

"Okay then, you'll call me tomorrow, the minute you talk to them?"

"As soon as I can, Zack. Sorry I haven't called. I've been up to my eyeballs in shit down here. I can't believe this thing," Micah wailed.

"Yeah, I know what you mean. It's fucking incredible," Zack agreed.

"How's the lady holding up?" Micah inquired.

"Marvelous, as always. Really pissed off about the plea bargain and lack of jail time. She'll be okay when we get justice in the civil case. Besides, I'm getting a germ of an idea on how to handle the criminal situation, as we speak."

"Care to elaborate?" Micah queried.

Zachary shared his idea.

"I like it!" Micah exclaimed. "It could work! In fact, I don't see any reason why it wouldn't. I'll talk to the man when I return from Florida."

"Micah?"

"Yeah?"

"Kick ass down there," Zack encouraged.

"I'll do my best, Counselor."

"I have faith in you, man. Micah?"

"Yeah?"

"I appreciate everything you've done," Zack cooed.

"Yeah, I know you do, but fuck that shit. Win the case and show me the money," Micah whooped.

"I'll do my best, Micah. I'll do my best."

"I know you will, Zack."

Chapter Forty-Two

Gerry Bartholomew sat in a coffee shop reading news accounts of the upcoming civil trial. This guy, Blake, turned out to be a better attorney than anyone expected. The church was on the run. Recovering from this episode would be far more difficult than the others. *What's wrong with me? Why can't I control myself?*

At the same time, he was proud of who he was, proud of his accomplishments, and hated that news reports called him a 'sexual predator.' *Fourth-degree criminal sexual conduct, probation, no jail time. A pretty good deal, considering the real circumstances, isn't it?* He knew fourth degree meant simple "touching." What was wrong with simple touching? *Why would anyone be sent to prison for that? Ridiculous!*

Bartholomew was relieved, of course, but should not have faced a prison sentence in the first place. He was a priest. He needed to minister to his parishioners. Those boys . . . those beautiful boys! He loved interacting with them, teaching them, helping them off with their clothing, gazing at their virginal bodies for the first time, caressing them, demonstrating the pure pleasure of intimate physical contact and connection.

Things were coming to a head. Did he want to be a priest or be with children? Must he choose? That old bastard who quarterbacked damage control for the church demanded change. He claimed things could not continue this way. Could he manage an assignment ministering to the elderly or to the infirm? Overseas? Transfer to an office position? *The priesthood is my life. They can't kick me out, can they? I need to minister to the faithful. I was born to minister to the faithful.*

His mind wandered, and he forgot where he was. He didn't realize he was muttering aloud. He scanned the small shop, gazing from one customer to another. Were these people staring at him? One glared at him over his laptop, another, over a pair of sunglasses. A couple of women were staring, alternatively, with hands over their mouths. Someone glanced over a newspaper.

Were they reading an account of this whole overblown, over reported fiasco? Were they talking about him? Did they recognize him from the news reports? He tried to hide his face when he walked in and out of court. Did everyone know him? He loved teenage boys—so what? Perhaps he'd be shipped out of town, like before, where nobody knew who or what he was.

Should I change my appearance? Grow a beard, a mustache, or change my hairstyle? Fucking parents! The kids love me! They love exploring their bodies, learning about physical pleasure, and the deep passion partners have for one another. But the damn parents keep getting in the way of these important relationships! And that damn Jew lawyer! They thought he was a lightweight. They thought they could buy him off. All they did was **piss** *him off, and he's better than they thought he'd be. The church will take care of it. It's only money. They've got plenty of that. The case will settle, quietly, like the others. I'll be okay. But damn those damn fucking lawyers and parents! Damn them! This is their fault . . .*

Gerry Bartholomew rose, tilted his head upward, nose in the air, and sauntered out of the coffee shop.

Chapter Forty-Three

Micah was shocked—an on-time arrival at Ft. Lauderdale airport. He'd have to fly the first thing in the morning from now on. Aside from the usual ten-mile trip—an exaggeration, nonetheless a long walk—in the Delta terminal at Metro Airport, the trip went off without a hitch.

Metro was a Delta hub. The terminal was large and confusing. The Ft. Lauderdale terminal, also a Delta hub, was much smaller and far less complicated. Micah deplaned, rented a car, and headed west on I-595 toward Coral Springs within twenty minutes of landing. *Try to accomplish that in Detroit.*

He had an address on NW 111 Way in Coral Springs. He toyed with the rental's navigation and quickly obtained coordinates and directions. He exited the freeway at University and drove approximately six miles into Coral Springs. Everything seemed fresh and new, palm trees everywhere. He understood why many northerners moved south.

After a series of lefts and rights on primary and residential streets, he found NW 111 Way. He had to double back a few times. The roads had similar names and numbers. The street system was quite confusing. Finally, he found the address. The house was a one-story stucco ranch with a screened-in pool. He looked up and down the block. Every house seemed identical except for the respective paint job. Every home had a screened-in pool. *Ah, Florida.*

What was life like with summer all year long? He wiped sweat from his forehead and put his nose to his armpits, immediately deciding that fall, winter or spring weren't so bad. He checked the address on the mailbox. The Pappas family lived here. Micah went to the front door and rang the bell. A tall woman in her late thirties or early forties answered the door. Micah recognized her immediately from a picture provided by a relative. This was Mrs. O'Connell.

"Hi, may I help you?" she chirped.

"Good morning, ma'am," Micah charmed. "My name is

Micah Love, and I'm a private investigator from Detroit, Michigan. Are you Mrs. Pappas?"

The woman's demeanor immediately turned cold.

"Yes, I'm Mrs. Pappas, and whatever you're interested in does not interest my family or me. Have a nice day." She started to close the door in his face.

"Mrs. Pappas," Micah pleaded. "Please? I've come a long way to talk to you. I'm begging you for five minutes of your time. If you're not interested in what I have to say, I'll leave. I promise."

Mrs. Pappas pondered his request. She seemed stressed and agitated, but what harm would a short chat do?

"Well, okay, five minutes. But that's it."

She'd be relieved to spill her guts to someone, but she's obviously been told to keep her mouth shut. Micah knew to tread carefully, but how could he *carefully* tell someone her family was in danger? He decided to be blunt and quick.

"Would you like something to drink, Mr. . . . ?"

"Love, Micah Love. Here's my card. No, thanks on the drink."

"Well then, what can I do for you?"

"I don't really know how to start, but . . ."

"But what, Mr. Love?"

"Mrs. Pappas, your family is in danger," he blurted.

Shock and fear registered on her face, but she remained silent.

"As I stated earlier, I am a private investigator. I was hired by the mother of two boys who were sexually abused by a clergyman in Farmington, Michigan. The clergyman is . . ."

"Gerry Bartholomew," she uttered, burying her head in her hands. "I've always known someone would come. I'm afraid you've come a long way for nothing. I can't help you, Mr. Love. Even if I wanted to, my husband would never let me. We must protect our kids. Besides, we made an agreement. How did you find us?"

"It wasn't that difficult actually. We installed unblocking equipment on your in-law's caller ID in Berea. We traced you through the phone number when your husband called his folks.

They're very worried about you, you know."

"I *do* know, but we had no choice. Leaving was the best thing we could do for our family. It had to be sudden, and we were sworn to secrecy. We weren't even permitted to tell our parents where we were going."

"Yes, I know," Micah revealed. "I know the whole story. But there are some things *you* don't know, related to your deal with the church, and what happened after you left."

"Please, tell me everything," she cried.

Micah could see the woman's experience in Berea was not easily forgotten. Micah sought to take advantage of her suffering to gain her assistance. It certainly made Jennifer tick. He hoped the same was true for the MacLean and O'Connell matrons.

Micah told her the whole story. Gerry abused the Tracey boys, and the church tried to cover it up. He went to Berea. They murdered the janitor, silenced the town, and entered into a plea bargain in the Michigan case, déjà vu all over again. The Berea cops and court system were stonewalling, and the church was going to get away with this again.

Mrs. Pappas/O'Connell listened, tearing up as he told the story. For the most part, however, she maintained her composure. "They promised us Gerry wouldn't be placed with children. He did this to *another* family? And poor Gus . . . kept to himself, the kids could be cruel, but he was a nice old man. How could they, Mr. Love?"

"Call me, Micah."

"Micah, then. Why would my family be in danger? We've done everything the church asked and more."

"I'm telling you, Mrs. O'Connell . . ."

"O'Connell! Oh, Micah," she sighed. "No one has called me by my real name in so long. It's nice to hear it again. Go on, sorry. You were saying?"

"I know how you feel. I know a lot of people who have been placed in witness protection. It's tough. Anyway, as I was saying, we believe they murdered Gus. He's the only other witness. Your family and the MacLean family are the only living witnesses to Bartholomew's prior conduct. They killed Gus. Is it such a stretch to believe they'd kill you guys, too? They know who and where you are. Who'd connect some house fire or auto accident befalling the *Pappas* family in Florida, with the incidents in Ohio and Michigan? It's a perfect set-up!" Micah warned.

"Oh, my God! It's impossible to comprehend! My church would actually have people killed?" She wailed.

"I know, Mrs. O'Connell, but everything I've told you is absolutely true."

"I promise to talk with my husband as soon as he comes home. I'll do my best to convince him to help you. There's not much more I can do. By the way, what exactly do you want from us?"

"Come to Michigan with your boys. Hopefully, you'll bring the MacLean family with you. Testify to what happened in Berea, the *whole* sordid affair. The truth will set all of you free. What can happen to you once you've testified? You'd be helping the Tracey family and protecting future kids from harm."

"I'll talk to my husband. I can't tell you what he would do, and I have no idea what the MacLean family will do," she warned.

"Set up a meeting for me with your husband and Mr. MacLean. That's all I ask."

"I'll do my best. You've convinced one of us if that's any consolation."

"It's a great consolation," he sighed. "Now listen to me. Whatever you decide, you must believe this: Your families are in serious danger. The bad guys may already be on their way. Go into hiding again, this time, from the church. The sooner you get to Michigan, where I can protect you, the better. Once you've testified, they no longer have the incentive to harm you."

"What about revenge?" She intimated.

"I can't fathom they've sunk to that level. Don't ask me why, but I'm almost positive your testimony will set you free."

The front door opened, and a large man walked in. He observed a stranger in his living room and went into immediate combat mode.

"Who the hell is this?" he demanded

Micah stood. "Mr. O'Connell?" He stated. "My name is

Micah Love. I am a private investigator from Detroit—"

"Name's Pappas. You're not welcome here," the man huffed.

"Pat . . ." Pam pleaded.

"Quiet, Pam." Pat interrupted. He faced Micah.

"Love, if that's your real name, I don't know what your game is, but you're trespassing. I want you to leave, right now. Don't make me call the police." He nodded toward the door.

"But, Pat . . ." Pam urged.

"I told you to shut up, Pam, and I meant it," he commanded. He turned back to Micah. "Mister, I'd like you to leave now!"

Micah started for the door. "Okay, okay," he capitulated, hands in the air as if a gun were being pointed at him. "I'm going. Don't do anything rash. Talk to your wife. Discuss my visit. I'm on your side, here to help. At the same time, there's a family in Michigan that needs you. You can help them and your family at the same time." He handed the man his card.

"Here's my card. The phone number's my cell. I'll be at the Holiday Inn on University in Plantation. Room 207. Talk to your wife, and then call me. We can handle this situation together, and you won't have to hide anymore."

The man started toward Micah and Micah hurried to the door. "Okay, I'm out of here, but please talk. Call me."

"No promises, Love," the man grumbled. "I don't like strangers coming into my house when I am not home and filling my wife with empty promises. Get the hell out of here."

Micah opened, exited, and closed the door in one quick motion.

***

Later that evening, Micah's cell phone rang.

"Love Investigations, this is Micah."

"Mr. Love? This is Pat O'Connell. You've got your meeting. I'm here in the lobby, with the MacLean family, my wife, and my kids. We're willing to listen. That's all I can promise. We will listen."

"That's all I ask," Micah gasped. "I'll be right down. There's a small conference room we can use, or we can use the coffee shop. Do you know if you were followed?"

"Don't think so. We're not experts, but we've been looking over our shoulders since we left Ohio."

"Understood. I'll be right out."

Micah literally ran out of the room, skipped the elevator and ran down the stairs, two at a time. He met the two families. Mrs. O'Connell made the proper introductions. The hotel clerk escorted them to a small conference room, asked if they needed anything, and then closed the door, leaving them alone. Micah told the families the entire story. As promised, they all listened. When Micah finished his narrative, he took a deep breath, sipped from a glass of water, and waited.

Mr. O'Connell broke the silence.

"Mr. Love, we'd like to talk privately. Please wait outside. We'll talk and then bring you back."

"Sure," Micah agreed, rising. "I'll be right outside the door."

He left the room and closed the door. As he waited, he heard voices but could make out no words. Voices were raised and agitated on a couple of occasions. Finally, the door opened, and Micah was waved in.

"We've decided to place ourselves in your hands, Mr. Love." Pat O'Connell was palpably relieved. "We've seen what these people are capable of doing. They ruined our lives. It does not surprise me someone was killed by these scumbags. It wouldn't surprise any of us if they came after us. Truth be told, we've been fearful of this ever since we left Ohio. They assume we're cowards. We sold out our families and our community for money. They won't expect this from us. We won't wait at home for them, like sitting ducks. The best defense is a good offense. If you promise to keep us safe, we'll come back with you."

"Once you testify, they will no longer be in a position to harm you," assured Micah.

"I hope you're right. What do you want us to do?"

"I want you to stay with me. Do not go home . . ."

"But our belongings, our houses, our money . . ." cried Mrs. MacLean.

"I'll take care of all that. Don't worry about a thing. It's too dangerous for you to go home. Trust me, please?" Micah implored.

"We trust you, Mr. Love. We are in your hands," Mr. O'Connell conceded.

"I won't let you down," assured Micah. "Now we have to arrange aliases and get you on a plane. I'll work out the details. We'll leave in the morning. I have to check out of here. We'll go to another hotel."

"Why?" Mr. MacLean wondered.

"Because I checked in under my real name. We have to be super-careful. We'll find a hotel on the beach somewhere, pretend to be tourists."

"Okay, whatever you say."

"Let's get going." Micah went to the front desk and checked out. Shortly thereafter, the two families and Micah drove southeast toward Ft. Lauderdale Beach. Micah found vacancies at a slightly rundown beachfront efficiency complex where rooms were rented by the week. Micah rented three rooms under an alias and paid cash in advance. Soon, everyone was safely tucked away in separate rooms. Micah sank into a recliner—satisfied he'd taken appropriate precautions.

***

He awoke to his portable alarm clock. He telephoned the families' rooms and informed them it was time to go. Then he called the rental car company to advise them where to retrieve their car. He promised to leave the keys with the hotel desk clerk. The rental car rep was not pleased. Micah appeased him by approving additional charges to his credit card statement. He didn't give a shit about the cost. He was more concerned about getting the hell out of Fort Lauderdale.

If the Voice and his troops were coming for the families, the odds were good they were already in Florida, staking out houses and running checks on credit card purchases. They'd check under the family names first. They didn't know Micah was in Florida so it wouldn't occur to them to check his credit purchases. At least, he hoped that was true. For the time being, he had the jump on them. He planned to keep it that way. Their very lives would depend on decisions he made from that moment forward. He called the Coral Springs Police.

A half-hour later, Micah met the families outside. He had a green marker in his hand. He went over to their minivans and used the marker to change their license plate numbers—threes became eights and ones became sevens. He was taking no chances. They left the hotel. Micah rode with the MacLean family. They drove west on I-595 toward the Florida Turnpike.

"I thought we were going to the airport?" John MacLean inquired, confused.

"We are, but not the airport or time they'd expect," Micah sneered.

The two vans hit the Florida Turnpike and went north, stopping only to pay tolls, buy gas for cash, or use restrooms and grab snacks for the kids. The kids were enjoying the great adventure. Micah studied them at a rest stop. They were running, laughing, chasing each other. *What resiliency! Jennifer should meet these boys.* There was life after heartbreak and turmoil, after this cruel betrayal of faith.

They drove several hours to the Kissimmee exit and Walt Disney World. They drove into the grounds and up to the Lake Buena Vista Resort.

"We're going to Disney World?" Mr. MacLean wondered aloud.

"Can you think of a better place to hide two families?" Micah beamed. "My office staff has purchased two three-day family vacations, including round-trip travel from Flint to Orlando and back to Flint. The MacLean's are the Hayes family, and the O'Connell's are the Johnson's, from Flint."

"What are we going to do here for three days?" Mrs. O'Connell inquired, aghast.

"Show the boys a good time. They're in for an ordeal in court. Why not enjoy themselves for a few days?"

"You're a good man, Mr. Love," Mrs. O'Connell marveled.

"Call me Micah," he grinned. "Let's go check in."

***

On NW 111 Way and SE 125th Street in Coral Springs, police cars pulled up next to surveillance vehicles sent by the Voice to watch the respective houses. The officers ordered the men to exit the vehicles and stand with their feet spread apart, palms on the hoods of their cars. Officers approached the houses and noticed both had been broken into. Nothing seemed to be missing, except, of course, the families. The officers interrogated the men, who claimed they were from out of town and got lost. Their license plates came back as rental car plates. They loaded the men into police cars and took them to headquarters for questioning.

Chapter Forty-Four

"Settle down, settle down," ordered the Voice. "This is an emergency meeting to update all of you on recent developments in the Tracey case. The MacLean and O'Connell families have disappeared."

"Good news, right?" crowed a member.

"No, bad news, I'm afraid. Someone else got to Florida before us. The families disappeared before our teams arrived. Local police were dispatched to the scene and discovered the houses were burglarized. Our surveillance teams were caught . . . well . . . surveilling.

"The police are holding our teams. They're being questioned as I speak. We had others staking out local airports but found no sign of the two families. They're gone. Blake and Love are behind this, I'm certain of it. This is a serious problem."

"What are we going to do?" a member quivered.

"We're going to find those two families and ensure their continued silence," assured the Voice.

"How are we going to do that? If they're with Blake or Love, they've decided to talk," a member reasoned.

"Deciding to talk and talking are two different things. I'll find them—and when I do, I'll make sure they remember our deal and all the money they were paid," the Voice promised.

"This is beyond crazy!" The original dissenting member fumed. "I've tried, time and again, to persuade this Coalition to finally do what's right. Who are we? Do we stand for the teachings of Christ, for compassion, goodwill, and charity? Do we feed the hungry and clothe the poor? Do we have missions, food kitchens, and health and educational organizations? Do we stand for the moral teachings of the Bible? Why do we use this office and this Coalition to shield criminal, degenerate clergymen from prosecution and cheat families of the children whose lives they ruin along the way? Where does this stop? It must stop!

"We should engage in the business of spiritual teachings and religion, not in cover-ups and child predator protection. I cannot believe or support what this Coalition has become! We were formed to protect the church from its enemies. I'm not naïve enough to believe we have none. However, we have now made our parishioners our enemies."

"Who among you agrees with the good father?" the Voice polled.

"I do," cried the brave cleric who voted with the dissenter the last time.

"Anyone else?" The Voice huffed. Silence overtook the room. "Very well, then. I move we locate the two families and ensure their silence. All in favor?"

"Aye."

"Opposed?" Silence. The two dissenters had left the room.

Chapter Forty-Five

While Micah was sleeping on a plane from Orlando to Detroit, Zachary was in Oakland County Circuit Court in Pontiac. Father Gerry Bartholomew was about to plead guilty to fourth-degree criminal sexual conduct. Saunders, the prosecutor, was present. Several men dressed in suits and cleric garb attended.

Jennifer was seated next to Zachary on the hard wooden bench. Zack spotted Walsh, sitting with the old cleric who attended the first settlement meeting he had with Walsh at Renaissance Center. It seemed ages ago.

Blake spoke to Costigan earlier in the week. The pastor told Blake the 'The Voice' called to advise he'd be appearing at the hearing on behalf of the church. So, Blake called Saunders. He asked who, aside from its lawyer, would be appearing for the church at the upcoming hearing. According to Saunders, Walsh provided the name of a particular cleric who would appear on behalf of the church. Saunders took note of the name and was pleased to pass it along to Blake.

So, this is the scumbag who has been orchestrating this elaborate cover-up for the church? The mysterious Voice was now exposed. Blake knew his identity. It was time to implement part two of his plan. He rose and walked over to the clerk's desk. The clerk pointed to a side door in the middle of the courtroom. Blake walked to the door, opened it, and left the room. On the other side of the door, a long hallway extended through several courtrooms. Clerks' offices, secretarial offices, and judicial chambers lined the corridor. Blake found Judge Shipper's research clerk and asked for a favor. Would the clerk follow Blake into the courtroom, talk to a potential witness, ask his name, and prepare a subpoena for that person to appear for trial? The clerk gave Blake the 'I'm-not-your-secretary' look. Blake became animated and agitated, and, in the end, for the sake of proper courtroom decorum, the clerk was helpless to disagree. Upon the clerk's capitulation, Blake thanked him, and the two walked into the courtroom. Blake pointed out the old man and returned to his seat.

Jennifer was about to inquire where he had been, but Blake put his finger to his lips. A short time later, the research clerk returned, holding an official-looking document. He approached the old man. A brief, heated conversation ensued. The clerk scribbled on the document and handed it to the old man. Walsh rose in protest. The back door opened. The bailiff rose and shouted, "All rise," as Judge Shipper entered the courtroom. After the judge was seated, the bailiff shouted, "Be seated! Court is in session. The Honorable Erroll Shipper presiding."

The clerk called the case, and Father Gerry Bartholomew was brought in through the accessible side door. Walsh walked up to the counsel table and stood next to Bartholomew.

The research clerk walked up to Blake and handed him a copy of the document he served on the old man. Father Gilbert Moloney was now served with Blake's subpoena and commanded to appear at the civil trial. The "Voice" was unmasked. Blake was elated. Moloney was furious. Judge Shipper interrupted their thoughts.

"We're here to take a plea in the case of *State v. Bartholomew*, is that correct?" Judge Shipper inquired.

"It is, Your Honor," Saunders responded, with appropriate deference and formality.

"And what are the details of the plea?" the judge queried.

"May it please the court, Your Honor, Joseph Saunders, assistant Oakland County prosecutor, appearing on behalf of the people?"

"Craig Walsh, appearing for the defendant, Your Honor," Walsh chimed in, with equal formality.

"Your Honor," Saunders continued, "Defendant Bartholomew was originally charged with two counts of first-degree criminal sexual conduct. After an exhausting investigation and several meetings with the victims, investigating police officers, and representatives of the defendant, we've decided to drop the charge of first degree, to accept a guilty plea of criminal sexual conduct, fourth degree."

"Fourth degree?" the judge vacillated.

Great actor, Zack smirked. "That's correct, Your Honor."

"Is that your understanding, Mr. Walsh?" the judge inquired.

"It is, Your Honor."

"Very well, then. Let's make sure the defendant understands his rights and what he's doing." Shipper turned to Bartholomew.

The judge asked Bartholomew if he understood the charge to which he was pleading guilty. Had the plea been coerced or had the defendant been promised anything in return for the plea? Judge Shipper advised Bartholomew he had an absolute right to trial by jury as guaranteed by the Constitution of the United States. Only the defendant could waive that right. Was this defendant making this plea freely and voluntarily and pleading guilty because he was guilty? Bartholomew answered all the questions appropriately and satisfied Judge Shipper he understood the rights he was giving up and was pleading guilty knowingly and voluntarily.

Shipper proclaimed: "I'm satisfied this plea is voluntary and is being made because the defendant understands and accepts his guilt." He faced and addressed Bartholomew and asked, slight contempt in his tone. "Gerry Bartholomew, on the days in question, did you, in fact, engage in the fondling or touching of the genitalia of two minors, Jake Tracey, age twelve, and Kenneth Tracey, age fourteen?"

"Yes, sir," the predator admitted.

Jennifer flinched. To hear Gerry admit even this, his smallest offense, made her blood boil. It was small vindication, but vindication, nonetheless. She envisioned Gerry in prison. She hoped the public was watching. She wanted the whole world to know about Gerry Bartholomew. Zachary told her to relax. He had a surprise for her. She wondered what it was—she hated surprises. The judge continued.

"I'm holding a presentence report, which recommends three years' probation and community service, extensive treatment, inpatient or out, in an appropriate mental health facility. Usually, I would withhold sentencing for a sentencing hearing, but I understand both sides have agreed to recommend the court adopt this presentence report, is that correct?"

"That is correct, Your Honor." Walsh and Saunders spoke in

unison.

"Very well, then . . ." the judge continued.

"May it please the court, Your Honor?" Zachary interrupted.

"Who might you be, sir?" the judge demanded.

"Zachary Blake, attorney for the victims, Your Honor. The victims' mother, Mrs. Jennifer Tracey, pursuant to the Victims' Rights Statute, would like to address the court before sentence is pronounced."

"I apologize, Mrs. Tracey. Of course, you may address the court. Please forgive the oversight." The judge corrected himself, happy to accommodate a voting constituent.

"Thank you, Your Honor. What you are about to do is not appropriate in this case or for this man. Gerry Bartholomew is a vicious predator of children. He cannot control himself, and the church refuses to control him. They would rather transfer him from town to town and permit his decadent abuse of children, wherever he goes. They've had ample opportunity to stop him, to arrange for professional help, to prevent my children and others from becoming victims. Instead, church officials have buried their heads in the sand and made the *victims* their enemies, while coddling this criminal.

"This defendant has committed more serious offenses against my boys and others. These offenses are much more severe than those to which he pleads guilty. This defendant has sodomized children. He has *raped* children. Children in every parish he has been will bear the emotional scars of his betrayal, perhaps for the rest of their lives.

"Your Honor, you must not ignore his many past and future crimes and victims. You must not return him to Lakes or any other parish. You must hold him accountable for ruining the lives of my children and countless others. You must sentence him to the maximum allowed. You must . . ." Jennifer broke down. Blake cradled her. She buried her head in his chest.

"Your Honor? Has this plea been accepted? Has Father Bartholomew been found guilty of fourth-degree criminal sexual conduct?" Zachary inquired.

"Yes, Mr. Blake. Had Mrs. Tracey spoken up earlier . . ." the judge quavered.

"Mrs. Tracey would like to present one more witness before sentencing is pronounced. Would that be permitted in the interest of justice, Your Honor?"

Jennifer turned to Zack and whispered, "I would?"

"Yes, you would," he whispered back. "The fun's about to begin. I promised a surprise, didn't I?"

"I object, Your Honor. The Victims' Right Statute does not permit a parade of witnesses. It enables *victims* to address the court. If this potential witness isn't a victim, his testimony should be barred," a terrified Walsh argued.

"I agree," Saunders chimed in. "However, Your Honor, I am curious about who the witness is and what he has to say."

"This witness's testimony has a direct bearing on sentencing, Your Honor. Furthermore, he could not testify until Father Bartholomew was found guilty," Zack explained.

"Very well then," Shipper ruled. "I'll hear the testimony and consider its relevance to sentencing."

Zachary motioned to the sheriff's deputy stationed at the back door. "Bring in the witness, please."

The deputy opened the door, and Phillip Jack strolled into the courtroom.

"Who's he?" whispered Jennifer.

"You'll see," Zack reassured.

Bartholomew turned white.

"State your name for the record please," the clerk demanded.

"Phillip Jack."

"Your Honor? May I have the witness sworn and ask questions as an officer of the court and attorney for the victims?"

"I object!" cried Walsh. He now understood why this witness was present. "I object in the most strenuous of terms. This is beyond the scope of Victims' Rights. This witness is not a victim. As such, he has no relevant testimony to offer."

"I agree, Your Honor," Zack concurred. "This witness is not a victim. However, he has very relevant testimony to offer on the issue of sentencing, and this *is* a sentencing hearing, is it not? Your Honor, you have discretion in these matters. I guarantee the relevance of this testimony."

"I will hear the testimony because it is in my discretion to do so. I will decide its relevance. You may examine, Mr. Blake, on behalf of the victims. The clerk will swear the witness."

"Your Honor . . ." Walsh protested.

"I've made my ruling, Mr. Walsh," Judge Shipper interrupted. "Your objection is on the record. Now, sit down before I find you in contempt!" His Honor roared.

Walsh sat down in disgust. Moloney shot him the stink eye.

"Carry on, Mr. Blake."

"Thank you, Your Honor." Blake turned to Jack.

"Sir, will you state your occupation for the court?"

"Yes, I am a detective lieutenant in charge of investigations for the Berea, Ohio Police Department."

"And in that occupation, Lieutenant—may I call you, Lieutenant?"

"Yes."

"And in that occupation, sir, did you have occasion to meet the defendant, Gerry Bartholomew?"

Blake turned to Bartholomew, who looked like he might crawl under a table or jump out the third-story window. Blake hoped for the latter.

"I did," Jack responded.

"Can you tell the court the circumstances of that meeting?"

"Yes, sir, I sure can." Jack was eager to expose Bartholomew.

"Please do so."

"Two families from Berea, members of St. Pat's Church, came to me and charged Bartholomew over there with sexually abusing their sons. I investigated the matter, confirmed, with hard evidence, the charges were true, and arrested Bartholomew on charges of criminal sexual conduct."

"What degree of criminal sexual conduct, Lieutenant?"

"First," Jack testified.

"What was the final result of those charges, Lieutenant?"

"The father copped a plea," Jack grunted.

"Copped a plea to what?"

"Fourth degree, Criminal sexual conduct. Damnedest thing I ever saw. He was permitted to plea off the record. The file was sealed. No jail time, three years' probation, everyone present was sworn to secrecy. My pension was threatened if I so much as uttered a word that the hearing even took place," he recounted.

"Were the victims and their parents present?"

"Yeah, they were there. Didn't speak, though. After the hearing, they disappeared. Took off in the middle of the night. No one's heard from them since. Word is they've been bought off and are now running scared." Jack enjoyed the moment.

"Scared?"

"Yeah, until tonight, when Bartholomew pleaded guilty, no police or court officer could disclose the plea bargain. The only people who might have talked were the victims. If they were eliminated, no one could talk."

"Objection! This is absurd. Eliminated? Sounds like something out of a Bond movie," cried Walsh.

"Yeah, well tell that to Gus, the janitor at St. Pat's. He turned up dead," Jack snarled.

"Your objection, Mr. Walsh, is overruled," ordered Judge Shipper. "Continue, Mr. Blake. I am finding the lieutenant's testimony quite interesting. May I also state, for the record, that before accepting this plea, I was assured there was no prior conduct of this sort by this defendant."

"I'm sure you were, Your Honor. That's the church's MO. Get rid of one charge, go on to the next. Transfer the guy from town to town in the meanwhile," Zack piled on.

"Objection!" cried an exacerbated Walsh.

"Sit down, Mr. Walsh, and don't get up again," roared Judge Shipper.

Walsh sat down in a huff. He looked over to the old priest. Zack caught a glimpse of Moloney's face. *If looks could kill . . .*

"Are you aware of any other charges and convictions against Father Bartholomew, Lieutenant?" Zack inquired.

"No, but I haven't checked with authorities at other locations he's been. I'd need a list of all his previous placements."

"You shall have one, Lieutenant," Judge Shipper commanded. "I've heard enough. I'm going to reserve the issue of sentencing until Detective Lieutenant Jack reports back to me regarding his investigation into Father Bartholomew's prior conduct. Lieutenant, I presume you wish to place the defendant in custody on his probation violation, am I correct?"

"You are, Your Honor."

"Objection! Your Honor!" Walsh screeched.

"Your objection is noted, Mr. Walsh. The defendant is remanded to the custody of Detective Lieutenant Phillip Jack of the Berea Police Department for incarceration on his probation violation. The lieutenant is to have the defendant brought to my courtroom for further sentencing upon completion of his investigation. I hereby order officials of the church to release to Lieutenant Jack copies of Father Bartholomew's personnel file with special attention given to locations and parishes where this defendant has previously served. Is that understood, Mr. Walsh?"

"Yes, Your Honor."

"Any violation of this order will result in contempt of court. The offending party or parties *will* be spending time in the Oakland County Jail. Am I understood?"

Walsh sighed. He managed a very quiet, "Yes, Your Honor."

"Very well, then, we're adjourned." The judge pounded his gavel.

"All rise!" shouted the bailiff. The judge rose and left the courtroom.

Zachary looked at Jennifer. She was beaming. "Blake, you done good," she gushed. Then, she hugged him, in open court.

Chapter Forty-Six

Micah and the two families arrived at City Airport and were greeted at the arrival gate by a limousine driver, arranged by Love Investigations. Micah instructed the driver to drive to the Doubletree Suites Hotel in Southfield. The driver headed west on I-94 to I-696 west and into the Southfield area. They passed the impressive Town Center complex, where Zachary Blake's office was located in his heyday. Micah pointed out the buildings to the families. The Doubletree was a short distance northwest of the Town Center complex. Love checked the families in under their aliases. He advised them to stay as close to the hotel as possible and promised to return shortly to check on them. He contacted his office and arranged for around-the-clock surveillance. He reentered the limo and directed the driver to Blake's eight-mile office. Zack and Jennifer were returning from court as the limo pulled into the pot-holed parking lot.

"Hey, Counselor, how go the wars?" Micah inquired.

"Micah! Damn it, man, I told you to call me!" Zack fumed. "Where have you been? What's going on? Did you talk to them? Will they testify? What—"

"Hold your horses, Zack. Let me explain." Micah adopted a pensive posture and told Zack everything—the arrest of the Voice's surveillance team, the Disney World gambit, the airport switcheroo, the families' current location, everything. Zack had to be impressed.

"Disney World, huh? Wow, Micah! Brilliant! Finding a family at a Disney resort would be like finding a needle in a haystack."

"You are correct, sir. I am a genius," Love agreed. He turned to Jennifer. "And how are you, madam?"

"I'm wonderful, Micah," she giggled. "Tonight has been filled with nothing but good news. Zack promised you were the best, and he was right! Thank you for everything." She planted a kiss on his cheek. Micah blushed.

"You're quite welcome," he managed. "What happened in

court?"

"Oh, Micah!" Jennifer exclaimed. "It was wonderful. I'll let Zack explain."

Zack replayed the court proceedings for Micah.

"Worked like a charm, just like you planned, huh? They had no idea Jack was testifying? Amazing! All of this undercover, cloak-and-dagger stuff, all that money, and it all came together, like clockwork. I've got to hand it to us. We do good work!" Micah boasted.

"It ain't over 'till it's over," Zack cautioned. "We've still got a week before trial. We must keep the MacLean and O'Connell families hidden and safe."

"Don't worry, Zack. Everything's under control," Micah assured.

"I mean it, Micah. We can't get overconfident. These families must testify. The plea in Berea is powerful stuff, but it still doesn't prove the church knew about the prior incident. The file was sealed. They could argue Gerry worked it out for himself, with his lawyer, and the church never knew anything."

"That's bullshit, Zack. No one would believe that," Micah snorted.

"Why not? With no one to testify to a church payoff, a jury might believe anything. The families *must* testify. Their testimony and Jack's are the keys to success," Zack insisted.

"How did the Detective Lieutenant perform in court?" Micah wondered.

"He was great," Jennifer beamed. "So was Zack. The judge was all set to rubber-stamp the sentence agreement until Lieutenant Jack walked in. A few questions and answers later, presto! Probation turns into at least five years. You should have been there, Micah. It was wonderful!"

"I'm sure it was, Jennifer. Well, I've got to get back to the hotel and check on my surveillance teams," Micah indicated. "I think I might move one of the couples. Keep them separate, you know. How's that sound?"

"Sounds smart," Zack agreed. "Take every precaution."

"All right, then. I'll check with you in the morning."

Micah took the limo back to the hotel. He informed the driver he would no longer need transportation, paid him, gave him a large tip, and sent him on his way.

Chapter Forty-Seven

Micah went to the eighth floor of the hotel where the families were staying in adjoining rooms. He found them together watching television. One guard was with them. Two others were in the adjoining room.

Micah didn't like switching things around, but Zack was the man in charge. "Listen, I think it's best to split you up. Put you in two different hotels."

"Why?" Mr. O'Connell protested. "Things seem perfectly fine here."

"And won't that stretch you a bit thin?" Mrs. MacLean added.

Micah rubbed his chin. "We're just being safe. I'll make a few calls, see what I can put together." He motioned to the guard, who joined Micah in the second room. Two guards in the adjoining room were also watching television, but not the same kind. They watched the lobby, seventh-floor, and eighth-floor video from the equipment they set up upon arrival.

"All quiet so far?" Micah inquired.

One of the men nodded. They'd booked a room on the seventh-floor and paid the clerk at the front desk to tell anybody who came looking for them that they'd booked that room. A costly maneuver on Love's part, but he was hoping it would pay off in the long term.

Love started scrolling through his phone for the number for another hotel when someone entered the lobby. Everybody in the room perked up. Three men went to the front desk, walking with precision and intent most weary travelers lacked when they entered a hotel. These men had no luggage, another red flag for Love. A few seconds later, three more men entered. Love couldn't hear what they asked the clerk, but his nervous glance into the security camera told Love everything he needed to know. The church wasn't about to let things go any further. Micah jumped to his feet in a second, barking out orders.

Chapter Forty-Eight

Kenny Tracey was a good baseball player. He played on his school team and was also involved in a weekly, hotly contested neighborhood-versus-neighborhood pickup game. Two boys, one from each neighborhood, were responsible for calling all the boys in their respective neighborhoods until each side had at least ten ballplayers. Ironically, the game was played every Saturday on Lakes' baseball field.

Jake frequently tagged along, as an extra player, although he wasn't a good ballplayer. On the Saturday before the trial, Kenny received the usual, "Wanna play today?" phone call. He asked Jake if he wanted to play, and Jake shouted an emphatic "Yes!" Kenny was less enthusiastic about the game. He was nervous about the trial but decided to play for Jake and the other guys in his neighborhood. Kenny Tracey was the ultimate team player.

As they walked to the park, Jake looked up at Kenny.

"Kenny?"

"Yeah, Jake?" His thoughts were elsewhere.

"Something wrong?"

"No, squirt. Just thinkin'."

"About what?"

"The trial. I guess I'm a little nervous. You?"

"Yeah, I guess. But this is important to Mom, and Zack seems like a good guy. Right? But what if they want us to talk about the things Gerry did to us . . . you know . . . the sex stuff? I don't want to talk about stuff like that in front of all those people. I know I'm supposed to be brave, but . . . I'm scared, Kenny."

Kenny relaxed and played big brother. "Me too, squirt. But it's kind of too late to back out now, don't you think? Besides, I don't want to let Mom down. A bad guy like this gets away with shit, and he'll do the same thing to some other kid. How bad can it be to talk about it? We got over talking about it to Doc Rothenberg, right?"

"You and Mom will be there the whole time, right?" Jake shuddered.

"Yeah, squirt, the whole time. Hey, come on. Let's not think about it." He changed the subject. "So, if there aren't enough players today, what position do you want to play?"

"I stink. You know that," Jake admitted, hanging his head. "I'll play wherever they put me."

"You don't stink, bro. These guys are older than you. You'll be better than these bums, one of these days, when you get older," Kenny cheered.

They arrived at the baseball field. There were barely enough players, so Jake got to play the whole game in right field. He got a hit and made a good running catch. He also let a ball go right through his legs for an inside-the-park home run—they didn't count errors—but that was baseball.

Kenny had three hits, played flawless shortstop, and hit a game-winning, walk-off home run in the bottom of the ninth. Jake was the first to greet Kenny as his brother crossed home plate. The whole team celebrated the sudden victory. This was the happiest the two boys had been since the camping trip. Best of all, not a single kid brought up the looming trial or anything about the case. Jake and Kenny walked home together, broad smiles on their faces, recounting game highlights. The trial was the furthest thing from their minds.

Chapter Forty-Nine

"Gone? What do you mean 'gone'? Where the hell did they go, Micah?" Zack was frantic. He'd just fallen asleep on perhaps the best night of his legal career when sleep was interrupted by a phone call. The Berea families were gone. The case, most likely, was gone with them. "Kidnapped?"

"It sure looks that way," Micah dreaded.

"What are the chances they escaped?"

"No clue. There were at least six men, probably more outside. Escape is possible, I guess, but doubtful. We've got some footage from the security cameras, but it doesn't show us what happened to the families," Micah conceded.

"Text it to me," Zack demanded. Two minutes later, his phone buzzed.

Zack studied video footage from a few hours ago. The screen split into three images—the lobby, the seventh-floor hallway, and the eighth-floor hallway. Micah had viewed it already, but for Zack, the whole thing was torture. Six armed men entered the lobby. In the eighth-floor video, two of the security men rushed into the hallway. Love and another man were left to guard the families.

The six assailants went up the stairs and were lost for a bit—Micah fast-forwarded the video. Four more men emerged from the seventh-floor decoy room. The elevator door opened, and a man got out, distracting the four guards. At the same time, six men burst out of the stairwell and stunned two of the guards with some kind of dart gun. The other two guards struggled with the seven men for a while but were completely outnumbered and outmaneuvered.

The assailants opened the room and found it empty. Immediately they split into three groups and headed for the stairs.

On eight, Micah led the families to the back stairway. They passed from view, and Micah turned off the tape.

"What happened next?" Zack demanded.

"We went out the back way and were ambushed by more of these guys. I took them down, but by the time I finished the last guy off, the families were nowhere to be seen. I don't know if they escaped or got kidnapped," Micah cringed

"Shit! Shit, shit, shit, shit, shit, shit, shit, *shit*! I've got the biggest trial of my life in a week, and my star witnesses are gone? Shit! *Shit, shit, shit!* What am I going to tell Jenny?"

"It's all my fault," Micah conceded. "I'll tell her."

"No, no, I'll tell her, and, Micah, what more could you have done? You've been amazing, man. I'm sorry I got so pissed off."

"You have a right to be pissed off, Zack. I blew it. I wish I knew how, though. I was so careful. I did everything right. God damn it! I promised those people! I looked them in the eyes and *guaranteed* their safety."

"Let's think this through," Zack paused. "If they've got them, they'll kill them or make them disappear. If they don't have them, maybe John or Pat will contact us before trial."

"No, they won't," Micah argued. "Why should they? I guaranteed their safety, and I fucked it all up. Why should they trust me? No, Zack, presume they aren't coming."

"Damn! We were so close. I could taste it!" Zack scoffed. "So, either way, they're gone. That leaves me with the guilty plea, Phillip Jack, Rothenberg, the Tracey family, the Farmington cops, Costigan, Glimesh, and Foley. I'll have to subpoena Foley. I can force him to admit to knowledge and the priors. I've got Bartholomew's deposition. He took the Fifth for almost every question, but it will piss off any jury. Jurors will assume his guilt."

"I thought that was a lock. I thought you were looking for priors to nail the church," Micah presumed.

"You thought right, but first, I still have to prove the charged offenses occurred," Zack explained. "Gerry pleaded guilty to Fourth Degree 'touching' only. It's still possible, if I get a large verdict against Bartholomew, the church might negotiate and pay the verdict for public relations reasons."

"That's true, Zack, but damn, those families! I *guaranteed* their safety. If anything happened to them . . ."

"And the impact of their testimony in front of a jury would

have been unbelievable," Zack ruminated. "Micah, you're a private investigator, right?"

"Right?"

"You find missing people, right?"

"Yeah?"

"Find them, dammit!"

"Way ahead of you on that score. My guys are turning the area upside down as we speak. If the families are still around town, we'll find them. We did it once—we can do it again." He tried to convince himself, as well as Zack Blake.

"That's what I want to hear! Go do your fucking job! Seriously, Micah, if you're doing everything you can possibly do to find them, what more can I ask? Keep me posted."

"I will, Zack. I won't sleep until I find them," Micah promised.

"I know you'll do your best."

Zack hung up the phone. What a colossal blunder! Micah had done a great job on this case. He found the priors, the investigating cop, the plea agreement, and the families, only to lose them.

Can I win the case without them? He doubted it. Oh, he'd win all right. He'd get a large verdict against the priest—a penniless scumbag cloaked with a vow of poverty. The church's contribution would be nothing compared to the size of the verdict. It might be a nice payday. He'd do the best he could with what he had and let the chips fall where they may. He still had a good case. The jury would hate Bartholomew. Perhaps they'd punish the church for the sin of *employing* him. The families might still show up. Did he have enough evidence to convince a jury the church knew of Bartholomew's propensities and covered it up? Jack could convince them of that, couldn't he? *Maybe.* His whole case was now reduced to a big maybe.

Chapter Fifty

Zachary Blake spent the rest of the week in his office, researching the law and preparing his trial brief. He constructed proposed jury instructions and *voir dire* (questions asked of proposed jurors to determine whether they were suitable to serve on the jury). He went over the proposed testimony with the Tracey family and Dr. Rothenberg. The boys still found it difficult to talk about their ordeal, but Rothenberg had done a marvelous job. In sample video testimony, the boys were articulate, direct, and sympathetic. Jennifer was compelling, describing shock and pain upon discovering the repulsive betrayal of faith and the severe emotional and physical harm done to her children.

Rothenberg was strong and professional. He was, with Zack's expert testimonial coaching support, able to describe the family's trauma understandably and humanly, without resorting to complicated medical terminology. Zack gave each of them copies of their depositions and instructed them to review the transcript so their testimony would be consistent with the depos.

Zack spent hours on the phone with Walsh, faxing proposed jury instructions, back and forth, in an effort to focus the areas of disagreement. The trial judge would appreciate the effort but would expect no less. The more trial lawyers agreed upon, the easier the judge's job. Zack did not want to try his case before a pissed-off judge.

Trial would begin the following day. Zack and Jennifer had just finished eating takeout dinner. He was working on the most crucial phase of the trial, his opening statement. Zack believed trials could be won and lost on opening remarks. Jennifer was scrolling through her phone.

Zack had difficulty with the opening. An opening statement is a promise of proof. The attorney informs the jury what the evidence will show. Make promises during the opening; keep those promises during the trial. He wanted to be able to prove everything he promised.

He could prove Bartholomew molested the boys and sought to cover up his acts. He could prove Bartholomew molested other children and covered up those acts as well. He could prove the abuse had a devastating and traumatic impact on the boys' lives and the life of their mother.

Zack could not directly prove, however, the church's knowledge of the predator priest's vile propensities prior to the boys' molestation. He had evidence to *suggest* knowledge and cover-up, but no smoking gun. The church would argue Bartholomew duped them, the same way he duped victims' families. Officials would claim as soon as Bartholomew's behavior was brought to their attention, they suspended him and offered treatment to his victims, performed brilliantly by the church's own doctor, Dr. Rothenberg.

It was a compelling argument. After all, who'd care to believe the church would sanction and cover up such abhorrent behavior? What direct proof did Zachary have to support his contentions? If he couldn't prove them, should he offer to do so in his opening? Hence, his dilemma, but what real choice did Zach have? He had to provide proof of the church's direct involvement. There would be no chance of a verdict against the church unless he made the offer of proof and figured out a way to prove it.

Concern about *substance* morphed into concern about *style*. Blake bought a full-length mirror and attached it to the back of his office door. He hadn't tried a jury case in years, and even when he was trying them successfully, he was never the great orator. The only way to overcome that problem was to rehearse, so he stood in front of the mirror, notes in his hand, uncomfortable with how he looked in his own eyes.

"This is the first of two opportunities I will have to address you directly, ladies and gentlemen," he began. *Is it too obvious a way to open? Don't the jurors already know that?* "This presentation is called the opening statement."

He saw Jennifer in the reflection. She'd stopped looking at her phone and was watching him. Their eyes met, and then she looked away, seeking something else to occupy herself. She settled on the remnants of dinner.

"It's my opportunity as the plaintiff's lawyer to tell you what I intend to prove," Zack continued. *No,* he thought, *that's using opportunity too much.* "Its purpose is for the lawyers to tell you what they intend to prove." *That's better.* "This is very important because the second—"

Jennifer dropped a paper cup, and ice spilled across the floor. "Sorry," she apologized.

Zack, distracted, tried not to break stride. "The second time I address you will be when we're all done here." *No, that's not right. Sounds too casual . . .* "will be at the end of the trial. That address is called the closing argument."

The ruckus of ice being dumped into the bathroom sink interrupted him a second time. "Sorry again," Jennifer squeaked, embarrassed, returning to the room. She crumpled up papers and bags from the table.

"At that time, I will summarize the evidence submitted in proof of the case. Why is this important? Because, and listen—"

He glanced at Jennifer, standing behind him, looking at him in the mirror. "Can I get by you for a second. I need to take out the trash."

It took every ounce of patience Zack could muster not to toss his notes into the air in frustration. "Listen," he sighed, trying not to sound as annoyed as he felt, "maybe you should head home for the night. I'm going to be at this for a while, and I need some quiet time."

"Oh . . ." she sputtered. "Oh . . . okay. I get it. I'll drop this by the dumpster on my way out."

She backtracked, gathered her purse and coat, and gave Zack a peck on the cheek. "Sounds good so far," she encouraged. "I'm sure you're going to do great."

After Jennifer left, Zack worked his way back into the proper frame of mind. When trying a case to a jury, He preferred to stand at a podium, pages of notes on its surface, politely shifting his gaze back and forth from the jury to his notes. Zack has no idea what Walsh's style was, but he wanted desperately to speak from the heart to this jury, in *this* trial. He spent hours fine-tuning the statement, pacing the room, talking to his invisible jury, critiquing his own performance. He was dissatisfied, but worse, he couldn't complete his masterpiece unless he could prove the church's involvement. As he was completing a final draft, the telephone rang. Blake picked up the receiver.

"Zachary Blake."

"Mr. Blake?"

"Who's this?" Blake queried, suspicious.

"A friend," a voice whispered, male, young perhaps, late twenties, early thirties.

"What can I do for you, friend?"

"More a matter of what I can do for you, Mr. Blake." The stranger offered an olive branch.

"Okay. What can you do for me?" Blake was cautiously intrigued.

"Within the church hierarchy, there's an organization known as 'the Coalition.' It operates in secret and handles matters that may embarrass the church. Its primary function is to prevent scandal so the church may continue to work to better society."

"Go on," Blake encouraged.

"Over the past several years, a disturbing trend began to surface among the clergy. We discovered an alarming number of priests worldwide had been sexually abusing young male parishioners. While the number is relatively small, the trend is disturbing. The ratio for our clergy is higher than that of abusers to normal men in other occupations."

"Gerry Bartholomew is one of those priests," Blake concluded.

"I'm afraid he is. His tendencies were known as far back as the seminary. After he received extensive treatment and our psychiatrists pronounced him fit for parish placement."

"Incredible," Blake exclaimed. "According to my research for this case, pedophilia is a treatable, but incurable condition. The worst place for a pedophile is a church."

"Probably true, Mr. Blake, but with a frightening shortage of priests and a forgiving platform, our natural tendency is to forgive, attempt treatment, and permit these men to resume their calling. Psychiatrists assured us, with treatment, these men learn to control their urges. We determined it was the human thing to do."

"When it endangers innocent, unsuspecting children and their families? Lives are being ruined," Blake grumbled.

"As I indicated, few placements were made, and only after treatment was declared successful. In many cases, offending priests graduate from the seminary without anyone knowing they are pedophiles. The church only discovers these predators after an incident occurs, the more common occurrence. In fact, Father Gerry is the only case I'm aware of where extensive treatment failed, and child sexual abuse resulted."

"Even giving the church the benefit of the doubt, Bartholomew should have been defrocked after the O'Connell and MacLean boys were abused," Blake stated the obvious.

"The Farmington placement was a horrible mistake in assignment. His placement was to a monastery. Somehow two assignments were accidentally switched. The results, of course, have been devastating."

"You think? Tell this to Jennifer Tracey! Talk to her sons," Blake snarled. "So, you guys screwed this up. Why not come clean, admit the mistake, and offer a fair resolution and an apology. That's all Jennifer ever wanted. Instead, we have two missing families, a dead janitor, a fucked-up priest, and a very angry Jennifer Tracey."

"The janitor is . . . is . . . dead? Are you sure?" The caller stuttered.

"Absolutely. You mean you didn't know?" Blake gasped.

"We were told he was taken care of. "

"Well, that's one way of looking at it. Where are the O'Connell and MacLean families? I need them in court tomorrow," he demanded.

"I have no idea. The Coalition was consulted and voted to ensure silence. Two of us dissented to this and other clandestine practices regarding this case. I argued the church should do as you have suggested—'come clean,' as you say, apologize, provide treatment, remove Bartholomew from the priesthood, and generously compensate the victims. After all, we are all church members, equals in the eyes of God. The vote was to ensure silence. If these people have disappeared, it may be the work of our leader. I can't be positive."

"This is all very interesting. It would make for excellent testimony at the trial and assure the 'generous compensation' you mentioned."

"I've called you at great personal risk, Mr. Blake. I'm not sure I can testify, but I'll contemplate it. Meanwhile, you've subpoenaed our leader, and you could pose these questions to him."

Of course! Blake remembered. *The old priest at the first meeting and the plea bargain!* He'd almost forgotten. How could he forget that smug face? The judge's research clerk served him at the plea hearing. *What was his name?*

"He won't be forthcoming," Blake opined.

"Let's see what develops. If I'm needed, I'll make myself known and testify."

"Sounds fair. How do I reach you?"

"I'll reach *you*, Mr. Blake. Goodnight . . . and good luck."

The caller hung up before Blake could thank him. Did this call move the case from the edge of defeat? If Blake couldn't get the old man to crack, this young priest—Blake assumed he was a priest—might testify to the church's clandestine placement and cover-up operations. *These guys handled and bungled this entire thing. Incredible!*

Blake finished writing his opening statement. He continued to recite to the mirror, repeatedly, pacing around a make-believe courtroom, well into the night. He couldn't sleep. Tomorrow was the biggest day of his life. He was ready, he decided. Tomorrow, Zachary Blake and the Tracey family would begin the end of their quest for justice. Blake turned back to the mirror.

"Ladies and gentlemen of the jury, my name is Zachary Blake, and I represent the plaintiffs . . ."

Chapter Fifty-One

" . . . Jennifer Tracey and her sons, Jake and Kenny."

Trial had begun. Trial briefs were presented to the court. Jury instructions were debated for most of the morning. Judge John Perry conducted *voir dire*. He even permitted the lawyers to ask various questions. Would wonders never cease?

Perry was an older man with greasy hair and a bad dye job. He was a smart judge, a former plaintiff attorney, and a perfect draw for Blake's case. Judge Perry was acutely aware religion would play an important role in the trial. Thus, the religious attitudes of the jury pool were vital to the attorneys, and Perry extended wide latitude to both attorneys.

After an arduous process, the jury was assembled. It was comprised of seven people – four women and three men, six jurors and one alternate. The alternate was not identified until the case was submitted to the jury. For the time being, all seven would hear the case.

Blake tried to select as many young mothers to the jury as possible. All four women selected fit the bill. He was much less confident of the men, but experience told him he wanted blue-collar, not corporate types. Two of the three men fit the bill. He was satisfied with the process and the selected jurors. Utopia, thought Zachary, would be for the alternate to be the lone corporate-type male. On the flip side, if the guy made the cut, he'd probably be the foreperson.

Blake scanned the courtroom. He saw no one who might be his mysterious caller. The trial was televised. Perhaps the caller would follow the proceedings on television. The Coalition leader sat in the first row of the gallery, clutching his subpoena. No sign of the MacLean or O'Connell families, Blake expected them to be a no-show.

Judge Perry invited Blake to proceed with his opening statement. Blake rose and introduced himself and his clients to the jury. He took a deep breath. *There was nothing at stake in front of the mirror.*

"This is the first of two opportunities I will have to address you directly, ladies and gentlemen. This presentation is called the opening statement. Its purpose is for the lawyers to tell you what they intend to prove. This is very important because the second time I address you will be at the end of the trial. That address is called the closing argument. At that time, I will summarize the evidence presented in proof of the case.

"Why is this important? Because—and listen carefully . . ." He walked over to the jury box, leaned on the polished wooden railing, and looked each juror in the eye. The technique proved effective. Each juror was poised, waiting for this important tidbit of information. "If Mr. Walsh or I promise to prove something to you in our opening statement, you must hear evidence supporting that promise during the trial. That evidence should be highlighted and reviewed in closing argument. If you haven't heard evidence proving that point, the attorney's burden has not been met. Opening statements are not evidence, nor are closing arguments. *Evidence* comes *only* from the testimony of witnesses and parties, and the exhibits presented.

Opening statements are still important, though. Why? They represent an attorney's roadmap for the case, his promise to prove the truth of *all* his assertions. If he strays off course, fails to prove what he promised, you must hold him accountable for this failure. If, however, he proves each assertion and identifies these proofs in closing argument, reward him and his client with your verdict.

Please listen carefully to my promises of proof. Listen to Mr. Walsh's offers of proof. I will prove each and every assertion I make in this opening statement. Hold me to this promise. Do the same with Mr. Walsh. If you do, you'll render a sizeable verdict for the plaintiffs in this case."

Challenged to listen carefully to Blake's opening, the jury did just that. Zack spun a riveting tale, starting with the death of Jennifer's husband, the boys' father. He described how the widow and her family turned to the church for comfort and received it for three years from Father Bill. Zack described Father Bill's sudden transfer, the subsequent arrival of Bartholomew, and of the ill-fated camping trip that shattered their lives. He described the elaborate cover-up, the hiring of Dr. Rothenberg, the telephone-tapping operations, and conversations with Costigan. Rothenberg would testify his phones were tapped. He would describe the boys' condition when he first saw them, the progress they have made, their present condition, and the traumatic events that caused their condition.

"The church knew of Bartholomew's propensities to molest children, before placing him at Lakes. Because of their perceived shortage of priests, church officials, with knowledge aforethought, covered up his history. They welcomed a child predator into the priesthood, but, worse, they placed this predator in a *parish,* with many young boys to prey upon. We will present testimonial evidence from a *member* of the secret church organization whose job it was to cover up these acts and save the church from embarrassment. We have video footage of certain parties, associated with the church, breaking into a hotel where families of the previous victims were staying. We will present testimonial evidence of Bartholomew's prior abuses in Berea, Ohio, the church's cover-up of those crimes, and their transfer of this predator to Michigan, with no public warning."

This was a risky promise. Zack could prove the prior predatory conduct through evidence of the plea bargain and Jack's testimony. Unless the MacLean and O'Connell families showed up and testified, he could *not* prove that the church knew of the charges or the plea. Phillip Jack could not attest to the church's direct knowledge.

Zack also promised to present testimony from a member of the Coalition. If the mystery caller refused to come forward, this testimony would have to come from Moloney, who would not be truthful. Zack hoped the jury would assume the truth, but he *prayed* for the miracle that all would show up and testify. This was the weakest part of his case, and the jury could easily reject his claims for lack of evidence.

He moved on to damages, describing the devastating effect these heinous acts had on the Tracey family. He promised testimony from the plaintiffs, family members, teachers, friends, Costigan, and Rothenberg to prove the traumatic result. Blake concluded a brilliant oratory by asking for a huge damages award, arguing the proofs would justify any sized award he ultimately decided upon. Blake thanked the jurors for their kind attention and advised he trusted them to do the right thing.

Zack returned to his seat, having delivered the best opening statement of his career. Jennifer patted his hand and smiled her appreciation. Judge Perry glanced at his watch and announced the hour was late. He adjourned for the day, a positive development for the case. The jury would now spend the night reflecting only on Zack's version of events, with no contradictions from the defense. If only he could deliver on his promises . . .

Chapter Fifty-Two

Walsh was low-key but impressive on opening statement. According to the evidence, Bartholomew was convicted of fourth-degree criminal sexual conduct, simple genital touching. Blake, Tracey, and the boys were grossly exaggerating the scope of conduct.

"Further," continued Walsh, "the church had no knowledge of the events in either the Berea or Farmington. Bartholomew hid his activities and proclivities from the hierarchy, and church officials are grateful to Mrs. Tracey for bringing the matter to their attention. After she did so, the church removed Bartholomew from the parish and placed him into treatment.

Church official volunteered to pay for treatment for the boys, despite having no obligation to do so. They referred the boys to Dr. Rothenberg, who Mr. Blake says has been terrific for the boys. The church is the single largest charitable institution in the world and does more good things for society than all other charitable institutions combined. A secret organization within its hierarchy, whose purpose is to cover up criminal acts and punish parishioners? An absurd premise!" Walsh invited the jury to use common sense to completely dismiss this notion.

"Something happened to the boys—there is no doubt of that. But the church is not responsible for the actions of a rogue priest. We are in this lawsuit only because the wrongdoer has taken an oath of poverty. The church, on the other hand, has deep pockets. A judgment against the church is against the great weight of the evidence. Such judgment will also pilfer money from a worthy charity.

"Mr. Blake says the church was involved in a cover-up, hold Mr. Blake to his promise and make sure he *proves* this serious accusation. Where are his witnesses? Where are the so-called previous victims? Mr. Blake must produce these victims, and they must testify the church was involved. Mark my words, ladies and gentlemen, they will not be at this trial because they do not exist." He returned to his table and sat down, never taking his eyes off the jury.

Zack thought Walsh's opening statement was fine. The jury was attentive. But, Zack felt Walsh lacked conviction, like his heart wasn't in it. The jury could believe the case was exaggerated, a veiled money grab, especially if the families failed to appear. After all, Walsh told them to make Blake *prove* his allegations, and Blake didn't have the proof.

After Walsh sat down, Perry instructed Blake to call his first witness. The show was about to begin in earnest. Zack was ready.

"Plaintiffs call Father Gilbert Moloney to the stand, under the adverse party statute." Zack read the name from the subpoena. The surprised older priest, seated beside Walsh at the defense counsel table, rose and approached. The anonymous Voice now had a name. He was not all-powerful and was no longer a mystery. He was a mortal, merely a man in a place where the person in power was Zachary Blake. The witness was sworn in and took the stand.

"Please state your name and occupation for the record?" Blake demanded, positioned at the jury box, so Moloney had to face the jury when answering his questions.

"Father Gilbert Moloney, employed by the church's North American Division."

"What, exactly, do you do for the division, Father Moloney?"

The title of respect was distasteful to Blake, but he believed the jury would view such lack of respect with disfavor.

"I supervise parish bishops, priests, and lay employees."

"Oh, and do you do this in a public or private fashion?"

"I don't know what you mean."

"Do the bishops and priests know you're their supervisor?"

"Some do, most do not."

"In fact, you operate in secret, don't you?"

"You could say that," Moloney conceded. He rolled his eyes to emphasize the meaningless point. Zack believed it was essential to confirm the existence of a hierarchy operating in secret. A secret organization within the church was vital to exposing the cover-up. He bore in.

"You guess?" Zack sneered. "'The Coalition,' the name of

your little group, is deliberately clandestine, isn't it?"

The Voice paused. If he was shocked, he concealed it well. He spoke calmly and succinctly.

"Secrecy is necessary for effectiveness. Coalition members attend services, church functions, outings, and so on, as parishioners rather than supervisors. We don't want employees showing off for their bosses. We want them to be themselves, to observe how they handle day-to-day job functions. The program works quite well. We have the finest clergy and lay staff in the country."

Zack was impressed with this reasoned response. Of course, the Coalition was necessary. This witness could handle tough questions and think on his feet. Zack would have to show the jury the Coalition's true calling.

"Except for Father Gerry Bartholomew," countered Zachary.

"Father Gerry expertly hid his activities from us, Mr. Blake. We can't be everywhere or prevent everything," reasoned Moloney.

Another good answer, Moloney is smooth! Maybe I could get him to admit that one man's "we can't prevent everything" was another's "negligence" and a verdict against the church . . . "It is my understanding the church knew of Gerry's tendencies toward pedophilia during his seminary years. In fact, didn't the church provide professional treatment for that condition?" He approached the witness and got as close to Moloney as Judge Perry would permit.

Zachary knew the statement was true. So did Moloney, but without the mystery caller, Zack couldn't prove it. Would Moloney admit it?

"That is absolutely untrue, Mr. Blake," the Voice lied. "The church turned over all its files on Father Bartholomew. There is nothing to substantiate such a charge. I know winning this case is important to you—there is a great deal of money at stake—but this charge is irresponsible."

Moloney was well-coached and saw an opportunity to go on offense. He mentioned money as a motive to sensationalize. The courtroom buzzed at the response and Perry slammed his gavel, ordering noisy spectators to be quiet.

"Order in the court. If you people can't behave yourselves, I will clear this courtroom."

"Objection, Your Honor!" cried Zack. "Move to strike everything after 'that is absolutely untrue' as nonresponsive and ask the jury be instructed to disregard. Please order this witness to refrain from making speeches and to limit his answers to the questions he is asked."

"So ordered," Judge Perry agreed. "All comments after 'That is absolutely untrue' are hereby stricken. The jury is admonished to disregard."

Perry turned to Moloney and glared down at him from the bench. "Father Moloney, please listen to the question, answer the question, and refrain from making speeches."

"Yes, Your Honor," Moloney whispered.

The courtroom fell silent. Blake and Moloney played cat-and-mouse throughout the morning. The Voice dodged numerous questions, but Zack began to wear him down and gained confidence in the process. Moloney's answers appeared to be rehearsed or practiced. There was arrogance about him, a 'you-can't-touch-me-or-my-church' tone that Zack hoped the jury picked up on.

On the other hand, according to Moloney, the church knew nothing of Gerry's previous propensities, and nothing about the MacLean or O'Connell families. Blake mentioned the previous victims by name, and Moloney didn't even flinch. The church knew nothing of Bartholomew's prior convictions and had no part in any plea bargain of the charges in this case.

As far as Moloney knew, the charges were reduced because Fourth Degree Criminal Sexual Conduct was the crime of which Gerry was guilty. Blake would need the families or the mystery caller to testify. Blake prayed the families were out there, somewhere, watching the proceedings on television. Perhaps the caller was too, equally angered by the Voice's smug testimony.

Walsh's cross-examination was brilliant. He developed the priest's curriculum vitae and went through his entire distinguished career, his parish work, his charitable work, and his work with children. Moloney counseled and nurtured the children. Moloney described personal community outreach for which he received citizenship awards and decrees.

Finally, he discussed the Coalition. He made it sound as though it was not clandestine at all. It was merely an effort to monitor parishes and respond to the needs of the community. When Walsh concluded his cross-examination late in the afternoon, Blake wondered if Moloney might be in line for sainthood.

Rather than start the testimony of another witness so late in the day, Judge Perry adjourned until the next day. It was not a good start for the plaintiff. Zachary needed help from someone, somewhere. He wondered about the missing families and the mystery caller. Then he realized he was being selfish and hoped, prayed, they were out there somewhere, alive and well.

***

Blake sat alone in his office, burning the midnight oil, preparing for the testimony of Jennifer, the boys, and Rothenberg. He couldn't decide which order to present these witnesses, so he prepared for all four witnesses at the same time. He also wanted Micah on the stand to discuss Berea. He was deeply engrossed with writing practice questions for Jennifer and Rothenberg when the telephone rang.

"Zachary Blake."

"I watched the proceedings yesterday, and today, Mr. Blake," advised the mystery caller. "Your tenacity is impressive. You couldn't shake Father Gilbert, though," critiqued the caller.

"You were in the courtroom?" Zack wondered. *Where? Who?*

"Yes, I was," the caller admitted.

Zack continued to search the crowded courtroom in his mind. "You're correct. I couldn't shake him much. He's a tough nut," Zack admitted. "But I thought he came across as smug and unfeeling."

"Very coached," the caller suggested.

"I agree," Zack was impressed with the caller's perception. "I hope the jury agrees. Nonetheless, I can't take that chance. He didn't give us enough on priors. I need you badly."

"I don't think so, Mr. Blake. I think you underestimate the jury."

"No, Father, you *overestimate* the jury. I can't leave this issue to chance," he warned. "Without the two families, I need you or someone like you to contradict the testimony of Father Moloney."

"I'll think about it."

"Think quickly. After the psychiatrist and the family, I need to get into priors. I can call Detective Jack and perhaps my investigator, but that's it. I'll need testimony of the church's involvement in the Berea cover-up at that time."

"How long do you think that will take?" the caller inquired.

"What?"

"The testimony of the witnesses who will testify before me."

"Two or three days."

"Then we still have some time."

"Please, ease my mind and say you will do it," Zack pleaded.

"I cannot make that commitment right now. It is very dangerous for me. You must understand."

"Oh, Father . . ." Zack noticed the caller hadn't protested earlier when referred to as "Father." This man was a priest. "I do understand. I also understand the only way to free you is for you to testify. If something happens to you after that, the public and the authorities will surely know the church is involved. Right now, you are the maverick who dissented and deserted, the mouth that needs to be shut before you expose the real work and function of the Coalition."

The caller reflected. Blake was right, but the caller was still justifiably apprehensive. After a long silence, he offered: "I'll think about it, Mr. Blake, and let you know."

Zachary heard the audible *click* of the telephone disconnecting. He stayed on the phone until he heard the dial tone. He slammed down the receiver several times.

"Damn it!" shouted Zack.

He tried to calm. He had lots of work to do. There were other witnesses and mountains of evidence to present. This was the fight of his life, and he had to keep his eye on the target. If the caller didn't testify, he'd have to find another way to convince the jury. *You can do it, Blake*, a little voice on the right side of his head told him. *Bullshit,* came the reply from the left. Zachary shook his head from side to side and returned to work.

***

Zack met Jennifer and the boys for breakfast on the morning of the third day of trial. He wanted to let Jennifer know about the mystery caller and get her take on the situation. They met at The Breakfast Club in Farmington Hills.

"So, how is everybody holding up?" cooed Zack.

"We're good, aren't we, boys?" Jennifer prompted, for Zack's sake.

"Kinda looking forward to this being over," Kenny fretted.

"Me too," Zack agreed. "Say, I wanted to ask you guys . . . someone called me. He won't tell me who he is, but I know he's a priest. He's a member of this Coalition organization within the church. He seems to know a lot about you. Did you see anyone who looked familiar in court? Do you know anyone in the church's hierarchy? I'm looking for anything I can use as leverage to get this guy to testify. He seems to be on our side."

"I have no idea." Jennifer quietly mulled it over. "Boys?" She glanced at both boys, turning from one to the other.

Kenny and Jake both shrugged in response.

"It could be a trick," offered Jennifer.

"I don't think so," Zack decided. "The guy seems very sincere. And I believe he can give testimony about Gerry's prior activity and the church's knowledge and cover-up. Those are the keys to a verdict in this case. It is so frustrating to be so close with no cigar," Zack grumbled.

"I didn't know you smoked, Zack," Jake peeped.

Zack smiled at the innocent youngster. *So young to be forced to go through something like this.*

"It's an expression, squirt," Kenny explained, always the smarter, big brother. His tone was harsh, but he quickly softened it. "He means like in baseball, when you're rounding third heading home, but you're not there yet. The outfielder throws the ball to the catcher. Will you score or be thrown out? Right,

Zack?"

"Exactly right, sport, great analogy," Zack noted, impressed.

"What's an 'alanogy?'" Jake inquired, botching the pronunciation.

Jennifer and Kenny put their hands over their mouths and stifled their laughter. Kenny spit food into his hands. Jake blushed with embarrassment.

"*Analogy*, Jake," Zack corrected, smiling, coming to Jake's defense. "It means something or someone who is very much in the same situation as the one you are in. We have the information we need, and we are heading home. But without testimony church officials knew about Father Gerry before he came to Farmington Hills, we may get a worthless verdict against a penniless priest rather than one we can collect from a corrupt hierarchy," he explained.

"You'll think of something, Zack. You always do," Jake brightened.

"Thanks, Jake. Hey, it's getting late. Let's finish our breakfast and get to court. It's a big day today. I'm putting Gerry on the stand."

"What's he going to say?" Jennifer shuddered.

"Probably nothing. He'll take the Fifth to every question. But I have some tricks up my sleeve. You'll see."

Chapter Fifty-Three

Zack had a reason for calling Gerry Bartholomew next. After Moloney, Blake figured he'd dispose of the other "hostile" witness before starting with the most persuasive testimony in the case, the Tracey family and Dr. Rothenberg. Father Gerry was sworn and turned over to Blake for questioning.

"State your name for the record please."

"Gerald Bartholomew."

"And where do you reside, sir?"

"At the rectory, Our Lady of the Lakes, Farmington, Michigan."

"And how long have you lived there?"

"Approximately one year."

"What is your occupation?"

"I am a parish priest."

A "parish" priest, not a "monastery" priest or any other kind, a "parish" priest, smug son of a bitch. "As opposed to any other kind?"

"As opposed to any other kind."

"Where did you receive your training?"

"At Sacred Hills Seminary in Detroit."

"How long have you been a pedophile?" Zachary let him have it with both barrels. A hush came over the courtroom; everyone leaned forward, awaiting the answer.

"I beg your pardon?"

"A simple question," Zack pressed. "Mr. Bartholomew, how long have you been a pedophile?"

"I prefer *Father Gerry*, thank you. As to your question, I refuse to answer on Fifth Amendment grounds."

"Your Honor, this man has pleaded guilty to crimes involving child sexual abuse in two jurisdictions. He's not in jeopardy, and I respectfully request the court instruct him to answer my question," Zack argued.

"Sidebar, Your Honor?" Walsh jumped to his feet.

"Approach," Judge Perry consented.

Both attorneys walked up to the side of the judge's bench, and a heated, off-the-record discussion ensued.

"Your Honor," Walsh began. "Father Gerry assuredly feels answering Mr. Blake's questions will place him in further jeopardy. He cannot be compelled to incriminate himself."

"But, Your Honor," Zachary countered, "he has already pleaded guilty. He is no longer in jeopardy for those charges as double jeopardy would apply."

"Not necessarily," Walsh argued. "If he pleaded guilty to lesser charges and then admits, today, to other acts that could get him charged for other degrees of criminal activity, double jeopardy might not apply, and he could be charged. Further, there may be acts not covered in his plea, and he is in jeopardy for those, if he testifies. For those reasons and any other reasons, he feels he may be incriminating himself and does not have to testify as to these matters."

"Step back," ordered Judge Perry, rankled. "I've heard enough."

He addressed the jury. "Ladies and gentlemen, if a witness feels his testimony will expose him to criminal liability, under the Fifth Amendment of the Constitution, he doesn't have to testify to those matters. What weight, if any, you decide to give to this refusal to testify is up to you, as the triers of fact in this case."

Savoring this favorable ruling, Blake moved in for the kill. "Did you have forcible sex with either Kenny or Jake Tracey, or both, at any time?" He demanded.

"I invoke the Fifth Amendment," Gerry repeated.

"Have you ever touched or fondled their private parts?" Two female jurors winced at the suggestion.

"I invoke the Fifth Amendment." Several jurors shook their heads, dismayed.

"Your Honor, this question goes directly to the crime in which this witness has pleaded guilty. He is not placed in jeopardy by answering the question," Zack argued.

"Objection, Your Honor." Walsh again jumped to his feet. "This witness . . ."

"Your objection is noted and overruled, Mr. Walsh," Judge

Perry ruled. "Mr. Blake is correct on the law here. Since Father Bartholomew pleaded guilty to the very act the question entails, the witness is required to answer. If he doesn't, I will take judicial notice of its truth, based upon his plea in the criminal matter. Furthermore, I will instruct the jury to assume this is a fact in evidence."

"And, my objection, for the record, is noted?" Walsh challenged.

"Your objection is noted. Father Bartholomew?"

"I invoke the Fifth Amendment." No surprise, there.

"Very well, then," began Judge Perry. "The jury is instructed Father Bartholomew did, in fact, fondle the private parts of either or both of these boys."

"Your Honor . . ." Walsh pleaded.

"Your objection is noted and continuing, Mr. Walsh."

"Thank you, Your Honor."

"I also find you in contempt of this court, Father Bartholomew. We will deal with that at a later time." Walsh started to rise. "I note your objection, Mr. Walsh." Walsh sat down in a huff. "You may proceed, Mr. Blake," Judge Perry ruled.

"Thank you, Your Honor."

Perry's ruling was better than if Bartholomew had testified. Walsh was befuddled, Bartholomew was hiding things from the jury, and the judge ruled in Zack's favor. Things were going well. Blake glanced at the jury box. Several jurors were troubled with Gerry's evasiveness. Zack was encouraged.

Gerry's testimony, if you could call it that, continued for most of the morning. Zachary asked Bartholomew every question about every sexual act he could muster. Bartholomew took the Fifth each time. Walsh objected each time, and Perry overruled him each time. It was monotonous but effective. Bartholomew was exposed as a criminal sexual predator, covering up criminal acts, hiding behind the Fifth Amendment. For purposes of money damages, the far more critical and difficult challenge was to expose the church cover-up.

Walsh didn't ask a single question. He knew who and what Bartholomew was. It was impossible to repair the damage, and

Walsh wanted the predator off the stand as quickly as possible. Walsh's strategy was to limit the verdict to Bartholomew and protect the deep pocket church. A verdict solely against Bartholomew and a no cause of action against all the other defendants would be an excellent defense result.

The trial recessed for lunch, and Blake took Rothenberg and Jennifer over to Jacoby's Tavern, a short distance from the courthouse. Zack loved their soup and ordered three different entrées for them to share.

"I've decided to change the order of your testimony," Zachary advised.

"What do you mean?" Rothenberg inquired.

"I'm going to take Jennifer and the boys first and follow with your testimony, Doc. I want the jury to hear Jen and the boys. If they become emotional, or whatever, I want to follow that up with expert testimony, explaining not only your treatment, diagnosis, and prognosis, but the behavior the jury just saw."

"Whatever you think is best, Zack," Rothenberg deferred.

"You were great today, Zack," Jennifer observed.

"Thank you, my dear," Zack blushed. He quickly changed the subject. "Let's finish our lunch."

"Don't you want to go over my testimony?" Jennifer wondered aloud.

"We've been over and over your testimony. Let's relax, enjoy our lunch and each other's company."

"As the only doctor present, I believe that is the perfect prescription for the present situation," Rothenberg chimed in.

"See, doctor's orders. Eat!" Zachary laughed.

They did what the doctor ordered. They relaxed, ate—stuffed themselves, for that matter—and enjoyed the moment. Getting to this moment in the trial was an exhausting experience for all. While there was now faint light at the end of a long and tortuous tunnel, there was still much work to be done and many painful moments ahead of them. They deserved a break.

After lunch, they returned to the courtroom. Blake spent most of the early afternoon in chambers, arguing with Walsh and Perry about the latter's rulings and proper courtroom decorum. It seemed Walsh didn't care for Perry's habit of overruling him before he finished his objection. After all, he had a client to represent and was entitled to make a record. Perry indicated he noted a continuing objection for Walsh, but Walsh continued to interrupt and was rude in the process. Perry correctly pointed out the courtroom was his, he had specific rules of decorum, and Walsh would adhere to them or find himself in the same contempt predicament as his client.

Blake was a mere spectator for the entire discussion. He enjoyed watching Walsh squirm. He was required to be there. In-camera discussions—those conducted privately, outside the presence of the jury and gallery—required all sides present to avoid the appearance of impropriety.

Perry finally adjourned the session, and the judge and the lawyers returned to the courtroom. Judge Perry reassembled the jury and Blake called Jennifer Tracey to the stand.

Chapter Fifty-Four

Zack was deliberate with Jennifer. He walked her through Jim's death and how, after Jim's accident, Father Bill and Lakes became a large part of her family's life. Bill's transfer was traumatic for her kids, but they were assured another fine young assistant pastor would replace him. In the boys' eyes, however, they were losing another loved one.

Jennifer testified about Gerry's arrival and how the boys never warmed up to him. He wasn't Bill. Zack paused. Time to discuss the camping trip that changed all their lives. He wondered how Jennifer would handle direct examination but was especially worried about Walsh's cross.

"Did there come a time when Gerry took the boys on overnight trips?"

"There weren't *trips*, plural. There was just one trip."

"When did that trip take place?"

"Spring, last year."

"What kind of trip was it?"

"A camping trip, in the Irish Hills."

"How long a trip?"

"A weekend."

"Friday night, Saturday and Sunday?" Zack sought to establish Gerry spent two evenings alone with the boys.

"Yes, they returned Sunday afternoon."

"Who picked them up?"

"I did."

"Where?"

"At our church."

"Did you notice anything unusual when you first saw the boys?"

"Well, I remember it was a beautiful day, the first of the spring. I got to the church and walked up to the rectory to pick them up. Kids were running and chasing each other all over the house, having a great time. But I couldn't find my sons." The jury was captivated, watching her recall this uncomfortable event.

"What did you do?"

"I found Father Gerry and asked him how the outing went."

"What did he tell you?"

"He claimed the boys had a great time and, as I could see, kids were still having a great time. He told me my boys were in the backyard and offered to get them for me. I went out on the front porch, and he brought them to me. I'll never forget the looks on their faces." Her eyes welled with tears. "They looked like they heard someone died. Gerry attributed this to fatigue. He ran the kids ragged, hiking, canoeing, and such. They'd be fine in the morning, he promised.

"For the ride home, the boys quietly got in the back seat. They usually fight over the front. They were silent the entire way home. I checked my rearview mirror. Kenny was glaring at Jake. He put his finger to his lips and ordered Jake silent. Jake had tears in his eyes. I couldn't imagine what was going on, but I knew, right then, something was terribly wrong." Jennifer winced at the memory.

"What happened next?" Zack probed.

"Not much. Their sullen behavior grew worse over time. They became more and more withdrawn. After two weeks or so, I decided to visit Father Gerry."

"Why?"

"Why what?"

"Why Father Gerry as opposed to anyone else?"

"Because I was convinced whatever was wrong had something to do with the camping trip. I thought maybe one of the other kids had done something to embarrass the boys. I wanted to see if Gerry knew anything."

"What happened next?"

"I went over to the church and found Gerry outside in the garden. I told him Jake had been silent and tearful, and Kenny was broody and silent. When I asked what was wrong, Kenny exploded at me. I asked Gerry if he had any idea what it was all about."

"What, if anything, did Gerry say?"

"He offered to come over and talk to the boys. I invited him

to dinner. I didn't know . . . how could I know?" Jennifer began
to cry.

"Would you like to stop for a moment?" Zack inquired.

"No." Jennifer composed herself. "I'm okay."

"You're sure?"

"I'm sure."

"What happened next?"

"That monster came to my house for dinner," she charged,
disgusted at the memory. She glared at and pointed to
Bartholomew.

"Objection, Your Honor. Please admonish the witness to
refrain from personal attacks in front of this jury. While I am
sure the jurors can imagine how Mrs. Tracey must feel, such
outbursts are inappropriate," Walsh argued.

"Your objection is sustained. The witness will answer the
questions posed and will refrain from editorializing," Perry
ordered, addressing Jennifer.

"What, if anything, happened at dinner?" Zack continued.
Inserting "if anything" into the middle of the question, on direct
examination, prevented it from being ruled a leading question.

"I didn't tell the boys Gerry was coming. I wanted it to be a
surprise. I thought they liked him. The boys came downstairs,
saw Gerry, and refused to come to dinner," she recalled.

"What happened next?"

She paused, searching her memory. "Gerry offered to go up
the boys' room and talk to them. God, help me. I sent their
abuser into their bedroom, alone!" she screamed. "I didn't know
. . . I didn't know . . . *I didn't know!*" She buried her head in her
hands, crying. *Thank God, the boys aren't in the courtroom.*

"Your Honor, a brief recess to allow Mrs. Tracey to regain
composure?" Blake urged.

"Mr. Walsh?" the judge inquired.

"No objection, Your Honor."

"Very well, then. We'll take a ten-minute recess. The jury is
admonished not to discuss the case until it is presented for the
verdict."

Zachary escorted Jennifer out into the hallway.

"Are you all right?" he consoled.

Jennifer dried her eyes with a tissue.

"I'm fine. Some guilt feelings I thought I had buried surfaced at the wrong time."

"Guilt feelings? What do you have to feel guilty about?"

"I sent the boys on that camping trip. They didn't want to go. I invited that animal to dinner and sent him up to their room. Perhaps if I had been more attentive to the signals my boys were sending me, this might never have happened."

"Jen, the only way this incident could have been avoided is if the church dumped Gerry long ago and sent him to a treatment center instead of to a parish. This is *their* fault, not yours, not the boys. Got it?"

"I got it. Aye, aye, Captain." She saluted.

"Jen—I . . . I . . ."

Jennifer put her finger to his lips and silenced him.

"Not now, Zack. I can't deal with anything but this trial and this moment. We can discuss anything, everything, in the future, but first, I need to get through the present."

She gestured at the courtroom, which held some of the keys for her, her sons, and any relationship she and Zack might have.

Jennifer fell silent and looked up at Zack.

"They'll be calling us back soon. I'm being as gentle as I can. Walsh will be much worse," Zack warned.

"I know. I'm fine. I've got to deal with the guilt and pain. Lakes is my church. It's been a rock for my family. It's supposed to represent God," Jennifer whimpered.

"And it still will, Jen. The parish isn't the culprit. People are the culprits. When people in power change their policies, the institution will be fine. But for God's sake, it certainly isn't *your* fault."

"You're right, of course. Thank you," she sighed.

"You're welcome. You ready?"

"Yes, let's go."

They returned to the courtroom, where Jennifer maintained her composure throughout the direct examination. Zack took her through Gerry's dinner visit and the boys' conversation she overheard after he left. They discussed Father Jon's visit, the offer of treatment with Dr. Rothenberg, and the visits to

Rothenberg capped by the stunning revelation that Gerry molested the boys. Jennifer described the absolute shock she experienced when Dr. Rothenberg first told her and the disgust she felt after being advised of the extent of the priest's conduct.

She recounted Rothenberg's conversation outside the clinic, and her total disbelief in discovering the Coalition was monitoring her house, the doctor's office, and her church. She described the meeting at Little Daddy's with Rothenberg and Costigan and their pact to turn the tables on the Coalition. Finally, she explained the boys' ongoing treatment and their progress.

"They aren't loving anymore. They're alternatively withdrawn and quiet, then, explosive or tearful. They don't kiss me goodnight. They were enthusiastic altar boys with Father Bill and Father Jon and were never discipline problems. After Father Gerry, their grades dropped. They display flashes of anger and argue over petty things. They have drastic mood swings and stay in their room for long stretches. They rarely play sports and have virtually abandoned their friends. They've lost confidence and self-esteem. They were happy guys, but not since this happened."

"Have you talked to the boys?"

"Oh, yes, when they'll let me," she commiserated.

"What do you talk about?"

"I tell them what happened wasn't their fault. I assure the boys they were *victims*, not criminals. For some reason, they feel *guilty*. I tell them I'll protect them, and nothing like this will ever happen again!"

"When you look over there, at Father Gerry Bartholomew, what goes through your mind?"

"Anger and disgust, pity, then anger again. I can't get the images out of my mind," she trembled.

"What images, Mrs. Tracey?"

Jennifer paused, took a deep breath, and glared at Gerry. The jury was on the edge of their seats in anticipation.

"God help me," she cried. "Gross, detailed images. Use your imagination! I can't clear these disgusting images from my mind! They are *haunting* me!"

"No more questions," Zachary snapped, turning the witness

over to a stunned Walsh.

"You may cross-examine, Mr. Walsh," Judge Perry stated.

"Th-thank you, Your Honor, may I have a moment?" He needed to recover from the end of direct testimony.

"Take your time, Mr. Walsh," Perry permitted.

After a few moments, Walsh took a labored breath and began his cross.

"Mrs. Tracey, I'm sure you understand it's my responsibility to ask you some questions."

Jennifer nodded.

"I'll be as gentle as I can, but I have an obligation to my client, understood?"

Jennifer nodded again.

"Y-you've never actually s-seen F-father Bartholomew abuse anyone, h-have you?" Walsh battled to regain composure.

"No, sir, I haven't, but the images are as real as they can possibly be."

"You don't know whether Father Gerry actually did the things you imagine, do you?"

"I know what my kids told me. *Those* are the images I see."

"You are a widow, are you not?"

"Yes, I am."

"And your husband died about four years ago, correct?"

"Just about."

"And after that, Father Bill became a father figure and he was transferred, correct?"

"Yes."

"Isn't it true, Mrs. Tracey, your boys took the death of their father very hard?"

"Yes."

"And they took Father Bill's transfer almost as hard, didn't they?"

As far as Zack could tell, Walsh was recovering nicely. He made an interesting point. Rather than attack Jennifer's story, he attacked the source of the boys' depression. Zack would have to counter. Even if the boys were mildly depressed before the camping trip, Zack decided, Bartholomew's assault made everything much worse.

He could make this a classic "eggshell skull" case. The argument was this: If your client has an egg for a head and the defendant's negligence causes it to crack, the defense can't blame the plaintiff's soft head. This theory is used to combat a defendant's use of a plaintiff's pre-existing condition as a mitigating factor in a personal injury case. In the Tracey case, "mild" depression becomes a far more severe diagnosis of major depression and post-traumatic stress disorder because of Bartholomew's sexual misconduct.

"Yes, I suppose they did," she conceded.

"Very well, then, after Father Bill left, Father Gerry replaced him, correct?"

"Correct."

"The boys *never* liked Gerry, from *day one*, did they?"

"No, they never had time to warm up to him."

Walsh was walking into a trap. He couldn't avoid the follow-up question. The rules of witness interrogation advise lawyers never to ask a question they don't know the answer. On *cross-examination*, lawyers should ask only questions that can be answered "yes" or "no." Witnesses should not be permitted to editorialize. Walsh's next question breached both rules, and he was severely punished for his lapse in judgment.

"Why is that?"

"Well . . ." Zachary and Jennifer rehearsed for this moment. "It took Father Bill about two months to gain the kids' confidence. He treated them special when he discovered they'd lost their father. The first breakthrough in their relationship was when Bill took the boys on an overnight trip. They came back happy, telling stories, laughing, and telling me what a great guy Father Bill was. The rest was history. Two months after Gerry arrived, he took the boys on an overnight . . ."

"Your Honor . . ." Walsh tried to stop her, suddenly aware of where she was going.

"You asked the question, Mr. Walsh. The witness may finish her answer," Perry ruled, suppressing a smirk. "Proceed, Mrs. Tracey."

"As I indicated, he took the boys on an overnight and *sexually molested them*! No, Mr. Walsh, they didn't like him. But they had a damn good reason, wouldn't you agree?" She grumbled.

Jennifer glared at Walsh, then Gerry, and then back to Walsh, as she and Zack had rehearsed.

Walsh paused and uttered, "no more questions." He sat down.

The gallery was buzzing. Moloney leaned over and began a heated conversation with Walsh. Zachary and Jennifer made eye contact and shared a quick smile. The judge pounded his gavel for order.

"Do you have redirect, Mr. Blake?"

"No, Your Honor, I'm quite satisfied."

"Call your next witness, please." Perry suppressed a grin.

"Your Honor, due to the lateness of the hour, I would respectfully request we adjourn until tomorrow," Zack suggested.

Zack wished to score points with the jury on two counts. Jurors were surely tired, and he wanted to send them home with Jenny's testimony as their last memory.

"Any objections, Mr. Walsh?" Perry requested.

Walsh turned from Moloney.

"None, Your Honor," he concluded, which prompted another lecture from the Voice.

"Very well, then. Court is adjourned until nine o'clock tomorrow morning."

The courtroom erupted in conversation after the judge and the jury withdrew. The press grabbed tablets and cellphones or typed laboriously on laptop computers. Walsh and Moloney were arguing. Blake, Rothenberg, and Jennifer stepped into the hallway and engaged in a group hug.

"That was amazing!" Rothenberg exclaimed.

"It worked like a charm," Zack beamed.

"It wasn't me, Zack. It was *you!*" Jennifer praised.

"How did you know he'd compare relationships with Father Bill and Jim?"

"Because he needed an alternate source for the boys' troubles, something for the jury to consider. Jim and Father Bill were obvious choices. Walsh helped by arguing the boys never gave Gerry a chance."

"It was perfect, Zack," Rothenberg agreed.

"How do you think it played to an outsider?" Zack wondered.

"All I can tell you is the jury ate it up. Jurors were on the edge of their chairs," Rothenberg opined.

"Do you really think so?" Jennifer challenged.

"Absolutely," responded Rothenberg. "I've been in court countless times, and I have never witnessed anything like *that*."

"We still have a lot of work to do. We have your testimony, Doc, and the boys to prepare for. Hopefully, the caller will show up or the Berea families, and I need to be ready." Zack brought them back to reality.

"You're right, of course," Rothenberg admitted. "But what a moment in sports history!" He declared.

"Hopefully, the first of many," Zack prayed.

Chapter Fifty-Five

Judges in all jurisdictions have one thing in common. They *always* ask the litigants and jurors to arrive at eight-thirty or nine in the morning, while *they* always arrive at nine-thirty or ten. Before reconvening, various emergencies and criminal matters must be disposed of.

Tracey v. Bartholomew was not a special case to Judge Perry or his staff. Perry completed the morning's business at ten-thirty. When the trial resumed, Kenny Tracey would take the stand. He sat in the hallway, dressed in a new gray suit his mom bought for the trial. He was nervous and very uncomfortable. Zack sat next to him on a wooden bench, going over his proposed testimony.

Jennifer watched the two of them from across the hall, a short distance away. She wondered whether she was doing the right thing. Her boys were on public display, forced to discuss things too repulsive for most *adults* to handle. How would two young boys handle this moment? Would the experience set their treatment progress back? Would they be able to articulate their feelings to a packed courthouse? These questions would be answered soon, but she found no comfort in the fact it would soon be over.

She was terrified for them and herself. If anything went wrong and they were harmed further, it would be her fault. The boys decided to pursue litigation. She insisted on leaving the final decision to them. However, Jennifer was the one who decided there would be no private deal, no confidential settlement. The boys weren't presented with the opportunity to settle or refuse to give testimony. Jennifer decided all of that for them. For the good of all children, she, alone, decided to use this case as a rallying cry for abuse victims. Gerry used and abused her kids. Was she now doing the same thing? That possibility was haunting her. She was having second thoughts.

I could settle this right now. The boys would be set for life and receive all the treatment they need. Why am I putting them through this?

The bailiff came through the courtroom doors to announce Judge Perry was ready to proceed. Jennifer was startled out of her thoughts. Blake, Kenny, Rothenberg, and Jennifer stood and entered the courtroom, closely followed by Walsh and Moloney.

Walsh tapped Zack on the shoulder and motioned him to join him in the inner hallway before the judge and jury arrived. Zack followed him into the hall.

"Before the boys are forced to testify, I've been authorized to increase my offer," advised Walsh.

"What's the increase?"

"We'll pay ten million dollars, plus lifetime treatment,"

Zack needed to sit, but there were no chairs in the hallway.

"Any conditions?" he managed.

"Nondisclosure of settlement terms, no admission of liability," Walsh continued.

"What about Gerry?"

"What about him?"

"Jennifer wants him defrocked, and she wants a guarantee he'll never receive a parish assignment again."

"They won't defrock him, Zack. I don't know why, but they won't," he sputtered, frustrated. He glanced up and down the hallway as if he was about to say something he shouldn't. "As for the parish assignment, he'll never be assigned to a parish. It's not possible, after the publicity generated by this trial."

"Will they guarantee that in writing?"

Walsh looked down at the floor. "I don't think so."

"For Christ's sake, Craig," Zack snarled. "Why the hell not?"

"I don't know. Arrogance? They won't be told what to do. They'll do the right thing, but not because someone *orders* them to. No one can dictate how they run their church except their brethren and God."

"That's the biggest crock of shit I've ever heard."

"Maybe so, but it is their position. Please take it to Mrs. Tracey."

"She won't accept. You know that, don't you?"

"Take it to her, Zack."

***

Zack and Jennifer returned to the counsel table after discussing the offer. Zack passed Walsh on the way and shook his head. Walsh stopped. He stared at Jennifer in disbelief. He leaned over to Moloney, who glared at Jennifer Tracey.

The bailiff yelled, "All rise." The back door opened, and Judge Perry entered the courtroom. The litigants and spectators rose and were seated when ordered. Perry asked about preliminary issues before bringing in the jury. There were none, and upon Perry's order, the jury members filed in and were seated.

"You may proceed, Mr. Blake," Perry permitted.

"Thank you, Your Honor. Plaintiff calls Kenneth Tracey."

The bailiff opened the doors to the back of the courtroom and motioned to the other side. Through the doors walked Kenny Tracey in his new suit, a fine-looking young man. He made no eye contact with anyone. Contrary to Zack's advice, he stared at the floor on his way to the witness box. The clerk swore him in, and he was seated as a witness.

"Your Honor, considering this witness's age and the delicate subject matter involved in this case, I request permission to ask leading questions."

"Mr. Walsh?" Perry inquired.

"Within reason, I have no objection, Your Honor," Walsh assented, prompting another glare from Moloney. Walsh's career as an attorney for the church was probably coming to a rough conclusion.

"Very well then, Mr. Blake. You have limited license to lead the witness. Don't abuse it."

"Thank you, Your Honor, and thank *you*, Mr. Walsh, for your kind consideration," Zack nodded a gesture of thanks.

"Your name is Kenneth Tracey?"

"My friends call me Kenny."

"Okay, Kenny, it is."

Zack walked him through hard times, the death of his father, the arrival and subsequent departure of Father Bill, and his introduction to Father Gerry. He handled most of the questions with relative ease. It was time to discuss the subject matter at the heart of the case.

"When Father Gerry invited you on the camping trip, what was your reaction?"

"I didn't want to go."

"Why not?"

"I don't know. I just didn't."

"Didn't you like Father Gerry?"

"Up to that point?"

"Yes, Kenny, up to that point."

"He was okay."

"Then why didn't you want to go?"

"Because I figured it would be like Father Bill."

"What do you mean?"

Zack did not expect that answer and didn't like the comparison of Father Gerry to a role model like Father Bill. Kenny knew what he was doing, though.

"I thought I'd get to like him, and he'd leave, like Father Bill. Everybody leaves, except mom." Kenny's eyes teared, and he glanced at his mother. She was proud of him and scared for him at the same time. Zack smiled. He *loved* that answer!

"That's why you didn't want to go on the camping trip?" Zack queried.

"Yes, sir."

"What changed your mind?"

"Mom *made* us go. She thought it would do us good." He recalled, distraught at the memory.

"Some bad things happened on that camping trip, didn't they, Kenny?" Zack prodded.

"Yes, sir," Kenny whispered. The judge, the jury, the gallery listened in rapt silence.

"Can you tell us, in your own words, what happened to you and what you witnessed happening to your brother on the camping trip?"

Kenny cringed. "Yes, sir. It's pretty disgusting."

Zack paused, allowing Kenny time to gather himself. "We can take it, Kenny. Take your time."

"I-I can't," Kenny labored.

"Let me see if I can help," Zack offered, gently tiptoeing

through this crucial testimony. He approached the witness box, amiably, and leaned on its ledge.

"Did Father Gerry ask you or your brother to remove your clothing on the trip?"

"Y-yes, sir," Kenny recounted, in torment.

The questions and answers continued, a deliberate, torturous process. Zack prodded Kenny to continue, and Kenny, cumbrously but courageously, responded.

"Where did this happen?" Zack pressed, eying the jury.

"In his cabin."

"What were you doing in his cabin?"

"He came into our cabin and announced that my brother and I won the contest." Kenny winced at the memory.

"What contest?"

"I didn't know. I-I didn't remember any contest. But I remember being excited we won."

"What happened next?"

"He told us we were special and got to sleep in the special cabin." Kenny glared at the floor, tightening his resolve.

"And that special cabin turned out to be his?"

"Yes, sir."

"What happened after he told you to remove your clothes?"

"We asked why."

"And what did he say?"

"'The Lord loves clean bodies, and so do I.' He made us take a shower before bed so we would be clean before the Lord."

"Then what happened?"

"We went into the bathroom and took off our clothes. We got into the shower." Kenny turned from Zack, the jury, and the gallery, momentarily closing his eyes in anguish.

"What happened next?" Zack continued.

"All of a sudden, the shower door opened, and Father Gerry walked in with us, *totally naked*! I couldn't believe it!" Kenny shook with fear and rage.

"Are you okay, son? Would you like to take a break?"

"N-no, sir. I'm okay," he calmed.

"So, the three of you took a shower together?"

Kenny glanced at the floor.

"Yes, sir."

"Did Father Gerry do anything in the shower that made either of you uncomfortable?"

"Objection, Your Honor!" Walsh was on his feet.

"What's your objection, Mr. Walsh?" Perry requested.

"The witness can only speak for himself, not his brother."

Zachary realized Walsh was correct. What he was actually doing was trying to disrupt cadence and distract Kenny.

Zack would not have it. "I'll rephrase, Your Honor. Did Father Gerry do anything to *you* in the shower to make *you* uncomfortable?"

"Yes, he did." Kenny continued, unruffled by the interruption. "He s-soaped up his hand and started washing Jake's and my private parts," he recalled, flustered by the memory, being forced to relive and recount it. Kenny trembled, head down, and continued to stare at the floor. Zack glanced at Jennifer. Witnessing her son's courageous, tormenting testimony was almost more than she could bear. *I was a fool to force my boys into this nightmare.*

Zack read her mind, shared her pain, but plodded on. "By private parts, do you mean your genital areas?" They entered the danger zone. While they rehearsed this testimony, Zack was apprehensive.

"Yes, sir." Kenny's eyes met Zack's. Zack counseled the boy to do this. They were two good friends, alone, engaged in an everyday conversation. But there was nothing usual about *this* conversation.

"Did he do anything else to you in the shower?" Zack continued.

"No."

"After the shower ended, what did Father Gerry do?"

"He insisted on toweling us off. He started rubbing my genitals with a towel—Jake's too." Kenny uttered. Zack wished he could stop, end the nightmare, this instant. But Kenny demanded the opportunity to tell his side, clear the air, and cleanse his soul.

"What did you guys do?"

"Nothing. We looked at each other, like 'What's going on

here?'"

"Then what happened?"

"He gave us nightshirts and underpants, and we started to get ready for bed."

"And did you finish putting these articles of clothing on?"

"No, sir."

"Why not?"

"Gerry grabbed our underpants. He told us we wouldn't need them— he was going to perform a special ritual and we needed to be naked underneath our nightshirts."

"What happened next?"

"He told us to get into bed."

"Did you listen to him?"

"Yes, we were *scared*!" He began to shake and sob, still in control.

"Kenny, we can take a break. Please, tell Judge Perry, and he'll give you a few minutes."

"No, I'm okay," he claimed. He wiped his eyes and cheeks with the sleeve of his suit jacket.

Zack walked over to the counsel table, and Jennifer handed him a tissue, which he carried to Kenny.

"Then what happened?" Zack resumed.

"He set up a small television with a built-in DVD and put on a DVD."

"What kind of DVD?"

"A dirty one. Men doing it to other men."

"Men doing what to other men?"

"You know . . ." He looked down at the floor. "Doing it, having sex. Gerry asked us if we ever did that."

"What did you tell him?"

"We told him no."

"Was that the truth?"

"Of course, it was."

"Is that still the truth?"

Kenny paused. "No! No, it's not!" he suddenly screamed. He trembled and tears rolled down his cheeks.

"Do you need to take a break, Kenny? I think you need a break."

"N-no, I want to finish." He wiped his tears with a tissue his mom gave him.

"Are you sure?"

"I'm sure."

"Why isn't what you told Gerry the truth anymore?" Kenny didn't like the use of 'Father' in front 'Gerry,' so Zack stopped using it.

Kenny paused. He took two deep breaths, picked up his head, and stared straight into the eyes of his predator.

"Because *he* did it to us and *he* made us do it to him!"

Kenny was highly agitated. He grimaced and pointed at Gerry.

"I know this is difficult, Kenny, but what did he do to you?"

"He did those sex things, like in the movie he showed us. He hurt us!"

"What kinds of things, Kenny?"

Kenny began to shake and sob, fighting to be brave, but losing the battle.

"God doesn't love me anymore . . ." Kenny blurted, disconsolate.

Zack was caught off guard.

"What? Why doesn't God love you, Kenny?" He prodded.

"Because I did bad things, Jake too," Kenny agonized, becoming hysterical. Jenny stood up in her place at the participants' table and gestured to Zack to end Kenny's suffering. Zack chose to ignore her.

"What bad things, Kenny? What did you and Jake do?"

"What Gerry made us do!"

"Then, Gerry is the bad one, Kenny, not you." Zack reasoned. Walsh jumped to his feet.

"Objection, Your Honor—calls for a legal conclusion. Behavior is for the jury to determine, not the plaintiff's counsel."

"Sustained. The jury will disregard Mr. Blake's last remark," ruled Judge Perry. He studied the boy on the stand.

Zack paused, desperately trying to give Kenny time to regain his composure. Kenny seemed to calm a tad, Zack continued, and Jennifer resumed her seat.

"Do you have trouble sleeping since this happened, Kenny?"

Zack inquired.

"Y-yes, sir," Kenny trembled.

"Why?"

"I have bad dreams."

"What are the dreams about?"

"Gerry." The rapid, rehearsed cadence seemed to have returned.

"What happens in the dreams?"

Kenny became distraught. "He does different things in each dream."

"Rather than go through each dream, why don't you tell us about the absolute worst one, okay?"

"Okay."

They practiced this testimony several times. Kenny also discussed this particular nightmare with Dr. Rothenberg. However, these nightmares were quite terrifying. Zack hoped the boy could maintain a modicum of composure in front of the jury. This was a crucial moment in his testimony.

"Okay. Uh . . . Gerry and I are in a cabin. He's dressed as a priest."

"Black jacket, black shirt, black pants, white-banded collar?"

"Yes, sir."

"What happens next?"

"He comes toward me. He . . .uh . . . p-pulls his clothes off with one rip, kinda like Superman, ya know?"

"Yes, Kenny, we know," Zack smiled. "Please continue."

Judge, jury, and the entire courtroom audience were hushed, immersed in each word, each sentence, affixed to the edges of their seats.

"He comes closer and closer," Kenny sobbed. "He has no face. He becomes a monster. He keeps coming, closer and closer. He's right on top of me," Kenny screamed, now hysterical.

He looked to Jennifer, then to the sky, standing, shaking. "Mommy," he pleaded, in agony, "make him stop! *Make him stop!*" he screamed.

Jennifer jumped from her seat. Kenny collapsed in a heap, trembling, slumped down in the witness stand. By the time Jennifer reached him, he had pushed through the door of the witness stand and fallen to the floor. He lay curled in a fetal position.

"No! *No!* Make him stop, Mommy!" He screamed, in delirious agony.

Jennifer stooped to the floor, sat and cradled her son in her arms.

"No more questions!" she shouted. "No more! This stops *now!*"

Bailiff, remove the jury, immediately!" snapped Judge Perry, springing into action. The court officer quickly escorted the jury out of the courtroom.

Walsh jumped to his feet. "Your Honor, if we are not allowed to cross-examine, we move for this witness's entire testimony to be stricken from the record, with the jury admonished to disregard."

The objection was cruel and heartless but shrewd and calculated under these exigent circumstances.

"We'll cross that bridge if and when we come to it," Perry suggested. "For now, we are in recess. Let's get this boy some help!"

Zachary and Rothenberg lifted Kenny off the witness stand and carried him out of the courtroom, through the private doors of the inner hallway, closely followed by a tearful, distraught Jennifer Tracey. The spectators watched in shocked silence. As the doors closed upon Kenny's exit, the courtroom was a den of excitement. Reporters scattered out the door to call in or write stories. Others frantically pecked on laptops and tablets.

If Kenny were unable to continue, Judge Perry could instruct the jury to disregard the testimony as though it had not been given. Cross-examination was an absolute right of the defendant in *any* case. Even if stricken, the testimony was riveting, unlikely to be forgotten by the jury, regardless of any cautionary instruction. This terrifying moment for Kenny Tracey was a powerful example of the impact of child sexual abuse.

Out in the hallway, the bailiff led Rothenberg and Blake into an empty jury room. They laid Kenny, gently, on a conference table. Rothenberg asked the bailiff for a glass of water. Rothenberg cradled Kenny's head and slowly put the glass of water to his lips. The water dribbled down his chin as he murmured and shook.

"He's in shock. We need to get him to a hospital." Rothenberg kneeled next to Jennifer, extending his support, the calm professional in a sea of panicked amateurs. "Call an ambulance," he directed the bailiff.

"Right away, sir." The bailiff appreciated the urgency.

Sirens could soon be heard, first in the distance, and then louder as the ambulance approached the courthouse. Paramedics arrived, and, with assistance from Rothenberg and Jennifer, carried Kenny to the ambulance and rushed him to Children's Hospital, a few blocks away.

Blake remained behind to confer with Walsh and Perry in the judge's chambers. Zack walked back into the courtroom where Walsh was engaged in conversation with Moloney. Zack motioned for Walsh to join him in the private hallway, and they walked together into the judge's office. Perry was standing at the outer secretarial office and, upon seeing the two lawyers, invited them into his chambers.

"How's the boy?" Perry wondered, concerned.

"I don't know, Your Honor. He's in shock. Paramedics took him to Children's," Blake advised.

"Children's is one of the best pediatric hospitals in the country. He's in good hands."

"Your Honor," Walsh continued his previous argument. "It is obvious this boy will be unable to continue. Furthermore, I bet his mother will refuse to allow his little brother to testify, under the circumstances."

"You can't make rulings based on defense counsel's speculation, Your Honor," Blake pleaded, disgusted to be having the conversation. "We don't *know* anything yet. I would request a short continuance at this time. Besides, if the boys are unable to testify, their depositions would be appropriate alternative testimony pursuant to the Michigan Court Rules."

"That's true. What about it, Mr. Walsh?" Perry tapped his fingers on the desk.

"I object to that, Your Honor. Until Jake Tracey takes the stand, and, perhaps, falters, we don't know he *can't* testify,"

Walsh opined, suddenly changing his tune.

"You would prefer to place the young man in the same situation as his older brother? Even if Kenny can't continue, and I exclude his testimony, that was quite troubling, don't you think? Do you want the jury to witness such an event twice?"

"I don't, Your Honor. That's why I move for a mistrial right now."

"On what grounds, Mr. Walsh?" The judge grumbled.

Blake maintained silence.

"On the grounds that Kenny Tracey's testimony was heard by this jury. Without cross-examination, it is highly prejudicial to the defendant, even with a cautionary instruction to disregard."

"If I instruct the jury to disregard and the depositions are read, there would be little, if any, prejudice, since the deposition testimony and the courtroom testimony was remarkably similar until the boy's breakdown. Your cross is preserved, and we can do the same for the younger boy."

"In my opinion, Your Honor, the harm is irreparable. The jury has heard too much. These jurors had their proverbial heartstrings tugged. We cannot repair the damage."

"The same damage would have been done if the depositions were read. The testimony was almost identical."

"But not in such dramatic fashion and not without cross-examination." Walsh began to realize this argument was hopeless with this particular judge.

"I disagree, Craig. If the boy can't continue, I will rule his testimony be stricken from the record and order the jury to disregard. Further, I will rule we use depositions in lieu of his live testimony. Now, what's your pleasure, gentlemen? Do you want the younger brother to try to testify live or do you want to stipulate to use his deposition testimony?"

"I want this ruling on the record," Walsh demanded. "I plan to appeal it immediately."

"As is your right. We'll put it on the record, but before we do, I'd like to clean this up and make the record clear. Do you want the younger boy live or not?"

"I'll stipulate to admitting deposition testimony, Your

Honor," Walsh conceded.

"I will also stipulate, Your Honor." These were Blake's first words in the entire conversation.

"Very well then," Perry glanced at a wall clock. "Let's go put it on the record. Afterward, we'll adjourn for the day. We'll pick up with the two depositions tomorrow at 9:00 a.m."

Perry rose and led the two lawyers out into the courtroom. As the judge stated his ruling for the record, Blake stood, at attention, in front of him, his mind wandering off. A perfect day for the case became a terrible one for his clients. He wondered how Kenny and Jennifer were doing. *I've got to get to the hospital.*

Chapter Fifty-Six

Kenny spent a restful, heavily medicated, night at Children's Hospital. Jennifer spent the night at his bedside and was not in attendance at the trial when it resumed the following day. In fact, Zack had to talk her out of dropping the lawsuit altogether. She was devastated. She underestimated the impact of public admission, and Kenny's breakdown was the ultimate evidence of her terrible mistake.

Zack argued the boys were no longer needed. Their testimony was preserved by deposition. Her mission to protect other innocent young teens from experiencing the same fate as her boys was still important. If she dismissed, Kenny's brave attempt to complete his testimony would be for nothing.

"Who cares?" she cringed. "Look at my son!" Kenny lay in a fetal position, virtually comatose.

"You don't want his trauma to be for nothing, Jen. Don't *do* this!"

"The cause doesn't mean much to me anymore, Zack. The money never mattered—take the ten million. Take your fee and donate the rest to a charity for abused children. I don't care which one. Do that! Look at my son! *Look at him!*"

"*He* would not want you to quit, Jen. Neither would Jake. Ask Jake, Jennifer."

So, Jennifer approached her sensitive, quiet youngest child, who convinced her to continue.

"Mom, Father Gerry is a bad, bad man. He hurt Kenny and me. Don't let him hurt anyone else. Please?"

She couldn't turn down that face. His look of longing was one only a mother—and everyone else in the world—could love.

"Kid would make a great lawyer," Zack joked.

Jennifer decided to continue with the lawsuit, making Zack swear her boys would never have to set foot in the courtroom again.

Zack arrived at the courthouse promptly at 9:00 a.m. The clerk greeted him and indicated Judge Perry wanted to see him in chambers. Zack went through the side doors and into the inner hallways leading to the judge's office. He found Perry and Walsh were waiting for him.

"How's the boy?" Judge Perry wondered, concerned.

"Still at Children's—he's semi-comatose, in shock. Dr. Rothenberg thinks he'll be okay, over time."

"I'm praying for him," Perry offered. "How are we going to proceed today? I'd like to complete the plaintiff's case today or tomorrow, if at all possible."

"I plan to present the two boys' depositions, and then Dr. Rothenberg, my investigator, and Father Jonathan Costigan. After those witnesses, I plan to rest and, perhaps, present a witness or two on rebuttal," Zack concluded.

He was bluffing. He had no one for rebuttal. Rebuttal was the plaintiff's answer to the defense case. Plaintiffs were permitted to present evidence contradicting the evidence presented by the defense. Plaintiffs have the first and last words in any civil trial.

"How long do you expect the defense case to last, Mr. Walsh?" Perry inquired.

"A day, maybe two, after the motion for a directed verdict."

A motion for a directed verdict was argued in almost every case after the close of the plaintiff's proofs. The judge evaluates whether the plaintiff has met its burden or whether jury issues still existed. In Zack's experience, he'd seen a few granted, but not in a case like this. There was sufficient evidence of abuse and cover-up for *this* case to go to the jury. Walsh put on his game face, but Zack was confident there would be no directed verdict.

The striking of Kenny's testimony and the admonishment to the jury to disregard that testimony was within the judge's discretion. Walsh could appeal, but the ruling was not reversible error. The lawyers headed out to the courtroom to await Judge Perry and the jury. They did not speak. Blake went straight to Rothenberg and Love for last-minute discussions of their testimony.

Moloney, the Voice, greeted Walsh, as he had every day of the trial. Obviously, he wanted to know what was discussed in chambers, out of his presence. Zack was surprised the Coalition hadn't bugged the judge's chambers. Then again, perhaps it had.

The judge and jury entered, and Perry launched into a detailed speech, instructing the jury to disregard Kenneth Tracey's testimony. Zack was now free to read the boys' deposition testimony into the trial record.

Zack presented the testimony through a reader, his former secretary. The secretary read the depositions with emotion, but could not produce the power, passion, and sympathy of live testimony. Still, through this reader, the boys graphically described the weekend camping trip and their repeated rape by a predator the church still chose to honor with the title of 'Father.'

The testimony was powerful and effective, and Walsh's reading of the cross-examination had little counter-effect. Walsh would have been considerably more aggressive had he known, at the time of the depositions, the testimony would be used at trial. His cross, for discovery purposes, was mild by comparison.

After the readings, Zack called Dr. Rothenberg to the stand. Dr. Rothenberg testified to the conversations he had with Moloney and the discovery his office was bugged. Over Walsh's objection, he compared it to the bugging of Daniel Ellsberg's psychiatrist's office during Nixon's presidency. According to Rothenberg, church hierarchy withheld the extent of the abuse.

The psychiatrist was shocked when the boys disclosed Bartholomew forced them into multiple sexual acts amounting to rape. Because Father Bill was akin to a surrogate father for the boys, Lakes had always been extended family. The church betrayed them, and the boys reacted like survivors of incest.

Bartholomew chose this particular family because it lacked a father figure. This type of family was his favorite target. Jim and Father Bill needed replacing—the boys were ripe for the taking. While Bartholomew didn't anticipate their rejection of him, he prepared for it. He swore the boys to secrecy, threatened harm to their mother if they disclosed the abuse.

The boys experienced severe repercussions from this experience, including crying spells, mood swings, nightmares, loss of confidence and self-esteem, a lack of desire to play, poor grades, disinterest in friends, arguments over petty issues— Jennifer Tracey and both boys provided graphic testimony about the frequency and severity of these conditions.

Rothenberg continued, "The boys also have experienced painful feelings of guilt. The church and the priest have successfully made these boys feel like criminals, as if the incidents were *their* fault and somehow they brought this on themselves. They have been locked out of their place of spiritual worship and have suffered a complete loss of faith. They were caught in a traumatic catch-22. Their respect for the church and their mother's faith precluded them from discussing the abuse. There was no escape. Bartholomew coerced the boys into feelings of desperation.

"Compounding these serious issues, Bartholomew preyed on boys who were just beginning to become aware of their sexuality. As shocking as this may sound, some of their experiences with Bartholomew might have actually been *pleasurable*. This creates even more confusion, since the boys, if aroused, would not be mature enough to understand those feelings. The raging hormones of puberty are totally disrupted by incidents such as these. I am gravely concerned they may have long-term, perhaps permanent, sexual issues.

"Many victims of sexual abuse experience symptoms later in life. These include depression, flashbacks, suicide attempts, alcoholism, drug abuse, aggressive behavior, and confusion of sexual identity. These are bad enough, but they are compounded by the fact that one support mechanism these boys turned to in bad times was the church. Here, the church was the culprit. Where do they turn to sort *that* out? This is a complicated situation, one that will require long-term, possibly lifetime treatment."

He went on to indicate the cost of treatment sessions and estimated long-term or lifetime treatment would cost perhaps millions of dollars. This was the trial's first mention of seven or eight-figure expenses or damages.

Walsh's cross-examination was rather simple. He stuck to the basics. "Psychiatry is not an exact science." "It's possible the boys may not need long-term care at all—only time will tell." Rothenberg had to concede these points. Walsh asked if psychiatrists often differed in opinions relative to treatment, prognosis, and diagnosis. Rothenberg acknowledged psychiatrists *often* differed.

"In fact," Walsh opined, "another psychiatrist could conclude, *in this very case*, that the boys' memories of these events will slowly fade, and their current problems, as acute as they are now, will be nonexistent in adulthood."

"He could come to that conclusion, yes, but he would be *wrong*," Rothenberg opined, looking Walsh straight in the eye. The commissioned defense psychiatrist, Dr. Unatin, came to that very conclusion. Rothenberg read Unatin's report and sought to soften the impact of his future testimony.

Walsh completed his cross-examination by asking Rothenberg if he had patients who surprised him and improved or were cured with far less treatment than anticipated. Rothenberg conceded the issue. Walsh decided to milk the issue dry.

"More than one patient?"

"Yes."

"More than two?"

"Yes, I've been in practice for almost thirty years."

"How nice for you. More than five?"

"Yes," he conceded.

"More than ten?"

"Yes."

"More than one hundred?"

"Yes."

"More than five hundred?"

"No, I don't think so."

"You don't *think* so? Don't you *know*?"

"I don't keep those kinds of statistics."

"Oh, so it could be, you just don't know. It could be thousands, for all you know, couldn't it Dr. Rothenberg?"

"No."

"Well then, how many?"

"Somewhere between two and three hundred, out of *thousands* of patients."

"That's a guess, though. It could be more?"

"Probably less."

"Could be more?" Walsh repeated.

"Objection, Your Honor!" Blake shouted, rising. "Asked and answered."

"He didn't answer, Your Honor," countered Walsh. "The question called for a 'yes or no' answer. I request you instruct the witness to answer 'yes or no.'"

"The witness will answer the question 'yes or no,'" Perry ruled.

"The answer is . . . yes," Rothenberg conceded.

"Thank you, Doctor. No more questions, Your Honor."

"Redirect, Mr. Blake?" Perry offered.

"Just a couple of questions, Your Honor." Blake was on his feet. "Dr. Rothenberg, you have been treating these boys for well over a year now, is that correct?"

"Yes."

"Would a psychiatrist who has a long-term treatment relationship with a patient be in a better or worse position to diagnose the patient's condition than a one-time evaluating physician who establishes no doctor-patient relationship?"

"The treating physician would be in a much better position to diagnose. He knows the patient far better than the one-time evaluator."

"Which of the two is better equipped to render a long-term prognosis or prescribe a treatment program?"

"The treating doctor, for the same reason."

"Is there anything in Mr. Walsh's cross-examination that would lead you to conclude you were wrong about the boys' need for long-term care?"

"No, absolutely not."

"Do you know Dr. Mark Unatin?"

"I do."

"Dr. Unatin examined the boys on behalf of the defense. He opines and will apparently testify the boys will not need long-term care to improve since memories of the events at issue here will fade as they reach adulthood. He wrote a report indicating long-term treatment would be counterproductive since it keeps bad memories active. Do you agree?"

"No, I don't. I respect Mark Unatin. He's a fine doctor and a friend of mine. But he's way off on his evaluation in this case. I presume he is trying to please the people who paid for his opinion."

"What do you mean?"

"He was paid, probably very handsomely by the defense, in this case, to render his opinion."

"Objection, Your Honor!" Walsh cried. "Dr. Unatin is a professional, a fine doctor, as this witness admits. Dr. Rothenberg may be offended a colleague disagrees with his diagnosis and prognosis, but he goes too far. He questions his colleague's integrity. His testimony in that regard is highly inflammatory. I move it be stricken from the record, and the jury be admonished to disregard."

The jury would be required to disregard a great deal of testimony in this case.

"Sustained. The testimony is stricken. The jury is admonished to disregard," Perry ordered. But, the point had been made.

"Call your next witness, Mr. Blake," Perry continued.

"Plaintiff calls Micah Love, Your Honor." Zack turned to the gallery.

Micah rose from his back-row seat, was sworn in, and took the hot seat. He testified to being retained—sounds better than hired—by attorney Zachary Blake to travel to Berea, Ohio, to try to locate Bartholomew's prior victims. Love told the jury that St. Patrick's in Berea was Bartholomew's previous placement before Lakes. Micah described activities in Berea, locating Pearl and Julius MacLean, interviewing the janitor, and then finding him dead. Eventually, the investigation led him to the two families in Coral Springs, Florida.

Micah tried to testify the families admitted Gerry sexually abused their kids and the church ran them out of town. Walsh objected to the attempted hearsay before Micah could blurt out the necessary words. Perry admonished the witness and threatened him with contempt.

Instead, Love told the jury a fascinating tale, detailing what *he* did and said. He met the families and convinced them they were in danger. As he was transporting the families to safety, Florida police, by *sheer coincidence,* arrested several men for breaking and entering the families' homes. Micah described the plane trip and limo ride, and the assault on the Doubletree Suites Hotel, where his agents were rendered helpless with dart guns. The families disappeared after the assault. Love told the jury he prayed they escaped. A court officer wheeled a laptop computer, projector, and screen into the courtroom. The jury was treated to a very graphic surveillance video of the entire episode, corroboration of Micah's testimony.

Walsh objected throughout Micah's testimony. He argued the testimony and video were highly prejudicial. There was no evidence of church involvement. In fact, he argued the church was unfamiliar with these families until officials were advised they were former churchgoers at St. Patrick's.

Perry overruled the objections. The witness never testified the church was involved. His testimony established a reason why a potential group of witnesses might not be presented for the jury's consideration.

"In fact," Judge Perry opined, "the very first time anyone in this courtroom mentioned a possible connection between the church and the Florida incident was when *you* mentioned it in your objection, Mr. Walsh."

Zack turned the witness over to Walsh. "I have just two questions, Mr. Love. You were hired by Mr. Blake, the attorney for the plaintiff, and you haven't uncovered a single shred of non-hearsay evidence the church was involved in anything related to Father Bartholomew's behavior in either Berea or Farmington, true?"

"Yes," Micah admitted. "That is true . . . but . . ."

"No buts, Mr. Love. Is it true?"

"Yes."

"As to the video that we just viewed—do you have any evidence anything we watched has anything whatsoever to do with this case or the defendants involved, Father Bartholomew, or the church?"

"No, I don't." Micah conceded. "But . . ."

"No further questions, Your Honor."

"Mr. Blake?"

"You were going to say something else, Mr. Love? But Mr.

Walsh cut you off. I'm sure the jury would like to hear what you were going to say?" Zack invited.

"Objection, Your Honor. He answered my question. There are no grounds for him to give a speech now."

"Sustained," ruled Perry.

"No further questions, Your Honor," Zack sighed.

"The witness may step down. Any more witnesses, Mr. Blake?"

"Plaintiff calls Father Jonathan Costigan."

Father Jon was sworn in and recalled certain key events. His conversations with the Voice were admissible hearsay. While they were out of court statements used to prove the truth of the assertions being made, they were also admissions against the interest of a party. As such, they were an exception to the rule.

Jon testified to his conversations with Moloney. He was advised of the camping incidents by Father Moloney and brainwashed into believing the church would be better served if Jon were discreet. Jon wanted Gerry out of his parish, but Moloney convinced him to consider the bigger picture, the future of *all* the children of the church, not only the Tracey boys. Moloney asked Costigan to "keep an eye" on Gerry, to limit his contact with children. The church would keep an eye on him off-campus.

At Moloney's insistence, Jon offered to counsel Mrs. Tracey and the boys, without disclosing his knowledge of the source of their troubles. He rationalized this request and convinced himself the boys would receive the help they needed while the church would avoid scandal. He recounted the meeting at Jennifer's house, where she confronted him about his involvement in the cover-up and the guilt he felt. He described his total shock when Jennifer told him the true extent of the abuse and his meeting with Rothenberg and Jennifer at Little Daddy's to discuss criminal and civil action.

Walsh's cross-examination centered upon whether Costigan was aware of any prior acts of sexual abuse. Walsh acknowledged the church's discreet methods of handling the Tracey situation were ill-advised. However, he asked if Father Costigan had ever heard *any* mention by *any* member of the church hierarchy that Bartholomew had engaged in inappropriate behavior prior to Lakes and the Tracey family. Jon had to admit he hadn't.

After Jon stepped down, Zack was forced to rest his case. He had no way of contacting the mystery caller. The Berea families weren't coming, even if they were alive. He was troubled. He poked around at the edges, but he failed to nail down the church's direct involvement or knowledge of Bartholomew's Berea escapades. He failed to prove the transfer to Farmington was made with knowledge of Gerry's decadent predispositions.

While Micah was attempting to trace the mystery caller, this couldn't happen soon enough to be useful. Zack was confident he secured a verdict against the priest. He was frantic that his efforts would fall short against the true financial source, the church. *What good is an uncollectible seven or eight-figure verdict?*

He considered the sealed files in the Berea civil case. Could he persuade a judge to unseal them? Provide evidence of the church's involvement in settling the previous case while relocating the families to assure their silence? *That proves prior notice, doesn't it?*

Would Perry grant him time to unseal the files to present on rebuttal? Would Foley tell the truth about the Berea incidents? *Too risky,* he decided. *Maybe, I can get these things in through the back door without the families, but can I do so in time?*

Zack telephoned Micah and instructed him to immediately begin the process of unsealing the civil files and preparing them for presentation in court. The next step in the trial was Walsh's expected motion for a directed verdict. Walsh would concede he could not get a *DV* for Gerry but *deserved* one for the church. He visualized Walsh's argument:

"Your Honor, there is not a shred of credible evidence to suggest the church had any knowledge of Gerry's propensities prior to these incidents in Farmington . . ."

Chapter Fifty-Seven

" . . . Furthermore, Your Honor, when church officials *did* discover Father Gerry's illness—pedophilia *is* an *illness*—it moved quickly to obtain treatment for Kenny and Jake Tracey and remove Gerry from Lakes and into a treatment facility. Perhaps they could have been more forthcoming to the Tracey family when they discovered the abuse. My clients have reflected on their policies and offered apologies to the Tracey family for not being entirely forthcoming.

"However, Your Honor, none of this has anything to do with this case. *This* case is about allegations the church *knew* about Father Gerry's illness and transferred him to Michigan, with knowledge of his illness. These allegations *have not been proven. Plaintiff* has the burden of proof, by a preponderance of the evidence, that the church was guilty of negligence *before* Father Gerry's placement to Michigan. Negligence, in this context, would require church officials knew or should have known about his illness. Again, Your Honor, there is no credible evidence of such knowledge. Gerry Bartholomew is a cunning, evil predator of children." Walsh cut all church ties with Gerry in his motion.

"He operates in secret. He obtains the silence of children by threatening them. How could anyone know about this until the predator was caught? Thank God he was caught! The church is investigating previous placements. Gerry will meet justice for every incident my clients uncover. However, a verdict against the church requires direct evidence of the church's knowledge or notice, and there is none. Thank you, Your Honor."

"Mr. Blake?" Judge Perry made eye contact. "I presume you wish to oppose this motion?"

"I do, indeed, Your Honor."

"Please proceed, Mr. Blake," the judge directed.

"Thank you, Your Honor. I'll be brief. Mr. Walsh is correct. There's no direct evidence the church was aware of Father Gerry's condition. There is *plenty* of evidence. However, they *should* have known or *probably* knew. You heard Detective Jack testify about the previous criminal charge and the silence surrounding it. It sounds remarkably similar to the conspiracy of silence in *this* case.

Is Gerry Bartholomew sophisticated enough to pull this off? Does he have the assets or cunning to orchestrate this type of criminal case resolution? You've heard the testimony of Micah Love. Who else but agents of the church had enough assets to arrange or stood to gain anything by the disappearance of these witnesses? You've also heard from Father Jonathan Costigan, an employee of the *defendant*. He testified he was *directed* by his superiors to help cover up Father Gerry's activities in Farmington.

"Rape is a *crime*, Your Honor. Failure to report an incident of child abuse is a punishable misdemeanor. Does the church's behavior in Farmington entitle us to infer the same type of cover-up that occurred in Berea and elsewhere? What's the real function of this *Coalition*? Why does it exist?

"We've seen the video evidence. The plaintiff would respectfully suggest this provides enough evidence to permit the unsealing of the Berea civil case documents. With those in hand, we will all know whether the church knew or should have known about Gerry's prior behavior. If Your Honor were inclined to grant the defendant's motion, we would ask, at the very least, for time to unseal and present these records in *this* case, to *this* jury. In a motion for directed verdict, the plaintiff is entitled to every reasonable inference. At the very least, we are entitled to wait until the close of *all* the proofs in this case. Thank you, Your Honor."

"Thank you, gentlemen," Perry turned from one lawyer to the other. "Both of you made strong arguments in support of your respective positions and clients. The defendant's motion is denied. I find the jury could reasonably infer the conduct suggested by the plaintiff from prior activities of the church relative to the issue of clergy abuse, particularly in *this* case, and a directed verdict is contraindicated. You may renew the motion at the close of proofs, Mr. Walsh."

He read the words from a piece of paper on his bench. His mind was made up *before* the motion was argued. Perhaps he had a similar cheat sheet for an opposite ruling. One never knew with judges.

"Are you ready to proceed with the case for the defense, Mr. Walsh?

"Yes, Your Honor."

"Please proceed."

"Thank you, Your Honor."

The case for the defense was simple. Walsh recalled Moloney to re-explain Coalition functions, ranging from charity work to promoting volunteerism, from checking on parishes and parish priests to public relations. The role of the Coalition varied, but they were not clandestine in the context argued by Blake. Whatever happened in Coral Springs or Berea had nothing to do with the Coalition. No official of the church was aware of Father Gerry's depraved condition until after the Michigan cases. When notified, the church took quick and decisive action to assist the Tracey children and remove the priest. "What more could we have done?" Zack could not lay a glove on him on cross. This guy was as smooth as they came. Zack was able to rehash all of the Berea subterfuge, a positive, only to have Moloney deny Coalition involvement in any of it, a negative.

Walsh next called Dr. Mark Unatin to the witness stand. Unatin, as expected, testified the boys would be *harmed* by long-term care, as it tended to reinforce painful incidents in their minds. With less treatment, there was a strong possibility the incidents' impact would lessen with time. He wasn't arguing for suppressing their feelings or withholding care, he was arguing care was not necessary over the long term. He also floated secondary gain as a motive to continue treatment. After all, long-term treatment would pad the pocketbooks of both Rothenberg and the Tracey family. This was Unatin's revenge for Rothenberg calling him whore on the witness stand.

On cross-examination, Zack used the same techniques Walsh used on Rothenberg. He established the treating doctor was in a better position to discuss diagnosis, prognosis, and treatment. Unatin repeated the treating doctor's opinion might be colored by secondary gain and fascination with the subject matter. Sometimes, a detached, independent evaluator renders a more reasoned and uncolored opinion.

Unatin also admitted he was not a *pediatric* psychiatrist and *never* counseled victims of child abuse. He admitted he might be wrong and Rothenberg right. Finally, he testified he was paid $20,000 to evaluate both boys, write narrative reports, and testify in court.

Walsh followed Unatin with Glimesh and Foley. The purpose of the clerics' testimony was to establish their lack of knowledge related to the Berea occurrences. The two testified they had no knowledge, whatsoever, of Bartholomew's illness, before, at the time of, or after the transfer. Bartholomew and his lawyers worked out the plea bargain, resulting in probation and a sealed conviction. Foley and Glimesh were out of the loop.

Foley further testified no parishioner ever approached him, including the MacLean or O'Connell families, to complain about Gerry for *any* reason, let alone child sexual abuse. As far as Foley knew, Bartholomew was a model assistant pastor, and there was no need to warn Farmington of anything. While this was a tragic ordeal for the Tracey children, only Bartholomew could have prevented it.

Zack's cross-examination focused on the unlikelihood Bartholomew retained an attorney without church assistance or whether his attorney would have thought to negotiate a private, sealed plea and probation without the political clout of the church. Both Glimesh and Foley assured him it was true. Zack turned to the jury and rolled his eyes. "No more questions," he shrugged.

After Foley's cross-examination, Judge Perry adjourned for the day.

***

For his first witness of the eighth day of the trial, Walsh called his investigator, Parks, to the stand. A computer and monitor were set up beside him.

Parks was asked about his experience and credentials. It

became quite obvious he testified in court many times before this appearance. Parks testified he was engaged to conduct surveillance on the Tracey family and their attorney. Zack jumped to his feet.

"What is the reason for surveillance of this unfortunate family and what is the relevance of testimony based on that surveillance?"

"I'll show relevance, Your Honor. As I indicated previously, it goes to credibility."

"Your Honor, I demand an offer of proof outside the presence of the jury," Blake argued.

"No, I don't think so, Mr. Blake. Mr. Walsh, I'll allow it, but be careful. Do not step on the integrity of these proceedings," Perry ordered.

"Thank you, Your Honor."

Walsh qualified Parks and reviewed his curriculum vitae, discussing his experience at conducting surveillance. Parks set up the computer and inserted a flash drive. On the screen, Jake and Kenny played in a park. They were, in various clips, throwing a ball back and forth, wrestling each other, playing tag, seemingly having a great time. The date at the bottom of the screen was August 16, four months after the Bartholomew incident. The video's purpose was to demonstrate the boys weren't sullen and angry on a 24-7 basis.

Zack wasn't surprised by the presentation. Insurance companies used these types of videos often. Investigators were instructed to conduct surveillance until they found an opportunity to cherry-pick one brief happy moment and use it against someone who claimed depression. They would video a disabled worker taking out the garbage or carrying groceries as if these moments somehow proved an ability to work. These videos were misleading and despicable, but they were often effective in front of a jury.

The scene switched to the Tracey's Farmington home. The date was two months before the start of the trial. The camera was placed on an outside window and peeped into the house. Zack, Jennifer, and the boys were having what appeared to be supper. Everyone seemed to be having a jolly time. The scene jumped again, to later that evening. Zack and Jennifer were on the couch, facing each other, Jennifer's hand in Zack's. Blake jumped to his feet, trying to ignore gasps and chuckles from the jury.

"What is the relevance of this, Your Honor?"

"Turn it off, Mr. Walsh," Perry ordered. "What *is* the relevance of this portion of the presentation?"

"Motive, Your Honor. This jury should know the only reason that Mr. Blake is pursuing this matter is that he has a personal agenda in pursuing the widow Tracey."

Zack tried to remain calm. He was losing the battle. "I'm not the one pursuing this matter. Jennifer Tracey and her sons are. There is no personal relationship depicted in this presentation. Besides, personal relationships are not the business of this court, this jury, or you! These videos are actionable invasions of privacy."

"Sue me!" Walsh mocked. "You'll sue anybody." The jury and the gallery chuckled at the comment.

"Gentlemen, I've heard enough. I agree with Mr. Blake. This portion of the presentation is excluded. The jury will disregard," Perry ruled.

"But, Your Honor . . ." Walsh whined.

"Mr. Walsh. I have ruled. Say another word and I'll exclude the entire presentation," Perry warned.

Walsh knew when to sit down and shut up.

"Are you through with this witness?" Perry grumbled.

"Yes, Your Honor."

"Any questions, Mr. Blake?"

Blake didn't respond. He sat at the counsel table, staring into space.

"Mr. Blake?" repeated Judge Perry.

Zack snapped to.

"Yes, Your Honor?"

"Do you wish to cross-examine this witness?"

"I sure do, Your Honor, thank you."

Zack quickly recovered from his momentary lapse in concentration. He tore into Parks. Did he know invasion of privacy was an actionable tort? How much was Parks' firm paid for its services? Did the church or the priest pay the bill? Was his firm retained before or after this lawsuit was filed?

"Mr. Parks, if the church didn't know about Bartholomew before this lawsuit, why did they hire a private investigator?"

"I don't know," Parks admitted.

Blake moved in for the kill. He asked Parks how long he tailed Kenny and Jake.

"We conducted intense surveillance over three months," Parks recounted, referring to his notes.

"And how many drives were used during this surveillance?"

"I'm not sure, maybe six?"

"And what was the duration of each drive?"

"I don't understand the question."

"No? How many hours of record time on each drive?"

"Oh! We use four-hour drives."

"Let's see now." Zack calculated. "Six drives, four hours per drive, right?"

"Right."

"Over these three months, how many days did you follow the boys?"

"May I refer to my surveillance notes?"

"Absolutely." Zack turned to the jury and smiled.

Several members smiled back.

"Over the ninety days, we were following them for approximately forty-five days."

"And as a result of those forty-five days, you were able to obtain these couple of moments of activity?"

"Yes, well, no. I mean, we recorded over several days. We probably shot a little bit every day; we had a clear view."

"Would you please reset the drive to the beginning?"

"Certainly." Parks left his chair, approached the computer, and reset it.

"Play the video again, please."

Parks pressed 'play.' Once again, the video of Jake and Kenny playing was shown. Zack did not watch. Instead, he focused on the second hand on his watch. Various members of the jury noticed and studied their own watches. The machine stopped.

"Twenty-five seconds. Twenty-five seconds!" He repeated

and turned to face the jury. "Would you agree with that, Mr. Parks?"

"More or less," Parks conceded.

"Which is it, more or less?"

"The presentation is twenty-five seconds long," Parks acknowledged.

"Let me get this straight. You recorded activity for forty-five days and found twenty-five seconds of these two boys being happy?"

"Well . . ."

"Do you have the other flash drives?"

"What other flash drives?"

"The other forty-four minutes and thirty-five seconds."

Parks shifted in his chair and looked downward. "No, I don't have them."

"Where are they?"

"I don't know, back in the office, I suppose."

"Why don't you tell this jury what's on those drives, or does Judge Perry have to order you to bring them in and sample them for us?"

"There is . . . uh . . . more video of the boys, similar to this one." He looked over at the monitor.

"Oh, they're happily playing like they are in the video you presented to the jury?"

"Not exactly."

"Well, why don't you tell Judge Perry and this jury what the boys are doing in these other recordings?"

"Nothing much."

"Can you be more specific?"

"Not really."

"Let me help you then."

"Do you have video of them arguing with each other or their mother?"

"Yes."

"Seldom or often?"

"Often, I guess."

"Do you have them being tearful?"

"Yes."

"Seldom or often?"

"Often."

"Did you video them at school?"

"Yes."

"Did they play with other children at school?"

"No."

"Did they play together at school?"

"No."

"Did they hang around with any of the other kids?"

"No, they stayed to themselves, as I recall."

"Did you ever, on any occasion, other than the one depicted in the video you presented in court today, observe these boys being just plain *happy*?"

"No, sir. I can't say I did."

"Over what period of time did you tail Mrs. Tracey?"

"About the same as the children."

"And what . . . what . . . oh, *never mind*. I have no further use for this *witness*."

Zack turned to the jury and made quotation signs with his hands at the mention of the word *witness*. Walsh did not dare to re-direct.

The final defense witness was Father Jonathan Costigan, who reluctantly admitted he received Gerry's personnel file when he was transferred to Lakes and saw nothing to indicate Gerry had problems with children. Conversations with his superiors were all positive. It appeared to Jon, at the time, that the church had no knowledge of Gerry's propensities.

On cross-examination, Zack again took Costigan through the cover-up efforts of the Voice and his Coalition.

"If Father Moloney had been able to enlist your support in the program he outlined, would you have been permitted to inform a subsequent parish of his pedophilia?"

"I suppose not."

"Perhaps your predecessor was under the same restriction?"

"Objection, calls for speculation!" shouted Walsh.

"Sustained," ruled Perry.

"Withdrawn," Zack capitulated. He made his point. "I have no more questions."

"Redirect, Mr. Walsh?" invited the judge.

"No, Your Honor."

"The witness may step down. Do you have any other witnesses, Mr. Walsh?"

"No, Your Honor. The Defense rests."

"Will you be presenting a rebuttal case, Mr. Blake?"

"Yes, Your Honor," Zack lied.

"How long do you think you will need?"

"Maybe one full day, Your Honor."

"All right, then. We'll adjourn until tomorrow."

Perry pounded his gavel, and the court was adjourned. Blake felt better about his chances with the jury. He seemed to connect with a few members. To hit a home run, though, he needed to nail down the prior notice issue. Tomorrow would be his last chance. If the mystery caller or the families were watching the proceedings, now was their time to step forward. If he had no rebuttal witnesses to present in the morning, he would rest. He'd visit Kenny and Jen and return to the office to prepare for closing arguments. His long battle for justice for the Tracey family was almost over.

Chapter Fifty-Eight

Zachary Blake sat in his office, reviewing his notes and recollections of the trial. He tried, without much success, to prepare his closing argument. It would be a lot easier if Micah found the missing families or tracked down the mysterious caller. Micah's call, twenty-five minutes earlier, to advise he had no luck on either score was aggravating, to say the least.

Zack's visit to the hospital was as positive as possible under the circumstances. Kenny was fully conscious, off medication, and could hardly remember the events that landed him at Children's Hospital. He'd go home tomorrow. Jennifer was briefed on the proceedings, although she seemed disinterested.

The toll of the lawsuit on her and her boys was a heavy one. She promised to appear the following day since Kenny was improving. Unknown to Zack, Jennifer told Kenny she'd drop the entire case if he wanted her to. His health was the only thing that mattered to her. If the case could cause him more harm, she'd drop it.

Kenny declined. He agreed with Jake. Both boys needed Gerry and the church to pay for their criminal behavior. And Kenny wanted no other child to suffer at the hands of Gerry Bartholomew. She was so proud of him at that moment!

Her boys felt strongly about continuing, but how did she feel? She thanked Zack for his hard work and managed a slight smile. Her attitude frightened him. Was she dismissing a possible future together? Was he only the family lawyer? *I'm paranoid.*

Back in the present, Zack found himself staring at his phone. "Call, damn it," he muttered out loud. But the phone stayed silent. Zack returned to his closing and worked into the morning hours. Tomorrow was the final day of the biggest trial of his life. Would he win the battle but lose the war? He could get a huge verdict against the priest, but would he be able to collect it from the church? This wasn't merely a possible result. The more he pondered trial events, the more he believed this was the more *probable* result. He'd obtain a big verdict—no money, no justice, and three very unhappy clients. He couldn't focus. He rose, turned off the lights, and dragged himself to the Z4. He looked over at the empty passenger seat and closed his eyes, imagining an occupant.

Jennifer?

Yes, Zack?

I love you.

I love you, too.

Zack opened his eyes and started the car. *Focus, Blake! Everything will fall into place. What would I have if I lost this case? I'd have nothing, no one—same as before.* On that pleasant note, he drove off into the night.

Chapter Fifty-Nine

Zack awoke to the loud beeping of his cell phone alarm. Without rising, he tried to focus, searching for the off button. He relaxed, several seconds later, when he found the button and hit it harder than necessary. This had been a morning ritual for as long as he had the phone. He longed for the days of his easy-to-shut-off alarm clock. *Sometimes, new technology is inferior to the old.*

He lay in bed, contemplating his morning. This could be the last day of trial. The judge would ask him if he wished to present a rebuttal. He'd say no, and the judge, surprised, would ask if he wished to present his closing argument. Again, he would answer no since he'd been unsuccessful in preparing it. Walsh would deliver a brilliant closing, the jury would be out only thirty minutes, and deliver a no-cause verdict for the defense. Jennifer would thank Zack for his hard work and say good-bye. *And I'll never see her again.*

Zack dragged himself out of bed, did his morning business, and crawled into the shower. Usually, this simple act of revival achieved its purpose, but not this morning. This would be the worst morning of his life. A hot shower could not brighten the mood.

He toweled off, moussed and brushed his hair, brushed his teeth, shaved, and quickly dressed. He contemplated himself in the mirror. He remembered the day in the bathroom at the RenCen, outside Walsh's office. He looked twenty years older. His stomach sagged from each day's assortment of fast food. He had heavy bags under both eyes. His hair was completely gray. The last time he studied himself like this, he still had some black hair.

I'm such a jerk. What would a beautiful, classy woman like Jennifer Tracey see in the likes of me? When the case was going well, he was her knight in shining armor, saving her kids. Under those circumstances and in a moment of weakness, she might have considered lowering her standards. Now that the case was over, especially with the expected negative result, the possibility of a relationship was over too.

Throngs of media people would celebrate his victory. But his large verdict against Bartholomew was uncollectable. Gerry had no defense. His fate at the trial was preordained. There would be a small measure of victory, Gerry's public humiliation, and the vilification of this creature, but it would not generate revenue. All his efforts, all the money he spent, trying to prove prior notice and cover-up against the church, had been for naught.

He was a beaten man, beaten by the evil forces of the Coalition. The Voice was laughing at him and would laugh long and hard after the verdict was read. Zachary might have dented the armor a fraction, but, in the final analysis, he did no serious or permanent damage. The Coalition would be assigned its next case and proceed along the same, sinister path it always followed. Sadly, because of Zack's failure here, there would be other abused children.

What was *wrong* with these church guys? Did they genuinely believe the greater good outweighed the suffering of innocent children and their families? Did they employ any preventative mechanisms to stop these sick freaks? Had any lessons been learned? Was the expense of cover-up and payoff less expensive than screening, training, education, or treatment? *For Christ's sake, this egregious conduct, from a major religious institution?* If he didn't know it was true, he wouldn't believe it.

He looked again at his reflection. Color rose in his cheeks. He tried to pump himself up. *I'll complete and deliver a terrific closing statement. I'll argue the obvious—the conspiracy to cover up Bartholomew's prior conduct was elaborate and successful. The church had enormous resources that enabled them to pull it off. But don't be fooled, ladies and gentlemen of the jury. Don't let the Coalition live another minute. Crush it with your verdict. Send this powerful message throughout the religious community: Society will not tolerate the sexual abuse of children. We can crush these perpetrators and those who attempt to protect or shield them. The power of we, the people, must be stronger than the power of any institution, including the church.*

He sat at his kitchen table, frantically writing, occasionally pausing to deliver oratory. The more he wrote and spoke, the more pumped he became. Finally, he declared himself ready. He'd deliver an eloquent and thought-provoking closing. Maybe he hadn't kept all the promises he made to the jury. But he could argue he was prevented from doing so by an elaborate conspiracy. The jury would understand. The verdict must be joint and several—against *all* defendants. Otherwise, it would have no impact. *The jury knows this, don't they?* For the sake of the children, Zachary Blake had to make them understand.

***

The courtroom was filled to capacity. Bridge chairs were strategically placed to handle the overflow. The outer hallway was packed with people who tried, unsuccessfully, to enter the courtroom. Wayne County sheriff's deputies were in the hall, literally pushing the crowd to the elevators, threatening arrests if order could not be restored. Reporters shouted, "Freedom of the press!" "Perry tramples on the First Amendment!" and other such slogans. The undaunted deputies suggested shut out reporters watch the proceedings on television at a local tavern.

Zachary and Jennifer arrived together and slipped through a side door not well known to the public at large. A small staff elevator carried them to the fourth floor, where the deputies were engaged in order-keeping activities. Blake opened an unmarked door that led to the inner hallway and pushed Jennifer into the privacy of the courthouse's inner sanctum before members of the locked-out press could get to her.

It was after 9:00 a.m. The trial would reconvene late because of the turmoil. Judge Perry issued an order from chambers that court would not be in session until complete order was restored, inside and outside the courtroom. Zachary and Jennifer stayed in the inner hallway while the battle to regain order raged on outside. Judge Perry's clerk saw Blake and summoned him into the judge's chambers. Blake entered and was surprised to see Perry and Walsh engaged in friendly conversation.

"Come in, Zack. Have a seat," Perry invited.

"Hi, Zack, how ya doin'?" Walsh chirped.

"Fine, Craig. Are you two having an in-camera conversation out of my presence?" Blake charged. The canons of ethics strictly prohibited such conversations for both judges and lawyers.

"No, Zack, we're just shooting the breeze," Perry explained. "When we finally get started today, how do you intend to proceed?"

"How do you mean?" Blake inquired.

"Rebuttal or closing argument?" The judge cut to the chase.

"Rebuttal, if my witnesses can get through the mess."

"Fine, fine. They'll get through. How many witnesses?"

"As little as one, as many as five. I haven't decided yet."

"You will be limited to three," Perry snapped.

"Why?" Blake wondered.

"Call it a compromise between one and five," Perry insisted.

"There is no precedent for this kind of limitation, I object," Blake postured.

"Your objection is noted, Mr. Blake," Perry uttered. "We will put the ruling and your objections on the record before we proceed."

"You don't have any rebuttal witnesses anyway," Walsh challenged. "It's all a bluff. You know it, and I know it."

"Is this true, Zack?" Judge Perry inquired.

"No, Your Honor, it isn't," Blake lied.

"What are the names of your witnesses?" Walsh continued.

"You'll see when I call them. They're on my witness list."

That was technically true. The MacLean and O'Connell families were on the list. The mystery caller was not—his name was unknown. Zack did add a catch-all to the list. 'Any, and all, employees or agents of the defendants' were part of his witness list. If the caller appeared and was willing to testify, Blake would get him in because of this designation.

"If you waste this court's time or have lied, Mr. Blake, there will be severe sanctions," Perry warned. "I'm already troubled by revelations you've engaged in a personal relationship with a client. I may be obligated to report this to the Bar."

"The video is misleading, Your Honor, which was the intent of playing it. This sleight of hand behavior has permeated the defense case. There is no relationship. But, do what you have to do, Your Honor. I can't stop you. We may be in the process of *beginning* a relationship, but that violates nothing. I won't apologize for having feelings. How about you also consider the way the defense spied on us? Pretty sleazy, wouldn't you agree?

"As to the witnesses, under these circumstances, Your Honor, with the circus going on outside, I can't guarantee they'll show, but I swear my intentions were and are honorable," Blake insisted.

"Well, we'll cross both bridges when we come to them," Perry softened. "What is the substance and purpose of their testimony?"

"To prove Bartholomew's prior incidents and the church's knowledge and cover-up of the same."

"You're bluffing," Walsh blustered.

"Am I?" Blake bluffed. "How would you know anyway? Unless you tampered with my witnesses."

"Your Honor, I resent that insinuation," Walsh groused.

"Your resentment is noted," Perry sighed. "Gentlemen, the trial is almost over. Cut the bullshit."

"Yes, Your Honor."

***

By 11:30 a.m., order was restored. The outer hallway was empty, and the sheriff's deputies were posted at every stairway and elevator. Only people who had business with Judge Perry or the other five judges on the floor would be allowed to pass. Inside the courtroom, proceedings were about ready to begin. The lawyers and litigants were seated at their respective counsel tables, awaiting the arrival of the judge and the jury.

Zachary scanned the gallery for anyone matching the description of the MacLean or O'Connell families or anyone he hadn't seen before who the mystery caller might be. He saw the same faces of the press and the usual court-watchers who were present throughout the trial. He glanced at Jennifer. She was as distant as she had ever been. Her thoughts were elsewhere.

Zack knew any chance the two of them had for a possible

relationship depended on this verdict. The verdict would be vindication that all they'd been through together was just, right, and worth the effort. To meet while fighting a losing battle, which damaged her children, would render any possible relationship unsalvageable.

"All rise!" shouted the bailiff, startling Zack from his thoughts. Judge Perry entered the courtroom through his private entrance, told the gallery to be seated, and asked the lawyers if there were any preliminary matters to discuss before the jury was brought in. Blake raised the issue of the judge's limitation on rebuttal witnesses, and they rehashed the entire conversation again, for the purposes of the record. Again, Walsh argued for severe sanctions, convinced Blake had no rebuttal witnesses.

Finally, after a half-hour of posturing and arguing, they were ready to proceed. It was 12:15 p.m. The jury had been in the jury room since 8:30 a.m. so Judge Perry decided to break for lunch. Rebuttal would begin promptly at 1:30 p.m. Perry apologized to the lawyers, litigants, and the gallery. He asked the bailiff to distribute passes to those in attendance so they might re-enter that afternoon. Only those with passes would be allowed re-entry. With the afternoon procedures established, the judge rose and exited the courtroom.

Zack turned to Jennifer. She was a million miles away.

"Jen? Jen?" He gently shook her arm.

She smiled, dreamily, as she looked at him and stretched. "Yes, Zack? What is it?"

"Court is adjourned. Do you want to grab a quick bite?"

"No. I'd rather stay here. I can't face all those reporters."

"I understand. How's Kenny doing?"

"He's fine. He's coming home this afternoon. Lynne offered to pick him up. I arranged everything so I could be here with you."

She looked at him and smiled. She was mellow and detached. *Drugs?*

"I appreciate that, Jen."

He put his hands on both of her shoulders and turned her toward him.

"What's the matter? You seem out of it this morning. Is

everything okay?"

"Well, since you asked, no, Zack, everything is not okay. My oldest son has been hospitalized. My youngest misses the only person he could always count on. Both have been traumatized, probably for life, and here I am, on some damn crusade to save the world's children. I should have been thinking about saving my own. How can I protect other parents' children when I can't even protect my own?"

She began to tear up, but Zack's question caused her to focus.

"You're being too hard on yourself, Jenny. There was no way for you to have known what Bartholomew was up to."

"That's not what I mean, Zack. What happened on the camping trip was *his* fault, his and the church. I can live with *that*. I can accept *that*!"

"What then?"

"I could have accepted the church's offer of treatment. I could have left things at that. I didn't have to drag my children through a public trial and cause them even more harm. What was I thinking? I could make a difference? What a joke! You can't fight these people, Zack. You did a great job trying. You really did. But in the end, money and power will always prevail."

"You're wrong, Jen," Zack argued, holding her shoulders, squaring her to face him. "That's conveniently cynical. This may sound corny, but sometimes, truth and justice *do* prevail. When I met you, I marveled at your faith, your capacity to believe. Believe in *this*, Jennifer. Believe I am going to win this case because I am. Believe the boys will get through this. They will be happy and strong someday soon. Believe, Jen! Believe!"

"I believe, Zack, but . . ."

Zachary put his finger to her lips. These were the words he wanted from her. There would be no *buts*.

"Hush, shhhh. I will take care of everything. Everything will work out. I promise. Trust me, Jen. I need you to believe . . . in *me*."

"I believe in you, Zack. I've always believed in you. That's not the problem . . ."

He put his finger to her lips again.

"Then, there is no problem. If you believe, we will succeed together."

He leaned forward and kissed her cheek.

"But the boys, Zack."

"The boys will be fine, Jen, as long as we see this through to the ultimate victory. They will receive the treatment they need. They will have their loving mother to support them in all future endeavors. They will see this verdict as an indictment of Bartholomew's conduct and vindication that they did nothing wrong. The verdict will help alleviate their guilt. And I plan to be there to see it all happen."

"You plan to be where?"

"Huh?"

"You 'plan to be there?' Plan to be where?"

"You caught that, huh?"

"You plan to continue to see us after the trial?" she wondered.

"What if I did? What would you say?"

"I'd say the timing was awful."

"Then, we won't."

"Won't what?"

"See each other. Besides, it was simply a rhetorical what-if kind of thing."

"What if?"

"Yeah, you know."

"No, I don't know. Why don't you explain it to me?"

She was toying with him, but he was too uncomfortable to notice.

"Jennifer, I-I-I . . ."

"I know, Zack. I know. I was kidding. We'll talk about this at a more convenient time, and you can explain the what-if scenario."

"Great idea!" Zack exclaimed.

They sat in silence as the courtroom began to fill up. Judge Perry would soon arrive and call for Zack's witnesses.

***

"All rise! Circuit Court for the County of Wayne is now in session, the Honorable John Perry presiding."

Perry entered while the bailiff trumpeted this familiar warning. Several men in suits, presumably lawyers, were standing at the clerk's counter to the right and below the judge's bench. The clerk started handing Perry paperwork that was handed to him by the suits. Perry scanned the documents, signed some of them, rejected others, and returned them to the clerk to complete whatever was necessary to satisfy the lawyers' requests. Blake wondered why judges couldn't set hours for these mundane procedures instead of making spectators, litigants, attorneys, and jurors wait for them to complete these tasks—unless, of course, Blake was the one who needed an order signed.

"Mr. Blake, are you ready to proceed with rebuttal?"

Judge Perry's question stabbed, like a knife, interrupting his thoughts. Zachary rose, scanned the courtroom, and saw all the same familiar faces.

"Your Honor, my witnesses haven't arrived yet."

"Did you inform them I begin the afternoon session promptly at 1:30 p.m.?"

"Uh, no, sir, I did not."

"Why not? May I ask?"

Blake felt drops of sweat forming at his armpits and forehead. Man, it was hot in that courtroom!

"Because, Your Honor, I have not been in contact with these witnesses for quite some time." Walsh sat back in his chair and made eye contact with the Voice. Both smiled broadly.

"Mr. Blake, would you please define 'for quite some time?'"

"Yes, Your Honor, since the beginning of these proceedings."

"These witnesses, who are they, what was their expected testimony, and have they been disclosed to the defense?"

"Yes, they have, Your Honor. One was a priest whose testimony was expected to reveal prior knowledge and cover-up of prior similar incidents involving the principal defendant and to expose a secret organization within the church whose job it is to cover-up such incidents on a broad scale. The others were

previous victims of defendant Bartholomew, whose testimony
would clearly establish he engaged in acts of pedophilia
previously, with other teenagers and pre-teens. The church knew
of these incidents, covered them up, and paid off the victims.
These were the victims at the Doubletree Hotel we saw in the
earlier video presented during Investigator Love's testimony."

Walsh rose.

"May it please the court, Your Honor? This priest is not on
the witness list, and we have been denied the opportunity to
depose these supposed previous victims. I would have objected
to the presentation of all or any of these witnesses. Where are
they? Was the video real? Do they truly exist? If they wish to
testify, perhaps in violation of some type of confidentiality
agreement, why aren't they present in court?"

"Your Honor, 'any, and all employees and/or agents of the
defendants,' is a designation on the Plaintiff's witness list. The
priest in question would surely qualify under that listing. As for
the other witnesses failing to appear, it is my firm belief, as an
officer of the court, buttressed by the video presentation of
Investigator Love, that their failure to appear results from an
obstruction of justice conspiracy perpetrated by the very forces
this lawsuit attempts to expose."

"Objection, Your Honor." Walsh leaped to his feet. "There
has been no evidence . . ."

"Sit *down*, Mr. Walsh. Don't rise again unless you're
instructed to do so by this court. These are serious allegations,
Mr. Blake. Do you have any evidence to support them?"

"Yes, Your Honor, I do. I can offer additional testimony
from private investigator, Micah Love, who was directly
involved in these events."

"Is Mr. Love still in the courtroom?"

"Yes, Your Honor, he is." Blake turned toward the gallery.

"Mr. Love," Perry ordered, "please step forward."

Love rose and walked to the podium, settling on a spot to
Blake's right. Judge Perry advised him he was still under oath.
Blake asked Love to retell the story in narrative form. Walsh rose
to object, but Perry's glare silenced him and sat him down.

This time, Love was permitted, out of the jury's presence, to tell the *entire* story, including parts inadmissible in the presence of the jury. Press members were frantically copying, in one form or another, everything he said. The story, if true, was headline news. Judge Perry focused attention directly on Micah Love. Walsh objected throughout Love's testimony on the grounds that Love was speculating the church was involved in these incidents. Walsh again argued his clients were unfamiliar with these families until they were advised they were once members of St. Pat's in Berea. There was no direct proof the church was involved in the Berea situation.

Blake followed Love's testimony with a presentation of the full Doubletree Suites video. Judge Perry stared at the video screen, paused, fought for control, and spoke.

"Having listened to the testimony and having viewed the full Doubletree video, in context, I find evidence of a possible conspiracy to obstruct justice. If I held an evidentiary hearing on the matter and invited hotel employees, private investigators, Florida law enforcement officials, and certain Florida residents awaiting trial for the B and E, I would probably hear enough evidence the church and its *Coalition* were behind this conspiracy.

"Therefore, I find sufficient probable cause to hold an evidentiary hearing to determine whether to charge Coalition operatives with conspiracy to obstruct justice and obstruction of justice."

"But, Your Honor," a stunned Walsh rose to protest.

"Sit down, Mr. Walsh. You will certainly be a witness at such a hearing. If you were involved in this circus in any minute way, I will have your license to practice law revoked and see you do time in one of our state facilities. Have I made myself clear?"

"Crystal, Your Honor." Walsh quickly sat down.

"Now, the more important question is what to do with this case and this jury. I'll see counsel in my chambers. Court is in recess."

Perry slammed down his gavel and left the courtroom. The two attorneys followed him out, and reporters scattered to call in the story. Blake and Walsh stepped into Perry's private office, and Perry, in a rage, immediately directed it at Walsh.

"God damn it! Such abhorrent behavior conducted and orchestrated by an official of my own church? I am ashamed, Mr. Walsh. What have you to say for your client and, for that matter, for yourself?"

"Your Honor, if these allegations are true, I'm as shocked as you are." Walsh groveled. "I am a member of the church, as well. I do not believe, however, the church had anything to do with these incidents. I certainly can advise you, as an officer of the court, *I* had nothing to do with them," he asserted.

Walsh could break rank in chambers. The Voice wasn't around to hear him, unless, of course, Judge Perry's chambers were bugged.

"As I declared from the bench—if you *were* involved, your career is over."

"I was not involved, Your Honor, and I believe the evidence will show the church wasn't involved either. I also believe you have a predisposition my clients *were* involved in a conspiracy to obstruct. As such, I believe you should recuse . . ."

"Don't go there, Craig!" Perry interrupted. "You're already treading on thin ice with this court. I've heard evidence from a single source. Common sense tells me and anyone else with half a brain, except maybe you, that no one else other than Bartholomew or the church stood to gain anything by murdering an innocent custodian, hiding or abducting two families, or planting listening devices in every participant's home or office. If Love's testimony is corroborated, there *will* be indictments. Do you understand me? If you want to have me recused, go for it! Know this, however. You will have an enemy on the Wayne Circuit Court bench for life!"

"Your Honor, I've changed my mind," Walsh capitulated. "I have confidence in your ability to render a fair and impartial decision in the obstruction matter."

"Now, Mr. Blake, what is your pleasure regarding the failure of these witnesses to appear? How do you propose we get the conspiracy evidence before the jury?"

"I'm not sure, Your Honor. Perhaps, Mr. Love can testify to the obstruction issues for the jury?"

"The evidence is uncorroborated, Mr. Blake. How long

would you need to arrange for the appearance of corroborating witnesses?"

"I have no idea, Your Honor. It's hard to know what other people are willing to do and when they might be willing to do it. Most of these witnesses are out of town. We would need to track them down."

"Would you like a mistrial?"

"God, no, Your Honor! My clients can't go through this again."

"Well, then . . ." Perry contemplated. "I will deliver a cautionary instruction to the jury that I have been provided with adequate evidence of witness tampering and obstruction of justice regarding the remaining proofs to be presented in this case. Zack will make an offer of proof, with or without the testimony of Mr. Love, as to what the absent witnesses were likely to say. The jury can decide for themselves whether this obstruction was or was not an act perpetrated by any of the defendants in this case."

"Your Honor . . ." Walsh tried to object.

"And you, Mr. Walsh, will keep your mouth shut!"

"Yes, Your Honor."

"How does that sound, Mr. Blake?"

"As good as I can expect, under the circumstances, Your Honor." Zack was cautiously elated. He was worried about the appellate ramifications of the ruling. *Will the Court of Appeals sustain this?*

"Very well, then. Let's go put this on the record and bring in the jury."

***

"All rise!" The bailiff shouted the familiar warning.

Perry stormed in. "Be seated," growled the judge, as he assumed his majestic position above the peons below. "Bring in the jury."

Jurors filed in, in order, as they had throughout the trial, wondering what was going on out of their presence. After they were seated, Judge Perry addressed them.

"Ladies and gentlemen, we apologize for all of these delays. They were unavoidable, as you will soon discover when you hear what is about to happen. Mr. Blake has produced credible evidence of deliberate witness tampering by specific agents of the defendants in this case. Witnesses Mr. Blake intended to call before you are unavailable due to this tampering. Therefore, this court hereby makes a judicial finding that justice has, indeed, been obstructed.

"Instead of calling these witnesses, I am permitting Mr. Blake to address you directly or through a witness whom you have heard from earlier, Mr. Micah Love, of Love Investigations. Mr. Love will recount, in detail, experiences that will essentially provide you with the sum and substance of the testimony you would have and should have heard from the unavailable witnesses. You are permitted to presume, in your own good judgment, whether this proffer is true or false and whether or not the obstruction was or was not perpetrated by the defendants or their counsel."

"Your Honor, I object!" cried Walsh, grandstanding for his clients.

Blake admired his guts, given Perry's attitude toward the video and the apparent complicity of the church depicted therein. Walsh was a worthy and challenging adversary.

"Your objection is overruled," Perry ruled. "Mr. Blake?"

Zack rose, preparing to call Micah Love to the stand. Suddenly, the back doors swung open, and a Wayne County sheriff's deputy rushed in, fast-walked over to Blake, and whispered something in his ear. Zack pumped his fist, elated with the news, and asked the court for a brief delay in the proceedings.

"Make it quick, Mr. Blake," the judge commanded. "Enough is enough. The jury is waiting."

He turned to the jury box, winked, and smiled.

"I'll be brief, Your Honor," Zack turned, walking backward, following the deputy out into the public corridor.

Zack pushed open the courtroom doors and there, in the corridor, stood the MacLean and O'Connell families.

"I can't believe this. Thank *God* you're all right!" Blake

yelped. "What happened to you? Where have you been? I have
so many questions. Are you here to testify?"

"Which question would you like answered first?" Pat
O'Connell smiled.

"The last one," Zack smirked.

"We're here to testify. We're tired of running—tired of
hiding. We're here to set the record straight."

"I've been terribly worried about you guys!" Zack
exclaimed. "I'm so relieved. I felt terrible our protection detail
failed you."

"Your protection detail saved our lives, Mr. Blake. It's nice
to finally meet you, by the way. Micah told us all about you.
You're a courageous man. I wish we'd known you when we had
our little go-around with Father Gerry. Your clients must be
proud to have you as their attorney," Pam O'Connell gushed.

"Excuse me, folks. There's something I must do." Blake
turned and burst into the courtroom.

"Your Honor, there's been a development! May we
approach?"

Perry motioned both attorneys toward him. "What's up?"

"The missing families have arrived, Your Honor. They want
to testify!"

"I object, Your Honor," Walsh screeched. "You've already
damaged my clients with this wild obstruction story. Now, here
are the missing witnesses—no obstruction! The jury is tainted.
No way! I won't allow it!"

"*You* won't allow it?" Perry gasped. "Who's the judge here?"

"Sorry, Your Honor. I didn't mean it that way. But it is
highly prejudicial to allow this testimony after practically
accusing my clients of conspiring to prevent it."

"No, it isn't," Zack interrupted. "In fact, it's to your
advantage. Your Honor, these witnesses have a story to tell.
They will be subject to direct *and* cross-examination. Mr. Walsh
can now cross them on any subject relevant to these proceedings,
including the obstruction charges. With the offer of proof
through Mr. Love, I would have been permitted, as I understood
it, to essentially offer what their testimony was *expected* to be,
without giving Mr. Walsh an opportunity for cross-examination.

Thus, it is to the advantage of the defense, especially now that the jury has been informed of obstruction charges, to cross-examine these witnesses and attempt to impeach their credibility."

"Sounds persuasive to me, Mr. Walsh," Perry analyzed. "What about it, Mr. Walsh?"

Zack's argument was brilliant, precisely what Perry expected. *Of course,* these witnesses would testify.

"Your Honor, I . . . I . . . believe these witnesses are tainted by their experiences. They will assume facts not in evidence." Walsh stuttered.

"And you can object and cross-examine to your heart's content," Zack reminded.

"Anything further, gentlemen?" Perry was ready to rule.

The two men shook their heads.

"Step back," ordered Perry. "Ladies and gentlemen of the jury, the witnesses, who were previously unavailable to testify, have arrived. Shortly, they will provide testimony on behalf of the plaintiff. The defense will have an opportunity to cross-examine these witnesses, and I will grant both attorneys wide latitude.

"You are permitted to decide what weight, if any, to give to this or any other testimony you have heard in this trial. Evidence comes from the witnesses and exhibits presented, not from speeches by the attorneys, not from me. Listen carefully to their answers on both direct and cross-examination. Do you understand?"

Whether they understood or not, every juror nodded in the affirmative. Now that the witnesses had appeared, Judge Perry cleverly appeased the defense by indicating "speeches" given by attorneys or him—including the one he made about obstruction—were *not* evidence. Thus, Perry's statement cured the record on appeal.

"Call your first rebuttal witness, Mr. Blake."

"The plaintiff calls Pamela O'Connell."

Attorney and witness plodded through the preliminaries and Pam's religious upbringing in Berea. They discussed her childhood memories, her marriage to Pat, and the joy of giving birth to healthy children. They discussed her positive relationship with Father Foley, other assistant pastors, and her devotion to her church.

Zack intended to establish Pam as a woman of the church, much like Jennifer, who was ultimately betrayed by church and Coalition operatives. Pam was *not* out to get the church. She had no unreasonable ax to grind. She was here to recount events in her life that began with the arrival of Father Gerry Bartholomew at St. Patrick's Church in Berea.

"What, if any, changes occurred to St. Patrick's, after Father Bartholomew arrived?" Zack inquired.

"When he first arrived, positive ones. Everything was wonderful. The boys liked him. Members thought he was wonderful. His sermons were moving and thought-provoking. Father Foley was aging. As time went on, he was less able to relate to the children and younger adults of the parish. Father Gerry was a breath of fresh air to those younger families."

"How long, after Bartholomew's arrival, did this harmonious period last?"

"For my family, about two, maybe three months. For almost everyone else, his entire three-year stay at St Pat's appeared *harmonious*, to use your word."

"Why were things different for your family?"

"Because Father Gerry took my children on an overnight camping trip to Cedar Point and sexually molested them." She trained her eyes on Bartholomew and delivered the words with little emotion. Bartholomew avoided eye contact and stared at the floor. The jury noticed the exchange. Murmurs rose from the gallery. Perry demanded silence and received it without pounding the gavel. Everyone present wanted to hear this woman's testimony.

"How did you discover they'd been sexually abused?"

"They came back from that weekend and were . . . I don't know how to describe it . . . different."

"Different, how?"

"They were quiet, aloof, tearful. There were violent mood swings. They lashed out verbally and physically at each other, my husband, and me. Their grades were in the toilet, and they refused to attend church or school outings. Their friends stopped coming around, but the boys didn't seem to care. They spent countless hours alone in their rooms. We knew they liked Gerry, so we asked if they were willing to discuss their problems with him."

"What was their reaction?"

"They refused. They called him vile names and said they never wanted to see him again."

"What did you do?"

"At first, I got angry. I taught my kids to respect the church and the clergy. I've never heard any of them talk that way about a priest. I thought it was blasphemous. I demanded an explanation. They told me he was a pervert. They turned and walked out on me in mid-conversation. They've *never* treated me with such disrespect."

Pam's eyes started to water. Judge Perry handed Zack a box of tissues, which he, in turn, handed to Pam. He waited for her to compose herself.

"Are you ready to continue, Mrs. O'Connell?"

"Yes, thank you."

"What did you do after the incident you describe?"

"I recounted the incident to Father Foley."

Yes! Zack beamed. *Notice to the church! Notice to Foley began the cover-up.*

"What did he do?"

"He recommended counseling."

"Religious counseling?"

"No, psychiatric."

"Did you follow his recommendation?"

"Yes, I did. He even recommended the therapist."

"Your kids went to see this person?"

"Yes, they did."

"Who paid for the sessions?"

"The church. I thought it was strange at the time, but Father Foley insisted."

"What was the result of the sessions?"

"They seemed to have no effect on the boys' behavior. Therapy centered on comfort through religion, and the boys wanted no part of that."

"Did they ever say why?"

"Not at first, but one day, probably two to three months into therapy, we had a family therapy session."

"What happened?"

"We were asking the boys why they hated church and school so much."

"What did they say?"

"They said it was because of Father Gerry."

"Did you ask why?"

"No, the therapist did."

"What was their answer?"

"My oldest started screaming and crying. He claimed Gerry was a pervert and did some disgusting things to him and his brothers. He was embarrassed to discuss them in front of me, so I was asked to leave the room. After I left, he advised my husband and this therapist that Father Gerry sexually molested him and his brothers."

One by one, the Berea parents walked into the courtroom and provided graphic detail of abuse, cover-up, and payoffs at St. Pat's. Perry ordered the family members sequestered, so no parent heard another's testimony. Perry wanted no suggestion that these parents were communicating with each other during testimony. As each testified, they were placed in the jury room, guarded by a Wayne County Sheriff's deputy.

Their stories were surprisingly similar to the Tracey family's experience. Their children spent an overnight outing with Gerry, and a sudden and startling transformation in their behavior and attitude toward Gerry and the church resulted. One by one, they revealed their shock and disbelief when the children told them Gerry sexually abused them. Disbelief became shock and horror when they learned the extent of the abuse. Their children never fully recovered, even with a change of scenery and a complete withdrawal from religion and religious activities.

Presuming Gerry was merely a rogue priest, the two couples demanded a meeting with Father Foley to advise him what they had learned. Father Foley gave them lip service.

"Suddenly, that man appeared," a parent cried, pointing to

Moloney. "He identified himself as a bishop, took over the conversation, offered treatment, significant money, and a change of scenery, in exchange for our silence. He argued the institution of the church would suffer greatly if these *allegations*, as he called them, were made public."

Notice to the church hierarchy—Zack was pumped. The Berea parents hammered the proverbial nail in the coffin.

The parents discussed Moloney's offer and agreed the church could not have been aware of Father Gerry's issues before placing him at St. Pat's. They assumed church officials would punish him internally, and prevent him from ever doing anything like this to another child. They accepted an offer of a new life in a new environment, with lifetime psychiatric treatment for their kids, in exchange for telling no one why they were suddenly and mysteriously moving out of state. They even promised not to tell their loved ones where they had gone.

They lost their homes, extended families, religion, and, in no small degree, their children. Their kids would never be the same despite the best care the church's money could buy.

In retrospect, they could not believe how gullible they'd been. How could that man—Moloney—have known the purpose of their meeting with Father Foley? What was he doing there if Gerry's propensities were unknown to the church? Why did they trust the church to do the right thing? *Of course,* church officials knew Gerry was a pedophile *before* his Berea placement.

They spoke of their painful banishment from Berea, moving away from friends and family. How foolish they were! Their kids were sexually abused and whisked away without an opportunity to say goodbye to family and friends. No wonder they blamed themselves. Why did their parents send them away, in the middle of the night, if all of this wasn't their fault? Their parents' own actions, trying to protect their children, created an ocean of unnecessary guilt.

The jury heard the stories of the families' escape from Coral Springs, minutes before would be abductors arrived. The families hid out on the beach in Ft. Lauderdale and at Disney World and then flew home with Micah Love, only to run into another abduction attempt in Southfield. Had they not escaped that night, they would not have been alive the following morning.

The sum and substance of their testimony continued, "We fled to Ohio. Can you believe it? We decided Ohio was the last place anyone would think to look for us. We hid out in flophouse hotels in Toledo, paid in cash, and never stayed in the same place for more than two or three days. We watched the proceedings on Court TV and tried to determine whether or not our testimony was needed. We decided to return to Michigan. *We* needed to tell our story, stop running and hiding, and return home to Berea so our kids could reunite with their grandparents, cousins, aunts, uncles, and friends.

"We needed to say to hell with the church and this mysterious man who paid us so much and cost us so much more. Most of all, we needed to stop Gerry. Had we spoken up in the first place, the Tracey boys would never have experienced his unique brand of *preaching*.

"For *our* crime, we will always owe a debt to this tragic family. We could have prevented their pain. Jennifer and her boys were severely and unnecessarily punished because of our stupidity, fear, and blind, misplaced faith. Jennifer, we are so sorry! Can you ever forgive us?"

As their direct examinations were completed, they were turned over to Walsh for cross-examination. A beaten man, Walsh concentrated on establishing the abductors were never identified, and witnesses could not testify that Bartholomew, the church, or Father Moloney retained their services. Beyond that, there was absolutely nothing he could do. He posed the same questions to each parent, sat down, and then buried his head in his hands. Blake had no questions on redirect and rested his case after the testimony was completed. Walsh had no additional rebuttal witnesses.

Trial adjourned for lunch. Perry ordered the attorneys to return promptly at one-thirty to begin closing arguments. He pounded the gavel, rose, and quickly left the bench.

Jennifer and Zachary immediately embraced the O'Connell and the MacLean families while Moloney and Walsh shuffled slowly out of the courtroom, muttering at each other. Zack suggested Jennifer take the two families out to lunch. He wouldn't be joining them. He had a new closing argument to write.

The courtroom was empty now. Zack took a deep breath, slowly exhaled, and scanned the courtroom. He was about to have his greatest triumph as a lawyer in this place. A silver-plated plaque above the judge's bench read, "Justice, Justice, Shalt Thou Pursue." He reflected on nine grueling days of trial, leaned back in his chair, and smiled.

He pursued justice for his clients with vigor. Would he secure it? He couldn't undo what was done to them, but he could secure their financial future by making the church pay for its misdeeds. If compensation wasn't justice, victory certainly was. A jury verdict would provide a measure of justice, and this victory would send Jake and Kenny a clear message: *Once and for all, what happened was not your fault*! Perhaps it would send the same message to the O'Connell and MacLean children.

He cleared his head, interrupting his own thoughts. *Time to finish my closing . . .*

Chapter Sixty

"Ladies and gentlemen of the jury, this is the first of two opportunities I will have to address you in what is known as the closing argument. You'll remember I made some specific promises during the opening statement. If I delivered on those promises, I told you I would summarize the proofs and prove I delivered. I asked you to render a significant verdict for the plaintiffs, only if you decided I kept my promises.

Our initial complaint demanded forty million dollars. Judge Perry will instruct you. You may award compensatory damages for the plaintiff's losses, *and*, if you decide they are appropriate, *punitive damages*, which *punish* the defendants.

The amounts we've demanded may seem exorbitant. We acknowledge this, but this case has never been about money. From the beginning, my clients sought to send a message to these defendants. Unfortunately, the only message these defendants can be sent is measured in dollars. To prevent similar conduct, this must be a strong and painful message. You may choose a higher figure, any figure you desire. My job is finished after I sit down for the last time. When I do, my clients' fates will be in *your* capable hands, ladies and gentlemen. Rendering justice will be *your* job.

"I must be honest—humble, but honest. This trial went *better* than we could have imagined. We have proven the defendant, Gerry Bartholomew, repeatedly sexually abused two beautiful young boys, Kenny and Jake Tracey." He turned and pointed at Bartholomew as he spoke.

"The boys were only fourteen and twelve years old at the time, happy-go-lucky, fun-loving boys, like your sons, nephews, or grandsons. Their whole lives were in front of them. Their worries and concerns were the simple ones of any twelve or fourteen-year-olds. Who are my teachers this year? Will I have friends in my class? Will Mom buy me an iPhone? Will the Lions, Tigers, Pistons, or Red Wings have good seasons? Will I do well in school? Will my parents be proud of me? Will I be invited to cool parties? Will I meet a girl? These should be the problems of Kenny and Jake Tracey. Instead, they worry about whether they can ever get the filthy and disgusting acts of this degenerate out of their minds." He pointed again at Bartholomew, who lowered his head.

"The boys worry other kids are looking at them funny or treating them differently because they had sex with Father Gerry. They did not have sex with this predator—they were raped! Never mind that Bartholomew used his church, his power, and his size to force two innocent boys to bend to his will. What matters to casual friends of Kenny and Jake Tracey is they had sex with *Father Gerry! Gross!* Kids can be cruel. You know this from your own common experiences.

"Kenny and Jake Tracey worry they will never trust or have faith again. Remember, ladies and gentlemen of the jury, these were religious boys, inspired by the remarkable faith of their mother. Today, as you've heard, they refuse to step into the church they were baptized in, where they attended services and experienced happiness all their lives. They've had more joy at Lakes than anywhere, but now, they are too disgusted and afraid to set foot in the place. Why? Because Lakes is the place where they met *him*!" He turned and pointed at Bartholomew, one more time. "Our Lady of the Lakes Church and School is the place responsible for bringing *him* into their lives. They can't go in *there*!

"Kenny and Jake Tracey are in a perpetual state of anguish. You saw their tortured agony as you listened to their deposition testimony . . ." Zack could not mention Kenny's emotional live testimony because Perry excluded it. However, Zack knew that no juror could completely erase those visual moments from memory. "They are moody, angry, disinterested in things that inspire every teenage boy—sports, hobbies, cars, music, girls, junk food, or school. Their grades have suffered, an issue, which, if not arrested, will have negative consequences in their adult lives.

"Ladies and gentlemen, you have heard the testimony of Dr. Rothenberg, a board-certified psychiatrist retained by *the Defendants*. He told you the boys have terrible guilt feelings.

Somehow, they feel they brought this abuse upon themselves.
Their guilt is compounded by their respect for their mother and
their church, which prevented them from discussing the abuse.
They buried the pain inside, coerced into feelings of desperation.
You heard Dr. Rothenberg say the boys were just beginning their
'raging hormones' period. Puberty has been totally disrupted by
these events, causing long-term, perhaps permanent, effects on
sexuality. Dr. Rothenberg told you many victims of sexual abuse
experience depression, flashbacks, suicidal thoughts, alcoholism,
drug abuse, aggressive behavior, and confusion of sexual
identity. Long-term, possibly lifetime treatment is in their future.

"You have heard the haunting and heartbreaking testimony of
Jennifer Tracey, who told of her shock and revulsion when
advised by Dr. Rothenberg that her boys were sexually abused.
She told you how the abuse has affected her relationship with her
own children. 'They aren't as loving anymore,' she told you.
Their grades have dropped, they don't play with each other like
they used to, they have drastic mood swings, they stay in their
bedrooms for long periods of time, they have no friends, they
don't pray anymore, and they won't give their own mother a
simple good-night kiss. She told you of the horrible images of
abuse she cannot erase from her mind. Please, remember her
riveting testimony, ladies and gentlemen.

"You have also heard smug and *dishonest* testimony from
Bishop Moloney. He lied under oath when he denied previous
knowledge of Bartholomew's pedophilia. The brave testimony of
the O'Connell and MacLean family proves Moloney committed
perjury. A bishop in the church swore on oath, to tell the truth in
this court, and then *lied* to you, ladies and gentlemen! Are we
surprised? What do we expect from a man who conspires to
obstruct justice, tampers with witnesses, plants listening devices
in people's homes and offices, and offers huge amounts of cash
in exchange for silence?

"And what of the testimony of Gerry Bartholomew, ladies
and gentlemen? When presented with an opportunity to explain
his so-called illness to you, to apologize to Jennifer Tracey and
her boys, what did he do? He hid behind the Fifth Amendment,
even though he'd already pleaded guilty to the acts in question.

"Father Gerry Bartholomew pleaded guilty because he *is* guilty. He committed unspeakable and perverted acts against defenseless children. Worse, this predator used his position in furtherance of his crimes and disguised his depravity as a religious ritual. This man will soon reside in an Ohio prison, where he belongs. He is not only guilty of serious crimes against children. He is guilty of a serious betrayal of faith.

"Finally, Ladies and Gentlemen, you heard compelling testimony from the O'Connell and MacLean families. These brave men and women risked their lives to travel to this place and present the truth about the church and its Coalition. It wasn't enough the church's agent, Bartholomew, destroyed the innocence of their children. It wasn't enough these families, because of their faith and trust in their church, accepted deceptive offers of support. It wasn't enough these families were forced, in the middle of the night, to move out of town and into seclusion from friends and families, like criminals.

"It wasn't enough for the church. Through its *Coalition*, church operatives planned to silence these families, abduct them from their homes and, perhaps, kill them. We may never know how low they would go. We suspect they killed one of their long-time loyal employees as part of their cover-up operation.

"I'm sure you've heard the phrase 'the truth shall set you free.' These simple, yet profound words apply to these two families. They are free to return home. Their silence is no longer necessary. Their safety is assured because if anything happens to them, suspicion will automatically be cast upon the church and its Coalition. Besides, I have a feeling a change for the better is currently in the works."

Zachary glanced over to and winked at Father Jon and Jennifer, side by side, in the front row.

"Ladies and gentlemen, Gerry Bartholomew's unconscionable actions and their devastating effect on the Tracey family present a unique opportunity to you. The church's prior knowledge of Bartholomew's depravity and its failure to sequester him from children presents a unique opportunity for you. The church's involvement in a conspiracy to obstruct justice and prevent you from hearing evidence presents a unique opportunity for you. You may send a strong message with your verdict. Consider this your unique opportunity to inform the church this kind of behavior cannot and will not be tolerated.

"Mothers and children will no longer go quietly into the night. Yesterday is over, forever. A new day dawns with the reading of your verdict. Let your word be the strongest possible deterrent to clergy-parishioner child abuse. After all, ladies and gentlemen of the jury, the children of today *and* those of tomorrow are counting on you. Don't let them down. Thank you very much for your kind attention."

Zack sat down, emotionally exhausted. Judge Perry was about to invite Walsh to begin his opening when an audience member rose and began to applaud. Perry banged his gavel for order. A second and third spectator rose, followed by another and another until the entire gallery stood and applauded. Perry pounded his gavel, rapidly, over and over, but the gavel was drowned out by thunderous applause. Perry turned his head toward the back wall and permitted himself a broad smile.

When order was finally restored, Judge Perry admonished the gallery for its outburst and ordered the courtroom cleared. He also instructed the jury to disregard the outburst and use their own good judgment in deciding the important issues of this case.

Walsh objected. He argued the outburst tainted the jury and demanded a mistrial. Judge Perry denied the request. After the court officers cleared the courtroom, Perry invited Walsh to present his closing argument. He delivered a professional, if not persuasive, closing argument. What could he say? Blake proved his case. He delivered on every promise. Blake beat him and his clients into submission. All Craig Walsh could do now was try to limit the verdict.

He emphasized Dr. Unatin's testimony and deemphasized Dr. Rothenberg's. He told the jury there was no credible evidence the boys would have long-term psychiatric problems. He argued many of Kenny and Jake's problems stemmed from the death of their father, and that Jennifer's continuing maternal love would ultimately make them whole again. "Love is the best medicine in the world," he testified with a smile. Finally, he argued he could not excuse or condone Gerry's acts but asked the jury to remember they were the depraved acts of a sick individual, who, like the Tracey boys, needed professional counseling.

"There has been no credible evidence offered," he claimed, "to prove these acts were known to anyone other than Gerry, until this lawsuit was filed."

Gallery members turned to one another, stunned, as did Zack and Jennifer, wondering, "Was Walsh present during the rebuttal testimony?" Apparently, he meant the Coalition didn't operate under the auspices of the church. This was an interesting hypothesis, but the time for presenting it was during the trial, and not during closing arguments. Walsh concluded with an anecdote, about money not achieving justice, and quietly sat down.

Zack delivered a few brief rebuttal comments and rested his case. After months of preparation and weeks of rigorous motions, briefs, arguments, and testimony, the case and trial of *Tracey v. Bartholomew et al.* was almost over. The only remaining tasks were Judge Perry's instructions to the jury, the jury's deliberations, and, finally, the publication of the jury's verdict.

The lawyers previously submitted proposed jury instructions to Judge Perry. The judge dismissed the jury, and the lawyers began the mundane task of arguing over, objecting to, and finally agreeing upon various instructions for Perry to read to the jury. Perry also had some of his own, which he routinely used.

When the attorneys and the judge finally agreed upon the instructions, Perry summoned the jury back to the courtroom, where he slowly and methodically instructed them on the law. He paid particular attention to the types of damages they were permitted to award in the case. When he finished delivering the instructions, he ordered the jurors to return to the jury room, choose a foreperson, and begin deliberations. At that time, he randomly selected and apologetically dismissed the alternate. The jury rose and filed out of the courtroom. The case was all over but for the waiting.

***

The courtroom emptied quickly. Jenny and Zack strolled out in silence. Zack was hoping she would say something about his closing—Was he effective? Did Jenny think they had a chance of getting what they wanted? To his dismay, she kept her eyes on the floor and her mouth shut. Her demeanor suddenly changed when she walked into the corridor. She looked up and her mouth opened in a gasp.

"Bill! Oh, my God, Bill!" she shrieked pure joy. She was gazing at a young priest, handsome, slender, well built, and tall. He had startling blue eyes, bluer even than Jennifer's. His hair was dark and wavy, parted on the right, the sideburns touched with a wisp of gray. He wore the traditional black on black with a cleric's collar. His smile revealed sparkling white teeth. But for the priestly wardrobe, this man could have made a fortune on the male model circuit.

"Jennifer!" he exclaimed.

"It's so good to see you! What are you doing here?" Jennifer cried, wrapping her arms around him.

"I don't know . . . moral . . . perhaps spiritual support for you and the boys . . . and some news." He terminated the embrace.

"And what?"

"Good news."

"What news?"

Jennifer was very excited. Zack hadn't seen her like this in weeks. Zack was trying to decide how to play the situation. He recognized the voice immediately. The mystery caller stood in front of him. But the cleric wasn't bringing this up, so Zack played along.

"Father Jon is retiring. I am the new pastor at Lakes."

"Oh, my God! What wonderful news! I mean, I love Father Jon, but—oh, did you hear, Zack? Zack! Father! Have you two met? Each other, I mean. This is wonderful news! Wait 'til I tell the boys. This may bring them back to me and, maybe, just maybe, begin to restore their faith! It's so good to see you. You look wonderful!" She gushed.

"Thanks, Jennifer. Under the circumstances, you are also looking well."

"Liar. I look awful, but thanks anyway. You'll come to dinner tonight? I can't wait to see the boys' faces when they see you and find out you're going to be back in their lives."

"I'd be delighted. Thanks for the invite."

Zachary was confused. Who was this guy to the Tracey family? Zack was beginning to feel a bit jealous. The two old friends chatted for a few moments before Jenny excused herself so she could catch up with Dr. Rothenberg.

"Mr. Blake?"

"Yes?"

"My name is Father William Stern. We spoke on the telephone."

"I thought so. Though I've got to say, things would have been a lot easier if you had let me put you on the stand."

The young priest nodded. "I watched the testimony of those four courageous people from Ohio. I'm not a lawyer, but I believe they've won your case for you."

"It's not my case, Father. It belongs to Jennifer and her sons. I'm just a caretaker."

"Seeing Jennifer, Kenny, and Jake on television was wonderful, but painful at the same time."

"I couldn't help but notice how excited she was to see you. How is it you know the Tracey family?" Zack was puzzled.

"Yes . . . well, you see, Mr. Blake. I am quite friendly with the Tracey family. I was Gerry's predecessor."

"You were what? Wait a second . . . Father William . . . Father Bill! You are *that* Father Bill?"

"Yes, Mr. Blake," Father Bill revealed, flashing his million-dollar smile.

Zack became angry. "Jennifer and the boys, they . . . they *love* you. How could you put them through this? How could you let things get so far? What the hell is the matter with you priests?"

"Please try to understand, Mr. Blake. I became a member of the Coalition after leaving Farmington Hills. Gerry's crime against Jake and Kenny was my first case. I was led to believe the organization monitored parishes and determined charitable needs or assisted priests who were having trouble with missions or addictions. I thought we were responsible for helping to match parish and priest and assuring community needs were met.

"I was not involved in Gerry's placement or the cover-up in Berea. There were mistakes made, and those mistakes were allowed to continue because certain people wanted to save face. When I found out what Gerry was, I was repulsed and scared. These were *my* kids who were exposed to his depravity. I almost quit the Coalition and the priesthood on the spot.

"After prayer and reflection, I decided my silence was more beneficial than my protest. I was only one new voice. My protest may have gotten me expelled. What help would I have been to the boys then? I decided to be silent, see what developed, gather as much evidence as I could, and expose Moloney and the Coalition for the criminals they are."

"Then why wouldn't you testify?"

"Hear me out, Mr. Blake. You have beaten the Coalition. It will not survive your verdict. I would have come forward if I didn't know this in my heart. A change in the focus of the Coalition is already in the works, a change from cover-up and conspiracy to exposure, censure, expulsion, and treatment. Instead of paying off victims and silencing them, the Coalition and the church will embrace them and their families, publicly vilify their abuser and provide spiritual and clinical counseling to all. The Coalition is developing a program to educate, screen, test, and counsel applicants for the priesthood, so clergy-parishioner molestation becomes a thing of the past."

"How do you know all this, Father?" Zachary wondered.

"Because I am the new national director of the Coalition."

"You're kidding, right?"

"No, Mr. Blake, I'm not. Moloney and his scandalous, murderous ways are out. He'll be prosecuted for the murder of the Berea custodian and for orchestrating cover-ups of Gerry's crimes in Ohio and Michigan. He simply doesn't know this yet."

"This is wonderful news, Father, but what does this have to do with your testimony?"

"There were two unpreventable consequences of my testifying. One, I would have been exposed as the mystery 'turncoat' of the Coalition, which would have had a very detrimental effect on my leadership."

"Why? I don't understand. You mentioned things are changing . . ."

"Changing, yes, Mr. Blake," Bill interrupted. "But they have not yet *changed*. There are still many hardliners who prefer to close their eyes and allow things to be handled the old way. Word of my testimony would have a chilling effect on the winds of change. Consequently, those hardliners might successfully quell the uprising of respectability to and fair treatment of victims and vilification of pedophile priests."

"You indicated there were *two* problems. What's the other one?" Zack wondered aloud.

"The Tracey family. They've suffered enough, don't you think? I'm the only religious figure who hasn't betrayed them. I may be the only one with an opportunity to restore their faith. Perhaps I can convince them to blame their experiences on the predators *responsible*, rather than God, religion, or themselves. If they found out I was a member of the hated Coalition during this trial, their faith in me could be destroyed. The revelation might cause a greater breach between them and their religion. They *need* their faith and their religious beliefs, Mr. Blake. My testimony may have gotten them a larger jury award, but it would have devastated this family."

"I understand. It's tough to reestablish a relationship when you're part of the problem," reasoned Zack. "Your secret is safe with me. What are your immediate plans?"

"Begin the healing process, Mr. Blake. A supportive member of the clergy will now be with them throughout jury deliberations, which should be helpful to them. I also wanted to bring news of Father Jon's retirement and my elevation as the new pastor of Our Lady of the Lakes. I could never have assumed the position if I had testified, Mr. Blake. Testimony adverse to the church would have made my transfer here impossible. Do you understand?"

"I do, Father. Under the circumstances you describe, I totally understand. What you are about to do for Jennifer and the boys will be more beneficial than any additional compensation the jury might have awarded as a result of your testimony. Thank you, Father, for everything you've done."

"You really care about them, don't you, Mr. Blake?"

"Yes, Father. I do. When this is over, I plan to pursue a relationship with Jennifer, if she'll have me."

"That's wonderful news, Mr. Blake, but a word of advice, if I may?"

"Sure."

"Take it slow. This family has been through significant trauma. Wait until the waters calm. If this blossoms into a love affair, I'll perform the ceremony myself."

"My rabbi might object."

"Oh . . . we'll do it together, then. I'll handle your conversion, though."

"I don't think so, Father."

"Kidding, Mr. Blake."

Chapter Sixty-One

After waiting over two hours for a verdict, Judge Perry sent everyone home. Zack speculated the jury had just enough time to select a foreperson and discuss liability. He doubted whether they'd deliberated long enough to consider damages. Jennifer and Father Bill spent the time renewing old acquaintances.

Jennifer was happy that the judge called it a night. She couldn't wait to bring Bill home and see her sons' reactions. Following their abuse, the boys were cold to anyone associated with the church. With Bill, it would be different. He was there for them in the aftermath of their father's death. He became a constant in their lives. They loved him and trusted him. Then, he left them.

Will they hold a grudge or blame Father Bill's leaving Lakes for what happened with Gerry? Has Father Gerry ruined things for the boys and any priest, even Bill? Her questions would be answered shortly. As Jennifer and Bill drove home, they talked about the boys. Jennifer explained their symptoms and Dr. Rothenberg's diagnosis and prognosis. Bill just listened. He never let on he knew everything.

They pulled up on the driveway. The boys were in front of the house, tossing a football. They ignored the truck, figuring Mom was home, no big deal. The tall, handsome priest exited the truck from the passenger side. Both boys saw him and shrieked with surprise and joy. Kenny ran to Bill and hugged him around the waist, followed shortly by Jake, who joined in a group hug. The boys completely ignored Father Bill's collar. He was not a priest or an agent of the church. He was Father Bill. Kenny and Jake loved him unconditionally. He put an arm around each boy, and the entire family walked into the house.

Zack drove back to his place alone. He felt abandoned by Jennifer after Bill's arrival. While he was not surprised she was thrilled to see Bill, he was unprepared to be entirely ignored by a woman he had feelings for on such an important night. He assumed he and Jennifer would await the verdict together. After seeing Bill, wrapping her arms around Bill, she completely neglected Zack. Jennifer and Bill walked arm in arm out of the courtroom, and never looked back.

Fuck! Zack felt like a jilted lover, replaced by his predecessor. He knew better, of course. How could he be jealous of a celibate priest? What of the boys? Bill was back in their lives. Was a relationship with Zack even possible? If the boys didn't care about Zack, why would Jennifer? He felt a migraine coming on. He arrived home. His telephone was ringing. He fumbled with his keys, inserted them in the lock, and burst into his house to grab the phone before the caller hung up. He was pleased to hear Jennifer's voice.

"Zack, with all the excitement over Father Bill, I forgot all about our date tonight. God, did I even introduce you two? Anyway, I brought Bill home. He's with the boys now, telling them his wonderful news. You should have seen their reaction when they saw him, Zack. They were my boys again, like none of this ever happened. Not even his *collar* bothered them. Bill will bring Lakes and faith back into the boys' lives. I know he will. That's half the battle. Zack. If you have faith, you can accomplish anything."

"I know you believe that, Jen. It's one of the things I love about you. This is wonderful news. I'm so happy for all of you. You deserve tons of happiness."

"Do you want to come over?"

"I don't think so. Let the boys have their evening with Father Bill. I'll see you tomorrow."

"Are you sure? I'll miss you."

"I'm sure, Jen."

"Whatever the outcome, thank you for everything. You were wonderful. You're the one positive thing to come out of this whole miserable experience. I couldn't have done this without you."

"If you have faith, you can accomplish anything," Zack chuckled.

"I'm serious. You're still my knight in shining armor. And, Zack?"

"Yes, Jen . . ."

He wanted desperately to hang up. She was torturing him, tossing him bones to make him feel good.

"When you're ready, I'd like to discuss the what-if scenario."

Tears began to form. *Does she mean it? Is this just another bone?*

"Seriously? You're not jerking me around, are you?"

"No, Zack. I'd like to talk about it."

"Well, then, we will talk soon. See you tomorrow."

"Zack?"

"Yes?"

"Are you all right? You sound blue."

"I'm fine, Jenny, just exhausted. It's been a long day."

"A long week and a half, you mean. Get some sleep. You probably haven't slept in over a week."

"It certainly *feels* that way."

"Well then, I won't keep you from your dreams any longer. Goodnight, Zack."

"Goodnight, Jen."

Zachary hung up the receiver and sat for a long moment, hand still attached to the receiver. He wondered if this was the beginning for him and Jennifer or the beginning of the end. *Time will tell.*

He hoisted himself up off the sofa and trudged into the bathroom. He turned on the shower as hot as the nozzle would turn. Slowly, he began to peel off his clothing, tossing articles haphazardly here and there. The air became thick with steam, and Zack began to sweat. He didn't notice. In the next few days, he'd receive his verdict. Win or lose, he feared Jennifer would soon be gone. He stood under the cascade, head down, until the water turned cold. Jennifer was correct, as usual. The money didn't mean a damn thing.

Chapter Sixty-One

Conventional wisdom says if a jury is going to no-cause the plaintiff— award no damages—the verdict will be swift. Similar logic applies to criminal trials where juries will, within hours, convict people, but take days to acquit.

In civil cases, this rule is more than courtroom legend. It takes longer to decide a plaintiff's verdict than it does to rule for the defense, for two simple reasons: A defense verdict requires one finding—the defendant was not responsible for the plaintiff's damages. A plaintiff's verdict requires a finding of liability *and* evaluation of damages, something not needed in a defense verdict. Thus, by sheer evidence evaluation, a jury has more work to do when rendering a verdict in favor of the plaintiff.

In *Tracey v. Bartholomew*, the jury had been out four days— usually a good sign for a plaintiff. Zack, however, was troubled by two considerations. The first was every rule had an exception. The six men and women could easily be stalemated over issues of liability and still be contemplating a "no cause." The second— and more probable—was the jury could be computing significant damages, but against *Father Gerry only*. Jennifer and the boys would win the battle but lose the war.

This issue was keeping Zack up at night, a concern from the moment Jennifer walked through his office door. The verdict was uncollectible against an impoverished priest. The boys would never see a dime unless the church decided to cover the verdict. *That* would only happen if significant concessions in money and future publicity issues were negotiated. Jennifer was unlikely to concede anything to those bastards.

He hoped this jury was deadlocked over *how much* money to award the plaintiff from *both* defendants. If a verdict was joint and several, the plaintiff could collect the entire award from either or both defendants. It was crucial for this verdict to be joint and several.

The three-plus days of jury deliberation were agonizing in light of anticipation of the verdict. The first full day of deliberation was spent in the courtroom. Zack, Father Bill, Jennifer, and the boys sat, paced, and waited with Walsh and a few local reporters who had followed the story from the beginning. Jennifer wisely brought a couple of board games. The boys sat at the counsel table and played the games. That they were playing at all, was a significant improvement brought about by the return of Father Bill. Zack couldn't quell rising feelings of jealousy.

By the second day, Judge Perry decided he'd return, as much as possible, to the other business of his court. He advised the parties he'd call them if the jury delivered a verdict or if an issue required the attorneys' presence.

Blake used the following few days to catch up on paperwork and unfinished cases. He also started to return a mountain of telephone messages resulting from his rekindled fame as a trial lawyer. Zack could build a practice again if he had the stomach for it. Whether he won or lost the Tracey case, he could soon be back on top.

However, he wasn't sure he wanted to return to that rat race. He hoped to have a choice. It was another reason this verdict was so important. A plaintiff's verdict against the church meant financial independence. He could cherry-pick his cases, take only the cream, and refer the milk to other lawyers for a standard one-third-referral fee. Or, he could hire younger associates and junior partners to do the grunt work. The right verdict would set him free.

He hadn't seen Jennifer since they left the courtroom at the end of the first full day of deliberations. He wouldn't call her. He agonized over possible reasons why *she* hadn't called *him*. His reason for not calling was sensible. He had a lot of work to catch up on. A lawyer can't try cases, go on vacation, or take sick days. The daily work is still there when he returns, waiting for him, like an unwanted visiting relative.

Damn it, why hasn't she called? The answer, of course, was Father Bill. Now that this man was back in their lives, the Tracey family didn't need Zack Blake. Blake sat back in his chair, not too far back. It was still broken. He'd get an expensive new one after the verdict. He'd move to a high-rise office building, hire an executive secretary, a paralegal, a couple of young attorneys, and renew his career. For the moment, however, he couldn't concentrate. He couldn't get *her* out of his mind. *What is she doing? Right now, right this minute.* The phone rang. Zack jumped.

"Zachary Blake."

"Zack, it's Craig Walsh."

"Hey, Craig, how are you? This waiting drives me nuts, you?"

"Yeah, it's no fun. That's for sure. You're about to receive a huge verdict for the plaintiff. The only question is . . . against whom? Will it be the church, the priest, or both? Obviously, that's of major importance. *That's* what should be driving you nuts."

Walsh knew Zack's pain point.

"You have a point," Zack agreed. "Do I sense you're about to make me another settlement offer?"

"Very astute of you, twenty-one million dollars, same terms as previous."

"Holy shit! But it requires confidentiality and no post-trial publicity or publication rights?"

"Correct, but who cares with all that money? That's a seven-million-dollar attorney fee, Zack."

"Thanks for doing the math, Craig. Actually, I can divide *any* figure by three—"

"What do you think?"

"It's an enormous amount of money, but the strings will be deal-breakers for Jennifer. She won't agree to a confidential settlement, period. I've told you a hundred times. For her, this is not and has never been about money—"

"I know, it's about justice and prevention," Walsh finished the line for him. "Hasn't there been enough publicity associated with this trial? How much more does she need?"

Blake remained silent. Craig wasn't wrong, but Zack knew Jennifer.

"Well, I tried," Walsh relented. "When the verdict is a hundred million against the priest, you'll wish you listened to me. Do you honestly think the jury fully grasps the distinction?

Do *they* know a damages award against the priest is the same as a no-cause?"

"We'll just have to wait and see," Blake suggested.

Walsh was right. How would the jury know the distinction? Walsh scared the shit out of him, playing on his worst fears. It really didn't matter, though—the decision was out of his hands. He would take the offer to Jennifer. He was her lawyer, and this was his duty. She would reject it because of the attached strings. The offer *did* give him an excuse to call her. He resisted the temptation to hop in the Z4 and drive to Jennifer's house. He checked his messages—there were none—and dialed her number.

"Hello?" Kenny answered.

"Hi, Kenny, it's Zack. How are you doing'?"

"Fine, Zack. You want to talk to Mom?"

He sounded more cheerful than Zack could ever remember.

"Yes, please. How's Jake doing?"

"He's fine. Hey, Zack?"

"Yeah?"

"You coming over? I haven't seen you in a while. We miss you."

"Come on, Kenny. Stop kidding around."

"No kidding, Zack. We were just talking about you, Jake and me."

"I figured I'd let you guys and Father Bill get reacquainted."

"Hey, Father Bill is great, like an uncle or big brother, you know? But, Mom, well, I think Mom really *likes* you. Know what I mean? So do we, Zack."

"I miss you guys, too," Zack choked up. "Let me talk to your mom. And, Kenny?"

"Yeah?"

"Thanks."

"For what?"

"For nothing. Let me talk to Mom."

He waited a few moments, and she came to the phone.

"Zack! Where have you been? I've been calling you for two straight days. I don't think your voicemail is working."

"Oh, I've been at the office, catching up on all the work I've missed during the trial and returning missed phone calls. I'm kind of famous now. Sorry I haven't called. I'll have to check my voicemail."

"That's okay. I *missed* you. That's all."

"I've missed you too."

"What's happening? Any news from the jury room?"

"The church has increased its offer of settlement."

"You're kidding, again?"

"Yep. They'll pay twenty-one million."

"Oh, my God!"

"*Oh, my God* is right. But, Jen, the terms are the same, complete confidentiality."

"We've come so far for a principle, Zack. You know I have tremendous faith, but this is so much money. This time, I'll let *you* decide."

Blake paused. She put the decision in his hands, right where he didn't want it. To this point, he could blame her for whatever happened. He had no accountability. It was easier to say no to Walsh's offers.

"Then the answer should be no, Jen. This case has always been about justice for the boys, never about money. It has been about faith. Let's wait for the verdict."

He couldn't believe the words came from *his* mouth.

"Zack?"

"Yes?"

"I'm proud of you."

"I'm proud of you too, Jen."

"Are you coming over?"

"Are you inviting me?"

"Zack, you don't need an invitation."

"Be right over."

***

Zack had a wonderful evening with the Tracey family. Father Bill, who was staying at the house, had to fly back to make arrangements for his return to Farmington. Zack was treated to a full-course meal and a high-stakes game of Monopoly. Kenny was the marathon winner, bankrupting everyone. The last to lose was Jake, who wiped the board clean with his arm, rather than giving Kenny the satisfaction of finishing the game as a winner.

Jake's antics reminded Zack of *his* childhood. His older brother, Larry, was as poor a loser as he was a winner. When he won, he'd gloat. When he was about to lose, he'd quit or swipe the board, much the same way Jake did. Zack smiled at the memory. He'd have to call Larry. They hadn't talked in a while.

After the game, the boys went upstairs, and Zack made cappuccino. He and Jennifer sat together on the family room couch, watching TV, sipping English toffee cappuccino, and reminiscing.

Finally, after the first relaxing moments he had spent in weeks, Zack looked at his watch and announced it was time to leave.

"Stay, Zack. Let's have that talk," Jennifer urged, gazing into his eyes.

She is so beautiful, Zack marveled. "What about the boys?"

"They don't mind, Zack. They like you, you know."

"I like them, too. So, the what-if scenario?"

"Would you prefer to talk about the weather?"

He agreed to stay. He was putty in her hands. Regardless of the outcome of the verdict, he hoped they would be together.

***

Blake awoke on Jennifer's couch, déjà vu all over again. The sound of his cell phone alerted him to a missed call. He cleared the cobwebs and staggered to the bathroom. He had to look twice at the screen for the missed call phone number, adjusting his eyes to the light pouring in from an overhead skylight. It was a 313 number, probably Judge Perry's chambers. Was it a verdict? He made sure the number was saved in his caller ID and returned to the family. Jennifer was sitting on the couch.

"What's up, doc?" She stretched and yawned.

"I think the court called. Maybe there's a verdict."

"That's good, isn't it? It's not too quick, is it?"

"Hard to say, Jen. I don't even know if it *is* a verdict."

He reverse-dialed the number, waited for a connection, and then spoke briefly to a clerk.

"We have a verdict," he remarked. "We have to get to the courthouse."

"Oh my God," Jennifer squealed. "I'm not ready." She looked in the mirror. "Look at my hair. I don't have anything to wear. I look like crap!"

"Calm down, Jennifer. All I have is the suit I wore *yesterday*. I don't even have a change of underwear. You'll look great. *I'll* look like shit."

"Then we'll look like shit together," Jennifer laughed. "You want the first shower or second?"

Chapter Sixty-Two

Word of the verdict spread quickly throughout the television, radio, and print media. By the time Jennifer and Zachary arrived at the courthouse, there were throngs of media types on the grounds, waiting to stick a microphone in the face of anyone involved in the litigation. As Zack pulled the Z4 into the city lot near the courthouse, he couldn't believe the media circus. He advised Jennifer to answer all questions with 'no comment' until the verdict was read. As they approached the entrance, a reporter spotted them and yelled, "Here's Blake!" The crowd of media types descended upon the couple.

"Mr. Blake, are you concerned about the verdict? It's only been four days."

"No comment," Zack grunted, continuing forward, fighting through the crowd.

"If the verdict is rendered against the priest alone, will you seek collection against him?"

"No comment." *How did they know collection was an issue if the verdict was against Gerry?*

"Are you satisfied with the way the evidence was presented, Mr. Blake?"

"No comment."

"Mrs. Tracey, are you pleased with Mr. Blake's performance, win or lose?"

"More than pleased," Jennifer proclaimed.

"No comment!" Zack whispered into her ear.

"Sorry," she whispered back, embarrassed.

"Are the two of you romantically involved?"

"No comment," they chimed in unison.

"What are you going to do with all this money, Mrs. Tracey?"

"No comment," Jennifer grumbled. She was a quick study.

They broke through the crowd and managed to arrive on the fifth floor without further incident. They watched from an outside window as the scene repeated itself when Walsh and

Judge Perry arrived. Attorneys, regulars at the courthouse, were being interviewed all over the lawn. They were happy to offer their 'expert' opinion on the potential outcome in exchange for having their names and faces plastered on the evening news and in the late editions of the *Detroit News*, *Free Press*, *Oakland Press*, and *Detroit Legal News*. Free publicity, negative or otherwise, never hurt any attorney's practice. Courthouse employees were being questioned for 'insider' knowledge. Television monitors and satellite dishes were placed all over the lawn to enable those who could not get inside to pick up Court TV and hear the verdict as it was read. Pandemonium reigned. Zachary and Jennifer were happy to be inside, looking out.

Litigants and attorneys, press members who won a lottery granting access to the courtroom, and trial participants on both sides, were soon settled in the courtroom. The press contingent and participants, like Micah Love and various church officials, were seated in the gallery. The parties and their attorneys were seated at their respective counsel tables. The bailiff read a stern message from Judge Perry, warning those present that outbursts, either before or after the verdict was read, would result in swift and severe penalties. Jennifer turned to Zack with a hopeful look and squeezed his hand tightly. Finally, the verdict was upon them.

"All rise!" shouted the bailiff. "Circuit Court for the County of Wayne is now in session, the Honorable John Perry presiding."

Perry entered with his familiar, "Please be seated."

"Before I bring in the jury, are there any preliminary matters to dispose of?"

"No, Your Honor," the lawyers concurred.

"Very well then, Deputy, bring in the jury."

The jurors filed in the courtroom, as they had on previous occasions. Members stared at the ground, expressionless, so as not to reveal any hint of their decision. When each stood in front of their appropriate seat locations, the judge invited them to be seated.

"Ladies and gentlemen of the jury, this has been a difficult and emotional case. The verdict you are about to read will be well-publicized and very controversial. You will be besieged by members of the press, both inside and outside the courthouse. We have attempted to address, as much as possible, the security concerns endemic to a controversial case. You will have a Wayne County Sheriff's deputy escort, both inside and outside the courthouse and to your vehicle. You will have the right to stop and talk with members of the press if you wish. This has been a relatively lengthy trial, and on behalf of the citizens of Wayne County and the litigants involved in this case, thank you for your valuable service. You deliberated long and hard. No one can accuse this jury of a rush to judgment. And now, ladies and gentlemen of the jury, have you reached a verdict?"

The foreman rose, expressionless.

"We have, Your Honor."

"Will you hand your verdict to the bailiff, please?"

The bailiff walked over to the jury foreman, who handed him the verdict form. The bailiff walked the verdict form slowly to Judge Perry and handed it to him. The judge silently read the verdict and handed it back to the bailiff.

"The record will reflect that I am handing the verdict form back to the bailiff, who is returning it to the jury foreman," Judge Perry described the process.

The courtroom was absolutely silent, in anxious anticipation.

"Mr. Foreman, what is the jury's verdict?"

"Your Honor," the jury foreman began to read, "We the jury find in favor of the plaintiff and order the defendants to pay compensatory damages in the amount of forty million dollars."

The gallery erupted. People rose. Some applauded. Some began to type on laptop computers or write feverishly in notebooks. Perry pounded his gavel, trying to restore order and threatening to have the courtroom cleared. Several Sheriff's deputies were on hand for this very reason, working the crowd, promising to evict those who disregarded the judge's orders. After several tense moments, order was restored, and Judge Perry repeated his contempt warnings.

"Mr. Foreman, will you continue your reading of the verdict, please?"

"Yes, Your Honor," the foreman assented. "We, the jury,

order the defendants to pay punitive damages in the amount of two hundred million dollars." The gallery uprising began again but was quickly quelled by the judge and the deputies.

Zachary sat at the plaintiff counsel table, dumbfounded. *A two hundred and forty million dollar verdict!* As order was being restored around him, he was in a state of absolute panic. *Did the foreman mention whether the verdict is joint and several?*

He thought he heard the foreman say 'defendants,' *plural,* not 'defendant,' *singular,* but wasn't sure. Judge Perry, however, was on top of the situation. After order was again restored, Perry addressed the jury foreman.

"Mr. Foreman, is your verdict against all defendants or any individual defendant?"

"Against all, Your Honor. Joint and several."

And there it was, the sweet music Zachary Blake waited to hear. He and his clients were awarded a *collectible* two hundred and forty million dollar verdict! The gallery was buzzing.

"Mr. Walsh, would you like me to poll the jury?"

Losing counsel was permitted to ask each juror whether the verdict, as read, was his or her verdict.

"Yes, Your Honor." Walsh was in shock. He could hardly utter the words.

"Juror number one, is this your verdict?"

"Yes, Your Honor."

This procedure was repeated for all six jurors, and each stated this was his or her verdict. It was now official. Judge Perry thanked and excused the jury for its service, and court was adjourned. Pandemonium re-erupted, and reporters besieged Zack and Jennifer. Those who could not reach Zack and Jennifer went after Walsh for a reaction. He issued a terse "no comment" and pushed his way out of the courtroom. Moloney was nowhere to be found.

For Zachary and Jennifer, the scene was different, euphoric. They politely answered all questions directed toward them. "Yes, we are ecstatic with the verdict. Yes, we were confident of a plaintiff's verdict throughout the trial."

"Yes," Jennifer cheered. "I never lost faith, and I always had the utmost confidence in Zack Blake. Yes, this is a verdict of

Mark M. Bello   345

vindication and victims' rights. Yes, we hope this verdict sends a strong message to all large institutions, not only religious ones, whose employees are directly involved with kids. Screen prospective employees carefully and effectively. Yes, we have a relationship. He's an attorney—I'm his client! Beyond that, we have no comment."

Zack and Jennifer were interviewed, live, on all of the local television and radio stations. Each station dispatched its top reporters. The verdict was big news in Detroit, all over the country, and even certain parts of the world. The principal defendant was a worldwide religious organization. The verdict was reported to be the largest of its kind in the history of Michigan jurisprudence. Finally, over two hours after the verdict was read, the last question was asked and answered. Zack and Jennifer embraced and exited the courtroom, arm in arm. A photographer jumped out at them and snapped a picture. They were getting a crash course in paparazzi journalism.

They walked to the parking lot and climbed into the Z4. Leftover film crews gave them smiles and thumbs-up signs as they filmed their departure. They drove up the Lodge to Jennifer's tri-level, to be greeted by two very happy boys.

"Wow! We're rich!" Jake shouted.

"Congratulations, Mom. Nice job, Zack," a mature-sounding Kenny added. Press corps and television crews began to arrive, and the family hurried into the house.

Later that evening, Zack prepared to leave. He couldn't fall asleep on the couch, *this* time, because the press would have had a field day. Jennifer fixed his collar and gave him a huge hug.

"Zack, this is amazing—*you* are amazing. Thank you for standing by me. Thank you for believing in me and for not telling me I was crazy for turning down all those fantastic offers. I know it was hard for you. Thanks for adding some stability to my otherwise turbulent life and for being there for my kids. Thank you for being you. Thanks for *everything*."

"No, Jenny. I owe *you* the debt of thanks. You and the boys are the best things that have ever happened to me. You saw what had happened to me since I handled your husband's case, but you took a chance on me anyway. I tried to sell you out for a quick buck. You were justifiably angry, but you stuck with me. I'm not sure why. My life and career were in the toilet before I met you and those wonderful boys. You guys turned all of that around for me. Hopefully, with a lot of love from their mother and stepfather, with professional help from Dr. Rothenberg, all this will become a distant memory. I'm falling in love with you, Jen. I want to discuss our life together."

"Oh, Zack, one step at a time, please? Let's get to know each other without the trial and the turmoil. Let's allow everything to settle down. The boys need to settle into their new lives, and I need to see how they do with Father Bill. Please, Zack, don't rush things. Be patient with me, okay?"

"For as long as it takes, Jen, for as long as it takes."

Epilogue

Two weeks after the verdict in *Tracey v. Bartholomew, et al,* lawyers for the church argued their formal Motion for Remittitur or a new trial. *Remittitur* is a formal request to the trial judge for the reduction of an excessive jury verdict. A new team of lawyers, specializing in post-verdict and appellate work, argued the motion to Judge Perry. The judge denied the motion, opining the verdict was consistent with the outrageous conduct of the priest and various agents of the church. This was a clear and convincing repudiation of the Coalition and Gilbert Moloney. Judge Perry also denied the church's motion for a new trial.

The church filed an appeal to the Michigan Court of Appeals, citing several points of error committed by Judge Perry, including erroneous instructions to the jury, admission of inadmissible evidence, refusal to admit admissible evidence, permitting emotional testimony without permitting cross-examination, allowance of testimony by witnesses who weren't on the witness list, and other abuses of judicial discretion. The Michigan Court of Appeals denied all points of appeal.

That decision was appealed to the Michigan Supreme Court. While the appeal was pending, Blake and church attorneys agreed to settle the case for $200 million, persuading the church to sign a nondisclosure agreement on the reduction of the award. Finally, after years of pretrial, trial, and appeals, *Tracey v. Bartholomew* was officially resolved.

Gerry Bartholomew was defrocked, placed in an Ohio state penitentiary, and began serving a lengthy prison sentence, suspended initially, but reinstated after his probation violation. He also received court-ordered psychiatric counseling, paid for by the church.

Craig Walsh was fired from Brodman Longworth and moved back to Louisiana, where he lived before being recruited to the silk-stocking firm.

Gilbert Moloney *retired* from his position as the director of the Coalition and left the priesthood. He recently left the United

States and was believed to be a security consultant with a prominent religious organization overseas. Federal and state law enforcement officials formed a joint task force to study and formalize various criminal charges against Moloney and other members of his Coalition. Their work was nearing completion and extradition papers were being prepared.

The MacLean and O'Connell families sold their homes in Coral Springs and returned to Berea, where they returned to their former jobs and lives. Their children were reportedly doing very well.

Micah Love was paid in full and received a handsome seven-figure bonus for his work on the Tracey case. He promptly retired to Florida, stopping in Berea to pick up Jessica Klein.

Because of the tremendous publicity generated by the Tracey verdict, the Law Offices of Zachary Blake became a high-demand personal injury law firm. Zachary purchased a gorgeous estate home on Lone Pine Road in the Cranbrook neighborhood of prestigious Bloomfield Hills. He closed his Eight Mile office and a new law office building on Woodward Avenue, a short distance from his new home. The building's previous owner, a defense law firm, had converted a beautiful Victorian home into a state-of-the-art law office.

Blake opened satellite offices at Southfield Town Center and Renaissance Center. In a short time, business swelled to a point where twenty experienced personal injury lawyers became partners with or associates of the firm. These attorneys employed fifty professional support staffers, executive secretaries, and paralegals. Each office location had an executive-size office for Zack, with deluxe furnishings and equipment, especially orthopedic approved executive chairs.

Zack also dove full-tilt into the *politics* of tort law, becoming a staunch advocate for civil justice causes. He accepted prestigious appointments to justice associations and contributed heavily to their *PACS*. Political winds were blowing to the right, and Zack was very concerned about the next election and how a potential candidate might affect citizens' rights in cases filed against insurance companies and large corporations. His practice was primarily a state practice, but an organization like the church, for instance, would be in a position to wield enormous influence over certain candidates, if any happened to become president of the United States.

Immigration and racial issues are *federal* issues—police misconduct and many criminal issues are decided in the *federal* system. Zachary decided to take a wait-and-see attitude, but he did not like the campaign rhetoric, the mood, or direction of the country.

One candidate, a well-known television business guru, promised to 'make America pure again,' and threatened immigrants from the Middle East and Mexico. Zack would do all he could to prevent this candidate from achieving success, but what if this was the will of the people? Time would tell.

Zack also began to pursue his what-if scenario with Jennifer. Many people, Zack included, expected Jennifer to sever all ties with the church. Instead, she became more involved. Aware of the potential for backlash against the church to harm its benevolent activities, Jenny started working with church charities and outreach programs. She contributed no small amount of her own award money to these services.

The church suffered financially. The size of the verdict was a contributing factor, but also, parishioners from all over the world were reluctant to donate to an organization that used donor contributions to cover up crimes or pay off victims. Despite Jennifer's assistance and compassion, the church was in for an uphill financial battle.

Father William Stern took the Coalition in an entirely new direction. All previous board members were replaced. A central database of employee records was established, and no placements or transfers were made, anywhere, without proper vetting and approval. The Coalition now functioned to provide discipline to those priests and other church employees who did not act in accordance with their vows.

The organization also offered financial, spiritual, and emotional assistance to parishioners, as needed. It was truly benevolent, doing the good work of the church. Perhaps, in time, such practice would be appreciated by the faithful, confidence would be restored, and parishioners would begin to provide financial support.

Jennifer, Kenny, Jake, and Zack, tapping some of his attorney fees, contributed portions of their recoveries to establish a foundation to provide counseling and treatment to victims of child sexual abuse.

Kenny and Jake Tracey continued treatment with Dr. Rothenberg and, at last report, were adjusting well to their new lifestyle. Kenny was a high school freshman, and Jake, a seventh-grader at the local middle school. Both boys carried grade point averages above 3.0. The boys continued to struggle with nightmares, long-term relationships, and trust issues. Except for an occasional favor for Father Bill, the boys expressed no interest in participating in religious activities or events.

Dr. Rothenberg was satisfied with their progress. Their prognosis, with continued therapy, was guarded. They experienced no suicidal ideations, and the doctor opined that their feelings of hatred for Father Gerry were appropriate under the circumstances.

***

Clergy-parishioner child sexual abuse is a significant institutional epidemic that has seriously damaged the lives of hundreds of young parishioners throughout the United States and Canada. Hundreds of millions of dollars have been paid to silence victims of this institutional embarrassment.

While this book and its characters are creations of fiction, and the Coalition is a fabrication of the author's wild imagination, the problem of clergy-parishioner child sexual abuse is a tragic and still ongoing problem.

END

Thank you for reading, and I sincerely hope you enjoyed *Betrayal of Faith*. As an independently published author, I rely on you, the reader, to spread the word. So, if you enjoyed this book, please tell your friends and family, and I would appreciate a brief review on Amazon. Thanks again.

Mark

Join Zachary Blake on his next journey into justice in Betrayal of Justice. Please continue for an excerpt. You can also buy it now from Amazon.

Betrayal of Justice

"My fellow Americans: I am very humbled yet emboldened by your vote to elect me as your president. I thank you for your support. I've earned your vote, and I will now embark on the task of securing your continued trust. I intend to do that by delivering on the promises I made during my very contentious campaign with Secretary Goodman. To accomplish these promises, we, the people, have to be vigilant and bold. We have to take this country in a new direction.

"This new direction starts with securing our borders. Under our current immigration system, our borders are porous, wide open for drug dealers, rapists, murderers, and terrorists to enter our country unchecked, able to move about freely to do all kinds of terrible things to law-abiding citizens. Other countries are not sending the best and brightest to our country. They are dumping 'human toxic waste,' and it is my job to clean up the mess.

"Furthermore, my ineffective predecessor has enacted recent unconstitutional restrictions on our citizens' right to bear arms through a series of illegal and unethical executive orders. These restrictions have left our citizens virtually defenseless against deadly, terrorist threats.

"My first order of business as your president will be to rescind these executive orders, restore full Second Amendment rights to our people, and encourage all of our law-abiding citizens to purchase weapons to defend against the scourge caused by our current, extremely ineffective, immigration system.

"My second order of business will be to secure our borders. No longer will drug dealers, pimps, pushers, rapists, murderers, or terrorists be able to freely enter our country through our southern border. I will build a second-to-none border defense system across our southern border, impenetrable border walls, and I will make Mexico and South America share the cost. I will do the same along our northern border. Canada will pay for our northern border defense system and help police it. If either or both refuse, we have ways of convincing them to ante up. These countries, indeed, all countries in the free and not so free world, rely on trade with the United States. We are their largest customers and trade partners. Let's see if they prefer tariffs on all goods entering the United States of America. We also provide serious aid and military support to many of these countries, and they will soon begin paying for that support, or it will be terminated. There will be no free rides from the John administration.

"The third order of business will be to beef up law enforcement in this great country of ours. We will increase border security and immigration and naturalization enforcement. We will create a new federal police force within the Department of Homeland Security answerable only to its secretary and to me. This force will be the finest of its kind and will be tasked with protecting our citizens from foreign interests seeking to destroy our country and our citizens.

"We will make America beautiful again. We will modernize our airports. We have the worst airports. Third world countries have better airports than we do. We will make our country's airports the biggest, brightest, most technologically advanced, and beautiful airports in the world. We will repair and replace our crumbling roads and bridges. Our crumbling infrastructure will be replaced using state-of-the-art equipment manufactured right here in the good ol' USA.

"We will put America back to work again, as these tasks will be performed by American-born workers. Advanced technology systems will require workers with twenty-first-century advanced technological skills. In with the new, out with the old, I say. Our natural resources will once again take center stage in the global economy. No more political correctness in energy production. We will put people back to work in Pennsylvania and West Virginia and produce energy for our people at a fraction of the current cost. How will we do this? By producing energy right here in America and curtailing our dependence upon foreign sources, especially those sources that sponsor terror. We will focus on price and American pride rather than the junk science and political correctness that has driven up the cost of our energy and ignores resources we can mine for-profit and supply to all corners of the globe. It is high time for America to assume its rightful role as a global energy leader.

"Finally, we will round up and deport all of those who have entered into and remain in this great country illegally. Round them up and toss them out. I have no use for criminals, and these illegal immigrants are a huge part of the criminal element that makes our law-abiding citizens less safe.

"We will combat terrorism and the global terrorist threat by taking the war to the shores of the terrorists and by banning all current and future immigration from any country I deem to be a sponsor of terrorists and terrorist activity. And, we will create jobs by assembling and training the best and the brightest national immigration and deportation force in the world. We will beef up federal, state, and local law enforcement departments, which will create more law enforcement jobs, manpower necessary to tackle the problems of local, state, national, and international crime. It is time to prioritize safety in this country. We will be the law and order capital of the world.

"We will make America safe again. We will make America strong again. We will put America first again. We will make America secure again. We will make America prosperous again. We will make America *pure* again. With your help and God's will, we will succeed in making America a shining city on a hill once again. Thank you . . .

***

" . . . God bless you, and God Bless the United States of America."

Arya Khan watched the Ronald John acceptance speech again and again on her laptop. Who was he talking to? She had been glued to the national television news stations for months, watching every report she could. She was fixated on social media and reviewed real news, false news, or *any* news she could find that would help her understand the issues and calm her fears that this man could actually become the President of the United States.

She tried to provide reasonable commentary when an article permitted comment. She engaged her friends and fellow students in thoughtful conversation. The polls seemed to favor Secretary Goodman, a decent, inclusive politician whose campaign slogan was "We are one America." The polls, as Arya had feared, were dead wrong.

The campaign battle was waged along racial and ethnic battle lines. John seemed to be the candidate of white Christians who, he said, were being shoved aside by politically correct politicians seeking to promote the rights of minority interests. The "minority interest" that bore the brunt of the new president's rage was the Muslim population. Throughout the campaign, he referred to terrorism as "Islamic." He vowed to stop the flow of Muslims into the country and to "weed out" those Muslim criminals that were already here.

But whom was he talking about? Not Arya and her family? She was born in the United States. She was an American citizen. Her parents were naturalized citizens and as loyal to the United States as any Christian person. Weren't they all endowed by the Constitution with the same rights and privileges as Ronald John? Didn't she have the right to life, liberty, and the pursuit of happiness? Could this evil man make good on these campaign promises?

Arya was an American citizen, born in Dearborn, Michigan, the daughter of devoted parents who fled war-torn Yemen in the mid-1960s for a better way of life in America. Arya's parents worked hard to establish roots in the multi-cultural Dearborn community. They owned and operated a popular local fruit market, purchased and built from the ground up with the sparse remnants of family money earned in the old country.

Arya's ancestors fled Northern Yemen at a time when the small Middle Eastern country was involved in a series of conflicts with Egypt and then-President Gamal Abdel-Nasser. Nasser sought regime change in Yemen as far back as 1957. In 1962, he offered the Free Yemen Movement financial support, office space, and airtime on the radio in an effort to bring about the change he sought. Nasser's prestige took a severe hit as the result of his falling out with Syria and the dissolution of his UAR (United Arab Republic). He sent expedition forces into Yemen, concluding a quick victory might assist him in regaining a leadership role in the region.

A quick victory was not achieved, and the country became embroiled in a war waged on multiple fronts, involving several governments, and political and geographic interests. By the middle of 1965, approximately 15,000 Egyptian men and 40,000 Yemenis were dead, and Egypt was facing a financial crisis. Despite billions in foreign debt, Nasser implemented his "long-breath strategy." He planned to reduce troop size from 70,000 to 40,000, withdraw from the east and the north where his positions were more exposed, and to concentrate on two particular border areas. The United States threatened to revoke some or all of a multi-million-dollar food and infrastructure aid package, and, still, Nasser refused to pull his troops out of Yemen. He vowed to stay in Yemen for twenty years if he had to. The "twenty years" never happened. Significant economic and political pressure prompted Nasser to negotiate a treaty in 1967 and Nasser withdrew his troops shortly after that.

In 1966, multiple gas bombings were reported, along with numerous injuries and fatalities. The most significant attack occurred in their own village, Kitaf, where gas attacks caused 270 casualties and 140 deaths. Arya's family was safely in America by then, embarking on a new life in the land of the free.

The family settled in Dearborn, home to the largest population of Arabs in the United States. The city's Arab community has been growing for at least a century, a growth that accelerated simultaneously with the Detroit area automobile industry.

Henry Ford, in the early and mid-twentieth century, recruited thousands of Middle Easterners to Dearborn to work at Ford's mammoth River Rouge plant. Contrary to the stereotype, many of those who fled the Middle East for a better life in the United States were not Arab, they were Iraqi Christians, Chaldeans, fleeing Muslim persecution. Dearborn, however, seems to be one place where Muslims and Christians have been able to live and thrive in harmony, peace, and prosperity.

The community has certainly not been without conflict and controversy. Orville Hubbard was Dearborn's most famous and longest-serving mayor. He served from the early 1940s to the late 1970s and embraced segregation. In 1985, a man named Michael Guido won the mayoral election in Dearborn after mailing pamphlets to constituents promising to address the city's "Arab problem."

A few decades before, the introduction of bilingual education was controversial, as were halal options in school cafeterias and the sight of traditional headscarves on Muslim women. Not so today, however, as the city, informally known as the Arab and Muslim capital of the United States, has elected its first Arab-American city council president and added its first Arab-American chief of police. Dearborn is the home of the largest mosque in the country, and a third of its population is of Arabic descent. Crime statistics and average annual citizen income figures are slightly less than the state median.

In the midst of all of this local peace and harmony, a man named Ronald John was now the President-elect of the United States. He campaigned on a platform that promised to "rid America of the Muslim scourge." *What does this mean?* Arya pondered. *Does this man seriously intend to engage in the process of deporting all Muslims, whether here legally or illegally, whether citizens or non-citizens? Isn't that unconstitutional?* Arya Khan was inspirited and . . . terrified.

The Zachary Blake Legal Thriller Series

About the Author

Mark M. Bello is an attorney and award-winning legal thriller author. After handling high profile legal cases for 42 years, Mark now treats readers to a front-row seat in the courtroom. His ripped from the headlines Zachary Blake Legal Thrillers are inspired by actual cases or Bello's take on current legal or sociopolitical issues. Mark lives in Michigan with his wife, Tobye. They have four children and 8 grandchildren.

Connect with Mark
Website: www.markmbello.com
Email: info@markmbello.com
Facebook: MarkMBelloBooks
Twitter: @ MarkMBelloBooks
YouTube: Mark Bello
Goodreads: Mark M. Bello

To request a speaking engagement, interview, or appearance, please email info@markmbello.com.

Printed in Great Britain
by Amazon